Ancient Expertise

We slowed down as we approached the ruins. The sun was hanging on the rim of the ocean horizon, a bloated red ball that threw long purple shadows among the blasted buildings and heaps of debris. We filed into the ruins gratefully, happy to feel some little protection from the decaying walls after being out in the open.

It had been a sizable city, I could see now that we were in it. Wide avenues were lined for several kilometers with buildings that must have risen quite high before they were blasted into rubble. How old? And what destroyed them?

"Radioactive background is nominal," Frede murmured as we picked our way through the debris littering one of the major avenues. She had unpacked the scanner from her equipment web and was holding it out stiffly in front of her, almost the way a blind man pokes his cane ahead of him.

"This city wasn't nuked," I said to her.

The troops automatically fanned out into two columns, one on either side of the shattered street.

"If it wasn't nuked," Frede asked, "how did it get blasted so badly?"

I thought I knew. "They fought a battle here. A long, bloody battle that went from street to street, building to building. Hand-to-hand killing, for weeks. Maybe months."

Frede shook her head, uncomprehending. "But that would mean the whole population was in the fight: civilians, children, e⋯

⋯irring in me. Troy. Stalingrad. The ⋯he bloodbath that followed.

⋯ I echoed. "In the siege of ⋯ulation died of starvation. ⋯ the zoo."

"Hell's ⋯

Tor books by Ben Bova

ORION AMONG THE STARS

BEN BOVA

A TOM DOHERTY ASSOCIATES BOOK
NEW YORK

ORION AMONG THE STARS

Copyright © 1995 by Ben Bova

All rights reserved, including the right to reproduce this book, or portions thereof, in any form.

Cover art by Donato

Edited by Patrick Nielsen Hayden

A Tor Book
Published by Tom Doherty Associates, Inc.
175 Fifth Avenue
New York, NY 10010

Tor Books on the World Wide Web:
http://www.tor.com

Tor® is a registered trademark of Tom Doherty Associates, Inc.

ISBN: 0-812-53511-1

First edition: August 1995
First mass market edition: December 1996

Printed in the United States of America

0 9 8 7 6 5 4 3 2 1 .

To Paul Spencer, Tommy Atkins, and all their cousins.

Yes, makin' mock o' uniforms that guard you while you sleep
Is cheaper than them uniforms, an' they're starvation cheap...

For it's Tommy this, an' Tommy that, an "Chuck him out, the brute!"
But it's "Saviour of 'is country," when the guns begin to shoot...

—Rudyard Kipling
Tommy

Prologue

This time death was like being in the center of a whirlpool, inside the heart of a roaring tornado. The universe spun madly, time and space whirling into a dizzying blur, planets and stars and atoms and electrons racing in wild orbits with me in the middle of it all, falling, falling endlessly into a cryogenically cold oblivion.

Gradually all sensation left me. It might have taken moments or millennia, I had no way to gauge time, but all feeling of motion and cold seeped away from me, as if I were being numbed, frozen, turned into an immobile, insensate block of ice.

Still my mind continued to function. I knew I was being translated across space-time, from one cusp of the continuum to another. Yet for all I could see or touch or hear, I was in total oblivion. For a measureless time I almost felt glad to be free of the wheel of life at last, beyond pain, beyond desire, beyond the agonizing duty that the Creators forced upon me.

Beyond love.

That stirred me. Somewhere in the vast reaches of space-time Anya was struggling against forces that I could not even comprehend, in danger despite her godlike powers, facing enemies that frightened even the Golden One and the other Creators.

I reached out with my mind, seeking to penetrate the blank darkness that engulfed me. Nothing. It was as if there was no universe, no continuum, neither time nor space. But I knew that somewhere, sometime, she existed. She had loved me as I had loved her. Nothing in all the universes of existence would keep us apart.

A glimmer of light. So faint and distant that at first I thought it might be merely my imagination obeying my desire. But yes, it truly was there. A faintest, faintest glow. Light. Warmth.

Whether I moved to it or it moved to me mattered not at all to me. The glow grew and brightened until I seemed to be hurtling toward it like a chip thrown into a furnace, like a meteor drawn to a star. The light blazed like the sun now and I threw my arms across my eyes to ease the pain, delighted that I had eyes and arms and could *feel* again.

"Orion," came a voice from that blinding, overpowering radiance. "You have returned."

It was Aten, of course, the Golden One. He resolved his presence into human form, a powerful godlike figure with a thick golden mane, robed in shimmering gold, almost too bright for me to look upon.

He stood before me in an utterly barren landscape that stretched toward infinity in every direction. A featureless plain of billowing mist that played about our ankles, an empty bowl of sky above us the color of hammered copper.

"Where is Anya?" I asked.

"Far from here."

"I must go to her. She is in great danger."

"So are we all, Orion."

"I don't care about you or the others. It is Anya I care for."

A faint hint of a smirk curled the corners of his lips. "What you care or don't care about is inconsequential, Orion. I created you to do my bidding."

"I want to be with Anya."

"Impossible. There are other tasks for you to perform, creature."

I stared into his golden eyes and knew that he had the power to send me where he chose. But I had powers, too, powers that were growing and strengthening.

"I will find her," I said.

He laughed scornfully. But I knew that whatever he did, wherever he sent me, I would seek the woman I loved, the goddess who loved me. And I would not cease until I found her.

Chapter 1

I found myself confined in a featureless gray enclosure, the curving wall of a smooth plastic cocoon so close upon me that I could not lift my head without bumping it. I lay on my back, disoriented, blinking eyes that felt gummy with sleep. My arms were pressed close to my sides; there was scant room for me to move them. But I edged one hand along the curving wall of my chamber. It felt blood-warm. Yet I was chilled, as cold inside as a frozen corpse.

I could remember dying, more than once. I recalled freezing to death in a frigid landscape of snow and ice and bitter, merciless winds. The numbness of the cold had been a mercy then; my body had been torn to bloody ribbons by a cave bear.

A mechanical click snapped me to the here and now. I heard a soft beeping sound, strangely annoying. Then the curved plastic cover abruptly swung open. Immediately a chill white mist enveloped me. I shivered and tried to sit up. It took an effort.

Propping myself on one elbow, I squinted through the icy mist. I was in a large room. Featureless gray walls. Low ceiling that glowed with cold bluish light. The floor was lined with large objects that looked to me like coffins. Dozens of them, a hundred, perhaps. And that irritating beeping sound, soft yet insistent, like a worry gnawing at the back of your mind. One at a time, and then in twos and threes, the lids of the coffinlike capsules swung back with soft sighing sounds, like

the slightest of breezes wafting through the nodding limbs of
a forest. Cold whitish mist drifted up from each of them. The
beeping stopped when the last of them opened.

Men and women began pulling themselves up to sitting
positions, rubbing their eyes, stretching their arms, looking
around the room. I could see that they were young, slim,
physically fit. They looked so much like each other that they
could have been brothers and sisters. At first I thought they
were siblings from two or three families. They wore nothing at
all. Completely naked, men and women alike. Just as I was.

The room suddenly jolted sideways, as if some giant hand
had slammed it. A dull, distant boom reverberated through
the mist-filled air. I almost fell off my bier. Several people
gasped or yelled out in surprise. An earthquake? No. Only
that one shock.

I swung my legs to the floor and stood up, tentatively,
testing my strength, keeping a grip on the edge of the coffin or
sarcophagus or whatever it was. A cryonic sleep capsule, I
realized, not knowing how I knew. That is what it was. The
room was crammed with row upon row of cryonic sleep capsules. The men and women in here with me had just been
awakened from death. Or the next thing to it.

"Who is in charge of this squad?"

I turned toward the challenging, impatient voice. And
stiffened with sudden fear and hatred. Standing in the hatch
was a reptilian, a bipedal lizard decked in green and gray
scales, insignia painted on its chest and shoulders, an equipment web strapped around its torso, the stub of a rudimentary
tail visible between its legs. It was only about shoulder-high to
me, not yet fully grown.

One of Set's offspring! Every nerve in me burned with
hatred, every muscle tensed for battle. But I had killed Set long
ago, in the howling agony that took him and his whole brood
of reptilian invaders. And he had killed me. I remembered
dying then, back in the age when dinosaurs roamed the Earth

and the Sun's dwarf companion star had not yet been crushed down to the planet Jupiter.

And this reptile was different. Its face was more lizard-like, with a snout full of teeth and a single bony crest atop its skull. The eyes were mere slits, glittering like a snake's, but they were set forward and scanned us with intelligent scorn.

"Come on! Shake out of it! You've been sleeping long enough," it said. Its voice issued from a tiny jeweled medallion it wore on a gold chain around its neck.

"Who's in charge here?" it asked again.

"I am," I said, realizing the truth of it as I spoke the words. "My name is Orion, captain of this hundred."

Those glittering eyes fixed on me. "Very well, Orion. Get your troops on their feet and ready for action—"

Another jolt rocked the room. This time it felt like an explosion. And sounded like one, too. The troops tottered and staggered. I grabbed the edge of my sleep capsule to keep from falling down.

The reptilian made a slight hissing noise. "You've got to be ready for action in one hour. That's an order, soldier."

It ducked back through the hatch. I realized that its equipment web was empty, mere decoration. We were going into action, all right, but it wasn't.

The mist from the sleepers was almost completely gone. The troops were standing uncertainly, still unsure of themselves, their minds still fogged with cryonic sleep.

"All right," I said, loudly and firmly, "you heard what the lizard said. We're going into action. Fall in!"

They eyed me suspiciously, sullenly almost, but pulled themselves together and formed files alongside their sleeper units. Sergeants stood at the head of each row, and three lieutenants—two of them women—marched barefooted to the front of the room and stood at attention before me. No one seemed distressed by their nudity.

I did not know these troopers. I had been placed in their

command just before the expedition took off, I recalled. Their
regular captain had been relieved of duty for reasons that had
not been explained to me. I had all the personnel data in my
head, of course, but those were merely cold facts from their
files. These hundred soldiers were all strangers to me.

I could remember! I marveled at that. As I marched my
hundred to the lockers for their clothes, armor, equipment and
weapons, I rejoiced in the fact that my memory had not been
wiped clean by the Golden One. I wondered why this time was
different. Aten always erased my memory after each of my
missions. Sometimes I had overcome his erasures, sometimes
I reclaimed my memories. Aten often smirked that he allowed
me to remember, that I could never have overcome his erasure
with nothing but my own efforts. I myself thought that Anya
probably helped me.

But now I could remember it all—or at least, I could
remember a lot. Anya. I loved her and she loved me. She was
one of the Creators, as far beyond me as a goddess is to a
mortal, but she loved me. She had risked her life to be with me
in all the ages I had been sent to by Aten. I wanted to find her,
to be with her, forever.

But there was a crisis, out among the stars, far from
Earth. Anya was out there fighting somewhere, as were the
other Creators. Fighting for their lives. Fighting for the survival of the human race. Fighting for the survival of the continuum.

Against whom? I had no idea. Was this the time of the
great crisis in the continuum that Aten and the other Creators
had feared so deeply? Is that why I was here, with my memories intact?

I wondered about that. How much of my memories were
with me? There was no way to tell. How do you know if you
don't remember a lifetime or two? I could hear Aten's mocking laughter in my mind. It seemed to say that I remembered
what he allowed me to remember, nothing more. I was his

creature, destined throughout all the lifetimes of the continuum to do his bidding.

"ORION TO THE BRIDGE." The order sounded from the speakers of the ship's intercom, overhead. "ON THE DOUBLE."

My troops hardly glanced at me as they pulled on their armor and equipment and hefted the heavy weapons we would be using planetside. They were veterans, despite their seeming youth.

I headed for the bridge without hesitation, finding my way through the labyrinthine passageways of the huge battle cruiser as if I had never been anywhere else. We were part of an invasion fleet, and our approach to the target planet was not unopposed. There was a battle going on, our invading fleet against their defenders.

At each double-doored hatch there was a sentry, a reptilian with insignia painted onto its scales and a sidearm buckled around its middle. Each time I flinched, remembering Set and his minions and how they had tried to make the Earth their own. But each of these sentries stiffened to attention at my approach and saluted with three-taloned hands.

They had one thing in common with Set's species: their size told their age, and their age told their rank. The bigger they were, the older and higher-ranking. I wondered what happened to reptilians who did not get promoted as they aged.

The bridge was small and cramped and eerily quiet with the tension of battle. Nothing but reptilians at the consoles, the cruiser's captain at the center bigger than all the others, of course. They were all absorbing data directly through the cyborg jacks plugged into their temples, their eyes covered with wide-spectrum lenses that showed them everything that the ship's sensors detected, far more than unaided eyes could see.

For me, though, there was nothing to see except these rapt reptilians at their duty stations, claws clicking on keyboards set into the armrests of their chairs. There were no screens for human eyes, nothing but blank metal bulkheads and consoles covered with dials and gauges that meant nothing to me. The bridge was uncomfortably hot, and had a strange dry charred smell to it, like a desert in a blazing noon sun.

Suddenly a hot glow blossomed off to one side of the bridge, burning through the bulkhead plates like a laser hit. I tried to call out a warning to the bridge crew but my voice would not work. The glow grew brighter, larger. I thought the ship's shields had been broken through; in another instant the hull would be ripped open to vacuum.

None of the reptilians noticed a thing. Behind their lenses and cyborg jacks they remained intent on the battle. The glow turned golden, too bright to look at, yet I could not turn my eyes from it. Tears began to blur my vision as the glow dimmed slightly and resolved itself to the human form of Aten, the Golden One.

"Tears of joy, Orion, at seeing your creator once again?" he mocked.

He looked calmly magnificent in the midst of that terribly tense, inhumanly quiet bridge. He wore a splendid high-collared uniform of dazzling white, with gold piping and sunburst insignia on his chest. His thick mane of golden hair glowed magnificently; his cruelly handsome face was set in a cold smile.

"Or perhaps you feel frustrated at not being able to view the battle," he said.

All at once I could see in my mind a planet nearby, and dozens of spacecraft swarming toward it. Defending craft were rising through its atmosphere, firing lasers and missiles as they approached our fleet. Three of their ships exploded soundlessly, vivid red blossoms of destruction against the planet's blue ocean.

"The battle goes well," the Golden One said.

The ship shook again from another blast, nearly knocking me off my feet.

"So I see," I replied dryly.

Aten arched a golden brow. "Humor, Orion? Irony? My creature is expanding his repertoire of behaviors."

"Where is Anya?" I asked.

His expression turned more thoughtful. "Far from here."

"I want to see her."

"Not now. You have an important task to accomplish."

"This is the crisis that you spoke of, long ago?"

His smirk returned. "Long ago? Ah yes, you are still bound by a linear sense of time, aren't you?"

"Don't play games with me."

"Impatient, too! Eager to see the goddess whom you love, I see."

"Where is she?"

"Your duty to me comes first, Orion."

"Who are these reptilians? Why are humans among them?"

"These lizards are our allies in the war, Orion. They are carrying your assault team in their ship."

And my mind filled with new knowledge. I saw history unreeling like a speeded-up film. Saw the first struggling efforts of humans to reach into space. Saw the first of them to stand on the Moon, and then the long hiatus before they returned. Saw the expansion through the solar system: scientists exploring Mars, industrialists building factories in space, miners and political refugees and adventurers spreading through the asteroid belt and the moons of the giant planets.

And all the while, scientists searched for signs of intelligent life among the stars. Fossils were found on Mars, primitive plant life beneath the ice shields of Europa. But for a century and more our radio-telescope scans of the stars found nothing; our calls into the vastness of interstellar space went unanswered.

Within two centuries of those first faltering footsteps on the Moon, humankind achieved the stars. Boiling outward from the confines of the solar system, brash and eager with the discovery of energies that propelled ships faster than light, the human race finally met its equals among the stars, other species fully as intelligent as we. They were thinly scattered through the vastness of the galaxy, but they were there: intelligent life, some of it roughly humanoid in form, other species quite different. But there were civilizations for us to meet, to exchange thoughts with, alien creatures as mature and as intelligent as we.

And as violent. Inevitably, there was war, a long, bitter, brutal struggle that had already killed billions and wiped whole planets clean of life.

My heart sank. Millions of years of human evolution, tens of thousands of years to build a civilization that can span the stars, and the result is war. Instead of learning and understanding one another, the so-called intelligent species of the galaxy slaughter one another.

"Why do you think I built your gift for violence into your kind, Orion?" the Golden One asked me. "There are only two kinds of intelligent creatures in the galaxy: those who can fight, and those who are extinct."

These reptilians were our allies. They called themselves the Tsihn, and they fought on our side against our mutual enemies in the cold, dark vastness of interstellar space. Allies or not, though, they still looked too much like Set and his race for me to feel comfortable.

Aten sensed my unease. "Orion, there are many, many different races in the universe, but only a few basic body plans. Reptiles and mammals share common ancestry; when they evolve into intelligent races they tend to stand erect, walk on their hind legs, and have their brains and major sensory organs grouped in their heads. The resemblance between these reptilians and Set's creatures is strictly an evolutionary footnote, nothing more."

"I would think the universe would be more varied than this," I said.

He chuckled condescendingly. "Your mind improves, Orion. Of course there are many other forms of intelligent life, based on body plans that look nothing at all like ours. But they are *so* alien that we have practically no interaction with them. Methane breathers. Sea-bottom dwellers. Interstellar spores. What they need we do not want; what we want they have no need for. We do not trade with them, we do not mix with them—and we do not make war with them. It would be pointless."

"So who are we making war on?" I asked.

"You will see, soon enough," he replied. "The planet we are approaching is crucial to this phase of the war. You and your assault team must seize a landing site, set up a transceiver station and hold it against all enemy counterattacks."

"With only a hundred?"

"More cannot be spared. Not now."

I wanted to laugh in his face, but I could not. A transceiver station down on the surface would be critical to the task of invading the planet and driving off the enemy. Equipment and supplies could be beamed from the fleet to the surface. People, of course, could not be. Not unless they were willing to die. It took an extraordinary amount of heroism—or desperation—to willingly enter a matter-transmission dock. The device disassembles you and transmits its scan of your body to the receiver. What comes out of the receiver is a copy of you, exact down even to your memories. But you have been killed, your atoms stored in the device for the next user. Your personality has been extinguished, you have ceased to exist. Perhaps the atoms that once made up your body will be used to reconstruct someone else. Or a drum of lubrication oil. Or a case of ammunition.

"A hundred is not enough to hold a transceiver site against enemy attack," I said.

Scowling, Aten told me, "You'll have support from the

fleet. Reinforcements will be sent as soon as possible. The planet is lightly held by the enemy. If you move swiftly enough, you should be able to get the transceiver working before they can attack you in force."

"And if I fail?"

"Then you will die, Orion. And your hundred with you. And this time I will not revive you. We are involved now in a crucial aspect of the ultimate crisis, Orion, the nexus that determines the course of the continuum. Everything else you have done pales to insignificance. Set up that transceiver and hold it until the reinforcements arrive. Hold or die."

Chapter 2

I got the command briefing as I assembled my troop and moved them into the landing vehicles. A flood of data and imagery flowed directly into my brain; the work of the Golden One, I knew. He was telling me telepathically what I needed to know to serve his purposes. And nothing more.

The planet's name was Lunga. The area where we were to land was jungle, low, swampy ground, ideal for defenders' ambushes and difficult for support from orbit. There were extensive oceans, rugged mountain ranges. No intrinsic intelligent life-forms: the highest order of living creatures was tree-dwelling nocturnal animals about the size of lemurs.

The enemy were humanoid in form, but much larger in build than any of us. Two and a half meters tall, they averaged, and very solidly built. They were not professional soldiers so much as a whole race of nomadic warriors. They called themselves the Skorpis, which in their language meant "Bred for Battle." Where they came from: unknown. Why they had allied themselves to our enemies: also unknown. They were starting to build a base on Lunga. Why, I was not told. What strategic value the planet had was also not in my briefing. My job, as Aten had told me, was to set up the transceiver and hold it. Or die.

We boarded the landers in squads, twenty-five young men and women per squad, each of them in green camouflage armor and helmets, bristling with weapons. Not much talk as they filed into the landers' narrow, cramped compartments. Most of the troopers looked grim, lips pressed together, doing what they were told by the numbers and trying not to let their fears show in their faces.

There were a few wisecracks, of course. Some of the kids covered up their jumpiness with wretched attempts at humor. And the usual gripes.

"How come we have to be the ones to go in? Why can't they send some other team? Why's it always have to be us?"

" 'Cause we're all heroes," came a reply.

"Yeah. We'll all get medals for heroism," someone else said, sourly.

"What's the matter, soldier, don't you like the army?"

"Maybe he's not happy in his profession."

"Well, you know what they say: *You've gotta be born to it.*"

At that they all laughed, even the one who complained. Their laughter seemed harshly bitter to me.

"Can it, you mutts," growled their sergeant. "Find your places and strap in. This isn't a joyride."

Kids. From my physical condition I was not much older than they, but I knew I had led many lives, died and been revived time and again. The Skorpis were bred for battle, were they? I had been created for battle. Aten built me to be a warrior, a hunter, a killer.

And so had these youngsters, Aten's briefing told me. Cloned from long-dead ancestors, gestated in artificial wombs, they were trained from birth to be soldiers and nothing else. They were raised in military camps, never seeing anything except military life, never allowed to mix with the civilian society that they were created to defend. They knew nothing but war, except for the brief periods between battles when they were trained for their next mission.

Some of their senior officers had been born naturally, to normal families, and joined the military voluntarily. But very few, even among the top officers, had homes and families outside the military. Like me, these troopers had been created to fight, to kill, and then to fight again until they themselves were killed.

I remembered the Sacred Band of ancient Thebes, the warrior troop made of pairs of lovers, men who would die fighting rather than let their partners down. And they had died fighting, down to the last one, when Philip's Macedonians met them in the battle of Chaeronea. I had been there with Philip and his son Alexander. I had taken part in the hand-to-hand butchery.

What about these youngsters? Would they also fight to the last man—or woman? I recalled the words of an ancient general to his men: "Your job is not to die for your country. Your job is to get the other poor sonofabitch to die for *his* country."

My job was to see to it that these young men and women won their battles with as few casualties as possible. I did not know them, not individually. Yet I was determined to be as good a commander for them as I could be. How good would that be? Would I be good enough, or would I get them all killed?

The testing time was fast approaching. Our landing vessel shot out of the cruiser's launching bay, acceleration flattening us back in our liquid-filled seats. There were no windows, no viewing screens in the landing vehicle's starkly utilitarian interior. Just the lurching and swaying of hypersonic flight and then the slamming shock of hitting the atmosphere, blazing through it like a falling meteor.

The whole squad was silent now. White-knuckle time. The enemy had thrown up nuclear missiles at the invasion fleet. We were supposed to be coming down on the far side of the planet, away from their only base. But what if they had more than the one base our scouts had detected? We had cleaned their satellites out of their orbits around the planet, but what if they had aircraft to intercept us? A single hit with a laser beam or the smallest of missiles would blow our hypersonic lander out of the sky. And us with it.

"Approaching jump zone," came the word from the cockpit, little more than a whisper in my helmet earphones.

The ship was still bucking and vibrating badly, biting deeper and deeper into the atmosphere, its outer hull glowing cherry red from the heat. I stood up, unsteady in the rocking, jouncing plane.

"On your feet!" the sergeant bellowed. I knew his name: Manfred, a veteran, hard-bitten and tough enough to forge his squad into a unit that would follow him anywhere without question—and take care of each other, whether under fire or in some brawling training camp.

My three lieutenants were in the three other landers. Our plan was to hit four drop zones in a relatively clear flatland, consolidate our four squads, and then start to assemble the matter transceiver while establishing a defensive perimeter around the site.

It was a night landing. That made no sense to me, since enemy sensors could detect us just as easily in darkness as in daylight. It made things more difficult for us, not the enemy. But the upper echelons had dictated a night landing for reasons that they did not deign to share with the landing force.

So we buckled on our flight packs, tightened our harnesses and helmet straps and lined up for the jump. I was at the hatch, the first to go.

"Jump zone in ten seconds," said the voice in my earphones.

The hatch slid smoothly open. A howling wind slammed at me, almost forcing me back a step. Automatically I pulled down the visor of my helmet. It was too dark out there to see anything with the unaided eyes, but the sensors in the visor lit up the scene quite well.

What I saw was not encouraging. A canopy of massive trees was whipping by, almost a blur at the speed the lander was maintaining. To jump into that jungle would be suicide.

"Jump!" rang in my earphones.

I jumped.

The flight pack vibrated against the small of my back, and suddenly I was hovering almost motionless in midair, falling slowly, floating almost. With my visor's sensors I could see the unbroken carpet of the jungle canopy coming languidly toward me, countless arms of countless trees. Where was the clearing we were supposed to land in?

I was drifting, the energy sphere generated by the flight pack resisting both gravity and inertia but not quite overcoming them, so that I sank slowly, like a leaf drifting to the ground. It was almost a pleasant sensation. But no matter how languid my fall, I was still falling, and if I crashed into those thickly intertwined trees my chances of reaching the ground uninjured were dim.

It must have taken only a few seconds, but it seemed like hours to me. And then I saw the edge of the clearing, where the trees abruptly stopped and the ground was a relatively smooth carpet of grass.

Turning onto my back, I looked up into the starry sky and counted twenty-five silhouettes tumbling through the air. And behind them, the bulkier shapes of the transceiver's components and our supplies and equipment. Out of the corner of my eye I caught a glimpse of our lander, wings tucking back now for supersonic climb, banking steeply away from us and lighting off its main engines, heading back to the cruiser in orbit.

I rolled over again and prepared to land in the clearing, working the flight-pack controls on my belt to bring me to a gentle touchdown on the grass. My boots touched the grass, all right, and then kept right on going. I splashed and started sinking.

"It's a swamp!" I yelled into my helmet mike. "Don't touch down. Hover and look for solid ground."

I tried to lift out of the quicksand-thick swamp but my

left leg had caught on something. I could hear Sergeant Manfred and some of the troopers calling back and forth:

"Looks like some rocks up there."

"Set down easy, see if it's solid ground."

"Boulders—yaargh!" A scream.

I was trying to pull free of the swamp, ratcheting up the power level of my flight pack slowly because my leg was caught and I did not want to wrench it or pop the tendons in my knee. At the same time I was searching across the open area, watching my troopers as they hovered, searching for a safe landing spot. One of them had screamed. Why?

"Look out! That thing's moving!"

What in the seven levels of hell was going on? And what was my leg caught on? The equipment packs were coming down now, splashing into the swamp like rocks falling in slow motion; sinking out of sight.

"It's alive!"

"Blast it! But don't hit Jerron."

I realized that my leg was not caught on anything. Something had grabbed the leg and was holding on to it. Tightly. Tight enough to bend the armor of my legging. I could feel it squeezing against my calf. Whatever it was, it was trying to pull me down into the grass-choked water.

I cranked the flight-pack power up higher and lifted up out of the swamp with something hanging on to my leg. I looked down and saw a nightmare tangle of tentacles and sharp snapping claws. It was climbing up my leg, trying to crack my armor and get at the meat inside.

Still rising slowly into the night sky, I pulled my pistol from its holster and took careful aim. Don't shoot your own foot off, I warned myself. I thumbed the laser power to low and tried to convince my would-be devourer to let go. It snaked another tentacle toward my wrist, pincer snapping audibly despite the rush of wind whipping past my helmet.

"It's you or me," I said aloud, thumbing the pistol up to

half power and slicing off the reaching tentacle. The creature made a growling sound and waved the severed end of its tentacle in the air, spewing dark blood.

Looking down again, I saw its face: a collection of clacking mandibles and glittering eyes, dozens of them. I fired at the eyes, raising the power of my pistol slowly, astounded that the beast—whatever it was—took the punishment for what seemed like an eternity to me. Just as I began to wonder if the laser beam was having any effect on it at all, it gave a howling shriek and dropped away from me.

Suddenly freed of its weight, I shot up even higher into the night sky. I gulped for breath and then started back down.

A full-scale battle was going on below me. I could see laser flashes and hear my troopers yelling and calling back and forth.

"The damned rocks are alive!"

"And *hungry!*"

"And friggin' hard to kill!"

The entire swamp was filled with carnivorous creatures thrashing, slashing, grabbing at our bodies as if we had been sent by heaven to feed them. My troopers splashed through the soupy water, shooting at the swamp creatures while trying not to hit one another.

And our equipment packs, the components of the transceiver and all our supplies, had sunk out of sight to the bottom of the swamp.

"Full power on the pistols," I called to them on the command frequency. "Whoever's got two hands free, unlimber a rifle and go after them."

Panting, battered, frightened, we finally fought free and made our way into the trees. The ground was firmer there and free of things that wanted to eat us. At least, it seemed that way.

We sprawled on the solid ground, massive trees rising in the darkness all around us, and caught our breaths.

"What the hell were they?"

"Think they come up onto dry land?" asked a worried voice in the darkness.

"They must have been figments of our imaginations," one of the women said, sourly. "The briefing tapes specifically told us that no threatening carnivores have been identified on Lunga."

"The highest form of living creature on planet Lunga," quoted another soldier from the tapes, "is a harmless furry tree-dwelling mammalian about the size of a tree lemur."

"So much for the scientific survey of *this* planet."

"So much for Intelligence."

"And the friggin' scouts."

"There's no intelligence in Intelligence."

"When's the last time you saw one of those bald guys away from his computer?"

Another of the women grumbled, "But they're so damnably smart about it. You notice they said no carnivores have been *identified* on the planet."

"Well, I identified a few. My goddamned armor's punched right through. Look at it!"

His chest plate was cracked where one of the tentacled claws had scratched across it. I looked down at my leg, surprised to see blood on my armor. My own, I realized. I had automatically shut down my pain receptors and clamped the blood vessels tight while I was struggling with the creature that had fastened itself to my leg.

"Sergeant," I called, "set up a perimeter and establish guards. I'm going to raise the cargo packs out of that swamp and float them over here. We'll rest here for one hour."

"Yessir," said Manfred.

I dialed the comm frequency of my helmet radio and called for the other squads. One by one they reported in, each of them telling a tale of swamp monsters. Two of the troopers had been killed on one squad. Several others injured.

I called up the map of the area and studied it in the view on my visor.

"We will rendezvous at point A-Six," I told the other squad leaders, picking a spot that seemed high and dry on the contour map. "In two hours. Any questions?"

"One of my men is too banged up to be of any help to us," said a lieutenant. "Can we call for an evacuation lift?"

"Negative," I said. "We bring our wounded with us. And our dead, too."

Chapter 3

While most of the rest of my squad grabbed a precious few minutes of sleep, I went to the edge of the swamp and worked the controls on my belt in an attempt to raise our equipment packs from the bottom of the bog.

One by one, slowly, reluctantly, they came up with big sucking sounds, like someone pulling his boots out of clinging mud. The flight packs worked even under water. I only hoped that their packaging was watertight. Dripping mud and slime, they hovered in the dark night air in response to my command. In the view of my visor's sensors they looked hot red against an eerie yellow-green background.

One of the swamp creatures snaked a tentacle to the nearest of the packs, touched it, decided it was not food and sank back into the ooze. They live in the water, I told myself. They won't come out of the swamp and up onto dry land. I fervently hoped so.

Then I wondered, If the planetary survey did not detect that this clearing was a swamp, if the scouts did not know that there are dangerous carnivores down here, how accurate is Intelligence's estimate of the enemy's strength and capabilities? It was not a pleasant rumination.

Sergeant Manfred rotated the perimeter guard every twenty minutes, giving each trooper about forty minutes' rest. He did not seem to sleep much. I had been built to need hardly any sleep at all. Had he been given the same strength? Could he control every part of his body consciously, even the involuntary nervous system, as I can? Could he slow down his perception of time when the adrenaline flowed, so that in battle his enemies seemed to move in slow motion? Could any of them?

I wondered about that until I saw him finally grab a catnap after the third set of guards relieved the second shift. No, Manfred needs sleep as much as the rest of them. He does not have my talents. None of them do. They are simply ordinary men and women, bred from cloned cells and trained to be nothing but soldiers.

After an hour the whole squad assembled and we glided through the forest toward the rendezvous point I had selected, the bulky equipment packs bobbing behind us. The trek was pure hell. It was hot and sweaty inside our suits, but when some of the troopers took off their armor, biting insects swarmed all over them. They put the armor back on, but the insects stayed inside their clothing, feasting on their flesh. It would have been funny, watching them trying to scratch themselves inside their armor, if they had not been so miserable.

The wounded were even worse off. As they floated in their flight packs, they moaned endlessly. One of the sergeants bawled them out in a vicious, half-whispered snarl:

"You whining bunch of mutts, you'd think your guts had been pulled out the way you're screeching. What are you, troopers or sniveling crybabies?"

"But Sarge," I heard one of the troopers plead, "it's like it's on fire."

"I've got four decorations for wounds, Sarge," another said, "but this is killing me."

Every centimeter of the way, as we groped through the dark forest, with the insects buzzing in angry clouds about our heads, the wounded troopers cried and begged for something to stop their pain.

Then we ran into the squad led by Lieutenant Frede, the unit's medical officer. Her wounded were whimpering and groaning just as badly as my squad's.

"I can't really examine them on the move, sir," she said to me. "Can we stop for ten minutes? And may I use a light to see their wounds properly?"

The enemy was supposed to be halfway around the planet. But what if there were other nasty surprises in this forest, like the swamp things that had tried to eat us? I glided among the trees in silence for a few moments, weighing the possibilities. Frede hovered at my side.

"All right," I said, my mind made up. "Ten minutes. Keep the light shielded."

I went with her as she examined the first trooper, a woman whose forearm had been cut when one of the swamp monsters punctured her armor.

The wound was crawling with tiny red ants feasting on her torn flesh. Frede jerked back with surprise as the ants, obviously bothered by the light, began burrowing into the woman's skin. The trooper screamed, whether in pain or fright I could not tell.

I took off the armor from my own injured leg and saw that the ants were chewing away. One of the drawbacks of inhibiting pain signals is that your body can no longer warn your brain of its danger.

Frede swallowed hard, then went to work on the wounded troopers. She had to flush out the ants with liquid astringents that burned so badly the troopers yelped and howled with pain. I stayed silent when my turn came and received admiring glances in the darkness of that tortured night.

It took more than ten minutes, but not much more. Frede was quietly efficient, once she got over her first shock of discovery. But as we powered up the flight packs again and started to glide forward through the trees, she said to me, grim-faced, "I hope those ants haven't laid their eggs under the skin."

A pleasant thought.

"I'll have to examine all of you once we set up base camp," she said.

We pressed on to the rendezvous point. The giant trees rose all around us in the pitch-black night like the pillars of a colossal darkened cathedral, but their lowest limbs were dozens of meters above the hummocky, leaf-littered forest floor. There was hardly any vegetation on the ground, only an occasional low-lying bush or shrub and thin grass. The high canopy of the lofty trees blocked sunlight very effectively, I realized, preventing much foliage from growing at ground level.

So we drifted through the massive boles of the trees like two squads of ghosts gliding through the sinister night. Muttering, complaining ghosts; clouds of biting insects still hounded us. At least the wounded stopped their whimpering once Frede got rid of the vampire ants. Now and then one of the equipment packs bumped gently into a tree or got wedged between two trunks and some of us had to go back and move it away, then find a wider avenue for it. After nearly two hours of this stop-and-go we finally reached the rendezvous point.

One of the other squads was already there, and the fourth showed up shortly after we did. Once Frede attended to the other wounded, I called a meeting of my lieutenants, leaving the noncoms to direct the checkout of the equipment packs and to make certain we had not lost any. The rest of the troopers began setting up our tents.

All three of the officers shared an uncanny resemblance. They were all about chin-high to me, and had broad, high-cheeked faces with clear blue eyes; they looked enough alike to be brother and sisters. In the dim light of our field lamps I saw that they even had nearly identical sprinkles of freckles across their noses. The army must have cloned them from the same genetic stock.

Lieutenant Frede, my medical officer as well as a squad leader, seemed levelheaded and not given to panic. Yet she looked plainly worried.

"Two of my troopers died," she said as she took off her helmet. The same short-cropped sandy brown hair as the other two lieutenants. "I haven't been able to do much more than give them a superficial look-see while we were on the march here, but it seems to me that the wounds those monsters inflicted on them were not serious enough to be fatal."

"Then what killed them?" I asked.

Swarms of insects whined all around us. She slapped at them. We were all scratching and trying to wave the bugs away.

"I think those swamp monsters must have injected a toxin into the wounds," Frede said, scratching inside the collar of her tunic.

"Poison?"

She nodded. "Poison. Which means that our other wounded may have been poisoned, too."

"Is there any indication—"

She did not let me finish my question. "The wounded are more sick than hurt. I think they've been injected with toxin. They seem to be getting sicker by the minute. Maybe those damned ants are poisonous, too."

I thought about that for a moment.

"I notice, sir," she added, "that you were wounded in the leg. How do you feel?"

"Fine," I said. Then I added, "My immune system produces antibodies very quickly."

Another nod. "Then may I recommend that we take a sample of your blood and use it to transfuse the antibodies into the wounded men?"

"Yes, of course. Good thinking."

So while the troopers began to assemble our transceiver and the dawn slowly lightened the leafy canopy high above us,

I lay down on a cot in Lieutenant Frede's medical tent and let her draw blood from my arm.

"Thank you, sir," she said, holding up the syringe filled with bright red blood.

I sat up and rolled down my sleeve. "If you need more, let me know."

"This should be sufficient, sir."

I got to my feet. The tent's bubble shape was barely tall enough for me to stand without stooping in its center. Four cots with sleeping wounded in them filled most of the floor space; the lieutenant's examination table and other medical equipment were arranged along the outer edge.

Frede stood up also and gave me a critical examination with her sky blue eyes. "You're not one of us, are you?"

"One of who?"

"The regular officer corps. You're from a different gene stock. You're bigger, darker hair and eyes, even your skin coloration is more olive than ours. Are you a volunteer officer?"

I made a rueful smile. "No, Frede, I'm not a volunteer."

She broke into a sly grin. "Then somebody at headquarters must be worrying about our sex lives."

"What?"

"According to the duty roster, you and I are paired for the duration of this mission. It'll be my first time with someone outside of our own clone group."

I must have stared at her like an idiot. Nothing in my briefings or my memories told me about sexual duties.

Her grin faded. "Just what I thought," she said somberly. "You're not a regular army officer at all, are you?"

I sat back down on the cot. "I've been selected to lead this mission by—" What could I say? A god? One of the Creators? An incredibly advanced descendant of the human race who regards us mere mortals as tools for his use, slaves for his whims? "—by the upper echelons," I finished lamely.

"It doesn't matter," she said. "Most of us have already figured out that this mission is some fucked-up brainchild of the higher echelons. Why else would they have replaced our regular captain?"

"Was he your regular partner?"

Her eyes widened. "You *are* a stranger, aren't you? Soldiers don't have regular partners. The army decides who you pair with, just like the army decides everything else in life."

I began to understand. These soldiers are created by the army, to serve in the army. They know no other life. No parents, no families. Nothing but the military way of life. Nothing but serving in the army.

"I wonder why," I mused aloud, "the army didn't do away with the sex drive altogether. Or even make its soldiers sexless."

Frede made a noise that sounded like an angry snort. "Might as well ask why they don't use robots instead of cloned humans."

"Well, why not?"

"Because we're *cheaper*, that's why! And better, too. Because we have emotions. Ever see a robot charge in where it's hopeless? Yeah, sometimes we get scared, sometimes we even run—but more often we stand and fight and kill our enemies even when we're dying ourselves."

I took a deep breath, considering all that. Then I said, "So the army allows sex as a form of reward, then."

For an instant I thought she was going to slap me. Her eyes blazed with fury. "Where are you from? The army allows sex because without it we don't fight as well. The sex drive is intimately entangled with human aggression and human protectiveness—both of them—at the deepest genetic levels. Don't you understand that? Don't you know anything?"

"Guess I don't," I admitted.

"By damn, I hope you know more about fighting than you do about the army."

"I know about fighting," I said softly.

"Do you?"

I nodded, then got to my feet again and left her standing in the middle of her tent, looking more troubled than angry. I knew about fighting, from the Ice Age battles against the Neanderthals to the sweeping conquests of the Mongol hordes. From the war against Set's dinosaurs and intelligent reptilians to the sieges of Troy and Jericho.

I knew about fighting. But what did I know about leading a hundred soldiers in a war that spanned the galaxy, a nexus in space-time that would decide the existence of the continuum?

I began to find out.

Outside Frede's medical tent, most of my troopers were busy assembling the transceiver that would be the hub of our base on planet Lunga. I could see from the number of modules they had already uncrated that we would have to knock down some of the trees to make room for the assembly. Two of the sergeants already had a team working on that, on the other side of what I now considered to be our base camp.

One squad was setting up the antimissile lasers, the only heavy weaponry that had been sent down with us.

"Nice of the big brass to send this down with us," one of the troopers was saying as she connected cables from the power pack to the computer that directed the lasers.

"Yeah, sure," groused the man working alongside her. "They don't want their nice shiny transceiver bombed into a mushroom cloud."

"Well, the lasers protect us, too, you know."

"Yeah, sure. As long as we're close to the transceiver we'll be safe from nuclear missiles."

"That's something, isn't it?"

"Yeah, sure. The brass loves us. They stay up nights worrying about our health and safety."

The young woman laughed.

Other troopers were setting up bubble tents and stacking our supplies. All of them had shed their armor in the morning

warmth and were working in their fatigues, which were rapidly
becoming stained with sweat. The insects that had plagued us
during the night had disappeared with the dappled sunlight
filtering through the canopy of leaves high above us. The little
camp sounded busy, plenty of grunts and grumbles and swear-
ing. In the background I could hear birds trilling and chirping.
Then the cracking, rushing roar of a giant tree coming down.
A thunderous crash. The ground shuddered and everything
went quiet. But only for a moment. The birds started in again,
the soldiers returned to their chores.

I walked past the construction crews, out toward the
perimeter where Sergeant Manfred was in charge of the security detail. He was in his mottled green armor, helmet on,
speaking by radio to the soldiers on guard through the woods.

"Anything out there?" I asked him. I myself wore only
my fatigues, although I had my comm helmet on and I kept a
pistol strapped to my hip. I remembered a time when I wore
a dagger on my thigh, out of sight beneath my clothes. I
missed its comforting pressure.

"There's something bigger than a tree lemur moving out
at the edge of our sensor range," Manfred said, his voice low
and hard.

"Intelligence claims there's nothing bigger than tree
lemurs on the planet."

"Those swamp things were bigger."

"But here on dry land?"

"Could be enemy scouts," he said flatly.

"Maybe we should dig in, prepare to fight off an attack."

"Does Intelligence know how many of these Skorpis are
on the planet?"

"They claim only a small unit, guarding a construction
team."

Manfred grunted.

I agreed with him. Intelligence had not inspired me with
confidence, so far on this mission. "I'll get a squad to start

digging in as soon as some heavy equipment comes through the transceiver. In the meantime, you—"

The blast knocked me off my feet, sent me tumbling a dozen meters. Clods of dirt and debris pattered down on me; acrid smoke blurred my vision. I could hear other explosions, and the sharp crackling sound of laser weapons.

Manfred slithered on his belly toward me. "You okay, sir?"

"Yes!" There was blood on my hand, but that was nothing. "Get your men back toward the base."

"Right!"

I lay there on my belly and squinted out into the woods as I yanked my pistol from its holster. Scarcely any shrubbery to hide behind in this parklike forest, but whole divisions of troops could be sheltered behind those massive trees. I wormed my way backward, looking for a depression in the ground that might offer a modicum of protection.

A laser beam singed past me, red as blood. I fired back before realizing that I should turn off the visible adjunct to the beam. The red light made it easy to see where your beam was hitting, but it also made it easy for the enemy to see where it was coming from. Tracers work both ways, I remembered from some ancient military manual.

Sure enough, a flurry of beams lanced out toward me. My senses went into overdrive as they always did in battle, slowing the world around me, but that was of little use against light-beam weapons. One of the laser bolts puffed dirt scant centimeters from my face; my eyes stung and I tasted dirt in my mouth. Another burned my shoulder. I hunkered down flatter, trying to disappear into the ground, spitting pebbles and blinking dust from my eyes.

A trio of grenades were arcing toward me. With my senses in overdrive I saw them wafting lazily through the air like little black grooved toy balloons. I popped each of them with my pistol while they were still far enough away for their explosions to harmlessly pepper the empty ground with shrapnel. Then a rocket grenade whooshed out of the woods; I had barely enough time to hit it.

I inched backward a bit more, still peering into the trees to find a trace of the enemy. Nothing. They were devilishly good at this. I heard a few muted explosions thudding far behind me, then silence. Minutes dragged by. Birds began to sing again, insects to chirrup.

I lay flat, staring into the trees, straining to catch some sight of the enemy, some trace of movement. Nothing. I carefully clicked off the visible tracer beam of my pistol, then fired into the general area where the grenades had come from. Still nothing. I held the beam steady on a bit of shrubbery until it burst into flame, but still no sign of movement, no sight of the enemy.

"Captain?" I heard in my earphones. My second-in-command, Lieutenant Quint.

"Go ahead, Quint," I whispered into my helmet mike.

"Are you all right, sir?"

"Hit in the shoulder. A few scratches. Nothing serious."

"They seem to have gone, sir."

I ordered the security detail to report in, by the numbers. Four of my troopers had been killed, six more wounded. No further reports of enemy activity.

I waited for nearly an hour. Nothing. The rest of the hundred had dropped their construction chores, of course, and grabbed their weapons to come out and reinforce our perimeter. But the enemy had vanished as suddenly as they had struck.

Finally we trudged back into the still-unfinished camp. I doubled the perimeter guard while Lieutenant Frede looked after the wounded and a burial detail froze the dead. Frede seemed puzzled as she applied protein gel to my burned shoulder.

"Your wounds are halfway healed already."

"It's a capability that was built into me," I said.

"But how? Biomedical science doesn't know how to do that. If we did we'd make all our soldiers this way."

I shrugged as she sprayed a bandage onto my lacerated hand. "I suppose I'm a new model. The first of a new breed."

She gave me a suspicious stare.

"Well, the important thing is that we beat them off," I said, trying to sound cheerful.

She still looked doubtful.

Outside her medical tent I saw Sergeant Manfred waiting for treatment. His face was nicked and one arm roughly bandaged with a blood-soaked rag.

"We beat them off," I repeated to him.

"They're still out there," he said somberly, with the flat assurance of a veteran. "That was just a probe. They'll be back. Tonight, most likely."

Chapter 4

Humans are diurnal creatures. We sleep in darkness and are active during the daylight hours. The Skorpis, my briefings had informed me, were descended from felines. They were nocturnal. All the more reason why our night landing made no sense. All the more reason to believe that Manfred was right; the next Skorpis attack would be at night.

I wanted to be prepared for it, but I was caught on the horns of a dilemma. The more men I put to guarding our perimeter, the fewer were available to assemble the matter transceiver. Without the transceiver we could not get the heavy weapons and sensors that we needed to make our make-shift base reasonably secure from attack.

We had one heavy weapon: the pair of antimissile lasers that, once assembled, could knock missiles out of the sky at ranges far enough to protect us from nuclear warheads. Or so the briefing tapes claimed. I shuddered at the thought of having nuclear weapons used against us. Apparently the high command had the same fear: hence the antimissile system. Our orders were to assemble it first, which we had very happily set out to do.

I gambled and put as many of the troops on the assembly task as possible. That meant roughly half of them. More would simply get in each other's way. The others guarded the perimeter while the construction job—heavy lasers and transceiver—hurried along.

I walked the perimeter myself, studying the landscape, searching for whatever advantages I could find in the natural fall of the terrain. If I had not been so preoccupied I might have enjoyed the afternoon. The forest was actually quite beautiful, the trees tall and straight and stately, the sunlight filtering through the leafy canopy so high up above dappling the ground with patches of brightness. Colorful birds swooped among the trees; insects buzzed and chirped. I even saw a few small furry things scampering across the mossy ground and climbing up the tree trunks. Too small to be one of Intelligence's tree lemurs, I thought.

I saw no sign of the Skorpis or any other enemies. Not a spent power pack, not a footprint on the soft ground. Several of the trees were singed or scratched from shrapnel, but that might just as easily have been from our own firing as the enemy's. For all the traces they left, the Skorpis might as well have been figments of our imagination.

But I did see something that interested me. A broad shallow gully that ran from a nearby stream toward the center of our base. A natural pathway aimed directly at the heart of our encampment. A stealthy battalion could crawl along that gully unnoticed by soldiers on either side of it, especially at night with a firefight going full bore. It had to be guarded, blocked.

Or maybe not. I began to wonder if the Skorpis had already scouted the area and noted the gully. Perhaps when they attacked—tonight, if Manfred was right—they would send a team to probe this sunken highway. If they found it undefended, they might send the main force of their attack along its length, to erupt deep inside our perimeter and shatter our defenses.

That's what I would do if I were in their place. Now how could I turn it into a trap?

I started back toward our lines, my head buzzing with ideas.

My three lieutenants were skeptical.

"Invite them to push along the gully?" Lieutenant Vorl

asked, her voice high with anxiety. "Let them penetrate our perimeter?"

We were in my bubble tent, squatting on the plastic floor like a quartet of Neolithic tribesmen. Again I was struck by the physical similarities among the officers. Sandy hair, freckles, sky blue eyes. Their skin was a light tan, almost golden, as if blended from all the races of Earth. Vorl and Frede could have almost been twin sisters. Quint, my second-in-command, their brother.

"We don't have the manpower to hold the entire perimeter against them," I said. "And we need another six hours before the blasted transceiver is operational. If we can trap a major part of their force and annihilate them, we might be able to break their attack and stay alive long enough to get the transceiver working."

"What about reinforcements?" Quint asked.

I turned to Vorl, my communications officer.

"No reinforcements," she said sullenly. "I worked my request all the way up to the admiral, and the damned lizard turned us down cold."

"We have to hold on until the transceiver starts bringing in the heavy weapons," I said, for about the twentieth time.

"But *inviting* the enemy to infiltrate down that gully . . ." Lieutenant Vorl shuddered.

"I agree," said Quint. "It goes against standard tactical doctrine."

"Lieutenant Frede, what's your opinion?" I asked.

She shook her head, said nothing.

"All right, then," I said. "Three against and one in favor. The ayes have it."

They looked surprised, almost angry. But they took my orders without further grumbling. We spent the hours of twilight setting up our perimeter defenses and mining the gully. I placed a weak screen of automated rifles about a third of the way down the gully, just to give the enemy the impression that the gully was not totally unguarded. I did not want them to discover that they were in a trap until it was too late for them to escape. At the end of the gully, a scant fifty meters from the edge of the transceiver itself, I placed ten of the steadiest troops with Sergeant Manfred. If the enemy reached that far, they had to hold them until the rest of us could come to their aid.

All work on assembling the transceiver had to stop when it became truly dark. We needed every soldier on guard, and I did not want our work lights to illuminate the area for the enemy. Not that they needed illumination. True to their feline heritage, the Skorpis could see quite well in darkness that would seem total to a human.

At least we had the antimissile lasers up and working. If the enemy tried to take us out with a missile attack, we were ready for them. I hoped.

Waiting was the toughest thing of all. The night was dark. No moon, and thick low clouds scudding across the distant twinkling stars. The biting insects swarmed at us again, making everyone miserable. Voices hooted out of the woods, night birds clacked and chirped with almost mechanical regularity. Now and then something would give out a weird, high-pitched howl.

Nothing bigger than a tree lemur had been identified on Lunga, I reminded myself. But those howls sounded as if something quite large was making them.

We scratched at our bug bites and grumbled and waited.

I was hunkered down in a shallow dugout a few meters to the right of the gully, in full armor—dented legging and all. My rifle rested on the sill of upturned earth in front of me. My belt and webbing were studded with grenades and spare power packs. Pistol on my hip, combat knife in my boot. I thought again of the dagger that Odysseus had given me; I missed its comforting presence, but it would have been of scant use strapped against my thigh, beneath my armor.

The sensors in my visor showed a tranquil forest. No sign of the enemy. I even saw an actual tree lemur, or something very like one, climbing slowly down one of the trunks, staring in my direction with enormous eyes, and then working its way back up the trunk until it finally disappeared into the foliage high above.

They have to attack tonight, I told myself. They want to knock out the transceiver before we get it operational. It makes no sense for them to wait until—

"Some movement in fourth sector," I heard a sergeant's guarded whisper in my earphones.

That was off to my left. I peered across the gully and into the trees out there. I could see nothing.

But when I swung my head back I saw a flicker of movement among the trees directly in front of me. They're out there, I told myself. Getting ready to hit us.

What if they use nukes? I had pondered that question all day. The transceiver components were shielded; nothing short of a direct hit would damage them. Our body armor could absorb a lot of punishment and protect us from radiation. But a tactical nuclear grenade could kill most of us very quickly and allow the enemy to walk in and dismantle the transceiver by hand, if they wanted to. We had no defense against tactical nukes.

Nor did we have any nukes of our own. Our mission was basically logistical, not attack. If anyone started throwing nukes around, it would be the enemy and we would be fried meat.

I saw more movement out among the trees. Of course, we had the automated antimissile lasers. They had been the first package we had set up. They could track a missile and zap it within microseconds, although how well they could track through the heavy canopy of the trees was a question I wondered about. Could they pick up a grenade at short range and destroy it? I doubted that.

Suddenly half the world lit up and a terrific roar shook the ground. My visor sensors overloaded and turned off. With my unaided eyes I saw that they had fired a barrage of rocket grenades at us, roaring in low to the ground, flat trajectories. Our antimissile lasers fired and blew away several of them in brilliant blossoms of flame.

Every sergeant tried to report in at once. The Skorpis were attacking around half the perimeter, charging forward into our guns.

And then they were hitting my sector, too. They came rushing out of the woods, firing and bellowing earsplitting battle cries. I grabbed my rifle and started shooting back. They were big, I could see that even at this distance, huge and heavily muscled with cat's eyes that glowed fiercely in the light of the battle.

I ducked down for a moment and worked the antimissile override controls on my wrist. Depressing the lasers to fire horizontally, I started them sweeping the woods with their heavy beams. My troops knew enough to keep down, stay flattened on the ground. The Skorpis walked into those powerful beams as they advanced. I saw them sliced in half, heads vaporized, trees blasted into flame. They dropped down to their bellies; their advance stopped.

We peppered them with our grenades. I saw white-hot shrapnel shredding the ground were they lay. But they did not retreat. They inched toward us, crawling on their bellies, dying and being horribly torn up by our fire but still coming at us, inexorably, relentlessly, like an unstoppable tide.

And the alarm on my other wrist tingled. Glancing to my left I saw that the automated laser rifles in the gully had found something to shoot at. Whole squads of Skorpis were slithering down the gully, just as I thought they would. The attacks on our perimeter were merely holding actions designed to keep our attention away from the gully.

Merely holding actions. Humans and Skorpis were dying all along our perimeter. The forest was in flames now. Rockets whizzed through the scorching air. Explosions shook the ground. Laser beams flicked and winked everywhere in a crazy crossfire. Men yelled and screamed at the enemy, who bellowed and roared back at us.

And the main weight of their attack was slithering down the gully. They were past the screen of automated rifles now, thinking that they had put the gully's defenders to rout. They were moving faster now, crawling on their hands and knees, almost to the point where Manfred and his ten would have to stop them.

I jammed my thumb on the stud that set off the mines. The whole gully erupted in a tremendous blast of flame and billowing dirt and smoke. I saw bodies hurled into the air, silhouetted against the flaming trees, and parts of bodies, too.

For a stunned instant everything went quiet. Absolutely still. Or was it that the shattering, overpowering roar of that explosion had simply deadened my ears?

"They're coming at us again!" It sounded like Lieutenant Vorl, who was stationed halfway around the perimeter from where I was. And, sure enough, more Skorpis were pushing forward toward my position, staying low to avoid the heavy laser fire, but still advancing toward us.

"Fall back," I said into my helmet mike. "Fall back and tighten up our perimeter." With a smaller circumference to cover we could intensify our fire.

For what seemed like hours we inched back and the Skorpis crawled forward. There was no end of them. I saw hundreds of their bodies sprawled in death all around us, yet their comrades still pressed forward, relentless, unheeding. My rifle became too hot to fire; it just refused to work. I pushed it aside and drew my pistol.

"Piss on it," muttered a trooper at my side.

I thought he was having trouble with his rifle, too.

"Piss on it," he repeated, adding, "sir."

And he demonstrated what he meant. With laser beams zipping scant millimeters over our heads, he wormed his penis out of his pants and armor and urinated on the coils of his rifle. Then he flattened onto his belly and resumed firing at the Skorpis.

"Cools the coils, sir," he said, without taking his eyes off the advancing enemy. "That's one advantage we men have over the women. Sir."

So I pissed on my rifle and got it working again, feeling slightly embarrassed in the back of my mind but glad to have the rifle functioning once more.

We were being forced back toward the heart of our camp. The Skorpis were evidently willing to spend as many of their warriors as they had to in order to destroy us. This was not a battle of attrition; it was a battle of annihilation. Either we wiped them out or they wiped us out.

Like all battles, though, there came a lull. We had fallen back to a tight little ring around the camp. Most of our bubble tents had been shot to shreds and the antimissile lasers had taken several blasts, but the screens around the transceiver were holding up. So far. The fires that we had started among the trees around our original perimeter had mostly died away now, although the air was still filled with a smoky, woody redolence.

I called my lieutenants together to see how we stood. We met in a muddy crater blown into the ground by a rocket grenade. Casualties were serious, but our weapons were still functioning; we had plenty of spare power packs for them. We were almost out of grenades, though.

"Report our situation to the fleet commander," I told Lieutenant Vorl. She edged away from the rest of us, opened up the wrist of her armor and started tapping on the keyboard set inside.

"The transceiver's still intact," I summed up, "but we can't afford to retreat any further. They're almost within hand-grenade range of the equipment now."

"The screens will still protect the equipment," said Lieutenant Quint.

"Yeah, but not us," Frede grumbled.

"It's only another hour or so until dawn," Quint said. "According to Intelligence, the Skorpis almost always break off their attacks when daylight comes up."

"And Intelligence has been a hundred percent on everything so far, haven't they?" Frede countered.

"It's the 'almost always' that worries me," I said. "They seem willing to fight to the last man."

"Theirs or ours?"

"Whichever comes first."

A laser beam lanced by over our heads. A grenade exploded somewhere.

"They're starting up again."

Vorl ducked her head back into our conversation. "Sir, I'm having a difficult time raising the fleet. A lot of interference on every available channel."

"Jamming?"

"Possibly. Or something's wrong with the comm equipment."

"Great," I muttered. "Just what we need, to be out of touch with the fleet."

More firing. But none of the sergeants were reporting in, so I assumed nothing major was developing. Not yet.

"How long can we sit here and hold them off?" Quint asked.

"As long as we have to," answered Frede.

"Do you have something else in mind?" I asked Quint.

He gave me a curious look: part worry, part eagerness. "The troop's morale is still high, sir. We've been killing those bastards all night long. But if we have to continue just standing here and taking it, morale will start to crumble. Especially if the Skorpis don't break off their attack at dawn."

"What are you trying to say?"

"I think we should counterattack them, sir. Battles are won by the moral factor as much as by attrition or maneuver. Hit back at them, run them off, scatter them and kill them. That's what we should do."

"You live longer on the defense," Frede said. "Attacking troops take higher casualties than defending."

"And we have no idea of how many of them are still out there," Vorl pointed out. "We could be charging into millions of them."

"That's the key point," I said. "We don't know what we're up against, how many of the enemy are facing us and what their intentions are."

A trio of rocket grenades slammed in around us, throwing us against the crumbling sides of the crater.

"Here they come again!" shouted one of the sergeants.

No more time for discussions. The enemy solved our argument for us. We crawled out of the crater and headed for our individual squads, or what was left of them. The Skorpis were charging at us now, bawling out their hideous war cries and running straight into our guns. We fired and fired and fired, pouring laser beams into them, knocking them down, severing legs and arms and heads, killing them by the scores, by the hundreds.

And still they came at us. The sky began to lighten, although I barely noticed it, I was so busy fighting. And the clouds of dust and smoke obscured the coming dawn.

My rifle finally gave out, its power pack drained completely. There was no time to replace it. I yanked out my pistol and fired point-blank at the huge Skorpis warrior who was charging down on me. The beam burned through his armor and went completely through his body, yet his momentum was so great that his dying body hurtled into mine, nearly knocking me off my feet.

It was hand-to-hand now, and the Skorpis had tremendous advantages of size. My senses went into overdrive again, slowing down everything around me to dreamlike slow motion. I reached down and grabbed my combat knife, a deadly thirty centimeters of serrated blue steel. And suddenly I was Orion the primitive warrior once again, shooting and clubbing and slashing at the enemies around me. The world dissolved

into a bloodred haze as I cut a swath through the swarming
Skorpis.

They were huge, much bigger than I, but I was far faster.
They seemed to move like sluggish mountains, arms the width
of my torso, shoulders wider than two normal men, their
catlike faces towering over me, contorted into snarling masks
of rage and pain and hate. Their body armor, designed to
reflect laser beams, was too light to stop my knife thrusts. I
fired my pistol at their slitted eyes, blinding them if nothing
else, and ripped at their throats or hearts with my knife.

They fought back, but I could see their massive arms
moving languidly to aim their pistols, see their eyes shifting,
see them stumbling and staggering as they tried to back away
from me. In vain.

Four of them were charging at me, laser pistols sparking,
making my armor glow. I shot one in the throat, then swung
my beam across the second's visor. I ripped open the gun hand
of the third and kicked the fourth in the chest hard enough to
make him stagger backward. The second one lifted his visor
and I shot him through his cat's eye, clubbed the one who was
clutching his slashed hand with the butt of my pistol, then shot
him in the base of his skull as he fell.

The fourth one threw his pistol at me; it must have been
drained of power. I saw it revolving lazily through the smoke-
filled air and flicked it away with the length of my blade. The
Skorpis howled and leaped at me, clawed hands reaching for
my throat. I sidestepped and fired a laser bolt into his neck.
His head twisted and he landed on his face with a jarring
thump. Before he could move I leaped on his back and drove
my knife through his armor and into his heart.

I jumped to my feet and turned full circle. It was all over.
There were no more of them to kill. I stood alone in the midst
of their fallen bodies, knife dripping their dark black blood,
pistol hot enough in my hand to scorch my flesh if I had not
been wearing battle gloves. They lay all around me, dead or
dying.

I blinked and turned again, every sense stretched to its utmost, every molecule of my body tensed for more danger, every atom of my being lusting for battle. It had been built into me; I had been created to kill. I swung around a third time, looking for more enemies. There were none.

A handful of my troops were left. Those still standing were gaping at me as if they were seeing an apparition. A hero. A monster.

Chapter 5

"They've gone," said Lieutenant Frede, her voice hollow with fatigue and pain. She was on the ground, propping herself up on one elbow, her face smeared, her legs soaked with blood. And a pistol gripped so tightly in her hand that even her glove seemed ghost white.

"Dead," muttered a standing soldier. "All of them."

"You killed them," Sergeant Manfred said. His right arm hung limply from his shoulder. That side of his face was burned black.

"We killed them," I said. "Or drove them off."

The sky was brightening from gray to pale blue. The sun would be up in a few moments. Gray smoke drifted in the air, acrid, stinging.

Frede rolled herself over to a sitting position. She was surrounded by bodies, ours and the more massive corpses of the Skorpis.

"*You* killed them," she said, with real awe in her voice. "I never saw anything like it."

The others who could still stand clustered around me. I was their savior, their hero. But also something of a maniac, a killing machine, a mindless merciless slaughterer. Hardened soldiers though they were, they were filled with admiration for my battle prowess, true enough, but also with something almost approaching fear.

"All right," I said, trying to break their mood and get

them back to normal, "let's get the wounded tended to. Where's Vorl? We've got to report to the fleet."

"She's gone," said one of the soldiers. "Grenade."

I pointed to the six least-injured men and women and told them they were the medical detail. Six others I put to checking out what was left of our camp, what supplies were undamaged. I myself tried to use the comm unit in my helmet to raise the fleet.

I got little more than static for my efforts. Which puzzled me. It could not be Skorpis jamming, not now that they were all killed or retreating. Unless they had set up automated jammers. That meant we would have to go through the woods searching—

"I hear you, Orion." Aten's voice was strong and clear. It seemed to be inside my mind, rather than coming through my earphones. "Pull down your visor."

I did as he commanded, and his image took form before my eyes. He was still in his splendid white and gold uniform, but he looked grimly unhappy.

"A huge enemy battle fleet appeared out of subspace and surprised our fleet. Most of our ships were destroyed, the others have fled."

"Fled?" I yelped.

"They were vastly outnumbered, Orion. They had to leave the area or be wiped out."

"But what about us? What about our support?"

"You and your assault team are on your own until the fleet can regroup and return to Lunga."

"How can you expect us—" But my question was too late. His image winked out. He was gone.

I slid my visor up and saw that my troopers were going about the tasks I had assigned them. None of them had heard my conversation with Aten. It was as if I had been in another dimension, walled off from them, while I spoke with the self-styled Golden One.

I let them work until we had sorted out our situation,

keeping the news of the fleet's abandonment to myself for the time being. Before anything else, I had to know what shape the troop was in.

The situation was bleak. Of our original hundred, forty-six had been killed and a further twenty-two so badly wounded that they expected to be sent back to the fleet as soon as a medical evacuation ship could reach us. Of the thirty-two remaining, all of us had suffered wounds of various severity, although we could still stand and fight. The only one among us to have gotten through the battle unscratched was Lieutenant Quint. I wondered about that.

Frede was in serious shape, both her legs smashed by a grenade. It would take a week or more for the automated medical regenerators to repair her shattered bones and rebuild the flesh. Others were just as bad off, and we did not have enough regeneration equipment to handle them all.

Sergeant Manfred's shoulder was badly burned, but aside from a loss of blood he was in walkable condition. I went to the patch of ground where he lay, with two soldiers kneeling over him with a transfusion kit.

"Manfred, you are now a lieutenant," I told him.

He glared up at me. "Sir, I don't want to be a lieutenant. I'm a noncom."

"You're a lieutenant, Manfred, until I can get someone else to head Vorl's squad. You will behave like a lieutenant and the squad will treat you like a lieutenant. End of discussion."

Clearly unhappy, he mumbled, "Yes, sir."

"How long will this transfusion take?" I asked one of the troopers.

She squinted at the readout numbers. "Nine minutes, sir."

"Lieutenant Manfred, there will be an officers' meeting in fifteen minutes, where my tent used to be. Report to me there."

"Yessir."

Both the troopers were grinning at him.

It was a pitiful officers' meeting. Manfred's shoulder and face were covered with spray bandages. Frede sat with her legs poking straight out, encased in regenerator packs up to the hips. And Quint looked strangely uneasy, as if he thought he ought to be wounded somewhere, too.

I had several nicks and burns on my arms, legs, and face, but nothing that required more than a smear of protein salve and a bit of time.

"What's the supply situation?" I asked Quint.

He took a deep breath. "Not good, at the moment. Practically everything was destroyed in the fighting. We have enough food on hand for three days, max. We're down to a dozen spare power packs. And the medical supplies are already stretched to the limit. We need more regenerators, especially. And fresh tents, cots, clothing, replacements for damaged body armor—"

"That's enough," I said. "I get the picture."

"When does the medevac ship arrive?" Frede asked.

"It doesn't," I said.

"What do you mean? We've got wounded here we can't even treat properly! They've got to be lifted back to the fleet."

"There isn't any fleet. They were jumped by a superior force and had to retreat."

"They ran away?" Quint's eyes went so wide I could see white all around them. "They've left us here and run away?"

"That's the situation," I said. "We're on our own."

It took several seconds for them to absorb the bad news. Frede and Quint stared at each other.

"Those goddamned lizards," Quint muttered.

Frede looked down at her encased legs. "I never did trust them, the cold-blooded bastards."

Manfred nodded to himself, as if he had expected nothing less. I was struck by the difference in looks between Manfred and the two lieutenants. The features of his face were sharper, harder. A hawk's beak for a nose, narrow eyes of dark brown, almost black. Thick bristles of black hair, cropped close to the skull. Even his skin was different from theirs, swarthier, stretched tight over his jutting cheekbones.

"We're going to die here," Quint whispered.

Manfred almost smiled. "What's the difference? If the fleet had taken us back they would've just put us back in cryo storage."

Quint glared at him. "You can be revived from cryo storage, soldier, sooner or later."

"Sure," said Manfred, "when they're ready to let us die for them."

"That's treasonous talk!"

"Hold on," I said. "We're not dead yet, and I won't have my officers squabbling." Turning to Manfred, I added, "Not even my new officers."

"Sorry, sir," he muttered. To me, not to Quint.

Frede asked, "If we only have a few days' rations and no prospect of resupply from the fleet, what chance do we have?"

"There's a Skorpis base on this planet," I replied. "They have plenty of food there."

"Raid the Skorpis base?"

"That's suicide!" Quint insisted.

I gave him a wintry smile. "Would you rather die fighting or starve to death?"

Manfred said, "Sir, with all due respect, that Skorpis base is on the other side of the planet. It'll take a helluva lot more than a few days to get there. What do we live on in the meantime?"

"We live off the land," I said. "Our briefings said that the local vegetation and animals are edible. Some of them, at least."

"What about our wounded?" Frede asked. "Some of them can't travel."

I said, "We can't leave the wounded here. They'd starve to death. And the Skorpis will probably come back; they still want to knock out our transceiver, I'm sure."

"Even without the fleet here to send us supplies?"

"The fleet might sneak a supply ship through, sooner or later. That's what the Skorpis must be thinking right now. They'll be back to finish the job."

Frede scowled at me. "So instead of waiting for them to attack us here you want to take all of us halfway across the planet and attack them in their stronghold?"

"If we wait for them here we'll be sitting ducks. I'd much prefer that they didn't know where we are."

Quint shook his head. "What difference does it make? We're dead anyway."

"That's the spirit," I said disgustedly.

The sudden whining hum of the antimissile lasers made all four of us look up. The lasers were powering up, swiveling, pointing skyward.

"Something's coming in," I said, scrambling to my feet.

The lasers fired, the crack of their capacitor banks sharp enough to hurt my ears. Seconds later we heard the dull rumble of an explosion, like thunder rolling in the distance. Another crack from the lasers, and then another clap of thunder, closer.

"This base is nothing more than a target now," I said. "We've got to get out of here."

None of them argued.

Battered, patched and bandaged, we gathered ourselves and what was left of our supplies and started the long trek through an unknown country toward the stronghold of our enemy. I led our vanguard, twelve of our least-wounded troopers. The twenty other relatively healthy men and women formed a guard around the flanks and rear of our wounded. All of us glided a meter or so above the ground on our flight packs. What was left of our supplies we carried along on the flight packs of our dead comrades.

We left their bodies at the base. It was a hard decision. Normally a troop cares for the bodies of its slain soldiers as well as possible, freezing them in cryo units when they can, in the hope that they can be repaired and eventually revived. Even if not, the bodies are treated with respect and eventually cremated with honors.

We could not bring the bodies of our forty-six dead with us; we simply did not have the strength for it. And besides, I figured that they would soon be cremated in a nuclear fireball. The Skorpis had tried to seize our base with their warriors and failed. Now they were determined to obliterate the base without risking further casualties.

Even as we moved the troop out into the dark, shadowy forest, the antimissile lasers fired again. And again. I wondered if the enemy was throwing that many nuclear missiles at our base, or if they were clever enough to send in dummy missiles, cheap unarmed rockets that gave our sensors the same signature as a nuclear-tipped rocket. Sooner or later our lasers would drain their power packs to exhaustion. Then a nuclear missile could be fired at us with impunity.

We started off near noon, local time, although the trees' high canopy hid the sun from us. It filtered down in mottled patches of brightness, breaking the cool shadows of the forest as we wended through the massive tree boles, a caravan of battered, grimy soldiers in green armor floating across the ground as silently as wraiths.

Dwindling in the distance we heard the insistent *crack! crack!* of the lasers, firing at incoming missiles. It seemed to me that the firing grew more desperate as the hours passed. The enemy couldn't be using up all that many nuclear warheads, I told myself. Most of those missiles must be decoys, dummies, meant to exhaust the system.

At last we drew too far away to hear the lasers. Either that, or their power packs had gone dry. If we had been there, and if we had fresh supplies coming in, we could replace the power packs and keep the base defended. But such was not the case.

It was nearly nightfall when we heard the vicious clap of thunder, sharp as a blow to the face. The shock wave of a nuclear explosion, palpable even at this distance. The sky behind us lit up and a low, grumbling, growling roar shook the air.

We all stopped, without a word of command or comment among us, and looked back. Through the trees, against the darkening twilight sky, we saw a mushroom cloud boiling up and up, bloodred in the light of the dying sun.

"There goes the base," someone said.

"You were right," Frede said. She was floating beside me, her encased legs dangling uselessly. "If we had stayed there . . ."

"Maybe the Skorpis think we did stay," I said. "Maybe they think we're all dead now and they've got nothing to worry about."

Frede said, "Maybe." But the tone of her voice told me that she did not truly believe that.

The nuclear blast set off a forest fire. We could see flames leaping through the distant trees. Thick dark smoke blotted out the stars. We hurried through the night, trying to put as much distance between us and the fire as possible. It was spooky gliding through the forest by the light of our helmet sensors. Every time I turned to look back over my shoulder the sensors would be momentarily overloaded by the bright flames; it was like glancing up at the sun.

Throughout that night we saw animals fleeing the fire. I thought I saw, out in those flickering shadows, creatures much larger than tree lemurs hopping and darting frantically to put as much distance as possible between themselves and the forest fire. Just as we were. The ground was rising, higher and drier as we advanced; the insects that had plagued us during our first nights on the planet seemed less annoying now. Or perhaps we had merely grown accustomed to their whining, bloodsucking company.

At last we came to a broad, swift-moving river. It surged quietly between steep banks, deep and wide, a good firebreak,

I thought. We skimmed across the water and made camp on the other side. It was close to midnight and we were all exhausted.

I posted a light guard, expecting no dangers. Nonetheless, we made no fire in our camp. I took a quick meal of tinned rations, bland and almost tasteless, but steaming hot once the tin was opened.

"Hey Klon," I heard a trooper whisper in the darkness to his buddy, "I'll trade you my 24-C/Mark 6 for your 24-C/Mark 3."

"What the hell for? They all taste like dust."

"I like the Mark 3 better."

"Lord God of Battles. Here, take the friggin' thing. What the hell difference does it make?"

Another voice chimed in, "Hey, don't you mutts know that these here rations have been prepared by the army's best scientists to provide all the nutrition a soldier needs in his daily requirements? It says so right on the label."

"He likes the Mark 3 better," Klon growled disgustedly.

"He *likes* this crap?"

"Yeah, I like it. So what's it to ya?"

"I dunno, Klon. What do you think?"

"You know what they say, pal—"

And a whole chorus of voices chimed in, "You've got to be born to it!"

They all laughed, and I wondered what made the punch line so funny to them.

After eating, I scouted around the area, glad to be on my feet again after a day of gliding in the flight pack. The guards were reasonably alert, and the forest seemed to offer a decent stock of small game. Even without the sensors in my visor I spotted several rabbitlike animals and a few smaller things nibbling on the foliage between the trees. There must be plenty of game here, even if those poor things running from the forest fire did not make it across the river. We would not starve.

Usually I need very little sleep. But the past night's battle and the strain of this day were catching up with me. Satisfied that the camp was secure, I turned over command to Lieutenant Quint and looked for a spot to lie down.

And almost tripped over Lieutenant Frede's encased legs.

Dropping to my knees beside her, I whispered, "I hope I didn't hurt you."

"Only a little," she whispered back.

"How are you feeling?"

"Tired, mostly. There's no pain from the legs, if that's what you mean."

"That's good."

"I'm afraid I won't be much good as a sex partner for a while."

"That's all right." I felt almost embarrassed, for some reason.

"You could ask for a volunteer, you know. We have four unpaired women in the troop, because of the casualties."

"I don't need one."

"It's within regulations to ask for a male volunteer, even if they're already paired with a female."

"I know the regulations," I said. But that was only partly true; I had not bothered to review all the army's rules, especially those regarding sexual practices.

"You're a celibate?" Frede asked.

I wished she would get off the subject. I temporized, "For the time being."

"Ohhh," she said. "You've got somebody waiting for you."

"Yes," I said, thinking of Anya.

But Frede had other ideas. "You know, of course, that the regulations on sexual assignments are equally binding on both members of the assigned pair."

"Yes, I know."

"That means that whatever your preferences, you are paired with me for the duration of this mission."

"I told you that I know that."

"You can call for volunteers while I'm on the sick list, but once I'm back to full duty, you are restricted to me."

"Right."

"Even if you have somebody waiting for you, back wherever it is that you come from."

I finally realized what she was driving at. "Oh! I see."

Frede laughed at my sudden discomfort, there in the darkness of the forested night. "Don't fret, Captain. I'll be good to you."

She was teasing me!

I reached out and clamped the nape of her neck, gently. "I'm looking forward to it," I whispered back to her.

Then I left her sitting there with her legs spraddled and a surprised expression on her face.

But the humor of the situation quickly faded from my mind as I stretched out on the mossy ground and closed my eyes. Anya. Where in all the space-times of the continuum was she? Why couldn't I be with her? Why must I be here with the troop of cloned soldiers, stranded, abandoned on some godforsaken world?

Godforsaken indeed. Forsaken by the would-be god Aten. Abandoned by the Creators, all of them. Had Anya abandoned me, too? Or had the others forced her to stay far from me?

I could not sleep. I wanted to. I closed my eyes and willed my body to relax. But I could not force my mind to stop thinking. I saw past lives, past missions on which the Golden One had sent me. I was Osiris in Egypt long before the first pyramid was built. I was Prometheus in the cold and snow of the Ice Age. I crumbled the wall of Jericho and helped to remove the Neanderthals from this timestream of the continuum.

All at the service of Aten, the Golden One. And always with the help of Anya, the goddess whom I loved. The Golden One hated me for that. Aten hated me because Anya loved me. Time and again she took human form to be with me. Time and again he tried to keep us apart. I had crossed eons and light-years to be with her. But always he schemed to keep me from her.

I am Orion the Hunter, created by Aten to do his bidding, hopelessly in love with one of Aten's fellow Creators. And here I was, stranded on some insignificant planet in the middle of an interstellar war, lost and abandoned with a troop of soldiers who were just as much slaves of their creators as I was of mine.

Why? Why had the Golden One placed me here and then abandoned me? To keep me away from Anya? Or for some other purpose, some part of one of his impetuous schemes for shaping the continuum to his own suiting? He had gone mad once, I knew. Perhaps he had become deranged again.

But no, I thought, what he's done now has all the earmarks of a calculated, deliberate plan. He put me on this planet Lunga for a reason. He simply has not deigned to reveal his plan to me.

The first rays of sunlight began to filter through the trees. I pulled myself up to a sitting position and gave up all pretense of sleep.

All right, I said to myself. If the Golden One won't tell me why he's put me here, I'll have to find out for myself.

Chapter 6

We resumed our trek across the world of Lunga, heading for the base that the Skorpis were building on the other side of the planet. I sent a few scouts ahead and out along our flanks, but none of them saw any sign of the enemy.

We came to the edge of the vast forest on the second day, and hesitated only long enough for me to consult the maps from the briefing files in my helmet computer. The display on my visor showed a broad stretch of open grasslands, then a range of rugged mountains. I did not like the idea of moving across the open grasslands; I had felt much safer beneath the screen of the forest's trees. The enemy's sensors could probe through the foliage, I knew, yet I felt instinctively that being out in the open was dangerous.

So we struck across the green, rolling country and headed for a fair-sized river that flowed out of those distant mountains—so distant that we could not yet see them. Trees and game lined the river's banks, and the fresh water was a necessity, since our recycling equipment had been left behind at our camp.

I began to live up to my name, and taught the troopers how to hunt. Laser rifles are hardly sporting, but we were after food, not entertainment. We began bagging the local equivalents of rabbits, squirrels, and birds.

"Wish there *was* something bigger than a tree lemur on this planet," complained one of the troopers.

"Something with more meat on it, anyways," said his buddy.

But for day after day, week after week, we saw nothing larger than the nocturnal tree dwellers. Slowly our wounded healed, all except two of them who died on the trek. We cremated them—we were building campfires each night, since we had no sign of any enemy presence. They might have put surveillance satellites into orbit, but if they had spotted us they had no move against us. And we could not risk eating our fresh-caught meat raw: cooking not only made the chewing easier, it killed parasites and microbes.

It was more difficult to maneuver along the riverbank than it had been to get through the big forest, because the trees along the river were smaller and the underbrush much thicker. Often we simply swung ourselves on our flight packs out over the river itself and glided along without obstructions.

"Here, there's things living in the water!" a trooper shouted one morning.

I should have berated her for looking down when a soldier should be looking out for signs of danger. Instead I told her that people catch fish and eat them. It was totally new information to her and to the rest of the troop, even the officers. Again I was stung at how narrow these soldiers' lives were. They had been given nothing except what they needed to fight with.

Soon enough, though, I made fishermen out of a few of them. Most did not have the patience. But each evening, as we made camp, my fishing brigade brought us back some wriggling protein.

At last we could see the mountain range rising up in the distance, blue and purple folds of bare rock topped with bluish white snowcaps. That evening Lieutenant Frede took the casts off her legs and gingerly tried walking around the campfire.

"Feels good," she said. The tentative expression on her face eased into a happy smile. "Feels fine!"

She slept beside me that night, snuggling close as the fire

guttered low. The next night Frede took me by the hand and
led me off into the trees, away from the camp.

"It's time, Orion," she said, sitting with her back against
a trunk. She pulled me down to sit next to her.

"Yes," I said, glancing back toward the camp. We were
well screened by bushes. "I suppose it is."

We started slowly, but very soon Frede was giggling
softly as she slithered out of her fatigues and helped me pull
mine off, all at the same time. I was surprised at my own
passion. I had intended to accommodate Frede, yet very
quickly I was just as frenzied and heated as she. A vision of
Anya stirred me, and I fantasized that is was my goddess with
whom I was making love: Anya, warm, daring, loving, distant
Anya, the woman whom I had sought across all of space-time,
the goddess who had taken human form for love of me.

The stars were glittering through the trees as Frede and I
lay side by side, sweaty and relaxed, and watched the moon
rise over the sawtooth silhouette of the mountains. It was a
tiny moon, far and cold and bleak, hardly throwing any light
at all onto the wide, silent landscape.

"What are you thinking about?" Frede whispered to me.

I shrugged my bare shoulders. "Nothing."

"Nothing, hell. You were thinking about her, weren't
you? The woman you're promised to."

There was no point in denying it. "Yes," I breathed.

"While we were doing it, too?"

"Yes."

"Good," she said.

"Good?"

"They don't tell you in training, Orion, but it's not smart
to make friends. Not among soldiers. Don't get yourself emo-
tionally tangled. Even if we live through this, they're just going
to pop us back in the freezers for retraining. When we come
out we'll be assigned to other partners."

"Do they wipe your memories when you're in cryosleep?"

"Sometimes," Frede said. "Depends. Mostly they just lay new training on you, add new data on the next mission."

Very much as Aten did to me, I thought.

"So don't get emotional about this," Frede said, very matter-of-factly. "It's not smart for soldiers to make friends."

Her tone of voice was so flatly unemotional that I wondered how certain Frede was about what she was telling me. She sounded like someone trying to convince herself.

I lay silent beside her for a long while. Then Frede slid a hand along my thigh.

"Ready for more?" she whispered.

I was, and so was she.

Afterward, I idly asked, "What happens when a soldier gets pregnant?"

She was silent for a moment, then replied softly, "That never happens, Orion. We're all sterilized. For a soldier, sex is just a way of letting off steam. We'll never have children."

And for the soldiers' masters, I knew, sex was a way of maintaining their army's aggressive/protective instincts. I remembered the bitter words of an old man who had been a storyteller, blinded by Agamemnon after the siege of Troy: "Lower than slaves, that's what we are, Orion. Vermin under their feet. Dogs. That's how they treat us."

I shook my head. Dogs are allowed to breed, at least.

I slept that night, curled up with Frede. And dreamed.

I could not tell if it was truly a dream or one of the Golden One's communications. Often Aten or one of the other Creators would summon me out of space-time to some other place in the continuum to speak to me, to give me orders, or to berate my performance.

In this dream—if a dream it was—none of the Creators appeared. I was alone, walking on the hard-packed sand of a wide white beach, breaking surf hissing and booming as the waves ran up to lap my booted feet, a hot sun burning in a sky of molten bronze.

At the edge of the sand was a line of tangled bushes, some of them bearing flowers of red and blue. And beyond them, the stumps of buildings, looking like candles that had burned down almost to their ends, melted and blackened. Ancient buildings. Somehow I knew that they had been abandoned for untold ages. Abandoned, just as I was.

A voice called to me. I did not hear the voice, I felt it in my mind. It did not call me by name, it did not even use words. But I sensed a presence that was reaching out to me, touching me mentally, examining me. I felt an intelligence, a curiosity— and then a loathing, fear and anger and disgust all mixed together. A rejection. The presence in my mind disappeared, winked out as suddenly and completely as a dolphin diving beneath the waves.

I stood alone on that distant beach and felt a yearning, a desperate desire for understanding, a sadness about who I was and what I was, a hollowness at the core of my existence.

"Anya!" I cried out. "Anya, where are you?"

No answer. The surf rolled in. The wind blew in my face. The sun beat down on me. For all I could tell, I was alone on that dream beach, alone on that planet, alone in the universe.

I wept.

Frede shook me awake. "Orion, what is it? Wake up!"

I sat bolt upright. We were in camp, under the trees, the first streaks of dawn breaking through low gray clouds over- head. The other troopers were still sleeping, sprawled alone or coupled, except for the sentries I could see down by the river- bank.

Frede wrapped her arms around my bare shoulders. "You were moaning in your sleep."

"I had a dream."

"And calling to someone. Anna."

"Anya," I corrected.

She pulled her shirt on. "Is she the one you're promised to?"

I almost smiled. "She's the woman I love."

Frede nodded matter-of-factly. "If we get out of this alive—you'll be going back to her?"

"I don't know. I want to, but I don't know if I can."

"The army won't pop you back into a cryo freezer until the next time they need you?"

I had to shake my head and admit, "I just don't know."

"That's what we've got to look forward to," Frede said. "Cryosleep or battle. With some training in between. It's a great life, Orion, being a soldier. You've got to be born to it."

So that was the meaning of the tag line. You've got to be born to it. A bitter joke, but it was just as applicable to me as to any of these cloned involuntary soldiers. You've got to be born to it. Or created for it. As all of us were.

"Come on," I said, getting to my feet. "Time to start moving."

She got up, but locked her gaze on me and asked, "Why?"

I stared back at her. "What do you mean?"

"Why do we have to start moving?"

"You know as well as I—"

"To attack the Skorpis base? Why should we? What difference would it make? Except to get the rest of us killed."

I knew that the troops had been conditioned to obey, to fight, to follow orders. That conditioning had weakened terribly during this mission, but it could be reinforced by a set of key words that every officer above the rank of lieutenant had memorized. I supposed, now that I thought about it, that higher ranks had other sets of memorized trigger phrases to use on the ranks below them. Aten had put those key words into my memory, and they sprang to my conscious mind now, just as if he were standing at my elbow, prompting me.

You are the tip of the spear, the point of the arrow. Those few words would drown Frede's dawning independence under a flood of mental conditioning, turn her from a frightened, doubting woman into an obedient soldier once more. A grumbling, complaining soldier, perhaps, but one who would no longer question the mission she had been assigned to, or waver at the thought of its impossibility.

I could not speak those words. Not then. Not to Frede. Condemned to a life she never had asked for, never had any choice in, she was beginning to show the first signs of independent humanity: she was afraid that she—and all of us—were not only going to die, but throw away our lives needlessly.

She misunderstood my openmouthed silence. "All right, you can break me down to private and put somebody else in my place. But I still don't see what good we're going to do, throwing fifty-two of us at an entrenched Skorpis base."

"What alternatives do you see?"

She took a deep, shuddering breath, as if afraid to say what was in her thoughts. But she squeezed her eyes shut for a moment, gathering her courage, and then said, "We can stay here. Live here. Forget the war, forget whatever the hell it's all about and just live the rest of our lives right here."

"Forget our orders?"

"They abandoned us, Orion! We didn't leave them, they left us!"

"Do you think the enemy will leave us alone?"

"We're no threat to them if we stay here. And they know we can maul them pretty good if they attack us. So why would they bother us as long as we can't hurt them?"

I thought about it for a moment. She was probably right. But if we remained here I would never find Anya. And as much as I hated the Golden One and all the other Creators, except Anya, I had to admit that there must be some purpose to his sending me here, to this place and time. Some reason.

"Frede," I said slowly, calmly, "my orders are to knock out the Skorpis base on this planet. Setting up the transceiver was merely the first step toward that objective, you know that."

Her face hardened. "And you're going to try to obey those orders, with fifty-two effectives?"

"That's what we're here for."

"Then you're going to get all of us killed."

"That's what we're here for," I repeated.

She glowered at me for a moment; then, strangely, she broke into a rueful grin. "You're sounding more like a real officer every day."

She marched off and started giving orders just as if nothing had been said between us. I was glad that I had not been forced to use the conditioning phrase. But I thought that Frede's moment of questioning was not the last discipline problem I would face. Indeed, it was probably only the first.

It got cooler as the ground rose toward the mountain chain. The nights grew chill, with a steady wind sweeping down from the mountains. It rained for several days in a row, until we were coughing miserably, sodden and muddy. But we doggedly slogged ahead, following the natural pass made through the mountains by the river as far as we could, until the river itself dwindled to a set of shallow gurgling streams that splashed over the rocks and tumbled into picturesque waterfalls.

The rain turned to snow, light at first but thicker every day. We left the streams behind and plodded cold and wet through the snow-filled rocky defiles, camping in caves each night. At least we could light fires and sleep dry. We could see the jagged mountain peaks rising above us, covered with snow. Some days the winds up there whipped the ice crystals into long undulating plumes that caught the sunlight in dazzling prisms of color. It would have been beautiful if it weren't so damnably cold. We floundered through snowdrifts hipdeep, shivering and hurting. Then at last we found more streams, unfrozen, gurgling through the snowbanks. We had crossed the mountain divide. Now our path lay downhill.

A week later we were out of the snow at last, sweating and

complaining about the growing heat as we descended the mountain range. Then we caught sight of the ocean. And the Skorpis base.

The base was not as huge or well fortified as I had feared. But it was big enough to make me wonder how my handful of troopers could even approach it. There must have been a thousand Skorpis warriors there, at least.

Studying it at the highest amplification my visor sensors allowed, I could see no trenches or fortifications protecting the base, although there were plenty of gun emplacements ringed in a semicircle around it. The base was built on the edge of the sea, along a bright width of white sand beach. Low buildings with roofs that glittered with solar power cells. Many rows of square tents, all neatly lined up with military precision. Some long metallic projections jutting out into the sea, like piers, with cone-shaped buildings dotted along them.

A tendril of memory tugged at me. I swept my gaze down the beach, past the outermost posts of the Skorpis, along the dunes and beach grasses for several kilometers, and . . .

There it was! The beach I had seen in my dream. The ruined city, blasted and burned down to stumps and scattered debris. It was real.

I pointed to it and asked my officers, "Can we get to those ruins without the Skorpis seeing us?"

Quint immediately shook his head negatively. Frede looked skeptical. But Manfred said:

"If we work our way along the ridge up here until we're past the ruins, and then come down there, where that river runs into the sea, we can edge up along the beach and keep the ruins between us and the Skorpis perimeter. Unless they send patrols out that far, we ought to be able to make it undetected."

"If they don't send out patrols," Quint echoed.

"And if they don't have surveillance satellites in orbit," Frede pointed out. "We'd show up nice and bright in infrared, I imagine."

"Not if we go along the beach in daylight," I said. "The beach itself will be pretty hot from the sun."

"Satellite sensors could still detect moving objects."

I considered the problem for another few seconds, then commanded, "We'll go that way. Start the troops moving. I want to be ready to get across the beach by midday tomorrow."

They all made reluctant salutes.

"And if we see any Skorpis patrols we lay low and let them pass. No firing unless they shoot first. I want to get into those ruins undetected, if we can."

We spent the rest of that day working our way along the ridge of mountains, down to the cleft where the river cut through on its way to the sea. With the fading light of dusk we maneuvered down to the riverbank, where we made camp for the night. No fires. And no Skorpis patrols in sight.

I did not even try to sleep that night. I skulked through the shadows, every sense straining, knowing that the Skorpis were at their best in the dark, wondering if they really were complacent enough to sit snug inside their base, wondering above all if they knew that we were near. The river made a rushing sound, as if hurrying to be reunited with the sea. The wind blew in off the water, warm and moist, like a lover's breath. The night was dark, moonless, and the stars scattered against the black sky meant nothing to me; I could not recognize any of the familiar constellations of Earth.

I saw the gleam of a light, far down the river, almost at the point where it widened into a broad and deep bay. An enemy patrol? Why would the night-loving Skorpis need a light? It couldn't be any of my troopers; they were all behind me with strict orders not to make a fire or even strike a spark.

I edged carefully toward the light, the rushing river on my left, keeping as much as I could to the brush and stunted trees that lined the base of the cliffs we had descended. I eased my pistol from its holster.

The light grew, brightened, and suddenly I knew what I was seeing. I knew who was there.

Boldly I left the protection of the foliage and slipped the pistol back into its holster. Sure enough, Aten the Golden One was standing in an aura of radiance, arms folded across his chest, an expectant smirk curling his lips. He no longer wore a military uniform. Now he was decked in a long white cloak atop a glittering metallic formfitting suit.

He looked like a god, I had to admit. Splendid of face and form, as ideal a human specimen as Michelangelo or Praxiteles could carve. Yet I knew that his appearance was an illusion, a condescension, actually. Aten's true form was a radiant sphere of energy; he assumed a human aspect merely to deal with his mortal creations.

"You are doing well, this time, Orion," he said to me, by way of greeting.

"Is this planet so important to your plans that my entire troop has to be sacrificed for it?"

"Obviously so," he answered. "Why do you think I placed you here? I have great faith in your abilities. After all, I created them, didn't I?"

We were temporarily outside the space-time continuum, I knew, wrapped in a bubble of energy that neither my own people nor the Skorpis could see.

"You created my soldiers, too?" I asked.

"Those things? Oh no! How little you must think of me, creature, to believe I would make such limited tools. No, they have been developed by their own kind, the humans of this era."

"And what is so important about this era?"

He smirked. "How to specify time to a creature who perceives it so linearly? You see, to those of us who *understand,* Orion, time is like an ocean—like the great sea that lies out beyond your pitiful little camp. You can be at one place on that ocean or another, but it is still the same ocean. You can travel across it, or even plumb it to its depths."

"There are currents in the ocean," I said.

"Very good! There are currents in the sea of space-time, as well. Quite true."

"And where in this ocean of space-time is Anya?"

His face clouded. "Never mind her. She is busy elsewhere. Your task is here."

"This is the ultimate crisis that you spoke of? Here on this planet?"

"This is part of it, Orion. Only a small part. Small, but critical."

"And you expect me to take the Skorpis base with fifty-two troopers, with no support, no heavy weapons?"

Aten made a condescending shrug. "I wish I could send you more help, Orion, but you must make do with what you have. There are no reinforcements to spare."

"Then we will fail. We will all be killed, with no hope of success."

"Perhaps I will revive you. If I can."

"And the others?"

"They are of no concern to me. I didn't create them; they were made by their own people."

"Who regard them as dirt. Expendable cannon fodder, cheaper than robots."

Again the shrug. "Tools, Orion. They are tools. You can't expect someone to pamper his tools. You use them as they have been designed to use."

"And when their task is finished?"

"You store them away carefully until you need them again."

"Or you throw them away because they've been damaged doing your work for you."

Aten shook his golden mane. "How emotional you are, Orion. Your emotions help to drive you, I know, but it does make it tedious talking with you."

"I want to see Anya. To speak with her."

"Impossible."

"Then I'll go out and find her."

He laughed in my face. "Certainly, Orion! Grow wings and fly away."

"I've traveled across the continuum on my own," I said.

"Really? On your own? Without any help from your beloved Anya? Or perhaps even from me?"

"On my own," I insisted. But I wondered inwardly if that was true.

"Do your job, Orion," he said harshly. "Demolish this Skorpis base, or as much of it as you can before your little troop is wiped out. Then perhaps I can bring you to Anya. If all goes well."

"But my troopers—"

"They'll all be dead, Orion. Then you won't have to worry about them any longer."

With that, he disappeared, winked out like a star eclipsed by a cloud. I was left alone on the bank of the river that rushed to the sea.

Chapter 7

We marched along the riverbank the next morning, and by noon had reached the area where it broadened into a wide calm bay. By midafternoon we reached the beach and stopped for a few moments of rest and reconnoitering.

From where we were, huddled beneath the trees and shrubbery that lined the river, we could not see the Skorpis base. The ruins of the ancient city stood between us and them. My hope was that they could not see us, and would not detect us as we marched across the open beach to the ruins.

"No sign of Skorpis patrols," Manfred told me, sweating from running to report in person. I had forbidden all radio communications for fear of being overheard.

"I'm sure they have satellites up," Frede said. Quint seconded her estimate with a worried bob of his head.

"Even if they do," I said, "we're not doing any good here. Those ruins will make a better defensive site, if we have to fight."

So we dashed across the kilometers of beach, skimming scant centimeters above the sand on our flight packs, hurrying, worrying, expecting a swarm of Skorpis attackers to swoop down on us at any moment. Frede kept squinting up at the brazen sky, as if she thought she could see any satellites up there if she only tried hard enough.

It was fun skimming that fast, so low to the sand, the waves to one side and the flowering shrubs on the other streak-

ing into a blur, the cracked and crumbling ruins rushing up
toward us, wind whistling past, breathless, racing, racing like
a flight of low-swooping hawks.

We slowed down as we approached the ruins and touched
our boots onto the sand, one by one, panting and laughing
from the dash we had just gone through. The sun was hanging
on the rim of the ocean horizon, a bloated red ball that threw
long purple shadows among the blasted buildings and heaps of
debris. We filed into the ruins gratefully, happy to feel some
little protection of the decaying walls after being out in the
open, vulnerable.

It had been a sizable city, I could see now that we were in
it. Wide avenues lined for several kilometers with buildings
that must have risen quite high before they were blasted into
rubble. How old? And what destroyed them?

"Radioactive background is nominal," Frede murmured
as we picked our way through the debris littering one of the
major avenues. She had unpacked the scanner from her equipment web and was holding it out stiffly in front of her almost
the way a blind man pokes his cane ahead of him.

"This city wasn't nuked," I said to her.

The troop had automatically fanned out into two columns, one on either side of the shattered street, the troopers
spaced out widely enough so the first shots of an ambush
would not take out more than one or two of us. Manfred had
taken the van, with four picked men and women; Quint had
assigned himself to the rear. I was starting to worry about
Quint; it was normal for a man to be afraid, but he was letting
his fears get in the way of his duties.

"If it wasn't nuked," Frede asked, walking beside me,
"how did it get blasted so badly?"

I thought I knew. "They fought a battle here. A long,
bloody battle that went from street to street, building to building. Hand-to-hand killing, for weeks. Maybe months."

Frede shook her head, uncomprehending. "But that

would mean the whole population was in the fight: civilians, children, everybody."

Memories were stirring in me. Troy. Stalingrad. The Crusaders' siege of Jerusalem and the bloodbath that followed.

"Civilians, children, everybody," I echoed. "In the siege of Leningrad most of the city's population died of starvation. They ate rats and all the animals in the zoo."

"Hell's fire," Frede murmured.

"Can you get a fix on how old these ruins are?" I asked her.

"Doubtful. Have to know the ambient ratios of radioactives for this planet, and that data isn't in our computer background data."

"You're sure?"

"I already checked," she said, tapping the side of her helmet where the earphones were. "I got curious about this city the first time we saw it, when we were still in the mountains."

So these "tools" can exhibit curiosity. They are more than mindless killing machines, despite the purposes of their creators.

We made camp in the littered basement of one of the crumbling buildings, with a thick concrete roof over our heads and solid walls around us. I let the troops risk a small cook fire, and while they were preparing the last of the food we had hunted in the mountains, I left them to wander through the buildings, seeking some clue to their age and origin.

I could find no pictures to help me. No paintings were left unburned, no statues unsmashed, no friezes or murals or mosaics were recognizable on the shattered remains of the walls that still stood. I found patterns of tiles here and there, tantalizing suggestions of what might have been decorations or even maps. But nowhere was there enough of a wall left intact for a whole picture to be seen.

As I picked my way through the debris-filled buildings, I

discovered something else. There were no animals scurrying about. No rats or even insects that I could detect. The destruction of this city must have happened so long ago that even the bones of its inhabitants had long since crumbled to dust and blown away on the winds of the nearby sea.

I stood in the middle of one ruin, in what might have been the lobby or entrance hall to a great building. With my booted foot I scraped aside some of the debris on the floor and saw that it was tiled in colors that once had probably been quite bold. Now they were faded with time, gray with clinging dust. I hunkered down on my knees and swept more of the debris away, seeking a pattern, a picture, any kind of a clue as to who built this city and when.

Nothing but a checkerboard of many-colored tiles. Perhaps, like the ancient Moslems, the creatures who built this city refused to draw representations of themselves.

What difference does it make? Once, long ago, the creatures who built this city fought an implacable enemy. And lost. Their city was ground down to dust. A civilization was destroyed. Another turn of the wheel.

Wearily, I took my helmet off and used it for a pillow as I stretched myself out on the rubble-strewn floor and gazed up at the darkening sky, those strange patterns of alien constellations. And with all my heart I wanted to be with Anya, to see her, to speak with her, to watch her fathomless gray eyes when she smiled at me, to touch her, hold her, love her and know that she still loved me.

Clasping my hands behind my neck, I said to myself, You boasted to the Golden One that you could find her without his help. All right, then, let's see you do it.

At least I could try.

I closed my eyes and attempted to remember those times when I had been translated across the continuum. The moments of nothingness. The cryogenic cold of the void between place-times. The endless dance of the atoms slowing, shifting, energies glowing and radiating in an endless coruscation, rising and waning like the tides, like the moon, like life itself.

Nothing happened. When I opened my eyes I was still in the shattered remains of the long-dead city, lying on the littered floor of one of its roofless bombed-out buildings. It was deep night; the stars had shifted noticeably above me. The luminous ribbon of the Milky Way twisted across the sky, clouds of stars, rich beyond counting. That pale, tiny, distant moon looked down on me sorrowfully. It seemed vaguely familiar, as if I had known it in another life, a different era.

Who are you?

I felt the voice, rather than heard it. The faintest thread of a question, inside my mind.

Who are you? it repeated.

"I am Orion," I answered aloud.

You are not like the others.

"What others?"

Those who call themselves the Skorpis. And their allies.

That made my chin come up. "Allies? What allies?"

We have seen you before. You were here yet not here.

"What do you mean? Who are you?"

No answer. Only a sense of utter revulsion. And then it was gone. I was alone again. Whoever—whatever—it was, it had left me.

I sat up and pondered. I had not imagined the contact; it was real. And it was here, in this space-time. It knew of the Skorpis. And it said that the Skorpis were not alone; they had "allies" with them.

"Who are you?" I called out.

No reply.

"I identified myself to you. It's only fair that you tell me who you are." The words sounded slightly ridiculous to me even as I spoke them. Some entity contacts me telepathically and I demand that they follow the rules of etiquette.

I sensed an amusement, although it might have been merely my own feelings of foolishness.

I waited there, squatting on the littered floor, until the sky began to turn milky pale above me. Admitting defeat, I got up and returned to the building where my troopers had camped.

Manfred was standing in the doorway at street level, rifle in his hands.

"Captain!" he snapped. "You're all right!"

"Of course I'm all right," I said.

"We spent half the night searching for you. When you disappeared—"

"I was inspecting the city," I said curtly. "If I had run into trouble I would have contacted you on the emergency frequency."

In the gray light of dawn Manfred's taut face looked half disappointed, half relieved. "Yes, sir, I suppose so. But still, we expected you to return and when you didn't . . ." His voice trailed off.

I clasped him on the shoulder. "You're right, Manfred. I should have told you that I was going to spend the night exploring. It's my fault. I hope you didn't lose too much sleep."

"No, sir. I'm fine." But now that I looked at him closely I could see that his eyes were baggy from sleeplessness.

The troop breakfasted on prepacked rations; then I sent them out by squads to check out the ruins and locate the best defensive positions they could find. Each squad went out under its top sergeant; I kept the officers with me.

"We need to scout the Skorpis base," I told them. "And, if possible, to get inside it."

Quint made a snorting laugh. "Sure. We'll just walk up to their perimeter and ask for a tour."

"Or tunnel from here to there," Frede suggested, grinning.

"I've done some tunneling in my time," I said, "but I don't think that would work in this case."

"Then what do you have in mind?" Quint asked. Then he added, "Sir."

I considered telling them about my telepathic contact but decided against it. I wasn't certain that I believed it myself. But the thought that the Skorpis might have allies inside their base was too important to neglect.

"I'm going alone," I said.

"You can't do that," Frede snapped. "With all due respect, sir, you can't go out on a suicide mission and leave your command to fend for itself."

"It needn't be a suicide mission, Lieutenant. I'm not a total fool."

"Then let me do it," she said without hesitation.

I shook my head. "I've had more experience at this sort of thing than you. I'll do it. If I'm not back by sundown tomorrow, you can consider me dead."

Frede looked as if she wanted to argue, but she knew it would be pointless. Manfred looked as if he thought I was crazy. Quint almost smiled. If I was killed, he would be in command.

Manfred cleared his throat. "May I ask, sir, how you intend to get to the Skorpis base? There's a couple of klicks of empty beach between the edge of these ruins and their perimeter."

"Wait until dark?" Quint asked.

"They see better in the dark than we do," Frede reminded him. "Any advantage we have, it's in daylight."

"Cross the beach in daylight?"

I smiled. "No, that would be like trying to sneak up on a pack of Tyrannosaurs."

"Tyranno-what, sir?"

"Very large carnivorous reptiles, ten meters tall, teeth the size of your forearm," I explained.

Frede looked as if she thought I was making it up.

Manfred brought us back to the subject. "Sir, if you can't

get across the beach without being seen, how are you going to get to their base?"

"Swim."

"Swim?"

I said, "Their base is laid out along the beach, isn't it? There are even some projections like piers that extend into the water, aren't there?"

"Yessir, but—"

"I'll double back to the bay, slip into the water there, let the current carry me into the ocean and then swim along the beach to the Skorpis base."

"That's a lot of swimming, sir," said Manfred.

"I'll use a flight pack. I assume they're watertight."

"Yessir, but salt water is very corrosive and—"

"What if there are animals in the water like the ones we met in the swamp?" Frede asked.

I hadn't thought of that. Sucking in a breath, I said, "I'll have to outrun them, I guess. Or kill them."

"It's suicide," she said flatly.

I gave her a tight smile. "I'm not asking permission."

Chapter 8

The water was surprisingly warm.

I had expected the bay to be cold, fed as it was by the river that came down from the snowcapped mountains. But instead the water was almost bath temperature, warmed by the sun during the long hot days.

The current was strong and swift, once I got away from the shore. I made a mental note to remember that for when I returned. I would have to struggle against that current unless I hugged the shoreline closely. The flight pack would help, of course, if it wasn't drained of power or corroded by the salt water.

With a final wave to Frede and Manfred, who had accompanied me to the edge of the bay, I ducked beneath the surface and let the powerful current carry me out to sea. I had stripped down to nothing more than shorts. The only equipment I carried was my pistol, my knife, and the flight pack strapped to my back.

I have strengths and abilities far beyond those of normal humans, even the cloned warriors that made up the involuntary army of this era. I could stay underwater for a quarter of an hour without difficulty, and even longer if I needed to; in an emergency I could squeeze spare oxygen from my body cells.

But I am not superhuman. I knew that if one of those tentacled swamp things got its grip on me now, underwater, I

would be face-to-face with death. My laser pistol would work
underwater, but only at very short ranges. The water absorbed
laser energy very quickly.

I wished that we had oxygen tanks with us, so that I could
remain submerged indefinitely. But we did not. Oxygen tanks
were not among the equipment we had carried to the planet
with us. I wished that the flight pack could push me through
the water faster, but I dared not drain its power pack too
quickly. So I had to be content with allowing the current to
carry me along, saving the flight pack for when my muscle
power alone would not be enough to propel me where I
wanted to go.

When I broke to the surface, I saw that I was already past
the curve of the shoreline. The sun was high overhead, the
swells of the ocean driving up onto the long white beach,
where the waves broke and boomed relentlessly. I swam out
beyond the surf, using the flight pack to help me against the
tide, and then struck out parallel to the beach, heading for the
Skorpis base.

The salt water was beautifully clear and lit by the afternoon sun. I could see brightly colored fish by the hundreds
sparkling and dashing about. A sleek, deadly-looking hunter
slid through the water farther out; it paid no attention to me
and I did nothing to change its attitude. None of those tentacled things from the swamps, thank fortune. I had no desire to
get tangled with one of those again.

When I came up for a gulp of air again, I saw that I had
made precious little progress toward the Skorpis base. Must
be a current running against me, I thought. Or perhaps the
tide is moving slantwise with respect to the beach. Reluctantly
I notched my flight pack to a slightly higher power and dived
beneath the waves again.

In the distance, through the crystal water, I saw what at
first I thought was a reef. Fish swarmed all around it, a glittering moving rainbow of coruscating colors and flashing movement. As I came closer, though, I realized that it was not a

natural formation but a set of structures built underwater and crusted over with coral and seaweed and a thousand other forms of shellfish and underwater plants.

I popped to the surface again to get my bearings. The ruins of the ancient city lay up above the beach. These underwater structures were part of that city, I guessed. Probably there were tunnels connecting the two. I tucked that possibility into my memory; it might be useful later.

I swam to the coral-encrusted structures. There were long arms reaching from the shore out to sea a kilometer or more, buttressed by stout pillars and cross-bracing. Whoever had built the city had built these structures, too. But why? I could discern no reason for them, no hint of their purpose.

Predators lurked there. As I glided along the structures, looking for something that might be an entrance, I saw a flicker of movement. A brightly colored fish suddenly disappeared in an eyeblink-fast snap of jaws. Looking closer, I saw a long gray eel-like thing hovering by one of the girders, its head filled with glinting teeth and a pair of beady eyes. Stretched along the girder, it was almost invisible until it moved. I reached for the combat knife strapped to my thigh. Its presence gave me some comfort.

I spent some time examining the ancient structures. If there were any hatches or air locks in them, they had long since been cemented over by coral and barnacles and other sea life. It was bitterly ironic. The intelligent beings who had built this underwater complex had long since vanished, probably self-destructed in a genocidal war. Now their magnificent structures served as homes for fish and crustaceans and seaweed and the lowliest forms of life on the planet.

Then I saw something big prowling through the water. Something with arms and legs.

Like the snapping eel, I froze in place beside a crusted buttress, hanging in the water with my feet dangling, holding my breath. By being still I could be almost invisible. Or so I hoped.

Three of them. Three human shapes gliding through the water a few dozen meters away. Skorpis? It was difficult to judge distance and size underwater. Two of the shapes were considerably larger than the third. They seemed to be escorting it as the three of them swam along. They wore bubble helmets and had flippers attached to their feet. As they came nearer I saw that each of them was encased in a skintight suit that bristled with equipment. Yet I saw no weapons on them. I could not make out their faces, but they seemed big enough to be Skorpis warriors. At least the two of them did. The third? A child?

I scanned my memory for information about the Skorpis. Yes, they traveled as tribes. Their society was matrilineal, their leaders all females. Warriors could be male or female, both were of the same size, there was no sexual dimorphism among the Skorpis. That meant that the third one was either a child or a member of a different species.

I was running out of air. Soon I would have to get up to the surface and fill my lungs. But I dared not move while the Skorpis were so close. Fortunately their attention seemed to be focused on the sea bottom. All three of them were looking intently downward as they paddled by.

As soon as they had passed me—by no more than twenty meters—I began slowly rising toward the surface, keeping the heavy buttress between me and them.

Tangy salt air tasted better than wine to me, but I had no time to spare enjoying it. My mind was torn between my original objective of reaching the Skorpis base and a new curiosity about the trio nearby. Where were they going? What were they looking for?

I took a deep breath, then dived back underwater and decided to trail this trio, at least for a little while.

I glided along behind them, watching from a few dozen meters away as they probed deeper and deeper among the jutting underwater structures. They certainly seemed to be searching for something. They inspected the ends of each of the long, tubular structures, spending several minutes examining one before moving off to look at the next. I had to go up to the surface twice while they intently studied the maze of long cylindrical tubes and their supporting buttresses.

I began to realize that many of those tubes had been broken off, smashed åt their ends. With all the sea life growing on the structures, that had not been evident at first. But now I could see that some tubes were far shorter than others, and their ends were ragged, as if they had exploded from within or been smashed from without.

At last the Skorpis trio, if that is what they were, swam out to the farthest tube. I dared not follow them all the way out there, for there was no cover to conceal me. The tube extended more than a hundred meters farther into the sea than any of the others. Perhaps it was the only tube to remain undamaged in whatever catastrophe overtook the others. In any event, I stayed close to the protective maze of girders and buttresses that supported the broken tubes.

The trio began to unlimber their equipment as hordes of curious fish swarmed around them, almost obscuring my view of them. In short order I saw the flash of a laser cutter and bubbles of heated water rising toward the gleaming surface above us. All the fish scattered away. The trio were engrossed enough in their work for me to rise to the surface several times for more air.

After a while the laser flashes stopped and I could hear through the water a cacophony of banging and the screeching of metal on metal. Then a long, tortured groaning sound, like a long-shut door being forced open on rusted hinges. The three of them disappeared from my view.

I waited long minutes. I went up to the surface for air. They were still gone when I came back down.

If that tube actually does connect with the ruins of the city, I thought, this could be a way for the Skorpis to infiltrate the city and wipe out what's left of my troop. Is that what they're up to?

I had to know.

I swam along the length of the tube to its end. None of the Skorpis were there, although much of their equipment floated in the water, tethered to the open end of the tube. They had opened it, I saw. They had pried open a small hatch and gone inside. I hung by one hand on the edge of that open hatch and debated my next move. It was dark inside the tube; I could not see much. The three of them might be waiting in there for me to walk into their trap, or they might be half a kilometer down the tube, searching its length to see if it brought them to the ruined city.

Remembering that the Skorpis saw in the dark much better than I could, I still squeezed carefully through that open hatch and inside the tube. I found myself in a water-filled chamber. The walls inside were smooth metal, untouched by the teeming sea life that had attached itself to the outside. I felt panic rising in me unbidden. It was one thing to be underwater in the open ocean. But in this confined chamber something like claustrophobia hit me. The only way out was through that narrow hatch and if it closed and trapped me in here—

My hands, blindly probing the ceiling of the chamber, found another hatch. I pushed against it and it swung upward. The gushing water drew me up through it into another chamber, this one lit a ghostly gray by luminescent walls. I kicked the hatch shut and the water drained out; I could hear the faint hum of pumps at work.

I stood on shaky legs and breathed again. The air was musty, damp, but breathable. Looking around this chamber, I saw still another hatch set into its curving wall. This was an air lock; it had been designed to let people go out into the ocean and come back inside again.

The Skorpis had done so and were somewhere up the tube now. Had they heard the pumps cycling? Did they know I was here? Were they waiting for me on the other side of that hatch?

I slid my laser pistol from its holster and leaned my free hand on the hatch. It swung open slowly. Whoever had designed this air lock had not been worried about enemies invading their city. The hatches opened at a touch.

I peered down the long, straight passageway formed of the tube's interior. It was more brightly lit, its curving walls glowing with luminescence, three sets of wet footprints clearly visible on its metal flooring. I even saw their three sets of flippers, left on the floor a few meters up the passageway.

If they were waiting to ambush me I saw no sign of it. The passageway was perfectly smooth, there were no alcoves or bends for them to hide in. I could see for hundreds of meters along it, but then it rose at a slight angle and I could see no farther.

Should I follow them or wait for them to return? They were far enough up the passageway that they probably did not hear the pumps recycling, so they most likely did not know I was behind them. I could wait here, keeping the hatch slightly ajar. When they returned I could shoot all three of them before they had a chance to blink their eyes. They would be dead meat in this featureless passageway; no place for them to hide. They were not even carrying weapons, as far as I could tell.

But they might be scouting out a way for the Skorpis to infiltrate the ruins and surprise my troopers. Frede must have been right; they had put surveillance satellites into orbit and watched us trek to that ancient city. Like spiders watching a band of weary, lost flies. They sat in the center of their web and invited us to come in.

I heard their footsteps before I saw them. Echoing down the metallic passageway, the soft wet padding of their bare feet came to me. Then their voices, low and rumbling like distant thunder. I pulled the hatch almost completely shut, leaving just a slit open for me to peer through. And shoot through. There was not an atom of cover for them.

Checking my pistol to make certain it was set at its highest level and still fully charged, I waited grimly as they came closer to me and their deaths.

They were talking as they walked down the passageway.

I found that I could understand their language, just as I had understood every language I had encountered on all of the missions the Golden One had heaped upon me. I could almost see his smirking expression of superiority, almost hear him telling me gloatingly that he had put the knowledge of the local languages into my brain the way one might insert a list of names and addresses into a computer.

"Another waste of time," one of the Skorpis was grumbling.

The smaller one, in the middle, said in a lighter, softer tone, "Absence of proof is not proof of absence."

The first one growled, "You may impress your fellow scientists with such talk, but all I see is a day spent searching for prey that doesn't exist."

"They exist," said the smaller one. "We're certain of that."

The third one spoke up. "Once I was certain that I could fly with no aid except a certain magical beverage that I had been drinking." His voice was heavy, sorrowful. "I was *very* certain. But I was wrong. Several broken bones showed how wrong I was."

"The aliens are here," said the one in the middle. Her voice sounded like a woman's. A human woman's.

"So you believe."

"We have evidence of their presence," she insisted.

"I am only a warrior, not a scientist. I believe what I can see, what I can touch or smell or hear or sink my teeth into. Your evidence"—he practically sneered the word—"is nothing but old myths and the tales of ancient ones."

They were getting close enough for me to see that the smaller of them was a human. A woman. Humans working with the Skorpis? I had thought that the human race was locked in a war for survival against the Skorpis and their allies. How could humans be allied to our enemies?

"We have more evidence than the mythology," the

woman said. "And these underwater structures were built for a purpose."

Neither Skorpis warrior answered her. Yet their silence was more eloquent than further arguing.

They were close enough for me to see clearly now. Unarmed. From the sound of their conversation, they knew nothing about my troopers in the ruins. They were looking for aliens, based on ancient myths.

If I gunned them down it would tell their leaders that enemies were near. When they failed to return to the Skorpis base, others would be sent to search for them. I could not hide their bodies. Sooner or later they would be found. The fact that they came out here unarmed told me that there were no predators in these waters that they feared. Their disappearance would immediately be suspect.

And, truth to tell, I found the prospect of shooting an unarmed human woman more than I wanted to deal with. Besides, I wanted to find out what she was doing with the Skorpis. There was much more going on here than the Golden One had told me.

Chapter 9

Softly I shut the hatch. Swiftly I opened the one in the floor and slipped into the water. Closing it behind me, I swam back out into the open sea and used my flight pack to drive myself quickly away from the end of the tube, back to the structures that could hide me.

If the trio suspected that someone else had been in the air lock, they gave no sign of it. They came out, with helmets and flippers back in place, gathered up their tools and swam back toward the Skorpis base. I waited awhile, then followed at a more leisurely pace, bobbing up to the surface every few minutes to gulp in air, rather like a dolphin.

There were underwater piers at the Skorpis base, too, but they were far smaller than the ancient ruins. Only two of them, and so new that hardly a barnacle had attached itself to them as yet.

I could see above me the shadow of a pier built over the water's surface, extending out the same length as this underwater shaft. Cautiously I rose to the surface for a fresh swallow of air. So far so good. I was almost inside the Skorpis base. Almost. It surprised me that the Skorpis had not set out electronic security systems underwater to protect their base from any possible seaborne threat. And the trio I had seen in the water had been unarmed. It was as if they expected no enemy attack, almost as if this was not a military base at all.

And there was at least one human working with them.

The sun was sinking into the sea, throwing a reddish gold glow over the wave tops. I treaded water for a while, bobbing up and down as each fresh crest of the incoming tide surged past me. I was close enough to the enemy to hear them walking along the pier above my head, to hear their voices as they worked and talked and complained about their situation the way all soldiers do everywhere, in any era.

"Protecting a litter of humans," one voice griped. "This isn't the life of a warrior."

"Maybe you'd rather have been with Second Battalion," said its companion.

"At least they got to use their claws."

"They're all dead. Is that what you want to be?"

"We should've sent in both battalions."

"No, we shouldn't have sent in either one. We should've nuked those hairless apes in the first place, not wasted a whole battalion trying to capture their damnable transceiver."

"Well, anyway, we're stuck with guard duty."

"Do you trust 'em?"

"Who?"

"The humans, who else? They say they're scientists, but do you think we can trust them? Or are they really spies?"

"How the hell should I know? They all look alike to me. The gray furs make those decisions."

"Like the decision to try to capture the enemy transceiver."

"Yes. Just like that."

There was more than one human in the Skorpis camp. And they were scientists, apparently. My head buzzed with the possibilities. Perhaps this was the way for me to penetrate farther into their camp.

I gave the matter a few moments' thought. No sense waiting until dark. Boldness might work where stealth would be detected.

Hoping that all humans truly did look alike to these Skorpis warriors, I wormed my shoulders out of the flight-pack harness and fastened it to the underside of the pier. With some feelings of trepidation, I also unbuckled my gunbelt and left the laser pistol and knife there, as well. Then I reached up, grabbed the edge of the pier and hauled myself up out of the water.

"Who the hell . . . ?" The two Skorpis on the pier were evidently sentries. They both had rifles, which they immediately unslung from their shoulders and pointed at me.

"Identify yourself!" said the larger of the two. Both of them were enormous, towering above my height and twice my bulk.

"Orion," I said, trying to smile disarmingly. "I got separated from the others and just made it back."

"I've never seen you before."

"Just arrived a few days ago," I said.

"There's been no resupply mission here for months," said the Skorpis. Both their rifles were pointed at my chest.

Drawing myself up on my dignity, I answered as haughtily as I could, "I was brought here on a special flight, at great expense. At least your superiors recognize the value of a scientist, even if you don't."

They looked at each other. It was difficult to read the expression on their feline faces, but to me they seemed uncertain, fully suspecting that I was lying through my teeth but unable to be sure. Then they did what all soldiers in every era do when in doubt: they marched me to their commanding officer.

Thus I was trooped from one giant Skorpis to another, from the pier to the command post at its base, from the command post to the quarters of the officer of the guard. From there to the offices of the chief of security, where a Skorpis wearing a chestful of ribbons on a cinnamon-colored uniform eyed me with enormous suspicion from behind an airport-sized desk. There were no obvious gender characteristics among the Skorpis, at least none that I could detect with their uniforms on, but I knew from my briefing information that this security chief was a female, as all Skorpis officers were.

"You come out of the sea with no clothes, no equipment?"

I must admit that I did feel slightly foolish standing in front of her with nothing but a pair of shorts that were still dripping wet. "I am with the human scientists," I said with as much dignity as I could command. "I was simply swimming near the base to check the structures that have been built underwater."

"And you claim that you arrived three days ago."

"Yes, that's right."

"There has been no flight into this base since the fleet departed after the battle several weeks ago," she growled at me.

"Take me to my fellow scientists," I insisted. "They'll vouch for me."

"There has been no flight in here for several weeks," she repeated.

"There was one. Perhaps you were not informed about it."

"That is impossible. Who are you and where are you from?"

I kept insisting that she take me to the other human scientists. She studied me the way a cat studies a bird chirping on a limb, just out of reach.

"The only other humans on this planet were the assault team that we wiped out. Perhaps we didn't exterminate all of you. . . ." There was a heavily gouged square of wood on her desktop. Unconsciously, she scraped the unsheathed claws of one hand along it. Or was it unconsciously? I got the impression she would like to use her claws on me.

I continued my bluff. "If you'll simply let me see my fellow scientists, I'm certain that all this confusion can be cleared up."

She shook her head in a very human negative.

"What harm could it do?" I coaxed. "One single human, unarmed, in the midst of a whole baseful of warriors?"

"You could be carrying an explosive device inside you. You could be an android. A walking bomb. The humans are very clever that way."

I shrugged carelessly. "Examine me, then. Probe me with search beams."

"You've already been probed," she replied. "While you've been standing here."

"Have you found any explosives? Anything at all but normal human organs inside a normal human skin?"

"You humans are very clever," she muttered again.

After nearly an hour of stubborn intransigence, she finally decided to march me personally—with a squad of six fully-armed warriors escorting us—to the part of the base where the human scientists were quartered.

"They sleep at night," she said disdainfully as we walked through the camp. It was bustling with activity, much as a human camp would in early morning. "This will disturb them."

It seemed to me that she did not mind disturbing the humans. Not in the slightest.

The humans were in a compound separated from the rest of the base by a fence of energy beams. Two Skorpis guards snapped to spine-popping attention as the officer approached. They turned off a section of the fence for us to walk through. The officer ordered our escort to remain at the fence. "Come if I call you," she commanded them. They saluted as one single organism.

It was quiet inside the human compound. Most of the buildings were dark, although lights showed through the windows of one long, low-roofed structure.

"The humans eat their meals together," the officer muttered, from somewhere in the darkness over my head. "They eat plants and pastes made by machines." Her voice reeked with distaste.

I was tempted to tell her that some humans hunt for their meals. But I refrained.

Without knocking she opened the door to the mess hall—for that is what it was—and stepped inside. Floorboards creaked under her mass. I came in behind her.

Twenty-two men and women, each of them in drab coveralls, stopped eating and turned to stare at us, spoons and forks in midair, mouths open and eyes wide with surprise.

The officer grabbed me by the scruff of the neck and nearly hauled me off my feet.

"This one says he belongs with you," she said, loud enough to rattle the windows. "Does he speak truth?"

A bearded man at the head of the table swallowed hard enough for me to see his Adam's apple work up and down.

"He belongs with us, yes," he said in a high, surprised voice.

The officer let go of me.

"When did he arrive? How?"

Before they could give a story that contradicted mine, I rattled, "On the special flight several days ago, just as I told you." Desperately I hoped that none of the other humans would give me away.

"I know of no special flight."

"It was only here very briefly," said the man at the head of the table.

"You might have been out at the perimeter," one of the women added, in a voice that trembled slightly.

"I can check all incoming flights in our computer records," said the officer. "If he is lying, he will die. If you help him lie, you will die with him."

The bearded man at the head of the table got to his feet. "You can't threaten us so easily. We were sent here by the Hegemony high command. The work we have to do here is too important to the progress of the war for us to be bullied by Skorpis warriors."

The officer hissed at him, just like a spitting cat. Then she said, with murderous calm, "The Hegemony orders us to protect you. If this human is a spy or a saboteur, he must be dealt with. If you help him, you are working against the Hegemony and you will be dealt with also."

"Let us take care of him," the bearded man said. "He's no threat to you or anyone else."

"You vouch for him? He is a scientist, as you are?"

The man started to nod, but one of the women down the table burst out, "We never saw him before! We don't know who he is!"

"Randa!"

"It's no good, Delos," she said to the bearded one. "What we're trying to accomplish here is too important to allow some spy to wreck everything!"

"You say he is a spy?" the officer thundered.

"None of us ever saw him before!" Randa fairly screamed. "Take him away. Open up his brain and find out who he is and why he's here!"

Chapter 10

Everyone in the mess hall froze, frightened, faces contorted with shock and uncertainty. Even the huge Skorpis security officer stood stock-still for a moment, just as stunned by Randa's revelation as the other humans.

In that flash of a moment I acted. It was either move or die, and I had no intention of dying.

I spun on the ball of my foot and punched the security officer as hard as I could on her chin. She staggered backward, knees buckling. Before she could recover I bolted across the mess hall, vaulting clean over the table while several of the humans shrieked and hurling myself through one of the windows. I crashed through and landed head-first on the hard-baked ground outside. I could hear the security officer bellowing like a lioness in heat as I rolled to my feet and ran for the energy fence that enclosed the human compound.

It was more than two meters high, but I cleared it with room to spare. Fear augments athletic skills. Now I could hear shouting behind me as I raced through the square tents and more permanent structures of the Skorpis camp. There were plenty of the huge warriors in sight, working, digging, marching in the darkness of the night. They seemed more surprised than alarmed as I sprinted past them, heading for the beach and the sea.

I knew the officer I had slugged would radio her security detail to head me off. And sure enough, I could see teams of warriors bustling out of the buildings at the base of the twin piers up ahead. More shouts behind me and a laser bolt crackling bright red lanced past my ear. A warning shot. They won't try to kill me, I reasoned. They want me alive for questioning. But that didn't mean they wouldn't gleefully burn my legs off.

I dodged behind one of the metal prefabricated buildings and started running off at a tangent to the beach. The piers were out, too well guarded. But if I could get to the water perhaps I could wait awhile, then swim back to the place where I had stashed my flight pack and weapons. If the Skorpis did not find them first.

As I bolted around the corner of another building, angling off toward the beach once more, a team of six Skorpis suddenly loomed ahead of me. All of them armed with rifles. I gave them no chance to aim at me. I dived into them with a rolling block, barreling into their legs, knocking several of them down. My senses were in overdrive, and I saw them tangling each other's arms and legs, cursing and snarling as they tried to pull themselves loose and get at me. I grabbed the rifle out of the hands of one of them, clubbed him to his knees with its butt, then flipped it around and fired into them point-blank.

I had no time to see how much damage I had done. Leaving them writhing on the ground, I dashed off toward the beach once again. To my left I could see a squad of Skorpis running along the sand in my direction. I had to get to the water before they saw me.

Too late. They saw in the dark much better than I did, and they quickly fired several rifle blasts at my feet, puffing up gritty pebbles and sand. I skidded to a stop and they ceased shooting and came running toward me.

I fired from the hip, one-handed, and knocked the closest two of them down. Then I flung myself face-first on the ground as the rest of them dropped to their knees and shot back at me.

There was no time for a firefight. If they pinned me down here for more than a few moments, the whole Skorpis base would be upon me. I had no choice. I leaped to my feet, firing as I ran, and raced for the water as fast as my legs would carry me.

My firing made them duck their heads a bit, but before I had taken a dozen strides a laser bolt seared my hip. I spun around, staggered, then drove on toward the water. Clamping down on the blood vessels, shutting off the pain signals, I limped toward the sea, only a tantalizingly dozen or so meters away now.

Another bolt hit my leg and I flopped down, rolled, and used my rifle to haul myself up again. I hopped, hobbled, staggered for the water as the Skorpis warriors came running toward me.

"Alive!" I heard one of them yell. "Take him alive!"

That was my one hope. I shot two more of the warriors as I tottered for the water. More laser blasts hit me, in the legs, in the chest. They were no longer worried about preserving me for interrogation; I was hitting too many of them.

I splashed into the surf, still firing, still being hit. Despite my rigid self-control I felt as if my legs had been burned off. Another bolt burned my shoulder so badly that I dropped the rifle. It hissed as its hot barrel struck the water.

The world was spinning. The surf surging against my bloodied legs, knocking me over as more laser blasts lanced past my head. They were shooting to kill.

I crawled into the waves, letting the water surge over me, cool and stinging with salt. Like a crab I scrabbled along the sandy bottom as the water flowed over my head, covering me, protecting me from their merciless lasers. I tasted salt water in my mouth, felt it filling my nose. I was deep enough now to float up off the bottom and let the current carry me out farther from the land.

There was not much skin on me that was unburned, I

knew. Despite my control of the pain signals, my body was telling me that it was almost gone. Legs useless, one arm burned to the bone, another searing wound in my chest.

I floated to the surface and gulped cool night air. I did not have the strength to swim. I was going to die again, and this time I knew that the Golden One had no intention of reviving me. I had failed in my mission. Failed him. Failed myself.

I would never see Anya again. Never look into her gray solemn eyes. Never feel her touch, hear her voice.

The Golden One had abandoned me to die here on this miserable planet. They had all abandoned me, all the Creators. Even Anya.

A bitter torrent of regret surged through me. Somewhere deep in my mind I could hear Aten's scornful laughter telling me that he knew I would fail him. I was merely a creature, after all. How dare I presume to love one of the Creators? I was made to be their tool, not their equal.

Regret. Love for Anya. Hatred for the Golden One. All these emotions flooded through me as I bobbed in the swells of that unnamed ocean, dying.

And something else. Something that I had never realized existed within me came to the front of my consciousness. Me. Myself. The individual who is Orion. Not the slave of the Golden One. Not even the lover of the goddess Anya. Myself. It did not matter how I was created or by whom. It did not matter who I loved or who loved me. I exist. I live and breathe and love and hate. I will not tamely die, mourning my failures, bemoaning my fate.

I pulled what little strength was left in my battered body and concentrated every atom of my will. There are paths through space-time, I knew. The continuum is like an ocean, and there are currents in it that can carry you from one place-time to another.

Squeezing my eyes shut, I thought back to all the times I had been translated through the continuum of space-time. Could I move myself voluntarily? Could I reach that city of the Creators, the city I had saved from Set's destruction, the city that they kept safe in its own protective bubble of energy?

With my eyes tight closed I could not see the stars in the night sky. My body grew cold, numb. I no longer felt the bobbing of the sea. Colder I grew, cryogenically cold for an endless moment.

And then I felt the warmth of sunlight on my naked skin. I opened my eyes and found myself lying in a meadow on a hillside. And below me lay the magnificent city of the Creators beneath its radiant sphere of energy, rising beside a calm blue sea.

A city of monuments and heroic statues, all dedicated to the Creators themselves. Pyramids and temples from every era, every culture of Earth. A city empty of people, except for the handful of Creators, the self-styled masters of the human race who had allowed themselves to be worshipped as gods. They had translated the monuments that adoring humans had built to them, accumulating them into this glowing city devoted to their own gratifications.

I rose to my feet. My body was whole and strong. The breeze from the sea was cool, the sun high overhead warming. I walked through wildflowers down the hill toward the city. Deer bounded in the woods farther off to my right. Rabbits hurried through the grass at my feet, stopping now and then to stare at me, noses twitching.

The city was empty. I knew that there were robots and mechanical conveniences waiting to be summoned by mere thought. But the Creators were not there, not one of them. I felt disappointed, yet not surprised. Aten had told me that they were scattered among the stars, struggling to resolve this ultimate crisis that they faced. Yet, to beings who can come and go through space-time at will, why were none of them here in their home base at this particular nexus in the continuum?

I wandered on, asking myself what I expected of this visit and getting nothing but a vague sense of uneasiness by way of an answer.

Past the Mayan Temple of the Sun I strolled, alone in the ageless city. Past the Parthenon and the great golden reclining Buddha that seemed to be grinning at me, knowingly. I walked through the city from one side to the other until I was at the base of the massive pyramid of Khufu, out beyond the Colossus of Rhodes.

I turned the corner of the great pyramid and there was the ocean, clean and glittering beneath the sun, waves washing up on the beach with curls of froth as they broke gently against the sand. The sea called to me and I walked into it, wading up to my hips before I slid in and began swimming slowly out toward the distant horizon.

"Welcome, friend Orion," said a dolphin that popped up beside me. "We are happy to see you back among us."

"Back among you?" I asked.

I saw that I was surrounded by the grinning sea mammals, gray and sleek and each as big as five men or more. It was no surprise to me that I understood their clicks and whistles. But I was surprised that they understood my tongue.

"It's been a long time since we hunted the fast-darting tuna together," said the nearest dolphin.

"Or went diving to the lair of the giant squid," said another.

"Where are the Creators?" I asked. "Do you know?"

"The other two-legs? They have been gone for long ages, Orion."

"They aren't much fun. They argue among themselves most of the time."

"They forget that we can hear them. Our sense of hearing is very acute."

"I know," I said, grinning back at them as I treaded water.

"Come!" said the nearest one. "There's a whole school of tuna not more than five kilometers from here. Let's feast on them!"

"Wait!" I begged. "I can't swim that far."

"No need for you to swim, friend Orion. Ride on my back the way you used to so many tides ago."

"If you don't mind carrying me . . ."

"Of course not! One hunter to another, we are all friends here in the sea."

So I slid one leg across his smooth back and clutched his dorsal fin with both my hands and off we went on a wild splashing ride, the dolphin racing powerfully, smoothly through the ocean, dipping down below the surface to run as fast as possible, then sliding up to blow steamy stale air through his vent and pull in a gulp of fresh air with a wet sucking noise. I did the same each time he popped to the surface. If the individual dolphins had names I never learned them; they seemed to know each other without the need for such tags.

They said I had gone hunting with them before, that we were old friends. I had no memory of it whatsoever, but I did not let that interfere with my enjoyment of this wild splashing ride through the ocean. The water was clear as air down to a considerable depth, with the sun lighting it up. If it weren't for the bubbles and the swarms of colorful fish darting all around us, I would not have thought we were underwater.

And then would come the splashing, frothing moment of breaking the surface, taking a fresh gulp of air. And then down below we would go again, sliding along smoothly on the powerful strokes of their tails.

Soon enough we came to the tuna school, big silver-gray sleek speedsters who turned and fled at the approach of the tribe of dolphins. Fast as the tuna were, though, the dolphins were faster. We split up into several smaller groups, circling around the school of tuna to set up a trap, much as the Mongols did on their great hunts each year. I slid free of my mount and hovered with a few of the older dolphins, treading water as I waited for the circlers to drive the prey toward us.

"Don't let them get past you!" my friend clicked gleefully as he dashed off. Underwater, I could not reply to him.

The tuna panicked and tried to evade the trap. The dolphins snapped them up in their grinning jaws by the dozens, by the hundred, gulping them down one after another. I grabbed one, more than enough for me to handle, bit through its spine to kill it and then let myself float to the surface with the big fish in my hands.

"Only one, friend Orion?" my friend teased. "This is the mighty hunter?"

I laughed as I tore at the clean fresh meat of the tuna. "How many deer can you chase down, legless one? How many rabbits can you outrun?"

I saw the dark fins of sharks circling in the distance, attracted by our slaughter of the tuna, but they kept away from the dolphins. As the sun began to slide toward the sea, we swam back to the beach by the Creators' city, with me riding my friend's back again.

Finally I was wading toward the beach. I stopped while still waist-deep in the water and shouted a farewell to the dolphins.

"Thanks for the hunt," I called.

"The sea is good, friend Orion. Too bad you aren't a dolphin, or at least a whale. You are a good companion, for a two-leg."

"And you are good friends, all of you. Thanks for sharing your hunt with me."

"The sea will always be your friend, Orion. It is good in the water."

With that, they turned and headed out to the deeper waters, leaving me to stagger back up the beach and throw myself on the warm sand for the lowering sun to dry me.

The sea will always be my friend, they said. Yet there was a place in space-time where I was floating helpless in the sea, wounded and dying.

I returned to that place.

Chapter 11

I had hoped that I could somehow return with my body repaired, strong and healed of my wounds. But that, I could not do.

I opened my eyes and saw the starry dark night and felt pain, wave after wave of agony throbbing through every part of my body. Even as I consciously damped down the pain receptors in my brain I could feel it sullenly glowering beneath my deliberate self-control.

I was floating on my back in the deep, dark ocean, just as battered and helpless as I had been before my trip to the Creators' realm. Had I really been there, cavorting with dolphins? Or was it all an illusion, a self-imposed dream, a feverish attempt at escapism?

My self-questioning quickly ended. I felt something brush against my badly burned leg. Just a touch, enough to make me twitch with alarm and get a mouthful of salt water in return. Then it was gone. But it would be back, I knew.

I remembered those tentacled horrors in the swamp, and wondered what predators this ocean harbored. Alone, half-dead, weaponless, I was going to be easy prey for some hungry hunter.

The sea will always be my friend, the dolphins had told me. I doubted it.

Another touch, making me flinch again. I remembered that sharks will often nudge their prey, bump it, almost play with it like a cat with a mouse before snapping it up in those horrendous tearing teeth.

Should I play dead or try to swim away? Would it make any difference?

It was no shark. This time I felt a tentacle delicately wrapping itself around the burned remains of my ankle. I shook my leg and it let go.

But not for long. The tentacle came back at precisely the same spot. This time it held fast. Quickly another slithered across my chest. I could feel its suckers attaching themselves to my burned flesh, delicately, almost tenderly.

I knew it was hopeless but I gulped down a big swallow of air as the tentacles pulled me below the surface. Bubbles gurgled in my ears. We sank down into the cold inky depths of the ocean.

Do not be afraid, friend Orion, I heard in my mind. *We will not hurt you.*

Now I'm hallucinating, I told myself. First I dream about dolphins and now I hallucinate that I can hear their voices in my mind. While I'm being pulled down to the bottom of the sea by some tentacled monster. If I don't drown the pressure will cave in my ribs soon enough.

Have a little faith, friend Orion, the voice in my mind said. It felt almost amused.

I lost track of time as we sank deeper and deeper into the sea. There was no light to see by, no sensation at all except the rush of water swirling by me.

Listen to the music of our world, said the voice. *Open your mind to it.*

I could hear more than gurgling, I realized. There were crackling sounds all around me. Hoots and whistles and soft thrumming noises. And off in the distance a faint melodic crooning that rose and fell. None of the clicks and whistles of dolphins, though.

Now open your eyes, Orion.

I hadn't realized I'd been keeping them shut. Involuntarily I gasped. I was surrounded by hundreds of soft glowing points of light, like being in the middle of a meadow full of fireflies or in the heart of a cluster of gleaming stars.

And when I gasped I had air to breathe.

"Can you hear me?" the voice asked. And I could. It was using sound rather than telepathy or whatever form of mind contact it had used before.

"Good," it said, without my answering. "The air globe is stabilized and you should feel more comfortable. We will see what can be done about your wounds." The voice was silky soft, warm and calm.

"Who are you?" I asked. "Where are we?"

The lights danced and twinkled around me, blue and red and green and yellow, but I could not make out any shapes.

"We are nearing the bottom of the sea, roughly a hundred kilometers from the shore where the Skorpis have made their base."

"You know about them?"

I sensed a tolerant chuckle. "Yes, we know about them. And about you." The voice grew darker, more severe. "And about the way you casually slaughter one another."

"I wouldn't call it casual," I replied.

No response. The lights flickered around me, as if they were dancing in a sphere all around me, binding me in a web of blinking colorful flashes of energy.

"You haven't told me who you are," I said.

"You may call us the Old Ones."

"What does that mean?"

Again that tolerant sense of amusement, like a grandfather watching a baby's hesitant first steps.

"You will find out in due course," the voice said. "For now, we must travel deeper into the sea."

I got a sense of motion, acceleration, a tremendous rushing through the dark waters. The lights remained all around me. I could breathe. I seemed to be floating weightlessly, almost like an astronaut in orbit. In the dim flickering light I could see that my wounds were scabbing over. The bleeding had stopped completely and I felt a little stronger. All the while I was moving through the inky depths, speeding deeper and deeper, farther and farther from the shore.

At last I saw more lights approaching. They glowed and pulsated as if they were living, breathing creatures. Whole avenues of light opened up before my eyes, as if I were flying toward a vast city, swooping along a highway of lights that led to its magnificent heart.

"How do you feel?" the voice asked.

"Bewildered."

"I mean physically. Your wounds."

I flexed my arms, looked down at my legs. They were healing rapidly.

"Everything seems to be going along fine."

"Good. We are pleased."

"Tell me more about yourselves. What is this city of lights that we are approaching?"

"This is our home, Orion. The home of the Old Ones."

"May I see you?" I asked, sensing that these lights were merely sparks of energy.

"You may be unpleasantly surprised," the voice replied. "You may be repelled by our appearance."

"Then tell me what to expect."

"A reasonable approach to the problem." The voice hesitated, as if checking with others before answering my request. Then:

"Orion, your Creators have told you that space-time is an ocean, have they not?"

"The one called Aten has taunted me more than once about my linear perception of space-time," I answered.

"Yes, we can see that. Yet your linear perception is not entirely in error, Orion."

"There are currents in the ocean of space-time," I said.

"And there is a flow, a very definite flow. Time's arrow exists. Entropy exists. Even though we may move back and forth across the ocean of space-time, we still cannot hold back entropy. The continuum unravels a little whenever we move through space-time. The greater our move, the more disorder arises."

"But what has this to do with the way you look?" I asked.

"Time's arrow," the voice replied. "There are earlier times and later times. There is a point in space-time when your planet Earth is barren and lifeless. There is a point where the human race begins—"

"Built by the Creators and sent to destroy the Neanderthals so that Earth can be inhabited by the Creators' creatures."

"Who in turn, over the millennia, evolve into the Creators themselves."

"Yes. They created us and we created them."

"There is a point in the evolution of our kind," the voice said, "when we had not yet developed intelligence, when we were far simpler beings living in the seas of our original world."

"Lunga is not your original world?"

"Oh, no. Not at all."

"Then where did you originate?"

I sensed a hesitation. "Does it matter? Suffice to say that once we were far simpler beings than we are now."

"Simpler beings," I said, beginning to understand what he was hinting at, "with tentacles?"

"Yes."

"And claws that can crack armor?"

"Do you think you are prepared to see us?"

I thought of those things in the swamp, with their clutching tentacles and snapping claws and dozens of beady eyes.

I took a breath and said shakily, "Yes, I'm ready."

"Very well."

The sea around me brightened and I saw that I was surrounded by dozens of writhing tentacled creatures. They were huge, immense, like gigantic pulsating jellyfish with long wriggling tentacles and lipless round mouths that opened and closed, opened and closed, coming nearer and nearer to me. My skin crawled and I felt panic rising inside me, surrounded by these enormous engulfing undulating horrors pressing closer and closer, tentacles reaching out for me, mouths pulsating. . . .

"Can you rise above your fears, Orion?"

I wanted to scream. Those enormous gaping mouths, like suckers big enough to swallow me whole, they seemed to be bearing down upon me, coming to devour me, coming to grasp me in those powerful tentacles and stuff me into one of those gaping maws. I could feel their digestive fluids burning into my flesh. I felt smothered, suffocating.

"Can you see beyond your terror, Orion? Can you look upon us as we truly are?"

I realized my eyes were squeezed shut, my fists pressed so hard against my temples I thought my skull would burst. They saved you! I raged at myself. They're healing your wounds. They are intelligent beings. Go beyond their appearance; look at them as they see themselves.

Shaking with dread, I opened my eyes and forced myself to look at them again. They hovered all around me, huge, engulfing. I took a deep, shuddering breath. They came no closer, floating silently in the deep waters. Yet they were so enormous that they filled my vision wherever I looked. There was no escaping them. I fought against the panic that surged through me, deliberately forced my heart to slow its terrified beat, calmed my breathing to something close to normal.

I stared at them for long, long minutes. They hovered all around me, pulsating slowly, lights flickering within their undulating bodies, patterns of color glowing and shifting rhythmically across their translucent skins. There was a certain dignity to them, I slowly recognized. Even a certain kind of beauty as they floated throbbing in the deep waters. They moved gracefully, I forced myself to admit, trying to avoid looking at those dilating mouths.

And they were watching me intently. Each of them pos-sessed two giant, solemn eyes that seemed focused on me.

"You are . . . beautiful," I managed to croak.

"We are glad you think so. After your experience in the swamp we were afraid that you would be biased against us. Xenophobia is one of the deepest traits of your species."

"We were created to be warriors," I replied. "It makes it easier to kill your foes if you are frightened of them."

"And yet the dolphins vouched for you."

"The dolphins?" I blurted. "Are they here?"

"Not in this era," the voice answered.

I realized that these Old Ones could travel through time the way the Creators could. The way I had myself.

"When we first made contact with you, Orion," the voice continued, "we sensed nothing but a warrior intent on slaying his enemies. But the dolphins told us you were a good friend to them, so we probed deeper."

It was the Old Ones whom I had sensed earlier, then. Yet I had no memory of how I got to be a good friend to the dolphins. Was I sent on a mission into the ocean, in another era?

"We find that although your basic instincts are those of a warrior, there are other desires struggling within you."

"I have a will of my own," I told them, "even though my Creator looks upon me as nothing more than a tool for his use."

"That is a part of the problem you present to us." The voice sounded slightly perturbed despite its silky smoothness. "We have been observing your kind since you first arrived. You humans are bloodthirsty as well as xenophobic."

"We were made that way," I admitted. "Although some of us have tried to rise above it."

"Have you?"

"Some of us have. There are humans at the Skorpis base who are scientists. They are not warriors, not killers."

"Why do you not regard the Skorpis as humans?" Although I heard only one voice, I got the impression that more than one of these sea creatures was speaking to me, or perhaps they were all speaking, and what I heard was a blend of their individual thoughts and questions.

"The Skorpis come from another world," I answered. "They are descended from felines."

"While your kind are patterned after primate apes."

"That's right," I said.

"What makes you think that the Skorpis come from a different origin than your own?"

"They couldn't . . ." I hesitated. "Do you mean that they were also—"

"Produced by your Creators? Why do you find that difficult to believe?"

"Not difficult. Just—a new idea. I hadn't considered it before."

"The universe is old, Orion. And your Creators have been very busy."

"But if the Skorpis were also made by the Creators, why are they fighting against us?" I asked.

"Whatever your Creators touch degenerates into violence," the Old Ones said. "They are a plague among the stars."

"But you," I asked again. "Who are you? What have you to do with the Creators?"

"We are a very old race, Orion. Older than your Creators by tens of millions of years. We have no desire to be dragged into the slaughters that your kind are perpetrating."

"Why should you be?"

"Because your fellow humans have discovered us. They have tried to make contact with us. They want us to ally ourselves with them against their enemies."

"I don't even know who our enemies are," I said.

"Other humans, of course. And species of similar levels of development, such as the Skorpis and the Tsihn."

I felt confused, stunned almost, at all this new information they were throwing at me. They sensed my mental turmoil.

"Do not feel anxious, Orion. We will explain everything to you so that you can understand it fully."

Why? I wondered. What do they want?

As if in answer, the silky voice told me, "You are going to be our ambassador, Orion. You will give our message to your Creators."

Chapter 12

The city of the Old Ones, down at the abyssal depths of the ocean, was a vast wonderland of delights. Actually, the term *city* is a misnomer, for the Old Ones had no need for buildings or structures. Yet they clustered together in this sea-bottom aggregation of lights and patterns, exchanging thoughts like very old and very wise philosophers. Aristotle would have been happy here; Plato would have found his republic of intellect.

For countless days I wandered through the city, buoyed in an invisible sphere that somehow always was filled with fresh air. I neither ate nor drank, yet I was nourished and refreshed. My wounds healed completely as I learned of the Old Ones, their origins and history, their place in the continuum, their relationship to the Creators and the war that was spanning this region of the galaxy.

The Old Ones had evolved from octopus-like invertebrates living in the early seas of their home planet. We humans have a prejudice that a species cannot become fully intelligent until it masters energy sources beyond its own muscular power. For a land-dwelling species such as ourselves, that first energy source was fire. Since fire is impossible underwater, we tend to dismiss the possibilities of intelligent sea creatures. Even the dolphins would not have reached true intelligence if human scientists had not augmented their native brains.

The Old Ones had manipulating organs: ten tentacles that could grasp and maneuver as well as human hands or better. They had large, intelligent brains and exquisitely subtle sensory organs. Instead of fire, they developed the abundant electrical energies they found in many species of fish and eels. Where we humans built tools and learned engineering, the Old Ones learned biology and incorporated the living forms they needed into a symbiotic existence within their own bodies.

They learned about the world around them. Over the millennia, over the eons, they slowly built up a body of knowledge about the sea and, eventually, the land and even the sun and stars. Long before the dinosaurs ranged across Mesozoic Earth, the Old Ones discovered the energies of space-time and learned how to move through the continuum.

By the time the primate apes of Earth began to develop into the earliest hominids, the Old Ones had explored the galaxy. By the time Aten and the other Creators decided to build their human tools and send them to the Ice Age strongholds of the Neanderthals on a mission of genocide, the Old Ones had decided to keep to themselves, content to contemplate the universe without tampering with it.

Where we humans, driven by our Creators, are constantly meddling with the flow of space-time, constantly trying to alter the continuum to suit our needs and desires, the Old Ones have withdrawn to their oceans and their thoughts. They are to us as a giant sequoia tree is to a chittering squirrel.

All this I learned from them.

"Friend Orion," said the silky-voiced one to me, "the moment has come for you to return to your own kind."

The Old One who addressed me was swimming alongside my sphere as we gently glided through an avenue of blue-white lights that flickered like fireflies through the dark water. In all the time I had spent with them I had never heard any of the Old Ones refer to one another by a name. They had no need of names, it seemed. I could tell them from one another by differences in their coloration and in the sound of their voices, although I never did learn how they produced sounds that I could hear.

"You know now who we are and what we are," said my companion and teacher. "Please tell your Creators that we refuse to be drawn into their slaughters. Our only desire is to live in peace."

"But what if one of our warring groups tries to force you to join their side?"

Again that sense of gentle amusement. "We will not be forced, Orion. We will not listen to their words. If they try to use weapons against us, their weapons will not function. We threaten no one. We will harm no one. But we will not allow our knowledge or strength to be used in war."

I recognized the hint.

"Will you meet us if we stop fighting? Would you be willing to exchange thoughts with us if we stop the war?"

A feeling of wry humor touched me. "Perhaps, Orion. In a million years or so, perhaps then you will be ready to share thoughts with us."

I felt myself grinning. "That's something to look forward to."

"Farewell, ambassador Orion."

I found myself sprawled on the beach near the ruins of the ancient city, where I had left the rest of my troopers. How long ago? I had no idea of how much time had passed. It was daylight, close to midday, I judged from the height of the blazing sun.

Getting to my feet, I started walking rapidly across the glaring sand toward the ruins. Within minutes a voice from one of the crumbling walls hailed me.

"Captain? Is that you?"

"Yes," I said, stating the obvious.

The trooper climbed up atop the broken edge of the wall. I recognized him: Jerron, the smallest man in the unit, often teased as the runt of the litter. He glanced behind him, and made a slight pushing motion with both his hands. I realized that his hands were empty. He was unarmed, not even a pistol on him.

I was about to ask him why he had no gun when a quartet of Skorpis warriors rose beside him. They were all fully armed. They pointed their rifles at me.

"Surrender or be killed."

The nearest bit of cover was the wall on which they stood. Otherwise I was totally unprotected, standing out on the bare beach in the noontime sun, wearing nothing but a ragged pair of shorts. Not even much of a shadow with me.

I surrendered.

"They came in the second night you were gone," Jerron told me as the Skorpis warriors marched us across the beach toward their base. "Just popped up in the middle of the ruins, outta nowhere. We never had a chance."

So the Skorpis had found that the underwater tunnels led into the heart of the ruined city, I realized. They knew we were there and they used the tunnels to take the troop by surprise.

"How bad were our casualties?" I asked.

"It all happened so fast we never had much of a chance to put up a fight. The guys on sentry duty caught it. Manfred, Klon, Wilma."

Manfred. The sergeant I had forced to become a lieutenant. A real lieutenant would not have been on guard duty. Manfred's old habits killed him. Then I remembered Frede's warning me that it's not smart for a soldier to make friends. Manfred was hardly a friend, but I felt his loss as if it were my own fault.

"How long have I been away?" I asked. "I've lost track of time."

"Four days, sir. The Skorpis knocked us off the second night you were gone, and then they've been waiting for you to come back ever since."

"So now they've got us all."

"Sorry to be the judas goat, sir." Jerron looked fairly miserable as we walked, struggling to keep pace with the giant Skorpis's strides. They were quite willing to nudge us with their rifle butts if they felt we were lagging behind.

"You've done nothing to be ashamed of, soldier," I said. "This whole mission was a disaster from the outset."

They marched us through their perimeter emplacements and into an open compound in the middle of the base, sealed off by electric fences, guarded by a dozen heavily armed warriors, surrounded by all the Skorpis on the planet. They were intent on keeping us from escaping, I could see.

Lieutenant Frede hurried to me as soon as the warriors pushed little Jerron and me into the compound.

"Orion! Captain! Are you all right?" There was real concern in her eyes.

"I'm unhurt," I said.

"From what we had heard, the Skorpis had fried you six ways from breakfast."

"They exaggerated their marksmanship," I said.

Lieutenant Quint pushed through the group that had gathered around us. "They claim you killed half a dozen of them," he said, with something like admiration in his voice.

"I didn't stop to count."

Frede said, "I don't know what they intend to do with us, but it won't be pleasant."

"How have they treated you so far?"

"Oh, okay, by their standards. We're stuck in this compound. No shelter. When it rains we get wet. We sleep on the ground. They feed us once a day, toward sundown."

"I haven't missed today's feeding, then."

Her expression grew more serious. "It seemed to me they were waiting for something. I guess they wanted to get you. Now they've got all of us."

Quint added, "Now they can do whatever it is they intend to do."

"Did you know there are other humans in this camp?"

"Others? No!" Frede said.

"I haven't seen any," said Quint.

"They seem to be scientists. And they're working with the Skorpis."

"Willingly?"

"I don't know."

"You there!" a deep Skorpis voice bellowed. "The one called Orion. To the gate. *Now!*"

I went to the gate, my officers and most of the remaining troopers trailing after me. The one who had called me was the security officer. I recognized her face and the insignia on her cinnamon brown uniform.

"Take him out of there," she commanded the guards. "I have a few questions I want him to answer."

I shot a glance back to Frede and the others. "Guess I'll miss today's meal, after all."

They marched me to the security officer's office and sat me in a chair that was a size too big for me.

"At least your uniform is dry this time," the security officer growled as she sat behind her desk. Two big guards stood behind me. My "uniform" was still nothing more than the shorts I had been wearing since she had last seen me.

"The other humans know nothing of you, even though some of them were willing to lie on your behalf."

"They are scientists," I said. "Not warriors."

"And you?"

"I am a warrior."

"Why did you come here?"

"To this planet? To set up a base from which we would attack you."

"And after your base was destroyed, why did you try to infiltrate this base of ours? One human, alone?"

"My orders were to destroy your base. I was scouting to see how I could accomplish that."

"Scouting alone?"

"Yes."

"And you intended to attack this base with fifty-two warriors, no heavy weapons, no support?"

"Yes."

She glared at me out of her yellow cat's eyes. "I don't believe you. Not even a human would be so stupid."

I temporized. "I knew you had nuclear weapons here. I thought I might set one off and wipe you out."

"And kill yourself doing it."

With a shrug I replied, "You're going to kill me anyway. What difference does it make?"

She radiated suspicion. "You came to this camp to make contact with the other humans. At least some of them are traitors, working against us. You will tell me which ones they are."

I shook my head. "I didn't even know there were any humans here when I infiltrated your camp. It was a shock to me. I still don't know what they're doing here."

"I don't believe a word you say."

"You have lie-detecting equipment, don't you? Or truth serum?"

Slowly she raised one hand and unsheathed her claws. "I can get the truth from you with these."

"You have the truth from me," I said, trying to remain calm. "No matter what you do the truth will remain the same."

"We will see." Then she added, in a growl, "You struck me. Then you ran away. Such a disgrace must be avenged."

The two guards grabbed my arms and twisted them painfully behind my back. The security officer rose from behind her desk, holding her hand full of claws in front of her like five surgical scalpels. If a cat could grin, she was grinning. I heard a low growling purr from deep in her chest as she came around the desk toward me, eyes glinting.

My senses went into overdrive as adrenaline poured into my bloodstream. My arms were pinned behind me by the guards, but I pushed myself to my feet so fast that they eased their grip on me slightly to grab my shoulders and force me down again. That slight easing was all I needed. I twisted violently enough almost to wrench my arms from their shoulder sockets, but the pain was nothing. I yanked one arm free, although the guard's claws raked bloody trails along its length.

I kicked the security officer in the chest, bowling her over backward against her desk while with my free fist I clubbed the guard still holding my arm. The other guard sank his claws into my shoulder, growling. I spun around and caught his chin with the heel of my hand, then drove a crippling blow to his windpipe. He sagged to the floor, gurgling blood, as I whirled to face the first guard, who was reaching for the pistol at his waist.

I grabbed his arm, twisted it so hard I felt bones snap, and shoved him into the security officer. She was still draped half across her desk. She pushed the howling guard away and pawed at her holster. I was much faster and snatched the gun out of her hand.

She glowered at me, blazing sheer hatred, as I held the pistol leveled at her face.

"I have told you the truth," I said. "I could kill you now but that would not change the truth of what I have spoken."

Another pair of guards bolted through the office door, saw that their commander was under my gun, and froze in their tracks.

"I won't willingly allow myself to be sliced up just because you want to find nonexistent traitors," I said to the officer. "I told you the truth. It was a total surprise to me that you have humans in this camp working with you."

I handed her the pistol. She grabbed it and started to swing it at me.

"And I bear a message from the Old Ones," I blurted.

She stopped in midswing. "The Old Ones? The creatures in the sea?"

"Yes," I said.

She hissed. But she put the gun down on the desk.

Chaper 13

They carried the injured guards away as the security officer fumed and snarled and slowly regained her self-control. At last she used the comm unit on her desk to speak to her superior, the base commandant. Within a few minutes I was brought to her office.

The bearded human, the one called Delos, was already there. The base commandant seemed older than the other Skorpis I had seen. The fur of her face and hands was graying. Her uniform was a pale blue, crusted with ribbons and decorations. The human scientist still wore gray shapeless coveralls.

"Is that all the uniform you have?" the base commander growled when they shoved me into her office.

"I've been swimming," I replied. "With the Old Ones."

Delos nearly jumped out of his chair. "The Old Ones? You've been with them?"

"I've spoken with them. They have a message for us."

The base commander waved the security officer out of the room. "I'll call if I need you."

Once she had shut the door, the commandant got up from behind her desk and indicated the table on the other side of her spacious office.

"Sit there," she told me. Delos got up from his chair in front of the desk and joined us. The table was too high, the chair too big, for me to feel comfortable. It was like being a child at an adult's table. I felt small, almost humiliated.

Delos did not seem to mind the furniture at all.

"What did the Old Ones tell you?" he asked eagerly. "How did you make contact with them? Where are they from?"

"Will they join us in this war?" the base commander wanted to know.

"They refuse to join either side," I said. "They reject all attempts to draw them into the war."

"Reject, do they?" the base commander rumbled. "A nuclear bomb or two exploded at depth might change their opinion, I think."

"Your weapons will not work against them," I said. "That is what they told me."

"Nonsense!"

"I believe them. They are far older and wiser than we."

"So were the Tsihn, and we bashed them halfway across the galaxy."

"And made eternal enemies of them," said Delos.

The commander's slitted eyes flashed, but she turned away from the scientist and said to me, "You must tell me everything that the Old Ones told you. I must know *precisely* what they said."

I repeated their message word for word, several times. The base commander sank deeper into a glowering unhappiness each time. The human scientist, though, seemed to grow more excited with each telling.

"Tens of millions of years older than humankind!" Delos said, almost smacking his lips with anticipation. "The things they can teach us! The things they must know!"

"They won't teach us anything as long as we continue killing one another. They regard us with loathing."

"But surely they would talk to scientists," Delos pleaded. "We're not fighters. We haven't killed anyone."

"Perhaps," I replied. "In time." I smiled inwardly, knowing that the Old Ones' contemplation of time was so far more leisurely than our own.

After repeating my story another half-dozen times, I was dismissed by the base commander. Outside her door, the security officer was waiting for me. If the Skorpis still had feline tails, hers would have been twitching with impatience.

"She believes you, does she?" she asked as she personally escorted me back to the prisoners' compound.

"How do you know that? Can you hear through closed doors?" The thought occurred to me that perhaps she had bugged her commander's office, under the guise of her security duties.

"No need to eavesdrop," she said grimly. "If the old tigress hadn't believed you, you would be chopped meat by now."

Before we were halfway to the prison compound, though, Delos came sprinting after us.

"The base commander's given me permission to house Orion in our quarters," he panted.

The security officer snorted, but we changed direction and went to the scientists' fenced-in area.

"He is your responsibility," she said ominously as she left me there with Delos.

He nodded and gestured toward the nearest of the low-roofed buildings.

"Wait," I said. Turning to the security officer, I asked, "What's going to happen to the rest of my troop?"

"The prisoners?" she made a movement with her shoulders that might have been a shrug. "Cryostorage, of course. We'll freeze them till we need them."

"Need them? For what?"

She bared her teeth. "For food, human. What else?"

"You eat humans?"

"They are made of meat, aren't they? Not as nutritious as some of the enemies we've fought, but they'll do in a pinch. With vitamin supplements, of course."

She seemed to be enjoying my consternation. I pulled myself together and said, "Well, until you put them in storage—or other arrangements are made for them—couldn't you find some shelter for them? And better rations?"

"No, I could not, human." And she turned abruptly and walked away from me.

The other scientists were just as eager to learn about the Old Ones as Delos was. They clustered around me once he had ushered me into their barracks. We were in a wide, bare room, furnished only with a long table and human-sized chairs and a pair of video machines off in one corner. A single row of windows on one side of the room looked out on the Skorpis camp, where purple twilight shadows were lengthening into night. The walls of the room were devoid of all decorations except for a single display screen showing an astronomical chart.

As I told my story still again I scanned the faces of the scientists around me. There were twenty-two of them, nine of them women. Most of them seemed young, the prime of their lives still ahead of them. Unlike my soldiers, they obviously were not cloned from one or two gene sets. They were tall and short, dark and fair, eyes of every shape and color, skin ranging from chocolate brown to pinkish white.

The woman called Randa, the one who had denounced me to the security officer, would not look directly at me. Either she felt ashamed of what she had done or she was angry at me for bringing danger to them. None of them commented on the claw wounds on my shoulder, matted with drying blood. I let it pass for the moment.

When I had finished my tale, though, I said, "Now I have some questions for you."

"Go ahead," said Delos. He was obviously the group's leader.

"What are you doing here on this planet, working for the Skorpis?"

"Working for the Skorpis?"

"What are you talking about?"

"We're not working for the Skorpis," said one of the men, with a considerable show of indignity. "They're working for us."

"The Skorpis are mercenary troops. They're here to guard us," said Delos, "while we try to study the Old Ones."

"Guard you against who?" I asked.

"Against you," Randa snapped. "And the rest of your homicidal maniacs who want to kill us all."

So it was anger that drove her, not shame.

"We had no idea there were other humans on this planet," I said. "All we were told was that there was a Skorpis base here and we were going to eliminate it."

"Typical military operation. They only tell you what they want you to know."

"Do you mean that humans are fighting against each other?" I asked. "We're involved in an interstellar civil war?"

"The Hegemony has been battling for its very existence for three generations now," said Randa. "Your so-called Commonwealth has been trying to annihilate us. You and your lizard allies."

"The Tsihn?"

"That's what they call themselves, yes," said one of the men.

"But how did the war start? What's it all about?"

"It started when Commonwealth fleets began attacking our settlements on a dozen different worlds."

"They wiped out whole biospheres. Killed everything."

"Burned planets right down to the bedrock."

"For no reason!"

"Without a declaration of war."

I shook my head. "It couldn't be for no reason. People don't attack one another for no reason."

"Lizards do."

"The Tsihn hate us. They hate all humans, anything that's not themselves."

"But you said that the Commonwealth is allied with the Tsihn."

"Against the Hegemony, that's right. But sooner or later the Tsihn will turn against the Commonwealth, too. You'll see."

There was real hatred in their voices, in their faces.

"I still don't understand how this could have begun," I said. "It doesn't make sense to me."   .

"You're just a soldier," Randa sneered. "How could you be expected to understand anything except killing people?"

That's what the Old Ones thought of me at first, I said to myself. But then they trusted me, they helped me.

Delos gave me a worried look. "Uh, if you really want to catch up on the history of the war, you can use one of our readers." He gestured to the video systems in the far corner of the room.

"Yes, why don't you do that," said one of the other women. "We need to discuss how we can use your information, what our next steps will be."

I could see that they wanted to talk among themselves without me. And I was burning with curiosity to learn how and why this seemingly endless war had begun. So I went to the video reader and sat in the contoured chair before its screen.

"I'll show you how to run it." I looked up, surprised. It was Randa.

"I can operate it," I said. "Soldiers aren't complete idiots."

"Oh." Her face reddened. "All right." She turned on her heel and fled back to the others, who were sitting themselves around the long table.

I turned on the machine and softly spoke my request to its computer. The screen glowed briefly.

And instead of the history tape I wanted, Aten appeared standing before me where the machine had been. He wore a

golden tunic and formfitting tights with calf-length boots. And
a frown. The golden aura of his presence enveloped me like a
warm mist. I knew that he had brought me out of the continuum into a bubble of suspended space-time where he could
interrogate me fully while the men and women across the
room neither saw nor heard us.

"The Old Ones made contact with you, Orion."

I nodded solemnly.

"And they refuse to help us?"

"They refuse to become involved in our war in any way.
Only after we stop the fighting will they even consider further
contact with us."

"I had hoped for more."

"They were quite firm about it."

"There *must* be a way to convince them to help us! There
must be."

"Perhaps you should try to contact them yourself," I
suggested.

His frown deepened. "I have. We all have. The only one
they responded to was you."

I must have smiled. "I'm flattered."

"Don't be," the Golden One snapped. "They saw you as
a helpless victim of our cruelty. They took pity on you, Orion,
nothing more."

"I disagree. When they first contacted me, in a dream I
had, they were repelled. They saw only a warrior, a killer, a
soldier who made war on other intelligent creatures. Later
they saw that there is more to me than a killing machine.
That's why they chose to speak to me."

"Remember, Orion, that *I* put those additional emotions
into you."

"No you didn't. Not deliberately, at any rate. You built
me to carry out your will, and for me to be able to do that I
had to be able to think and act for myself. I've learned much
about the world, Golden One. Much about the Creators and
myself—and my fellow humans."

"Really?" Aten crossed his arms over his chest.

"Really. I'm more than your tool. I'm an individual. How many times have you berated me for not following your orders?"

"Stubbornness is not godliness, Orion. Only we Creators have full freedom of action. You obey me, whether you think so or not."

"You have full freedom of action?" I actually laughed at him. "Then why this desperate war? Why this need for help from the Old Ones?"

"That involves forces that your mind could never understand," he said. "I didn't build such capabilities into you."

"You didn't have to. I'm learning them on my own. The Old Ones speak to me and not to you. I am learning and growing."

"And someday you will challenge me," Aten mocked. "You sound like a frog planning vengeance on an elephant."

I decided it was foolish to carry on this vein. Changing the subject, I asked, "How did this war start? What is the reason for the fighting?"

"It was inevitable. As the human race expanded into the stars they met other intelligent species. Xenophobia is a basic emotion among all intelligences."

"Xenophobia doesn't start wars."

"Doesn't it?"

"Then how are the humans allied with the Tsihn? And how are the Skorpis working with . . ." My words choked in my throat. Suddenly I understood what was happening.

Aten slowly unfolded his arms, studying me like a zookeeper who had just added a new specimen to his collection.

"This war—" I hesitated, thinking furiously. It was the only explanation I could see. "This war is really between you and the other Creators. You are fighting among yourselves, and using us as your pawns."

His utterly handsome face twisted into a smirk. "Of

course. I'm surprised it took you so long to figure it out. You who prides himself on his growing wisdom."

"But why? Why would you have such a falling-out with the other Creators?"

"It's not only me, Orion. Our little family has split into two almost equal camps. Equal and opposite. Much as we did over Troy, except that this time, instead of a paltry few Greeks and Trojans, we are dealing with interstellar civilizations."

"And you drive them to war?"

He shrugged carelessly. "There was no other recourse. The other Creators would not listen to reason."

"They would say the same of you and your allies, wouldn't they?"

"I imagine so."

"You still haven't told me why you've split; the source of the conflict."

"We have reached the ultimate crisis, Orion. A dilemma so crucial, a turning point so critical to our survival, that we Creators could not agree on how to handle it. I told you that this war was part of the ultimate crisis, and so it is. Until I can force the other Creators to agree with my plan for handling the crisis, we will be powerless to face it when it finally falls upon us."

"So you're sending billions to slaughter, destroying whole planets, to decide how to deal with this final crisis."

"It is necessary. For our survival."

"You make war on each other by using us—and other races, as well."

"Why not? Do you expect us to fight each other, to kill one another?"

"And Anya? Whose side is she on?" But I knew the answer even as I asked the question.

Aten's face clouded over. "I'm afraid she is not among my allies. In fact, she is leading the opposition."

"Then, to serve you I must fight against her."

"It's her own fault, Orion."

I did not care whose fault it was or which of their sides was in the right, if either of them was. All I wanted was to find Anya, even if that meant working against Aten.

I looked into his gold-flecked eyes and saw that he understood precisely what was going through my mind. I could not hide my thoughts from him.

"The last thing in the world that you want to do is find her," he warned me. "She is far beyond the paltry romance that you once had with her. She has reverted to her true form, Athena, the warrior goddess. She no longer cares to don human shape. She no longer loves you."

"I don't believe you."

He made an indifferent gesture with his hands. "What you believe or fail to believe makes absolutely no difference."

"Doesn't it?"

"No, Orion, it doesn't. You can chase across the whole galaxy seeking your beloved goddess. You can think me an egomaniac who sends his own creations to slaughter. No matter what you think, if you find Anya now she will kill you. Without a second thought."

"No! She loves me."

"Perhaps once she did. But she has outgrown you, outgrown the foolish desire to take on human form. She is truly the goddess of death, Orion. Your death. Believe it."

Chapter 14

For the next several days, as I worked with the human scientists, my mind kept spinning around the revelations that Aten had heaped upon me.

Anya was fighting against the Golden One. The Creators were split apart, and they had split the human race into two warring factions. They had even enlisted alien races in their ever-expanding war.

And Anya no longer loved me. That I refused to believe. She might hate Aten, she might be fighting against the Golden One with every quantum of her strength and knowledge, but she would never turn against me.

Yet I was a soldier in Aten's army. War washes sentiment away in torrents of blood. I could be killed as impersonally as a man swats an insect, light-years away from her, and she would never know it. I would be merely another casualty among the Creators' human pawns.

No! I could not accept that, could not believe it. Anya loves me, we have loved each other across the millennia and the light-years of space-time. She still loves me, just as I love her.

Can I find her? Can I reach her, wherever she is? Why must I fight this senseless war on Aten's side, instead of hers?

These were the thoughts that flooded my mind as I dutifully tried to help the human scientists at the Skorpis base on Lunga. In vain.

They had been sent to Lunga to establish contact with the Old Ones and enlist their aid in the interstellar war. The planet's only strategic value was that the Old Ones had a settlement here. My mission, at Aten's devious direction, had been to prevent the Hegemony from making an alliance with the Old Ones while he tried to establish contact with them himself.

My mission seemed oddly successful. The Old Ones refused to have any form of contact at all with the Hegemony scientists. We swam in the ocean for days and even had a full-sized submersible sent down to the Skorpis base. But no matter how far we went into that ocean, no matter how deep we dived, we saw no trace of the Old Ones.

"Maybe they've left the planet altogether," Delos suggested gloomily as he bent over the display screens in the cramped sensor center of the sub. Each of the screens showed an ocean teeming with sea life and no trace of the Old Ones.

"You say they had a city down here?" Randa asked me. In the confines of the sub's compartment we were practically pressing against one another. I could smell the faint trace of perfume in her hair. And a musky odor of perspiration.

Nodding, I replied, "A big city, although it really was more of a collection of lights than a set of structures."

"Well, there's no lights nor structures anywhere in view," Delos said with an exasperated sigh.

"Perhaps the sensors are being blocked in some way," I suggested. "Screened."

We sent out swimmers. I went out myself. Nothing. It was as if the Old Ones had never been there. Yet I got the distinct feeling that they were nearby, watching us, perhaps amused by our frustration.

The one good thing that I was able to accomplish during those discouraging days was to get better quarters for my troopers. I refused to be housed with the scientists, insisting that I was a soldier and I would share the treatment the other prisoners received. At the same time I pleaded with Delos and the Skorpis base commander, whenever I was brought to her presence, for a roof over the prisoners' compound.

One morning, just as I was about to be escorted to the scientists' buildings again, a Skorpis skimmer pulled up at the gate of the prison compound, loaded with sheets of plastic and bags of connectors.

"You will build yourselves a shelter," said the sergeant who drove the skimmer. "No tools are needed. Get to work."

By the time I returned that evening the shelter stood, neat and square. There was even bedding inside, I saw.

"Now we need partitions," Frede told me, quite seriously. "For privacy."

It astounded me how the troopers could adapt to their situation. They had slept on the bare ground and eaten one thin meal a day and been grateful that they were still alive.

"Now we need to escape," I said back to her. "Before they put us all in their larder."

Her eyes widened.

"To the Skorpis," I told her, "prisoners are food. The only reason we haven't been frozen so far is that the scientists want me to work with them and I told them that the price of my cooperation is to keep all of you alive."

"But as long as you work with the scientists . . ."

I had to tell her, "I don't think it's going to be much longer. They're coming to the conclusion that there's nothing they can do to reach the Old Ones."

"Then we've got to get out of here pretty quickly."

"Yes," I agreed. "But how?"

That was a problem without a solution that I could find. There were forty-nine of us, unarmed, under constant watch, in the middle of a camp of at least a thousand Skorpis. I racked my brain for days on end trying to come up with a plan that might have some faint chance of working. Nothing.

Until one night it hit me. We don't need to escape. We need to be rescued.

I lay on the plastic floor of our prison, Frede next to me,

staring up at the blank ceiling. I still had no clothes except the shorts I had been wearing for weeks. I closed my eyes and called silently to Aten.

There was no answer. Nor had I expected one, at first. Summoning up my will and my memory, I translated myself to the empty city of the Creators and stood once again beneath the warm sun on the hillside overlooking the city and the sea.

To those who can manipulate space-time, it matters little if you are in a certain place for a moment or a millennium. You can always return to the place and the time where you started.

"I can wait," I called the cloud-flecked blue sky. "I can wait as long as you can."

I did not have to wait long. Almost immediately a silver glowing sphere appeared before me, so bright I could not look at it, yet I felt no heat from its brilliance. It coalesced, took the form of a man. The Creator whom I thought of as Hermes: dark-haired, lean, the hint of mischief in his ebony eyes.

"Orion, the disturbance you make in the continuum is like a toothache."

"When did you ever experience a toothache?" I countered.

He grinned at me. "What is it? What brings you here all hot and impatient?"

"Are you part of this interstellar war?" I asked.

"Of course. We all are."

"And whose side are you on?"

His trickster's face took on a sly, cunning look. "Does it make a difference to you?"

"Can you take me to Anya?"

He thought a moment, then shook his head. "Better not to, Orion. She bears the weight of our future on her shoulders. She would not be glad to see either one of us."

"You serve the Golden One, then."

"I serve no one!" he blazed. "I have put in my lot on Aten's side, though, that is true."

"Then tell him that he must rescue my troop from the Skorpis base on Lunga."

"Tell him that he *must?* By your word?"

"If he expects me to serve him further," I said.

Hermes actually blinked at me. "You bargain with your Creator?"

I smiled back at him. "No, *you* bargain with him. I must return to my troopers."

And I opened my eyes in the prison shack at the Skorpis base, with Frede sleeping soundly beside me.

The rescue attempt, when it came, was just as fouled up as every other aspect of our mission to Lunga.

It was early afternoon. I was out in the submersible with nine of the other human scientists, including Delos—who went on every cruise—and Randa, who still seemed hostile and distant most of the time, although she could thaw slightly, especially when there was some interesting science to talk about.

The Skorpis warrior who accompanied us, so big that he could barely squeeze through the sub's hatches, filled the tiny comm compartment with his bulk. If humans felt uncomfortably dwarfed in Skorpis furniture, this warrior seemed ridiculous with a comm set clamped to his furry head. It was designed for human ears and human dimensions, but the warrior had managed to get the earphone to stay in his cuplike ear by slapping a strip of gummy tape across his head. It must have hurt when he pulled it off. I could see the pale scars of earlier tapes etched into his greenish fur.

"Return to base," he rumbled.

Delos, in the next compartment bent over the sensor displays, jerked his head up so suddenly he banged it on the metal overhead.

He yelped with pain, then said, "Return? Why?"

"Orders," answered the Skorpis.

Rubbing his head, Delos reached an arm into the comm compartment. "Please give me the other headset."

The Skorpis warrior complied and Delos held the set against his ear. Standing next to him, I could hear the communications operator on the other end.

"Enemy fleet has been observed approaching the planet. Return to base immediately."

The rescue mission, I thought. My heart began to race.

"But if there's a battle we'll be safer here in the sea, submerged, than at the base."

"Orders are to return to base. Immediately."

Delos wanted to argue, but the Skorpis at the comm console was already leaning his thick fingers on the keypads that activated the automated controls. We were returning to base, following orders.

And the Golden One was coming to rescue my troopers.

We broke to the surface a scant kilometer from the shore and cruised to the pier. As I clambered through the topside hatch and out onto the sub's deck, I could see no action. The sky looked clear and serene. But there was an air of electrical expectancy at the base that we could all feel as the human scientists who had remained ashore ran out onto the pier and helped tie up the sub.

We rushed back toward the scientists' compound, escorted by two fully armed warriors who had met us at the pier and the Skorpis who had run the comm console in the sub. His two comrades handed him a rifle and a flexible reflective vest as they ran.

"There's a shelter beneath the main building," Delos told me, panting with exertion. "The Skorpis insisted on building it even though I thought it was silly. Shielded and everything."

I saw that the base was buttoned up, braced for an attack. No one walking about, none of the usual drilling or workaday chores going on. Out by the perimeter the guns were manned. Automated laser batteries were already pointing skyward.

"I've got to see to my troopers," I said.

"Don't be foolish," Delos said. "Come with us where you'll be protected."

"I belong with my troop." I veered off, sprinting toward the prison shack.

No Skorpis tried to stop me, although Delos yelled, "Bring them to our shelter if you can."

I waved and ran faster toward the shack.

It was empty. Had the Skorpis already moved the prisoners to safety? I was surprised, doubtful.

Then I saw, to one side of the shack, a pile of canisters. "No!" I shouted. "They didn't!"

A high-pitched screeching shrilled through the air, the Skorpis equivalent of a siren, barely audible to a human. The attack was imminent.

No need to count the canisters. I knew what they were. Cryonic containers. The Skorpis had spent the morning freezing my troop. There was a big skimmer parked on the other side of the pile. They were going to move them to their food lockers when the attacking fleet was spotted.

I pounded the side of the flimsy shack hard enough to make it shake down to its plastic foundation. They're frozen! Frozen!

A heavy hand gripped my shoulder. Turning, I saw it was the security officer.

"Get to shelter," she commanded. "Attack is starting."

As she spoke, a rash of laser blasts splashed against the energy dome shielding the base. The usually invisible dome flared flame red for an instant, then orange. It cleared, but I could see it shimmering above us.

"To shelter," she hissed. "Now." She wrapped an arm around my waist, lifted me off my feet and started running, carrying me like a sack of groceries.

More laser blasts splashed against the shield, and I heard the lightning cracks of the Skorpis lasers firing back. The whole world shuddered and we were knocked flat as a nuclear

warhead hit the base of the shield. The shield absorbed most
of the energy, but the kinetic pulse conducted by the ground
was like the shock of an earthquake.

I scrambled to my feet; the security officer got to hers a
bit more slowly. Through the shimmering shield I could see
lights glinting in the sky, far overhead. Our ships, still in orbit,
catching the light of the sun up there.

More nukes exploded and we staggered across the base,
between buildings that swayed dangerously with each new
explosion. The shield was flaming deeper and deeper into the
red now, as more laser beams fired against it. It was only a
matter of time until the shield was overloaded. Another blast
knocked us to the ground again. Dust and grit filled the air,
burning my eyes.

Spitting dirt from her begrimed face, the security officer
pointed in the direction of the scientists' compound. "Shelter," she said. "You go there."

"What about you?"

"I have duty station." She hauled herself to her feet and
started off in the opposite direction just as another nuke
pounded outside the shield, making the shield go black for
eons-long moments. The ground shook violently and several
buildings collapsed. A heavy support beam cracked loose
from one building and fell like an ax across the back of the
security officer, flattening her beneath its weight.

I staggered over to her, through the choking dust, as more
explosions shook the ground. The shield was visibly wobbling
now, blinking red and orange and bubbling like water on the
boil.

She was conscious, but barely. The beam had crushed her
ribs, maybe broken her back. I strained against it, summoning
up every reserve of strength in me, and hauled it off her. It fell
to the ground beside us with a thunderous clunk.

I dared not turn her over. Her tunic was a mass of blood
from her shoulders to her waist. She lay facedown, one cheek
in the dirt, the other caked with grime.

One yellow eye gazed steadily at me. "You do not follow orders," she muttered.

"I'll get help."

"No one will come. I am dead. Go to shelter before you become dead, too."

Her eye closed. She stopped breathing. I felt for a pulse in her throat, in her wrist. Nothing. She would have gleefully ripped me to ribbons a few days ago, yet I felt an enormous reluctance to leave her there, to admit that she was dead and there was nothing more that I could do.

Another blast and the twisted, crazily leaning side of the building next to us began to groan and shudder. I jumped to my feet and started running, glancing over my shoulder to see the whole building collapse in a thundering heap on top of the Skorpis' dead body.

For a moment I was disoriented. I stopped, blinking in the swirling dust while explosions thudded around me and the energy screen crackled and hissed like a badly tuned video.

There! I recognized the scientists' compound. Its buildings still stood, although the electrical fence around it seemed to be turned off. The Skorpis must be feeding all the base's power into the energy shield, I thought. Once that shield is overloaded and shorts out, the attackers can blast the whole area with nukes.

But what good would that do? I asked myself as I dashed past the dead fence and into the largest building in the compound. The fleet's been sent here to rescue me and my troop, not annihilate us.

Or so I thought.

I had no idea of how to find their shelter. Must be a doorway or a hatch somewhere, but I could see none in the dim twilight caused by the dust sifting through the air outside. Another explosion shook the building so hard I nearly was knocked to my knees.

"Where's the shelter?" I bellowed as loudly as I could. "It's me, Orion!"

Almost immediately a section of the floor cracked open. "Down here," a voice shouted back. "Quick!"

I dashed for the trapdoor and yanked it wide enough to squeeze through just as a greenish light filled the room and I felt a dizzying, nauseating sense of vertigo that made my head swim.

Then everything went utterly black.

Chapter 15

When I came to my senses once more I was hanging in midair almost three meters above the team of human scientists, who stood craning their necks upward toward me.

I landed in their midst with a painful thump, knocking several of them to the metal plates of the flooring. I rolled over and sat up. Looking around, I saw it was obvious that we were no longer in the Skorpis base.

"What happened?" asked one of the scientists.

"Where are we?"

"Transceiver beam," answered Delos. He was sitting beside me, rubbing the small of his back with both hands. He was one of the men I had bowled over when I fell.

"We're aboard one of the fleet vessels, then," I said.

"Looks that way, doesn't it?"

Indeed it did. We were in a metal chamber, bare except for a slit of an observation window set high in one wall and a tightly closed hatch opposite it. I could feel the humming vibration of a starship's engines through the deck plates.

Transceiver beam, I thought. The attacking fleet must have saturated the Skorpis defensive shield at last and then squirted the beam down to snatch us. The beam scanned our molecular patterns, annihilated us, then reproduced us here on the ship exactly as we were on the planet. That was why I materialized nearly three meters above the others; they had been in the shelter and I was at the lip of their trapdoor when the beam found us.

The transceiver beam had killed us, all of us, then rebuilt us here aboard the starship. No one willingly allows himself to be transported by a matter transceiver.

But we were not asked.

"We're prisoners, then," said Randa.

"Maybe not," I said. "They may not understand who you are."

"Welcome to the *Blood Hunter*," came a voice from above us. Looking up, I saw a red reptilian face glaring down at us from the observation window. This was a Tsihn ship, I realized.

I got to my feet and helped Delos and the others to theirs. The hatch swung open and a pair of reptilians entered the chamber, scaly green and lightly built, so alike I could not tell the difference between them.

"You will come with us," said one of them through the translator it carried on a thin chain around its neck.

The scientists were put into a fairly spacious compartment lined with bunks, like a barracks. I saw toilet facilities at the far end of the chamber.

"Which of you is the one called Orion?" asked one of the twins.

"I am," I answered.

"You will see the captain on the bridge." So I followed the green little reptilians—after they had carefully closed and locked the hatch to the scientists' barracks.

The bridge was compact and quiet. The reptilians do not make noise the way we mammalians do. I found it almost eerie the way every station was manned with reptiles of various size and hue, yet hardly a sound issued from any of them. There was no air of tension on the bridge. Only two of the lizards had their cyborg connectors plugged into the ship's sensors. The battle seemed to be finished.

The Tsihn captain was almost my size. It sat in its command chair and looked me over the way a snake studies its prey. Its scales were mottled green and yellow with some gray spots here and there. Much of its upper torso was covered with insignias and markings of rank. Its snout was wide and filled with tiny needle-like teeth.

"You have no uniform?"

I realized I was still in my threadbare shorts. Before I could reply, it said, "We will provide you with a proper uniform."

"Thank you," I said.

It seemed decidedly unhappy. "I have lost many capable Tsihn to rescue you and the other humans."

"You arrived too late," I said. "The men and women of my assault team have been frozen by the Skorpis."

The reptile's tongue darted out from between those teeth, flicked back and forth for an instant, then retreated.

"So your team goes into the Skorpis bellies."

"You can still pick them up, if you haven't destroyed their base altogether."

"Not destroyed," it said. "My orders were to locate you and bring you and the other humans to my ship. This I did. I bombarded the Skorpis base, overloaded their shield, and snatched you from them. It cost me a dozen Tsihn killed, many more wounded."

"But my troopers are still down there on the planet, frozen!"

"No concern. I have obeyed my orders. You are the one I was commanded to rescue. And those with you."

"But those are not my troops." I tried to make it understand. "My troops are still with the Skorpis."

"Yes, frozen, I know." The tongue flicked out again; then it asked, "So who are the humans with you?"

"Scientists," I said.

"I was told you would be with an assault team, not a pack of scientists."

I hesitated. If I revealed to the reptilian that these humans were enemies, what would it do?

It saw through my silence. "Scientists of the Hegemony, is that it?"

"They were studying the planet, trying to make contact with intelligent creatures in the sea. They are not soldiers," I said.

"But they serve the enemy."

"The Skorpis were there to protect them."

The captain hissed in a way that almost sounded like laughter. "Some protectors! We snatched them right from between their claws!"

"But my troop is still there," I repeated. "They're the ones you were supposed to rescue. You must go back—"

"Go back!" it snapped. "By now the Hegemony has a whole battle fleet swarming around Lunga. I have only four ships, two of them badly damaged by the Skorpis ground defenses. My mission was to sneak in and rescue you, not to take on a Hegemony battle fleet. We don't go back. We run away as fast as we can."

"But my troopers—"

"Can't be helped. Not now. This is war, human. Losses are to be expected."

Not my troopers, I said to myself. Not Frede and Jerron and the rest of them. They've suffered enough. They've been through battle and done everything we asked of them. I'm not going to leave them to feed the Skorpis.

"Tell me about these scientists," the captain was saying to me. "They must have valuable information in their heads, no?"

"They're not military scientists," I said, warily. "They don't know anything about weapons or strategy."

"Still, they are a good prize to bring back to headquarters. A bonus. I will be praised."

"You'd be praised more if you brought back the troopers you were sent to rescue," I grumbled.

Its red eyes seemed to burn. "Orion, I was sent to rescue *you.* That I have done. My orders said to bring up any humans with you. That I have done, also."

I stood my ground and glowered back at it.

It shifted in its chair, then raised one taloned three-fingered hand. "Take the helm," it said to its second-in-command. Then it curled one of those taloned fingers and said, "Come with me, Orion."

Mutely I followed it through a hatch that we both had to duck through and into a small, dimly lit compartment. I saw a wide bunk built into one bulkhead, a desk with a blank display screen above it. The captain's quarters, I guessed, spare and spartan.

"Sit," it commanded. There was only one chair, a stool, actually, in front of the desk. The captain eased its bulk onto the bed. It reached to a panel at the head of its bunk and a section of the bulkhead turned transparent.

I gasped. We were out in deep space, nothing to see but stars that were stretching into elongated streaks of light because of our ship's relativistic speed.

"We run with our tails between our legs, Orion," the captain said good-naturedly. "Soon we reach lightspeed and then there is nothing out there to see."

I looked back at it and saw that it was holding a metal drinking cup out to me.

"Alcoholic beverage made from grain," it said. "I keep this for human guests."

"Thank you." I accepted the cup.

It reached into the compartment in its bunk again and poured something else into another cup. "Tsihn prefer drinks with blood in them."

We touched cups and drank. The liquor was smooth and warming.

"Many intelligent species have rituals of sharing food or drink to show friendship," said the captain. "I want you to know that even though I cannot rescue your assault team, I wish to be friendly with you."

"I understand," I said.

"War is never pretty. But maybe for your troops this is a better fate than they might have expected. They are frozen now. They feel nothing."

"But they must have known what the Skorpis intended when they were put into the freezer cells," I said. "Their last thoughts must have been hell."

I realized that its darting tongue was the Tsihn equivalent of a sigh. "So what better did they have to look forward to? Your Commonwealth does not regard warriors with honor. The Hegemony, too. Humans treat their warriors very strangely, Orion."

"They treat them as if they're less than human," I admitted.

"Yes. Send them to do fighting, then freeze them when fighting's over." It shook its head. "Your warriors are treated like machines. Worse."

"I would still like to save them, if I could. I'd like to help them, find a place where they could live in peace and safety, without the Commonwealth forcing them to go into battle, without being frozen like some unwanted slabs of meat until they're needed again." I was thinking out loud now, letting my thoughts spin out to this stranger who was not human in form but more human than my own Creators in its sympathy.

"Put it out of your mind, Orion," said the captain. "I would like to retire to a planet I saw once, green and lush and so humid that steam rises from the swamps every morning of its year. But I will die in a metal egg, Orion. I will spend my life aboard this ship or another like it and one day, somewhere, I will be killed. That is the life of a warrior. That is what we are, Orion, you and I and all those others of so many different species. We were hatched to fight our peoples' battles. There is no other life for any of us."

I sat in that cramped compartment sipping at the whisky this reptilian captain had given me while we grew more morose and bitter. At last I pushed myself to my feet and asked it to excuse me. It ordered one of its bridge crew to show me to my quarters, which turned out to be a compartment almost identical to the captain's. The Tsihn showed me how to manipulate the controls to make the bulkhead transparent and to tap into the ship's communicator and computer systems. It slid back a panel and I saw a closet with two sets of uniforms hanging in it.

Once the reptilian left me alone, I slid the closet shut and stretched out on the bunk. It was a little short for me, but I did not care. I had no intention of sleeping in it.

I summoned the Golden One. I called across the currents of space-time to him. Speak to me, I urged. Give me a moment of your attention.

Nothing. He would not answer. I could have translated myself back to the Creators' city, but what good would that have done? Aten would not deign to see me there. The last time he had sent his messenger. I did not want a messenger, I wanted Aten himself, the Golden One.

But he would not reply to me. When I closed all my senses and tried to reach out to him with my mind, I received nothing but emptiness.

Wait! There was something. A tendril of thought. The faintest whisper of a contact.

Friend Orion, said the Old Ones. *You have survived the battle.*

But my troopers, I called to the Old Ones. *They have been frozen. They will be killed.*

You want to save them.

I can't do it by myself. Can you help me?

We do not interfere in any way, Orion. We have made that pledge and we will keep it.

But my troopers . . .

We feel your pain, Orion. You are gaining in wisdom. Pain is the price of wisdom.

Is there no way they can be saved?

That is for you to determine, friend. Use all your resources. Reach out to grasp the opportunities that surround you.

What opportunities? I asked.

But there was no further response. The Old Ones had said what they wanted to say and departed from my mind.

Use all your resources, they had told me. Grasp the opportunities that surround you.

I swung my legs off the bunk and reached across the narrow compartment to activate the ship's computer. Through the transparent bulkhead I could see that we were still flying at relativistic velocity, not yet beyond lightspeed. I called up the tactical program and saw that there was indeed a full squadron of Hegemony battle cruisers chasing after us. The tactical plot showed that we would reach lightspeed before they came within weapons' range. Once past lightspeed we would be safe.

We would also be unable to send back a ship toward Lunga to pick up my troopers. Whatever I was going to do, I had to do it before we got to lightspeed.

I had less than two hours to act.

Chapter 16

I spent nearly half that time at the computer screen, learning every aspect of the *Blood Hunter,* from engine rooms to weapons systems. I was particularly interested in the auxiliary ships that this cruiser carried. They ranged from tiny scouts to shuttles big enough to carry assault teams to a planet's surface.

I found one that might serve for what I had in mind: a survey ship that had an adequate carrying capacity and enough range and life support to make it all the way back to Lunga. If I could get it off the *Blood Hunter* before the warship reached lightspeed.

I had to act quickly. I felt a momentary pang of regret that I would have to act against the captain who had tried to befriend me. But, as the reptilian itself had said, war is never pretty.

I had no weapons, but at least I had a decent uniform to wear: the blue of Earth's sky, with a high choker collar and a wide belt of gold. The buckle was a sunburst symbol, I saw. The emblem of the Golden One. I grimaced with distaste but cinched it around my waist, wishing I had a pistol to hang on it.

Out into the passageway and straight down to the level where the Hegemony scientists were being kept. I passed several Tsihn of various sizes and hues; none of them tried to stop me or even acknowledged my presence in any way. Good. Let me be a nonperson among them.

The hatch to the scientists' compartment was locked but unguarded. I simply unlocked it and ducked through. They seemed to be preparing for sleep; most of them were sitting on their bunks, a few huddled together in a corner of the chamber, talking.

"On your feet, all of you!" I snapped. "We're getting off this ship. *Now!*"

They dithered a bit, but once I told Delos that I was taking them back to Lunga he got them organized in quick order. Now came the hard part: getting all twenty-three of us down to the hangar bay where the survey vessel was docked.

"Stay close together and follow me," I told them. "If we're stopped, let me do the talking."

It almost worked.

We marched along the passageway and down the power ladder to the hangar level. A few Tsihn passed us, but none bothered to ask what we were doing. There were no guards posted inside the ship, but we found a quartet of mechanics working on a damaged scout ship in the repair bay down at the hangar level.

"Nonessential personnel are not allowed in this area," said the biggest of the mechanics.

"We're just passing through," I said.

It was not put off. "Security!" it called to the microphone built into the hangar bulkhead. "Unauthorized humans in the hangar bay!"

I smiled and said, "You've done your duty very well. The captain will be pleased with you."

And walked my gaggle of scientists past him, toward the pod where the survey vessel was housed.

It sat in the pod, a bulky ungainly conglomeration of spherical crew habitats, cargo holds, equipment containers and propulsion engines. It was a true spaceship, never meant to fly in an atmosphere or land on a planet's surface.

"Get your people aboard quickly," I said to Delos as I flipped open the cover of the pod's door controls.

"SECURITY TEAM TO HANGAR POD FOUR," bellowed the ship's intercom. "ON THE DOUBLE."

No time to study the door controls. The Tsihn would override the electronic system from the bridge, anyway. I just reached in and smashed the control panel with my fist. Then I grabbed the overhead door and pulled it shut manually. It moved grudgingly, but within a few seconds I had it closed and manually locked.

The air-lock hatch was another matter. I sprinted into the survey ship and squeezed through its hatch.

"Seal the hatch once everyone's through," I said to the nearest scientist as I made my way forward to the cockpit. Delos was already in the pilot's seat, powering up the ship's systems. I slid into the other seat.

"You're going to get us all killed, you know," he said from between gritted teeth. But his fingers were flying across the control boards. Indicators were lighting up; I could hear the ship's generators whining to life.

"We've got to open the air-lock hatch," I muttered, directing the computer screen to list an inventory of the ship's equipment.

"A ship like this doesn't carry weapons," Delos said.

But it did have a digging laser, I saw on the inventory list. A couple of touches of my fingertips and the computer showed me where the digger was stored.

I pushed out of the cockpit, commandeered two of the strongest-looking men, and went outside the ship to unpack the digging laser. Tsihn crewmen were pounding on the pod doors, and the intercom blared:

"ORION, THIS IS THE CAPTAIN SPEAKING. HAVE YOU GONE INSANE? STOP THIS MADNESS AT ONCE OR I WILL BE FORCED TO ORDER MY WAR-

RIORS TO BLAST THEIR WAY INTO THAT POD AND KILL ALL OF YOU!"

"Captain," I shouted, "I'm taking these humans back to Lunga to exchange them for my troopers."

"THAT IS IMPOSSIBLE. YOU HAVE NO ORDERS TO DO SO."

"I'm going to crash this ship through the air-lock hatch," I bluffed.

"THAT WILL DAMAGE MY VESSEL AND KILL YOU."

"This survey vessel is built pretty solidly. I think I can make it through the air lock." I was working furiously as I spoke, helping the others to unpack the laser.

"MADNESS!"

"You could save a considerable amount of damage to your ship by opening the air lock," I said.

"THAT WOULD ALLOW YOU TO ESCAPE."

"That would save your ship from damage. Who knows, maybe this survey ship's engines will overheat and explode when I try to push her through the air-lock hatches."

By now we had pulled the laser equipment free of its container and were starting to connect its power pack and alignment optics.

"YOU ARE THREATENING TO DESTROY MY SHIP!" the captain bellowed.

"I only want to get back to Lunga and barter these scientists for my troopers," I said.

"I COULD ALLOW YOU TO LEAVE THE *BLOOD HUNTER* AND THEN DESTROY YOU ONCE YOU ARE A SAFE DISTANCE AWAY."

I hadn't thought of that. "Yes, that's true. You could."

"Look!" shouted one of the scientists.

I followed his pointed finger and saw that the pod door was turning a dull red. The crewmen were working on it with a torch.

And then, with a rumble, the inner air-lock hatch began to slide open.

"PUMPING DOWN TO VACUUM," said an automated computer voice. "THIS AREA SHOULD BE CLEARED OF ALL PERSONNEL IN TEN SECONDS."

We left the digger sitting in pieces on the deck and jammed through the ship's hatch. I pushed past the scientists crowding the main habitat sphere and went up to the cockpit. Randa was sitting alongside Delos.

"The captain's going to let us out," I said. Through the cockpit's observation port I saw that the outer air-lock hatch was opening. I could see the stars out there.

"Yes, and then he'll blow us to eternity once we're clear of his precious ship," Randa muttered.

"I don't think so," I said, thinking of the captain who shared a drink with me.

The air lock was fully open now. Delos touched the propulsion master-control key and the ship seemed to lurch once, then slide smoothly toward the open hatch, beyond it and out into the dark starry void.

I leaned between them and punched at the communicator panel until the Tsihn captain's red-eyed face glared up from the screen at me.

"I'm sorry to betray you this way, Captain," I said. "But this is something that I must do."

It hissed. "I'm not even going to waste a shot on you, traitor. Let the Skorpis blow you to hell. There are plenty of them heading your way."

I grinned at it. "Thank you, Captain."

Its slitted eyes closed briefly; then it said, "Go with honor, Orion."

Minutes later the *Blood Hunter* winked out of sight with a soundless flash of blinding white light, safely in superlight velocity, beyond pursuit by the Skorpis.

Which we decidedly were not. As soon as Randa turned

on the ship's long-range sensors, half a dozen battle cruisers showed on our tiny screen, heading our way.

Delos immediately began taping a message to be beamed to them. "This is Dr. Delos of the University of Farcall, chief of the scientific research team on the planet Lunga. We are returning to Lunga aboard a survey vessel. We are unarmed. Our entire complement of crew is scientists and the human named Orion. I repeat, we are unarmed and are returning to Lunga."

Then we waited to see if the approaching Skorpis cruisers would listen to his message or shoot first and ask questions afterward.

They listened, and I could hear the sighs of relief echoing through the whole ship.

The commander of the Skorpis squadron spoke at length with Delos as the ponderous battle cruisers took up formation all around us. We headed back toward Lunga surrounded by the cruisers, a minnow being escorted by killer whales. It was almost ludicrous.

The scientists seemed tremendously relieved. Only as they gathered around me and thanked me for rescuing them from the Tsihn did I realize how much they had feared being prisoners.

"Those lizards make my blood run cold," said one of the women. "They don't have a shred of human decency."

I thought of the Skorpis and their eating habits and wondered how much political expediency shaped her attitudes. Your alien enemies are inhuman; your alien allies are extraterrestrials.

And beyond them all, beyond all the human factions and the alien intelligent races locked in this interstellar war, were the Creators—descendants of the human race but evolved far beyond human form. Were there other far superior races involved, too? I wondered. Aten had spoken of the ultimate crisis as being something far more catastrophic than this "mere" war in which billions were being slaughtered and whole planets devastated.

I knew that the Old Ones existed, but they wished to play no part in the struggles that ensnared us. Might there be other races, far older, far superior to us? Was that the ultimate crisis Aten and the other Creators feared?

I had scant time to reflect on those matters. We were approaching Lunga again. Now I had to bargain for the lives of my troopers, which meant that the scientists who had just thanked me for saving them would soon be cursing me and trying to kill me.

Chapter 17

"Who are you, really?" Delos asked me.

We were alone in the cramped galley of the survey vessel, no more than an hour away from taking up orbit around Lunga. The commander of the cruiser squadron escorting us had suggested putting a Skorpis crew on board our vessel. I had refused, assuring her that we were returning peacefully to Lunga and did not need her help.

"I am Orion," I answered as I poured myself a cup of a stimulant processed out of alkali crystals from the gleaming vat built into the bulkhead.

Delos shook his head and smiled at me. "Look, I could say that I am Delos. But that tells you nothing except what to call me."

His eyes were inquisitive, not demanding. The smile on his bearded face was gentle.

"I see," I replied. "You are Dr. Delos of the University of Farcall, chief of the scientific research team on the planet Lunga."

He poured himself a mug of the steaming brew as he said, "I am also the son of Professor Leoh of Albion and the Lady Jessica, director of the Farcall Institute of Exopsychology, science laureate of the Golden Circle, and husband of Randa."

That last piece of information surprised me. "You and Randa are married?"

"Didn't you know?"

From the way they seemed to take the opposite position on every question, it had not occurred to me that they might be husband and wife. I was almost amused by the thought.

"Now that I've told you who and what I am," Delos said, returning to his original question, "just who and what are you?"

I had to shrug. "I am Orion. A soldier."

"There's more to it than that."

If I told him that I was created by a half-demented egomaniac from the far future, built to be sent on missions of murder and carnage through all the eras of space-time, he would undoubtedly think I was either insane or joking with him.

So I said, "No, there's not much more to it than that."

"Your parents?"

"I'm a soldier," I repeated. "Do the soldiers of your Farcall have parents? Aren't they cloned and raised on military preserves? Aren't they kept apart from the rest of your society, frozen when they're not needed, revived and given their orders and sent out to do battle for you?"

He scratched at his beard. "Well, yes, I suppose so. I really don't know that much about the military. This field trip with the Skorpis is the closest to the war that any of us have come. Believe me," he added fervently, "it's been close enough for a lifetime!"

"You've been at war all your life, and for a couple of generations before you were born."

"Yes, but that's the military's business. We're scientists, we don't get involved in fighting."

"Yet you expect your military to protect you."

"Of course. That's what they're for."

I felt an unhappy sigh filling my chest. "Well then, think of me as one of those soldiers."

He studied me a moment with those inquisitive soft brown eyes, then said, "No, Orion, that won't wash. There's more to you than that. I want to know what you're hiding and why."

"What makes you think I'm hiding anything?"

"Because the Old Ones spoke to you," he hissed, and his eyes suddenly blazed, revealing his true feelings. "My team and I have been on Lunga for two months with no contact whatsoever, no matter how we tried to communicate with them. You come along and the Old Ones speak to you within hours of your reaching the ocean."

I had to smile. He was jealous. "I could be lying," I said.

"No, you're not lying. And you're not a simple soldier, either. Who are you, Orion? Why were you sent to Lunga?"

"I wish I knew," I told him. I drained my mug, feeling the hot liquid burn its way down inside me, then turned and left the galley, leaving Delos standing there seething with curiosity and resentment.

Randa was still in the cockpit with one of the other scientists. I told them both to get out.

"I'll take over the controls," I said.

She shot me a skeptical glance. "Are you sure you can handle it? Inserting a ship into planetary orbit isn't as easy as you may think, Orion."

Her meaning was clear. Even the slightly tolerant smile on her lips betrayed her thoughts. I'm a scientist, she was saying, and I can understand how to pilot a survey vessel by studying its control panel and calling for instructions from the ship's computer. You're a soldier, you can't be expected to know anything or to do anything you haven't been specifically trained for.

I reached down and grasped her arm. Lifting her gently from the pilot's seat, I said, "I can pilot a dreadnought if I have to. Go on back to the galley and ask your husband if he thinks I'm capable of running this little tub."

She looked surprised, annoyed. But she came out of the chair without resistance and started back toward the galley, casting a resentful look at me over her shoulder.

"You too," I told the scientist in the other seat. "I'll handle this by myself."

He huffed a little, but he left me alone in the cockpit. Scanning the control board, I saw that the vessel had an automated orbital-insertion program built into its computer's memory. Sensors were already estimating Lunga's mass and distance. All I had to do was touch a pressure pad on the board and the ship did the rest by itself.

I activated the communicator, instead, and asked for the Skorpis base commander. Several underlings tried to talk to me, but I refused to speak to anyone until the base commander's grim, gray-furred face appeared on the display screen before me.

"You are surrendering, Orion?" She made it sound more like a statement than a question.

"No," I said. "I have returned to offer you an exchange."

"What have you to offer that I would desire?"

"Your team of scientists."

Her lips pulled back slightly to show her teeth. "You captured them and now you return them?"

"I saved them from the Tsihn and now I offer them back to you."

Unconsciously she began grooming the fur of her face. "They must be of very little value to you if you offer them back to me."

I almost smiled, remembering the wonderfully fierce bargaining that would go on in the bazaars of cities the Mongols had taken or even in the boardrooms of interplanetary corporations.

"Their value to me is not so important as their value to you," I said.

"What value are they to me? They cannot fight. They cannot entertain. They cannot be used for food. They have not succeeded in their mission. Because of them I have lost nearly two whole battalions of warriors."

I jumped on that point. "Your orders were to protect

these scientists. You fought honorably and well to protect them. Unfortunately, you must tell your superiors that you failed. The scientists were captured, despite your spending nearly two whole battalions to protect them. It is very sad."

If a cat could smile, she did it then. "I have not lost the scientists. They are on your ship."

"But not on yours."

"Meaning?"

"Meaning that I will blow up this ship, with the scientists in it, if you do not agree to my terms."

"You will kill yourself, then?"

"Yes, and no Skorpis will ever eat my flesh. I will blast this ship and all of us into an ionized gas cloud."

Her massive shoulders moved in a very human-looking shrug.

"Go ahead, then. It is no fur off my face."

"But what will your superiors say when you report to them that you failed to protect the scientists? What will they say when you report that you refused to take them back after they had been captured and returned? You will be meat for their larders, I'm afraid."

That brought out a snarl. "We can take your ship—"

"Not before I blow it to atoms."

She just stared at me. Even though it was only an image on the display screen I could feel the fury of that yellow-eyed stare. At that moment she would like nothing better than to sink her fangs into my throat.

"But I will happily return the scientists to you," I said, trying to sound carefree and cheerful.

"Under what terms?"

"That you return my troopers to me."

"They are prisoners. They surrendered with hardly a fight."

"So they are worth very little," I taunted. "How much courage can you ingest from soldiers such as they?"

"Then why do *you* want them?"

I had to think fast. "I want to revive them and train them to be true soldiers, worthy of their calling. So that the next time you meet them they will offer you a better meal than their miserable carcasses offer now."

Now it was her turn to do some thinking. She undoubtedly thought that I was lying, that there was something else going on. But actually, what I told her was as close to the truth as I could say. My troopers needed better training—and better leadership—if they were to survive their battles.

"I must consider this carefully," said the base commander. "The prisoners have been frozen. They belong to the larders of those who captured them. I must determine what payment those warriors should receive if they give up their food."

Nodding, I replied, "I'm inserting this vessel into a stationary orbit around the planet. In one hour I will set off the engines and blow up the ship."

"I will give you my response in less than one hour, Orion."

"Good." I cut the connection, and saw that my finger trembled slightly.

"You can't be serious."

Turning in the pilot's chair I saw that Randa was standing behind me. She had not gone back to the galley. She had heard my conversation with the base commander.

"I'm completely serious," I told her.

"You'd kill us all for the sake of a handful of soldiers? Soldiers? Why, they're little better than machines."

"They're quite human," I said, holding on to my temper.

"And you think that we'll just sit here quietly and allow you to murder us?"

There were no weapons among them, I knew. Even the tools that the ship carried were in cargo containers outside this crew habitat module.

I grinned up at her. "There are twenty-two of you and only one of me. But I doubt that more than three or four of you could squeeze into this cockpit area at one time. And I can handle three or four of you without raising much of a sweat."

"You're insane!" Randa snapped. "We're *scientists*, you big oaf! Each one of us is worth a hundred of your miserable soldiers."

I let that pass. I merely said, "If you keep your cool and don't do anything foolish, you'll be back at the Skorpis base within an hour or so. Or what's left of the base, anyway. If you try to stop me I'll blow this ship to hell right here and now."

She stared at me, horrified. "Don't you care about your own life?"

I found myself shaking my head. "No. I don't give a damn. Death doesn't frighten me in the slightest. In fact, it would be a relief."

Randa shuddered, turned, and fairly ran toward the galley and her fellow scientists.

The Skorpis commander called me when there was less than five minutes remaining in the hour. I could imagine what she had been going through: trying to determine if there was some way they could take this survey vessel or incapacitate me before I blew up the ship; weighing the worth of the forty-nine frozen prisoners against the worth of the twenty-two Hegemony scientists; deciding how much recompense to give the warriors who had captured my troopers. Idly I wondered if they ate any of the reptilian Tsihn they captured in battle.

She agreed to the trade, reluctantly. The forty-nine cryo units were carried to my orbiting vessel by a trio of Skorpis landing shuttles. I would not have my troopers destroyed by a matter transceiver. Once I was satisfied that all of the bulky sleeper units were properly attached to my vessel, I allowed the scientists to board the last of the Skorpis shuttles.

Delos stood beside me and watched his team file through the air lock that connected to the shuttle.

"Where will you go now?" he asked me.

"To find someplace that has the facilities to revive my troopers."

"And then?"

"I don't know," I admitted.

"Continue the war?"

"I suppose."

Randa was the last of the scientists in line. As she placed one hand on the rim of the air-lock hatch, she turned slightly to look at me.

"Would you really have killed us all for the sake of a gang of frozen corpses?"

I heard the words she did not speak: a gang of frozen corpses who are nothing but soldiers, not quite human, fit for nothing but to fight and eventually die on some ball of rock out among the stars.

"If I had to," I said.

The corners of her lips curled slightly in a malicious smile. "And how do you know that those pods actually hold your precious soldiers? Maybe the Skorpis commander put forty-nine of her own warriors in them, to take you by surprise."

I made myself smile back at her. "The Skorpis commander made an honorable agreement with me. She's a warrior. She'd kill me if she could but she wouldn't deliberately lie to me."

"You think not?"

"She doesn't have the same set of values that you do," I said.

Randa's eyes shifted from me to her husband. "Let's go," she said to Delos, "and leave this madman to his frozen soldiers." With that she ducked through the hatch.

Delos looked up at me with eyes that were almost sad. "Somehow I get the feeling, Orion, that I would learn a lot more about the universe by going with you."

"Be my guest," I said.

But he shook his head. "I wish I could. I'm not a soldier, but I have a duty to perform. And I know my place."

"Maybe you can help to end this war."

"How?"

"I wish I knew."

He put out his hand to me. "We're on opposite sides, I know. But—good luck, Orion. I wish there really was a way to end this war."

"Search for it," I said, taking his hand.

Chapter 18

Part of my agreement with the Skorpis commander was that she allow me to leave the Lunga system. Alone now in the survey vessel, I broke orbit and headed in the direction that the Tsihn fleet had taken. The Skorpis battle cruisers remained in orbit, but I knew that as soon as their commander decided to, they could overtake me and blast me into vapor.

The survey vessel was not capable of lightspeed. The only safety I could hope for was to find another Commonwealth ship in normal space. A forlorn hope, I realized. Space is vast, and most of the ships traveling through it go to superlight velocity as soon as they can, which puts them completely out of touch with turtle-boats such as mine.

But I had another means of communicating.

I put the ship on autopilot, with instructions to warn me if any Skorpis or Hegemony vessels appeared nearby. Then I leaned back in the pilot's chair, closed my eyes, and reached for contact with the Creators.

This time it was easy. The Golden One appeared immediately, decked in a magnificent glowing robe. He seemed to be hovering in the emptiness of interstellar space, a splendid god radiating power and glory.

"What a strange ape you are, Orion," he said. "Threatening to kill yourself if the enemy refused to return your troopers to you."

"I've died before," I said. "There's no great trick to it."

"But you expect me to revive you each time."

Vaguely I recalled a slight, soft-spoken Hindu with dark skin and large liquid eyes. "It would be a relief to be taken off the wheel of life," I said.

"You seek nothingness? Oblivion?"

"It would be an end to pain."

Aten smirked at me. "Your nirvana is not to be, Orion. Not yet. I have further chores for you."

"First revive my troopers," I said. "Awaken them and allow them to live normal human lives. They deserve that much, at least."

"They will be revived, I promise you. I haven't given up hope of enlisting the aid of the Old Ones and similar ancient races. Your troopers will help you to establish the next point of contact with them."

"End this war," I urged him. "Stop the killing. What's so important that it makes you send billions to their deaths?"

"What's so important about those billions that it matters when and how they die? They're creatures, Orion. Creatures. My creations. I can use them as I choose. I use them as I must."

"Why should we help you to carry on this war? What's the point of it? Why can't you stop it?"

Aten shook his head as if disappointed in me. "How little you understand, my creature. Don't you think I would end the war if I could? It isn't that easy, Orion."

"Why not?"

"If it takes two to make a fight, it also takes two to make peace. Anya and her ilk won't stop fighting. They want their way, and that way will lead us all to utter disaster."

"She must think differently."

"She is wrong!"

I thought, If only I could find Anya, speak with her, learn why she is fighting, what her goals are.

But the Golden One read my thoughts as easily as if I had spoken them aloud. "She would kill you out of hand, Orion.

The goddess you love now seeks only blood and vengeance. Anyone serving me is her enemy and she will destroy them. She is my enemy, Orion. And therefore she is your enemy."

No, I thought. She could never be my enemy.

"Fool," spat Aten. And he disappeared from my awareness.

I was back in the cockpit of the survey vessel. Warning lights on the control board were blinking red, the contact alarm beeping annoyingly.

The screen showed a lone vessel, a sleek scout ship moving at nearly lightspeed toward me. Cranking up the sensors to maximum magnification, I saw that it bore the hexagonal symbol of the Commonwealth.

It was a Tsihn ship. Its captain appeared on my display screen, small and slight, scales rippling pink and pale yellow.

"You are the survey vessel from the *Blood Hunter*," it told me, rather than asking me. "The humanoid known as Orion."

"That is correct."

"Good. You will be attached to my ship and then we can haul our eggs out of this region before a Hegemony cruiser spots us."

I stayed aboard the survey ship while the Tsihn scout sent out an EVA team to grapple my vessel and attach it to theirs. Once we were safely linked to them, the scout ship accelerated to lightspeed and made the jump to superlight velocity.

The Tsihn captain did not invite me aboard its ship. It seemed to want to have as little to do with me as possible. Its orders had been to penetrate the area where I had jumped away from the *Blood Hunter*, find me and bring me back to the nearest Tsihn base. Its orders did not include hospitality or even civility.

The Tsihn base was not a planet, but a massive motile station nearly a hundred light-years from the Lunga region. It hung in the emptiness of interstellar space, outlined against a distant bright swirl of gas and dust glowing red and blue in fluorescence stimulated by a cluster of newborn hot, blue stars a few light-years away.

There was a human section to the station, and I was brought there by a Tsihn escort, not knowing whether I was going to receive a medal or a court-martial.

I got neither. The human chief of the section was a grizzled old brigadier named Uxley with prosthetic legs and a permanently bleary expression on his baggy, sagging face. I was brought to his office by my Tsihn guards, who wheeled about and left without a word or a salute. I stood before his desk at attention.

"You're being put in charge of a battalion, Orion," Brigadier Uxley told me, with no preliminaries. "Don't ask me why. Somebody higher up in the chain of command must either have enormous faith in you or wants to see you dead. Maybe both."

He was clearly unhappy over me. I had no rank, not even a record in his personnel files. As far as he was concerned I was the protégé of some high-ranking officer or politician, with no real military experience. He was, of course, more right than he could know.

"There's a little piece of rock called Bititu," he said, flashing an image of a black, pitted asteroid on his wall screen. "What its strategic value is, no one in the upper echelons has seen fit to tell me. But it's to be taken by you and your thousand. And damned quick, too."

"Sir," I said, still at ramrod attention, "I would like to have the survivors of the Lunga mission as part of my command."

He fixed me with a bloodshot eye. "Why?"

"I know them, sir, and they know me. We work well together."

"Do you?" He looked down at the display screen on his desk for several moments. I could not see the screen, but from the reflection of light on his face I could tell he was paging through a considerable amount of data very quickly.

Finally he looked up at me. "You pulled them out of a Skorpis depot? Single-handed?"

"I negotiated for them, sir."

His attitude softened appreciably. Leaning back in his padded chair, he pointed at me with a rock-steady finger. "You're not regular army, are you?"

"No, sir."

"Yet you went in there and got your troops away from the Skorpis."

I said nothing.

"All right, you can have them with you. I'll even add them to your command, since you're already slated for a full battalion. The sergeant outside will show you where your quarters are. Better start spending every waking second on studying Bititu and the Hegemony's defenses of it."

"Yessir." I saluted and left his office.

And went straight to the cryonics center where my troop was being revived. It was a big chamber very similar to the one where I had first awakened in this era. The medics had removed forty-nine of the chamber's regular cryosleep units and placed my troopers' capsules on their foundations. They were all plugged in to the chamber's environmental controls and computer system. Frede was in one of those pods. And Quint, Jerron and the others. Frozen inside dull metal canisters inscribed with Skorpis symbols. The capsules looked old, heavily used. But I saw no vapor leaking from them; battered they might be, but they still worked as they should.

"They won't be coming out of it for another six hours, at least," said the medic on duty at the control station. Her voice echoed off the metal walls.

"It takes that long?" I asked.

She waggled one hand in the air. "Slower is better, once the body cells have been defrosted. Pump nutrients into them, stimulate their brains to restart, let them dream and sort out whatever memories were locked in short-term storage when they went under."

Their short-term memories must be terrible, I thought. The last thing they would remember would be the Skorpis freezing them for their food larders. Did they struggle? Try to fight? Or go under resigned to their miserable fate, convinced that they had been abandoned by their leaders?

"And besides," the medic added, "we just got orders to feed some new training into them. So while we're letting them come back gradually we can program this new material into their neural systems."

I didn't bother to ask what the new training material was. I knew they were being programmed with everything the army thought they needed to know about Bititu. I decided to go back to the cubicle they called my quarters and start to study up on the asteroid, too. It wouldn't do for my troops to know more about the operation than I did.

But first I asked the medic, "Could you call me when they wake up?"

"I'll be off duty then," she said.

"Well, how long will it take? What time will they start to come out of it?"

"Another six hours. I already told you."

I thanked her and hustled back to my quarters. I spent the six hours studying Bititu, grateful that I did not need sleep. What I learned of the asteroid was not encouraging.

Bititu was an asteroid in the Jilbert system, a seven-mile-long chunk of barren rock, roughly kidney-shaped. Jilbert itself was a dim red dwarf star with only one true planet, a gas giant orbiting so close to the star that they were almost a binary system. The rest of the system was nothing but asteroids, an unusual state for the planetary system of a dwarf star.

The Hegemony had apparently fortified Bititu heavily. According to the reports I scanned, the asteroid was honeycombed with tunnels defended by a full regiment of spiderlike creatures that the reports referred to only as the Arachnoids. Very little was known about them; even their intelligence was in some doubt. Some scientists believed that individual

Arachnoids were not intelligent, in the sense of being self-aware and motivated, but were instead part of a collective hive mind, as many species of insects have proven to be.

The most discouraging part of the reports was the admission that not much was known about the Arachnoids because none had ever been taken alive. They always fought to the last member. Not a happy prospect for those who had to do battle against them.

Then I saw that the Commonwealth's scientific community requested that we take as many of the Arachnoids prisoner as possible, for them to interrogate and study. The phrasing of their request made it clear that they thought we soldiers slaughtered all the Arachnoids deliberately.

"Despite their nonhumanoid appearance," the scientists' request read, "the Arachnoids are to be treated as fully sentient, intelligent beings. Indiscriminate killing of these creatures is punishable by military code."

I turned off the video reader with a feeling almost of disgust. Bititu would be a bloody mess, it seemed. There was no way to take the asteroid except by direct assault, and the enemy was well entrenched and willing to fight to the bitter end. I doubted that the Arachnoids would willingly allow themselves to become prisoners and objects of our scientists' eager investigations.

With my mind full of foreboding I went down the metal passageway of the station back to the cryonic center.

A different medic was on duty now, a gray-haired male whose face was also a grayish pallor, as if he had not seen the sun in years.

"They're coming around," he whispered as I looked out across the big room filled with the cryonic capsules. His attention was focused on the dozens of display screens set into the curving panel before his chair like the faceted eyes of a giant insect.

I felt the chill of cryonic cold seeping into my bones. "Shouldn't it be warmer in here?" I asked.

He shot me a disapproving glance. "I know what I'm doing, soldier."

"Yes," I said. "Of course."

"They're going to be disoriented for a bit. The briefings they've been getting while we're pulling them out will be mostly subconscious, until they're brought to the surface by trigger phrases."

The trigger phrase, I knew, was simply the name of the target asteroid: Bititu.

"The last real memories they'll have will be whatever they saw when they were put under."

Skorpis warriors forcing them into the cryo pods. Knowing that they were nothing more than food to their captors, that if they were ever awakened it would be for ritual execution.

"Isn't there some way we can tell them they're safe, that they're not prisoners of the Skorpis anymore?"

The medic glared at me. "Is that what happened to these soldiers? They were frozen by those damned cats?"

"Yes."

"Shit on a goddamned mother-loving sonofabitch sandwich," he snarled, his fingers suddenly playing across the control keys. "Nobody tells me any pissing thing. Same old army. If there's a way to screw things up . . ." His voice sank to a disgruntled mumble.

At last he looked up from the controls and displays. "It's too pissing late. There's nothing I can do. They're going to start waking up in a few minutes and they'll still be thinking that they're prisoners. If we don't have a couple of heart attacks among them it'll be a pissing miracle."

My mind raced. Was there anything I could do? Could I reach out to them mentally and assure them that they were safe, that they had nothing to fear?

Too late. A heard a click and a sighing sound. Looking across the chamber, I saw one of the capsules pop open, white vapor issuing from it like fog seeping across a graveyard at midnight. Another clicked and sighed. Then more.

Someone moaned. Someone began to sob like a motherless child. Which we all were, of course.

I rushed to the nearest capsule. I saw a trooper struggling to a sitting position, eyes wide with fright.

"It's all right," I shouted, my voice echoing off the chamber's metal walls. "You're safe. You're not a prisoner anymore."

One by one the pods opened up and my troopers awoke. Many of them were ashen-faced, trembling. Others sat up with fists clenched and teeth gritted, ready for a fight. I saw that most of them were bruised, lips split, eyes swollen, clotted blood matting their hair. They had not gone into those pods peacefully.

I searched through the capsules for Frede's pod. She was just opening her eyes when I found it.

"Orion?" she asked as I leaned through the vapor steaming out of her capsule. "They got you, too?"

A heavy blue-black bruise swelled her cheek. I saw slashes on her arms where her sleeves had been torn.

"No," I told her. "I got you back from them. You're safe. It's all right."

"Safe?"

"We're in a Tsihn station. I got you back from the Skorpis."

I helped her up to a sitting position. She seemed dazed, disoriented. "We're not prisoners? Not . . ."

"You're not prisoners anymore. You're safe."

She looked around, blinking her eyes. "Sheol, do I have a headache," she muttered. Then she threw her arms around my neck and kissed me so hard that the rest of the barely revived troopers whooped and whistled.

And then someone screamed, as if in agony or mortal terror. I pulled away from Frede's embrace and sprinted to the pod. It was Lieutenant Quint, screaming horribly, still lying on his back with his eyes squeezed shut, his hands raised defensively in front of him, his legs churning as if he were trying to run away.

"Quint, it's all right!" I yelled into his contorted face. "You're safe."

He kept on screaming as if he could not hear me. I reached into the capsule and grabbed the front of his shirt, yanked him halfway up and shook him violently. Still he screeched, eyes closed, gibbering incoherently.

I slapped his face. Even as I did, I noticed that he was unbruised. Shaking him again, I shouted, "Wake up! It's me, Orion. You're safe."

He was trembling uncontrollably, but he opened his eyes and stared at me.

"You're not among the Skorpis," I said, more gently. "It's all right. There's nothing to be afraid of."

A few of the other troopers had gotten shakily to their feet and gathered around Quint's capsule. I smelled something foul, and realized that Quint had emptied his bladder and his bowels, either when the Skorpis had shoved him into the pod or just now, as he awoke.

I waved the other troopers away before they smelled it. "Fall in," I said. "Give the lieutenant a minute to pull himself together."

I had them line up, leaving Quint in his capsule. They were bruised, cut, uniforms tattered and dirty, but alive and grinning at me.

"There must be a sorrier-looking bunch of mongrels somewhere in the army," I said to them, "but if there is, I hope I never have to look at them. Sergeants, get these mutts cleaned up, find their assigned quarters, and see that they're issued fresh uniforms and kits. Officers, come with me."

I knew that the remaining sergeants among my troop were experienced veterans who knew how to maneuver their squads through a camp, whether it was on some alien planet or an interstellar way station, such as this was. I wanted the troopers out of the chamber before I dealt with Quint.

He was a mess, both physically and mentally. Frede was the only other surviving lieutenant, and it took the two of us to coax Quint out of his pod and down to the medical rehab center. The gray-faced medic who had supervised the revival process came with us.

"I've seen this before," he told me as a pair of robot nurses took Quint gently in their metal grips. "He won't be fit for active duty until he's been completely deprogrammed and retrained. Maybe not even then."

"What will happen to him, then?" I asked.

The medic shifted his shoulders beneath his white jacket. "Oh, they'll assign him to some desk job, I suppose. He'll be perfectly adequate to send other troopers into battle; he just hasn't got the stuff in him to face battle himself, anymore."

I should have felt pity for Quint, I know. Instead I felt a smoldering resentment, almost anger.

Frede read my face. "He can't help it," she said. "He's not goldbricking."

"How do you know?"

She shrugged. "What difference would it make?"

I realized she was right. What difference would it make? Despite all the training, despite being gestated specifically to be a soldier, despite a lifetime of nothing but the military, Quint had taken all the fighting he was ever going to take. I should have seen it coming. I should have realized that while we were fighting for our lives on Lunga he was hiding in a hole somewhere, keeping his head down, unwilling or unable to face the death that the rest of us did not even think about in the heat of action.

"It's not a good thing for soldiers to think too much," Frede told me as we left Quint to the medics and went to find our quarters and the rest of the troop.

"Maybe not," I muttered, thinking of Randa, who did not really believe soldiers were capable of thinking at all.

"You're now my second-in-command," I told her as we walked along the metal passageways, guided by the computer displays on the bulkheads. Most of the others in the passageways in this section of the station were humans, although we passed several Tsihn and even a few other species.

She nodded. "Are we going to stay here on this station, or will they ship us to an R-and-R center?"

"No R-and-R," I said. "We've got a new assignment."

"Without a rest and refit from the last one?" She was immediately indignant.

I suddenly realized that it was my fault. "I asked for you," I said, "when I got the assignment."

"What assignment?"

"Bititu. It's an asteroid in the—"

I stopped. Frede's eyes seemed to glaze over for a moment. The trigger word. I could have kicked myself. All the data from the subconscious briefing came surging up into her awareness.

"Sheol," she murmured. "They don't give you the easy ones, do they?"

"I shouldn't have asked for you," I started to apologize. "Maybe I can get you released for R and R."

"Not now. Not once we've been briefed. They'll either ship us out or freeze us."

We started walking along the passageway again. I didn't know what to say. It had never occurred to me that the troopers deserved a spell of rest and recreation after their ordeal on Lunga. Bititu promised to be even worse.

"There's one glitch in the planning that I'll have to fix," Frede told me as we approached the section where we would be quartered.

"What's that?" I asked.

"The sleeping arrangements. They've paired each of us off with other people."

"That's standard procedure, isn't it? The army doesn't want us forming emotional attachments that are too close."

"Right. But you're battalion commander now and rank has its privileges."

"I don't know if I should—"

"Not you," Frede said, her eyes twinkling mischievously. "If I'm your second, then I can pull *my* rank to supersede the bitch they've assigned to you."

Chapter 19

So when we boarded a Tsihn troopship for the flight to Bititu, Lieutenant Frede was my second-in-command and my bunkmate.

Our ship joined a sizable battle fleet of cruisers and dreadnoughts. The plan was to make the run to the Jilbert system at superlight velocity, so we could not be detected until the very last moment, when we slowed to relativistic speed. Navigation was going to be tricky, but the Tsihn admiral assured me that they could get us to within a few light-hours of Jilbert.

"In that way," it told me at one of our conferences in its quarters, "the Hegemony will have no warning time to reinforce the system."

Its conference room was hot and dry; like being in a sunbaked desert, except that we were seated around an uneven conference table. Half of the table was set at a height to make humans comfortable, the other half several centimeters higher for the comfort of the big senior officers among the reptilians. The admiral, of course, was the biggest of them all: nearly three meters tall when standing, the dun-colored scales of its chest almost completely covered with symbols of rank and distinction.

The walls of the conference room were filled with holograms of arid rocky country and a blazing bronze sky. I was tempted to shield my eyes from the sun, but the brightness actually was never high enough to cause real glare.

"The nearest Hegemony base to Bititu is in the Justice system," I pointed out. "That's only a dozen light-years away. The enemy could send a battle fleet to Bititu before we've secured the asteroid."

The admiral flicked its forked tongue in and out almost faster than the eyes could follow, its way of working off nervous energy.

"We will remain in the Jilbert system until you have secured the asteroid, never fear," said the admiral. "My fleet is powerful enough to take care of any Hegemony attempt to reinforce Bititu."

I remembered the way the Tsihn fleet had bolted from Lunga and stranded us.

"In point of fact," said the admiral, tongue flicking blurrily, "we are hoping that the Hegemony will attempt to interfere. It will give us an opportunity to destroy one of their fleets."

I was glad to hear that it was so confident. Glancing along our end of the conference table to Frede and my other officers, I saw that none of us humans shared its opinion.

My battalion spent most of the flight in training. We converted the troopship's passageways and compartments into mock-ups of the tunnels and caves we expected to find on Bititu and practiced storming through heavily defended positions, day after day. There was no room for subtlety in our tactics. It was just brute force and firepower. I knew the casualties would be high.

"Why doesn't the fleet just blow the goddamned asteroid out of existence?" Frede asked one night in our bunk. "Why do we have to take it?"

I had no answer, except, "Maybe the Commonwealth wants to use it as a base for themselves after we've driven out the Hegemony."

"You know what I think," she asked, then went on without waiting for my reply, "I think it's those double-domed scientists. They want Arachnoid specimens to study, so we get stuck with the job of trying to capture some of them."

"But according to our briefings, the Arachnoids fight to the last one," I said.

"Tell it to the scientists."

"Still," I said, thinking aloud, "the fleet could bombard the asteroid before we go in, pound it as hard as they can. It wouldn't hurt the Arachnoids deep inside the rock, but it could knock out any of them up by the surface."

"And make our landing easier," Frede said.

But when I took up the question with the admiral's chief aide, a reptilian about my own size with beautiful multicolored scales, the answer was: No preliminary bombardment. It would merely alert the Arachnoid defenders and delay our landing.

"But once we show ourselves in the Jilbert system, several light-hours away from the asteroid, won't that alert them?" I asked.

"No preliminary bombardment," the reptilian repeated. "The plan is set and will not be changed."

I demanded the right to ask the admiral about it. Permission denied. I got the impression that the strategists who had planned this operation wanted to capture Bititu as intact as possible. They were perfectly willing to spend our lives in exchange for killing off the defenders without wrecking the asteroid itself.

I had other ideas.

I assigned Frede and my other officers to studying the pictures of Bititu as minutely as possible. I myself spent most of my nights going over those images, pinpointing each spot on that pitted bare rock that looked like an air-lock hatch or a gun emplacement. Then, one by one, I assigned each of those targets to one of our heavy-weapons platoons.

My plan was to knock out those surface defenses as we rode toward the asteroid in our landing vehicles. Instead of sitting inside and waiting passively until we touched down on the surface, I ordered my weapons platoons to zero in on specific targets and destroy them while we were in transit from the troopship to the asteroid.

Otherwise, I feared, the Arachnoid defenders would blast our ships out of the sky before we reached the rock.

As we neared the Jilbert system I worked the troopers harder and harder. Little sleep and less rest. We raced through the ship's passageways every day and almost every night. When we were not physically assaulting our mock targets we were studying the imagery of Bititu, familiarizing ourselves with every crevice and hollow of its surface, picking out the precise spots where each landing vehicle would touch down on its surface.

Some of the troopers began to complain that by the time we reached our target they would be too tired to fight. I drove them harder.

"We go relativistic in six hours," the Tsihn liaison officer told me at last. "Then two or three hours to the point where you embark for the asteroid."

I got my troops ready. We marched to the loading docks where our landing vehicles waited, singing ancient songs of battle and blood. We got into our armored space suits, using the buddy system to check each other carefully. The suits had been anodized white at my insistence; in the dimly lit tunnels of Bititu we had to be able to see each other. No one knew what the visual range of the Arachnoids was, whether white stood out as clearly to them as it did to us, but I was determined to avoid killing ourselves with friendly fire.

I put the heavy-weapons platoons in the first of our forty landers, with the other platoons' landers coming in behind them. I put myself in the first of the weapons platoons.

As the troops clambered aboard the landers, awkward in their heavily armored suits, Frede came up beside me, her helmet visor raised, an odd, expectant smile on her face.

"Well, we're as ready as we can be," she said, her voice trembling ever so slightly.

"Make certain your weapons team hits every assigned target," I said. "Especially the air locks. Maybe those spiders can breathe vacuum, but I doubt it."

"I never liked spiders," she said.

"Now's your chance to kill a few thousand of them."

She nodded inside the space helmet, then slid the visor down and lumbered off to her landing vehicle. I clamped my visor and sealed it. I had done everything I could think of. Now it was us against them, with no mercy expected either way.

The landing vehicles were little more than armored shields with handgrips for the troops and propulsion units hung off their sterns. We pushed off the troopship, forty landers, and slid out into the darkness of space.

"Here we go," said one of the troopers. I heard his tense, shaky voice through my helmet earphones.

"Another free ride, courtesy of the army."

"Enjoy your trip."

"Yeah. You gotta be born to it."

No one laughed.

The sullen red star off in the distance gave very little light. The dark, pitted rock of Bititu seemed to float out there among the stars, a long way off. And we seemed to be hanging in the middle of the emptiness, barely moving. As I clung to the handgrips behind the forward armored shield, in the midst of the heavy-weapons platoon, I had to turn my entire body around to see the troopship we had just left. Farther in the distance hovered hundreds of battle cruisers and dreadnoughts, sleek and deadly, with enough firepower to atomize Bititu and its fanatical defenders.

We slowly, agonizingly drifted toward the asteroid. I felt naked and alone despite my armored space suit and the soldiers surrounding me. Not a sign of life from the asteroid. Not a glimmer of light. It merely hung there, growing slightly larger as we slowly approached it, a massive elongated chunk of rock, pockmarked with craters and scored with strange grooves, dark and solid and ominous.

I checked the watch set into the wrist of my suit. I had set it to count down to the instant when we would begin firing at the surface facilities. A hundred and nine seconds to go. A hundred and nine eternities.

At last I saw something glint on the asteroid's surface. The reflection of sunlight? No, Jilbert was too faint and red to make that kind of glitter. Then another, and the front shield of one of our landers flared with the impact of a laser blast. Missiles were leaping from hidden fissures in the asteroid, blazing toward us. Our bombardment plan was instantly forgotten as we began to shoot at the missiles. They exploded in silent fireballs, each one closer to us as we drove onward toward the asteroid.

A lander was hit, bodies and fragments scattering, tumbling, flailing through the dark emptiness. Another, and then another. Dying voices screamed in my earphones.

"Fire at the surface targets!" I bellowed into my helmet microphone. "Heavy weapons, fire at the surface. All other platoons, antimissile fire."

My well-trained troops began shooting at the targets we had picked out. But the enemy was firing missiles from spots that had looked like nothing but bare rock until a few moments earlier. A missile exploded scant meters from my lander, I could feel the heat of its flare even through the armor of my space suit. Fragments ripped into us, clunking against our armored suits. A trooper's oxygen tank exploded in a brief deadly flare of flame, killing him instantly.

We were hitting the ground targets, I could see. Explosions peppered Bititu's surface. Missiles were still blazing toward us, several more landers were blown away, but we were hurtling toward the surface now. We would be there in a few seconds. Smaller weapons were blasting at us now; I could feel the lander shuddering as small solid slugs racked us. A trooper was hit just next to me, space suit erupting into fountains of gushing blood that froze in the vacuum into solid red pellets.

We huddled behind the lander's forward shield as lasers and projectiles racked the vehicle from one end to the other. Half the troops on the lander had already been killed by the time we thudded onto the asteroid's rocky surface.

I jumped in the negligible gravity, rifle in hand, and blasted a partially open hatch set into the rock. It snapped shut. It took an effort to keep from soaring into space; I adjusted the flight pack on my back to negative and felt some semblance of weight that helped me to flatten onto my belly while laser beams and volleys of slugs zipped over my head.

My earphones were ablaze with frantic voices:

"They're all around us!"

"I've got seventy-percent casualties! We've got to get off this rock!"

"Where's the weapons platoon? I need backup. *Now!*"

I slapped a magnetic grenade on the hatch and backed away. It blew noiselessly in the vacuum, smoke dissipating almost before my eyes registered its presence.

"Get into the tunnels!" I yelled into my helmet mike. "The only troops left on the surface are going to be the dead. Get inside! Move!"

I rolled another grenade into the opening of the blasted hatch, then slid into the tunnel headfirst, spraying rifle fire into the murky shadows to clear out any defenders who might have survived the grenade.

The tunnel was barely wide enough for me to crawl through and so dark that I had to turn on my helmet light, despite the infrared sensors in my visor. I heard something slithering behind me and rolled onto my back, aiming my rifle down the length of my torso.

"It's just me, sir!" came a trooper's voice, and I saw a space-suited figure, as anonymous as a faceless sculpture, crawling down the tunnel behind me.

Rolling onto my stomach again, I came face-to-face with my first Arachnoid. It was black, fully a meter wide, with eight spindly legs covered with what seemed like barbs. It held an oblong object in its front two claws, something with fins and a glasslike lens pointing at me. Behind that weapon I saw a face with horizontal mandibles clicking rapidly and eight glittering eyes, no two the same size.

I ducked my head, digging my visor into the bare rock of the tunnel, and pulled the trigger of my rifle at the same time. I felt a blast of heat against the armored top of my helmet, heard a high-pitched wail and the scuttling sound of claws on rock.

When I looked up the spider was gone, but there was a patch of sticky pus-yellow goo on the tunnel floor where it had stood. I saw a side tunnel veering off from this one. Pulling a rocket grenade loose from my belt, I set it for impact and fired it down the side tunnel. It exploded almost immediately, showering me with a hail of pebbles and dust and smoke.

I crawled past the side tunnel, ordering the trooper behind me to take his buddies along it. My earphones blazed with frantic voices:

"There's millions of 'em!"

"They're behind us! They're all around us!"

"We've gotta get out of here! There's too many of 'em!"

There was no way out of here. We could not get back aboard the landers even if we wanted to; they had lifted off the asteroid as soon as we had disembarked.

Slithering forward on my belly, I peered deeper into the tunnel. For a few moments I saw nothing, but I realized I could hear scraping noises and eerie, whistling screeches. Somehow there was enough air in the tunnel to carry sound, or maybe the rock itself was conducting sound waves. Farther off, I could hear the *crack, crack* sound of lasers firing so rapidly that it became an almost continuous clatter of noise. And explosions, some of them big enough to shake the tunnel. Dust and screams and voices shouting.

"There's more of 'em!"

"It's like a trapdoor. Look out!"

The tunnel was widening. The light on my helmet was deep red, not much help in seeing, but Intelligence hoped that the Arachnoids' eyes could not see that end of the visible spectrum. It occurred to me that if we could produce sensors that detected wavelengths our eyes could not see, the Arachnoids might similarly have developed technology to aid their natural senses. So I switched off the lamp and inched along the black tunnel, depending on my visor's infrared sensors to warn me.

Something exploded somewhere behind me, too big an explosion to be one of our grenades. A cloud of dust roiled along the tunnel. Then I heard that scraping, skittering noise again and a spider popped out of another side tunnel. I blasted it in half with a bolt from my rifle. Edging to the lip of the tunnel entrance, I peered into the darkness. My visor showed the faint outline of something in there, inching slowly toward me. I waited until it became clear. Another spider. I killed it with a shot in the middle of its eye cluster.

I worked my way past the sticky remains of the Arachnoid. The tunnel was almost high enough for me to get to my hands and knees, and getting wider all the time. The Arachnoids, I realized, needed more width than height to accommodate the shape of their bodies.

"My squad's down to six effectives. We've got to get out of here!"

"Keep moving toward the center of this rock," I bellowed into my helmet mike. "Nobody's getting off until the last spider's killed."

"Look out, sir!"

I rolled over and saw half a dozen Arachnoids dropping out of a hatch in the top of the tunnel, behind me. The trooper who had shouted the warning fired at them. Two of the spiders rushed at me. I shot the first one in the belly, it was that close. The second was on top of me, jamming its pistol against my chest and firing point-blank. I knocked the gun away with the butt of my rifle as the beam cracked my suit armor and burned my flesh. With a roar of pain I pressed the muzzle of my rifle against the spider's underside and fired. The Arachnoid exploded, spattering the tunnel and me with sticky yellowish pieces.

The trooper behind me was dead, his head blown off, but there were two dead spiders beside him, and another of them twitching its legs helplessly. I finished it with a quick blast from my rifle. My suit was sealing the hole the laser beam had made, fluid edges of the perforation flowing together and quickly hardening. I could feel the medical systems inside the suit spraying a disinfecting analgesic on my burn.

But my thoughts were on the sixth of those Arachnoids. The one that was not accounted for. It must have scuttled down one of the trapdoors that lined these tunnels. Was it lurking just behind one of the hatches, waiting for me or some other unsuspecting trooper to pass it so that it could pop out again and kill more of us?

In the distance ahead of me I saw a dim light and made my way toward it. Several tunnels came together in a hollowed-out area; the walls were smeared with something fluorescent that gave off a faint, sickly greenish yellow light.

I hesitated. I could hear sounds of lasers firing and the dull thumping explosions of grenades echoing down the tunnels. This little cavern seemed to be a nexus of some sort, yet it was apparently deserted, undefended. I heard screams of pain and shouting from one of the tunnels, and then a trio of Arachnoids came scuttling backward toward the cavern. They turned around as they came into the wider area. One of them slid a claw into a crack in the tunnel floor, and a hatch—cleverly concealed to look like a natural piece of the rocky floor—slid open.

Just as the spider did that, its companions spotted me. I fired at the two of them as the third popped down the open hatch. My rifle blast blew the first Arachnoid to pieces and chopped a leg off the second. It fired back, charring the shoulder of my suit. My second shot killed it.

I realized that the spiders did not seem to be wearing any protective clothing. Maybe they *could* breathe vacuum, I thought, although there was definitely air of some kind in these tunnels. I had no time for investigation. The third one lobbed a grenade at me. My senses shifted into overdrive and I saw it soar slowly up from the open hatch, hit the ground once and bump along in my direction. I pushed myself backward, down the tunnel along which I had come, as the grenade went off in a shower of rocks and dust. The blast tore the rifle from my hands; flying debris peppered my armor, denting and cracking it along the shoulders and helmet. But it held. I was unhurt, though momentarily stunned.

The spider edged above the lip of the hatch to fire its laser weapon at me. But I was faster, grabbing my rifle and squeezing its trigger even as I dragged it along the ground toward me. The blast caught the Arachnoid in its eyes. It screeched and dropped out of sight.

I crawled to the edge of the hatch and saw a squirming mass of Arachnoids below, dozens of them, with their wounded companion wriggling its barbed legs in their midst. Before they could react I dropped a grenade on them and slammed the hatch shut. The explosion forced it open again.

Several troopers came crawling down tunnels into the cavern. Their armor was stained, scuffed, bloodied. One of them was missing an arm. They collapsed, exhausted, on the rocky floor.

"Officers report," I said into my helmet mike.

One by one they called in. In several platoons the sergeants or even ordinary troopers were the ones to speak; their officers had been killed or wounded. I heard nothing from Frede until almost the end.

"Frede here. We're down to five effectives, all of them wounded. I'm the only one still in one piece."

Studying the locator map on my visor and the red dots

that represented the positions of the reporting soldiers, I saw that we had more or less cleared out two levels of the tunnels that honeycombed the asteroid. There were at least four more levels to go. Maybe more. And I was down to about thirty percent of my original landing force.

Chapter 20

It grew eerily quiet. In the dim underground shadows, dust sifting through, the fighting had stopped for the moment. The Arachnoids seemed content to wait for us to push deeper, into the next level of tunnels.

I had the medical officer set up his aid station and told the troopers to take a quick squirt of nutrients from the nipples in their helmets. The nutrients included neural stimulators designed to counteract the effects of physical exhaustion and mental fatigue. The troopers called it "joy juice," or "mother's milk," or worse.

I sent a team back to the surface to bring down all the grenades and explosives from the magazines that the landers had left. They caught a few Arachnoids out there, hiding in the wreckage of some of the crashed landers, waiting to snipe at unsuspecting humans.

"We got 'em all," reported the sergeant who led the ammunition detail. Then he added, "I think."

"Were they wearing any kind of protective suits?" I asked through my helmet radio.

"No, sir," said the sergeant. "None that I could see."

The scientists would be interested in that, I thought. I had the grenades and heavier explosives distributed among the surviving soldiers and gave them orders to blanket the tunnels with explosives before moving into them.

"Blast every hatch you see," I told them, "and then blast

whatever's on the other side of the hatch. Check every crevice, every crack in the rock. Go slowly, make certain you've cleared the area around you before advancing. Now let's move."

It was slow, painful going. Hours dragged into days. We inched along the tunnels, probing for trapdoors and hidden nests of spiders waiting to pounce on us. I called up to the fleet and requested more explosives.

"Do you have anything that can produce a high-temperature flame?" I asked.

The Tsihn weaponry officers conferred among themselves, then called back to me that they could send down drums of chemicals which, when mixed together, burst spontaneously into flame.

"Good!" I said. "Send down all you can."

The Tsihn hesitated. In the image on my visor I could see its tongue flicking nervously.

"These are very volatile liquids," it said. "Very dangerous to handle."

I laughed at it. "What do you think we're doing down here, having a picnic?"

It did not understand my words, but my tone was clear. Within a few hours a shuttle craft took up a parking orbit a scant hundred meters off the asteroid and off-loaded dozens of large, bulky drums. A Tsihn officer came down to the second-level cavern that I had turned into my command post. It was clad in an armored space suit just like the rest of us; the only way we could tell it was not one of us was from the fact that its suit was clean and undamaged.

It explained that the liquids in the drums were hypergolic: mix them and they burst into flame hot enough to melt aluminum.

"Fine," I said. "That's just what we need."

The drums were identified by Tsihn symbols. They looked like abstract pictures to me, little black blots spattered on the curved sides of the big gray drums.

"You must be very careful with these chemicals," the Tsihn officer kept repeating. "They are very dangerous."

"That's just what we want," I assured it.

The Tsihn left as quickly as it could.

We went to work on the tunnels, pouring a whole drumful of one chemical down one hatch and then tipping over its hypergolic counterpart and moving out of the way—fast!—as a river of flame burst down on the shrieking, skittering Arachnoids. One by one we cleaned out the tunnels, advancing as soon as the flames had died away, crawling through smoke so thick and oily and choking that we sealed our visors and went back onto the life-support systems in our suits.

Down level after level we crawled, through the sooty smoke, through the charred heaps of hundreds of spiders. Their flesh crackled and broke apart in brittle chunks as we crawled past them. Even sealed inside our suits we found the smell nauseating. This was no longer a battle, it was extermination, I thought. The Arachnoids don't have a chance against the liquid fire. I could see, even in the dim light through my helmet visor, that the fire was so intense it had fused the tunnel walls into a slick, glassy surface.

But they were not finished yet. Not quite.

We had made our way down to the core of the tunnel complex, a large cavern near the heart of the asteroid, big enough for us to stand in. Five major tunnels converged here, and five rivers of flame had poured down into this cavern to turn it into a pit of hell. The floor, the walls, the domelike ceiling were blackened. There had been equipment down here; I could see the charred remains of boxes and consoles, plastic melted and dripping.

But no bodies.

I walked upright, boots crunching on the burned litter, rifle cradled in my arms. Frede and a dozen other troopers were behind me, visors down, gloved fingers on the triggers of their rifles.

"You'd think they'd make their last stand down here," Frede said.

I shook my head inside my helmet. "Not if they're smart. They would have figured out that the fire rivers would all converge here and—"

Four camouflaged doors in the ceiling dropped open and dozens of spiders jumped down on us, firing, screeching weird high-pitched cries. One of them landed on my shoulders, heavy enough to buckle my knees and knock the rifle out of my hands. I saw a horrific set of mandibles snapping at my visor and felt a laser burn my arm. Grabbing at the spider, I yanked it away from me and smashed it against the cavern wall. Its hard shell took the shock, several of its arms sinking their barbs into the armored sleeve of my suit, another two firing pistols into my torso.

I staggered back, still clutching the thing by one of its barbed arms, and reached for the pistol at my hip. My right arm was badly burned, but I shut off the pain signals and yanked the pistol out of its holster. The Arachnoid tried to block me with one of its arms but I clubbed the arm away and fired into its clacking, snapping mouth. The beam sawed through the creature's head and came out the other side, splashing against the wall.

Turning as it dropped away from me, I saw another spider clinging to a trooper with several arms and flicking the detonator of a grenade with one free claw. The explosion killed both of them and knocked the rest of us to the floor of the cavern.

With my senses in overdrive I fired at two more of the Arachnoids, pulled a third off Frède's back and blew its head off, then swept half the cavern with the beam of my pistol.

The attack ended as suddenly as it had begun. Four of my troopers were on the ground, dead or dying. None of the spiders was left alive.

Through the suit radio I could hear Frede gulping for air.

"Thanks," she gasped. "It was going to set off a grenade, I think."

"Suicide fighters," I said. "We won't have any prisoners for the scientists to study."

Frede laughed bitterly. "Tough shit," she said.

I was able at last to tell the Tsihn admiral that Bititu was secure, after four days of intense battle. My casualties were nearly eighty percent. I myself was burned in the chest and right arm.

The admiral congratulated me, although its image in my visor showed no sign of pleasure or even of approval.

"The Hegemony has not seen fit to attempt to reinforce Bititu," it complained. "My fleet has waited here for nothing."

As we were being ferried back to the troopship I wondered why the Commonwealth thought this barren chunk of rock was important enough to kill hundreds of troopers. Apparently the Hegemony did not want to hold on to Bititu badly enough to send help to its Arachnoid garrison.

I shook my head wearily. Was there some real strategic meaning to this fighting, or was it all a game that the Creators were playing among themselves, using us and the other alien races we had encountered as pawns for their entertainment?

What difference did it make? Sitting there in the shuttle craft on the way back to the troopship, grimy and bloody and utterly exhausted, I did what all the other troopers were doing. I leaned my head back against the bulkhead and dozed off.

"It is not a game, Orion."

The Golden One appeared before me, radiating light so blindingly bright that I had to shield my eyes with my aching, weary hands.

He seemed deadly serious, none of his usual mocking tone in his voice, his face somber, almost grim.

"The balance of forces in this war is tilting the wrong

way," Aten told me. "Anya and her ilk are slowly overcoming my Commonwealth."

"But we took Bititu," I protested, like a child seeking its father's approval. "Isn't that something?"

"Not enough," he said. "The Hegemony did not go for my feint. The fleet waited, but the enemy did not step into the trap we had prepared for them."

"Feint? All that killing was nothing more than a feint?"

"Not quite, Orion. A good strategist always has more than one objective in sight." Some of Aten's old haughty self-importance crept back into his expression. "The military aspect of your exertions did not pay the dividends I expected, but the political consequences may yet bear fruit."

"What do you mean by that?" I asked.

He folded his arms across his chest. "You will see, in due time."

I blinked and was back on the shuttle, amid my wounded, bone-tired, snoring troopers. The shuttle shuddered and thumped as it docked with the troopship, waking all but the most determined dozers.

"Home sweet home," somebody cracked.

"You know," said someone else, "that cryosleeper's gonna look damned good to me."

I frowned. Cryosleep? Is that what was in store for these troopers?

They let us rest for two whole days. The severely wounded were sent to sickbay while the rest of us were examined by medics, patched here and there, and allowed to return to our quarters. We slept, we ate and we slept some more.

On the third day we were handed dress uniforms and ordered to assemble in the ship's biggest cargo bay. It had carried supplies and ammunition on the trip to Bititu; now it was empty. Human officers I had never seen before—all of them in magnificent spotless uniforms heavy with braid and decorations—put us through a marching drill and then paraded us around the big cargo bay to the tune of martial music piped in through the ship's intercom.

They stood us at attention in front of a makeshift dais, and the human officers, together with a handful of Tsihn, made a series of speeches at us, praising our courage and loyalty. Even Brigadier Uxley was there, obviously reading his prepared speech from a screen built into the rostrum that he leaned upon. He had flown out from the sector base to rendez-vous with us at one of our navigation points, where we slowed from superlight velocity for a few hours.

"They're piping this ceremony back to Loris," Frede whispered to me as we stood at attention through the long, boring speeches.

Loris. The Commonwealth's capital planet, my memory told me. The only Earthlike planet of the Giotto system, 270 light-years from old Earth itself.

Then the Tsihn admiral read off a unit citation and handed out medals. It seemed like a miserably poor reward for such hard fighting, but the troopers were pitifully grateful for the recognition.

At the end of the ceremony Uxley smiled beamingly at us and announced, "You are relieved of all duties for the remainder of this trip back to sector base six. There you will be reassigned. Dismissed."

Frede came up to me as the troop broke up into chatting, laughing little groups.

"Ready for some R and R?" she asked.

"Not much to do aboard this bucket," I complained.

"We can grab some sack time."

I caught the gleam in her eye. "For the whole trip back?"

Frede laughed. "That would be fun, Orion, but we've only got another twelve hours."

Puzzled, I asked, "What do you mean? The commander said we're relieved of all duties—"

"That means we're going back into cryosleep," Frede

said, her tone sobering. "You don't think they're going to feed us the whole trip back, do you? A few watts of electricity to keep the nitrogen liquefied is a lot cheaper than having us underfoot."

"But I thought—"

She gripped my arm, making me wince slightly.

"Oh, I'm sorry! I forgot your arm is still healing."

"You mean that after all the fighting we've done they're going to pop us back into the freezers?"

Frede gave me a sad smile. "We got a unit citation and individual medals and congratulations from the admiral. They beamed the ceremony back to the capital for all the civilians to see. We're official heroes. What more can a trooper ask for?"

I shook my head. "I guess you've got to be born to it."

"Yeah," she said. "Come on, let's make out while we're still warm."

Chapter 21

I was an officer, and not a regular army officer at that. I received special treatment. I was allowed to remain awake for the trip back to sector base six.

There was a handful of other human officers on the ship, but they seemed to deliberately avoid me. They were staff officers, not line. I got the feeling that they regarded fighting soldiers as beneath their dignity. Or perhaps they were inwardly ashamed of their soft jobs and did not wish to be reminded that the memos and charts and requisitions they dealt with represented real, living, bleeding men and women who were sent into battle at the touch of a keystroke.

Brigadier Uxley remained on board, riding with us back to the sector base. Uxley was cut from a different cloth than the staff officers. He had been a frontline soldier; lost both his legs in battle. He was a gruff old buzzard who drank too much and liked to talk far into the night. We became friends, of a sort. I could drink with him because my metabolism neutralized the effects of alcohol almost as quickly as I digested it. And I needed very little sleep, after resting several days from Bititu.

We spent the long nights of the flight back to sector base six in the brigadier's quarters, drinking his favorite liquor. The Tsihn quartermaster complained about using the ship's limited supplies of energy to make unauthorized refreshments with the matter-transceiving equipment. Uxley overrode the reptilian's objections.

"Damned lizards think they own this sector just because their fleet is operating here," he grumbled to me as we drank the night away.

He liked to tell war stories, and his memory for them became better with each glass of whisky he downed. Unfortunately, he seemed to forget that he had told me several of his favorite stories more than once. He repeated them, night after night, although each retelling was slightly different.

"You're lucky," he said one evening, slurring his words as he poured himself another drink and refilled my glass.

"Lucky?" I asked.

Bobbing his reddened face up and down, Uxley said, "You fought those damned spiders. And the Skorpis before that."

"I wouldn't call that lucky," I said.

Waving a finger in the air, he explained, "You don't understand. You haven't had to fight humans. It's easier to kill aliens. Humans—even those bastards of the Hegemony—that's a little tougher, believe me."

I grimaced inwardly. I had fought humans, killed them face-to-face with swords and knives, fought for the Greeks at Troy, for the Israelites at Jericho, fought in a thousand different times back on distant Earth.

"I fought humans," Uxley said, leaning close enough for me to smell his alcoholic breath. "That's where I lost these." He thumped on his prosthetic legs.

"It must have been very painful," I said.

"You don't feel the pain. Not at first. Shock. I had both m'legs burned out from under me and I never knew it. Just flopped down on my belly and kept on firing at those Hegemony bastards. Bastards took my legs. I wanted to kill 'em all, every one of them. I got a bunch of 'em, don't think I didn't. When the battle was over I was surrounded by piles of enemy dead. I held my position and killed 'em by droves."

I sipped at my whisky.

"I can still hear 'em," he said, his voice sinking to a whisper. "At night, when I go to sleep. I can still hear the wounded moaning and screaming. Every night."

One evening he asked me if I would like to see the recording of our ceremony, as it was shown to the populace of Loris and all the other Commonwealth worlds. When I hesitated, he laughed.

"Don't worry, you won't have to sit through all the speeches. The news media trimmed our ceremony quite a bit."

I really had no choice. I pulled up a chair next to his as he ordered the voice-activated screen to show the news recording from Loris.

I saw my troop, looking clean and fresh in the dress uniforms they had issued us. Instead of being in the cargo hold of a troopship, we appeared to be out on the surface of an Earthlike planet, beneath a bright blue sky, flags and pennants snapping in a brisk breeze. And we were only one tiny unit on a parade ground that held massed ranks by the tens of thousands. The ground was black with Commonwealth soldiery that had been added to the scene by computer.

I glanced at the colonel. "They make it look good, don't they," he muttered.

The computer-created band played stirring martial music while a commentator identified my unit as the group that "annihilated the defenders of a key planet in a conquest that took only four days."

Only four days, I thought. Four days in hell.

The entire show was over in less than ninety seconds.

"What do you think?" Uxley asked me as the screen went dark.

I felt anger simmering inside me. "A kernel of fact wrapped in a big phony sugar coating," I said.

He nodded and began to pour his first drink of the evening. "Got to keep the civilians happy, Orion. Got to keep up their morale."

"Really?"

He looked at me through bloodshot eyes. "Hell, man, most of 'em don't even realize there's a war going on unless we show them stuff like this."

"Then why don't they show them combat scenes? Why don't they show some of the tapes our helmet recorders took on Bititu? Then they'd see there's a war being fought!"

Uxley shook his head. "Don't want to scare them, Orion. The deep thinkers upstairs, the psychotechs and politicians, they don't want to upset the civilians with blood and pain. Just tell 'em that we're winning, but there's a long haul ahead. Light at the end of the tunnel. That's what they feed the civilians."

"Crap," I said.

"I suppose it is," Uxley agreed calmly. Then he took a big swallow of whisky. "I believed in this war, Orion. I really believed it was important to fight for the Commonwealth. That's why I joined up. Volunteered. No one forced me. I left my family as soon as I graduated university and joined the army."

"What did your family think of that?"

He shrugged, his sorrowful eyes looking into the past. "Father was proud. Mother cried. My sisters thought I was crazy."

"And now?" I avoided looking at his legs.

"Who knows? Haven't seen any of them in years. We would hardly recognize each other, I suppose. Too much has happened, we've moved too far apart."

"Wouldn't you like to go home?"

He gulped at his whisky. "The army's my home, Orion. I have no other home now. Just the army."

Another night we got onto the subject of his legs.

"They tried regeneration, but something in my metabolism fouled up the process. These plastic jobs are all right, though. I can get around just fine and they only hurt if I have to be on my feet for more than an hour or so."

Then he started once again on the story of how he lost his legs.

"Training, Orion," he told me. "That's the important thing. Training. It's not rational to expect a man to stand and fight when he's being shot at. A sane man would turn and run for safety. Takes training to make him fight."

"Even our cloned troopers?" I asked.

"Yes, of course. They're humans. They want to live, cloned or not. Got to train them to stand up to battle, not to run when all hell's breaking loose on them."

"And train them to kill," I said.

"Oh, yes, killing's an important part of it. No one's figured out how to win a battle without killing, despite all the scientists and computers."

"Brigadier, what's going to happen to my troop?"

"Happen?" He blinked his bleary eyes. "They'll be reassigned, what else?"

"Don't they get any time for R and R? Furloughs?"

Uxley sat up straighter in his chair. "You're talking about troopers, Orion. They were made to fight. That's what they're for. They're not real people, like you and me. We've got families and friends and a life back home. They don't. They're nothing but soldiers. What would they do with a furlough? They've got no place to go, no families, no home except the army."

"But you said you've drifted apart from your family, your home," I pointed out.

"So what? I've still got 'em. They're still there if I decide to go back to them. You've got a family and home, don't you?"

I wondered what to say, finally decided on, "No, I don't. I'm—an orphan."

"Too bad. But the troopers, they're just clones. We made 'em to fight, not to mix with society."

"There's nothing in their lives except battle and training for battle."

"We let 'em have sex, don't we?" he countered with a broad wink.

"Because some psychotechs decided they'd fight better if their aggressive/protective instincts were reinforced by sexual relationships. Is that all they mean to you? A bunch of instincts to be trained and used like weapons?"

Uxley began to look uncomfortable, his face flushing slightly. "Listen to an old veteran, Orion. Being a soldier consists of long months of boredom punctuated by moments of stark terror. We've eliminated the boredom for them. They ought to be grateful."

"And left them nothing but the terror. Is that fair to them?"

"Fair?" His face reddened even more. I didn't know whether he was going to burst out laughing or roar with anger. "Fair? We're fighting a war, man! We need the biggest number of troops we can generate. And the cheapest. We can't go around worrying about their feelings. It'd make them soft, lower their fighting morale."

I tried to make him see the troopers as human beings, fully as human as he himself was, or as he thought I was. But it was useless. Night after night we talked about it, and he always came down to the same statement. "They were made to fight. Otherwise they would never have been made at all. They ought to be grateful that they're alive and able to serve the Commonwealth."

Yes, I thought. Just as I should be grateful that I have been given life after life, all for the privilege of serving Aten and the other Creators.

"What will their next assignment be?" I asked one night.

Uxley shrugged. "Headquarters hasn't decided yet. Or at least, I haven't been informed."

"Aren't they being retrained while they're in cryosleep?"

"Not yet," he told me. "Not as far as I know."

I began to wonder. And to think. As I lay awake in my bunk after bidding the colonel good night, I began to consider what the Golden One had told me and what I had seen with my own eyes of this era, this time of interstellar war, this battle among the Creators themselves.

The Golden One had told me that Anya had rejected me, rejected human form, that she was leading the fight against him. I was programmed to believe him, but deep within me there was a shadow of doubt. Anya and I had loved one another through the eons, in every era to which I had been sent. Why would she change now?

The Golden One said that if I found Anya she would kill me as quickly and casually as a man swats an insect. And he would not revive me; perhaps he would be unable to do so, more likely he would be unwilling.

Very well, then, I thought. If I seek out Anya, wherever she is among the stars, and find that what Aten has told me is the truth, then I will be killed and that will be the end of it. The end of all suffering. The end of all my hopes and pains. The end of love.

But if he has been lying to me, if Anya still loves me and wants me with her, then it is lunacy for me to remain locked into this servitude. I should go out and find her.

Love or death. The ultimate stakes of life.

I began to plan.

The Golden One had his own plans for me, I discovered.

Once we reached sector base six I supervised the off-loading of my troop's cryosleep capsules. I wanted to begin retraining them for the mission I had in mind, and began to look into how I might tap into the computers that programmed the sleep training systems for the base.

But as I started cautiously playing with the computer terminal in my cramped quarters, Aten appeared to me once more. One instant I was sitting at the desk in my quarters, hunched over the keyboard and display screen.

The next I was on that grassy hillside above the Creators' mausoleum of a city. The sun shone warmly, the wildflowers nodded in the breeze from the nearby sea. Waves washed up on the beach. I knew there were dolphins out there who regarded me as their friend.

A golden sphere appeared in the air before me, blazing radiance, forcing me to throw my arms up over my face and sink to my knees.

"That's better, Orion," I heard Aten's arrogant voice say. "A properly worshipful position."

When I dared to look up, the Golden One had assumed human form, standing before me in his immaculate military uniform.

"You did well on Bititu," he said, almost grudgingly.

"It was a slaughter."

"Yes, but necessary."

"Why?"

"You mean you haven't puzzled that out for yourself, Orion? You who claim to be almost as good as your Creators? You who scheme to find the goddess you're so infatuated with? Why would the Commonwealth want Bititu?"

Not for itself, certainly, I reasoned swiftly. Then it must be valuable for its location. But there was nothing else in the Jilbert system except the fading red dwarf star itself, a single gas giant planet orbiting close to it, and the scattered debris of other asteroids, dead chunks of rock and metal. . . .

I looked into Aten's gold-flecked eyes. "There was once another planet in the system. You destroyed it."

"Two others, Orion," he answered. "We destroyed them both."

"How many were killed?"

He shrugged carelessly. "The Hegemony had planted colonies on those worlds. They were turning them into powerful military bases."

"But what did that threaten?" I asked. "There's no Commonwealth world for a hundred light-years or more."

"So?" he taunted. "Think, Orion. Think."

The only other planet in the Jilbert system was the gas

giant, a huge blue world covered in clouds. Beneath those clouds the planet's gases would be condensed by its massive gravity field into liquids. A planetwide ocean. Of water, perhaps.

It hit me. "The Old Ones."

Aten actually clapped his hands. "Very good, Orion. The Jilbert gas giant is a world on which the Old Ones have lived since time immemorial. Perhaps it is their original home world."

"The Hegemony established their bases in the system in an attempt to establish contact with the Old Ones."

"And to prevent us from making such contact," the Golden One added.

"Now that we've driven the Hegemony out of the system," I reasoned, "you want to try to reach the Old Ones."

Like a patient schoolteacher, Aten prompted, "And since you are the only person the Old Ones have seen fit to talk to . . ."

"You want me," I finished his thought, "to attempt to contact them again."

"Exactly."

My mind was churning, trying to set this new factor into my plans without letting Aten realize what my true objective was.

"In that case," I said, "I will need a ship and a crew."

"I can send you there without such paraphernalia," he said.

"And have me tread water in that planetwide ocean until the Old Ones deign to speak to me?" I retorted. "Can I breathe that planet's atmosphere? Can I eat the fish that swim in that sea?"

He nodded. "I see what you're after, Orion. You want the survivors of your assault team to be retrained as crew for your vessel. Touchingly virtuous of you, to be so loyal to such creatures."

"They are human beings," I said.

"Manufactured to be soldiers. Weapons, Orion, nothing more."

"Your ancestors," I reminded him.

Aten laughed derisively. "So are tree shrews, Orion. Do you feel pangs of conscience for them?"

Before I could answer, the entire scene disappeared as suddenly as a snap of the fingers and I was hunched over my computer screen again in my quarters at sector base six.

The computer beeped and my orders appeared on the display screen: I was to command a scout ship and return to the Jilbert system where I would contact the Old Ones and invite them to join the Commonwealth.

I saw to it that my cryosleeping troopers received the training they needed to run a scout vessel. I myself spent almost all my time in the training center with a crown of electrodes clamped to my head as the training computer poured information into my brain. I wondered if this was the way Aten trained me for my various missions throughout space-time, while I was unconscious.

In a week my troopers were revived and our ship arrived, a sleek disk-shaped scout named *Apollo*. I frowned when I first learned the name; the Golden One had styled himself Apollo to the awestruck ancient Greeks and Trojans. Aside from the name, though, I found the vessel trim and fit, and my troopers transformed by their cryosleep training into a crew that at least appeared to know what it was doing.

Frede was still my second-in-command, and *Apollo*'s navigation officer. Little Jerron was now chief engineer. Ordinary mutts who had been little more than cannon fodder on Lunga and Bititu now found themselves classified as ship's officers, in charge of weapons, logistics, damage control, communications, medical services. They grinned at their newfound stature, but they took their new duties quite seriously.

And, one by one, each of them thanked me for getting them better duty. Emon, our weapons officer, put it best:

"The longer we stay with you, sir, the better off we'll be. If we live through it."

I believe he was entirely serious.

We spent two days directing the robots that outfitted and stocked *Apollo* with supplies; then we left sector base six and started our run back to the Jilbert system.

Except that we never got there.

Chapter 22

Frede and the others were happy to be awake, alive, and running a starship rather than fighting as expendable infantry.

"This makes us more important to the Commonwealth," Frede told me. "More valuable."

"And it's easier duty," said weapons officer Emon. As a sergeant, he had been wounded twice during the assault on Bititu. Frede's official title was now "first mate," which set off a lot of jokes because she once again had jiggered the sleeping assignments so that she shared my bunk.

The bridge was compact, built more for efficiency than comfort, with only five duty stations jammed in cheek by jowl. Tactical command and all the ship's information systems were tied together in the consoles and data screens that surrounded us. From my command chair I could see anything in the ship I needed to see, call up all of the computer files, activate any system aboard the vessel.

We made the transition to superlight velocity as smoothly as if the crew had spent years aboard the ship. As far as their memories and reflexes were concerned, they had. Neural training, whether awake or in cryosleep, leaves virtually the same imprint on the brain and nervous system as actual experience would.

"What if we could just fly this ship forever," Frede whispered to me one night in our bunk. "Just forget the war and everything and go out among the stars for the rest of our lives."

"Would you like that?" I asked.

"Yes!" She clutched at my bare shoulders. "Never to be frozen again. To be free. It'd be wonderful."

"To be free," I murmured, knowing that in all the eras of space-time in which I had existed, I had never been free.

"There are others," she whispered. "You hear stories about them."

"About who?" I asked.

"Renegades. Units that disappeared, just walked off into the jungle and never were heard from again. Ships that took off on their own, split from the fleet and ran away forever."

I knew all about renegades. Lukka and his squad of mercenaries, fighting for their lives in the shambles of the Hittite empire's collapse; Harkan and his band of thieves roaming the mountains of Anatolia, searching for his enslaved children; guerrillas from a thousand wars in a thousand different eras.

"And the war," I asked her gently. "Our duty to the Commonwealth?"

She hesitated for a moment, realizing that she was speaking to her superior officer even though we happened to be lying nude in bed together.

"How long have you been serving the Commonwealth, Orion?"

I evaded a direct answer. "Time loses its meaning."

"I've been serving all my life," Frede said. "So have we all. It's all we know, the army. It's all we have to look forward to, until the day we're killed."

There was a trigger phrase, of course, that came with my orders. Whenever the crew began to show signs of humanity, indications that they were thinking of themselves instead of their duty to the Commonwealth, all I had to say was "Remember Yellowflower."

The planet Yellowflower, according to the Commonwealth's history of the war, had been suddenly and ruthlessly attacked, destroyed by Hegemony forces without a declaration of war, scoured down to bedrock. Four billion human beings had been killed, the planet's entire biosphere totally obliterated. Yellowflower had been the start of the war, three generations earlier.

According to the Commonwealth's history. I recalled the human scientists on Lunga telling me that it had been Tsihn attacks on Hegemony worlds that had started the war.

I stroked Frede's short-cropped hair. "It's not so bad now. We've got this fine ship. As long as we stay in superlight no one can touch us."

"But sooner or later we'll drop back to relativistic speed and reenter the war."

"Maybe," I murmured, not yet ready to tell her what I was hoping to do.

She fell asleep and I lay on the bunk beside her. As captain of this vessel, my quarters were small but comfortable. Frede was right: the galaxy is huge; one ship could lose itself among the stars. But what of all the other ships, all the other assault teams and regiments and armies and battle fleets? What right did we have to run away and hide while others were fighting to their deaths, humans and aliens, Commonwealth and Hegemony?

There has to be a way to stop this killing, I told myself. There has to be.

A warning, Orion.

It was a voice from the Old Ones, in my mind. I recognized it instantly. Closing my eyes, I felt a moment of utter cold, the wild plunging sensation of nothingness, and then I was swimming in the warm sea of their ocean once again. A dozen or more of the Old Ones glided through the deep, dark water with me, pulsating colors, tentacles waving as if in greeting.

"Is this the planet in the Jilbert system or am I back on Lunga?" I asked.

"What difference?" came their reply. "In a sense, we are on both worlds—and many others, as well."

I thought I understood. Each of the Old Ones swimming around me came from a different planet. They had all come together to meet with me; each of us was light-years from all the others, yet we swam together in this fathomless ocean.

"You said you wanted to warn me of something?"

Their response seemed to come from all of them, even though I heard it as only one voice.

"Orion, your war grows deeper and more violent. It troubles us."

"I have been asked by one of my Creators to encourage you to join the Commonwealth," I said. "Their reasoning is that, with you on their side, they will quickly end the war."

"In victory for the Commonwealth, at the expense of the Hegemony."

"Yes."

"Since this slaughter began," they said, "we and others of our maturity have remained totally neutral."

"Others?" I asked.

"There are many, many races among the galaxies, Orion. And even between them. You humans have met and interacted with species of your own youthful stage of development. You interact with your own intellectual peers. You trade with them. You fight with them."

"While you older species remain aloof from us."

"From you, and from the Skorpis, the Tsihn, the race you call the Arachnoids, and all the others who have not yet achieved the wisdom to avoid slaughtering one another."

I got the impression of a group of gray-haired elders watching a gaggle of noisy brats fighting in a sandbox.

"But your war grows more violent," they repeated.

I agreed. "There seems to be no end to it."

"From the outset you slaughtered billions of your own kind, eradicated all life-forms from entire planets, blasting them down to their rocky mantles.

"Then you escalated the violence. Whole planets were blown up, as were the two outer worlds in the Jilbert system, blasted into fragments."

"I know," I said.

The voice became grave. "Now the violence is about to escalate again. The Commonwealth has perfected a weapon that can destroy a star. The weapon creates a core collapse of the star; a supernova explosion is the result."

I felt a hollow sinking sensation in the pit of my stomach.

"This must not be allowed."

"If the Commonwealth unleashes this weapon," I told them, "then the Hegemony won't rest until it develops something similar."

"We will not permit stars to be destroyed."

"Not permit . . . ?"

"Give this message to your Creators, to the leaders of both warring factions: Tell them that if they attempt to destroy a star they themselves will be eliminated from the continuum."

"Eliminated?"

"The human race, the Skorpis, the Tsihn, all the warring species will be extinguished."

"How? What do you intend to do?"

"The older species have maintained neutrality throughout your squabbles. But we cannot allow you to destroy the very stars on which the continuum hinges. Attempt to attack a single star, and we will eliminate you—all of you—completely."

They spoke with one voice, an implacable finality in their tone.

"Go back to your Creators and tell them what we have said, Orion. The fate of many species depends on their reaction to our warning."

I sat bolt upright on my bunk. Frede lay sleeping peacefully beside me, a little girl's smile on her relaxed face.

The Old Ones were using me as a messenger again. It's not enough that Aten manipulates me, the Old Ones use me to manipulate him and the other Creators.

But then I smiled. Did the Old Ones know my inner thoughts, my plans? I had hoped to use this scout ship to find Anya, somewhere deep in Hegemony territory. Now the Old Ones had given me a reason for seeking her. I had to warn her about the Commonwealth's star-wrecker.

The third watch still had an hour to go when I came onto the bridge and relieved Dyer, my logistics/damage-control officer, who had the command. The watch was almost entirely perfunctory; as long as we were in superlight velocity there was nothing to worry about except a possible internal malfunction.

Taking the command chair, I ransacked the ship's computer records for information about the Hegemony. Where was their capital planet? What kind of defenses guarded it? Would they honor a flag of truce on a Commonwealth ship?

The computer could not tell me, of course, if Anya was in the Hegemony's capital. The data screens showed their capital planet, Prime, in the Zeta system. I viewed their cities and learned their population, history, economy, social customs, politics, military capabilities—much data, little understanding.

The screens showed Prime itself to be a gray, forbidding city of massive stone buildings rising out of dark cliffs into a heavy cloudy sky. Its streets were almost empty, swept by gusts of rain and sleet. Giant Skorpis warriors seemed to be at every intersection, serving as police or militia guards. The people of Prime looked grim, dour, humorless.

"Why the interest in Prime?"

I looked up from the screens surrounding my chair and saw Frede standing beside me, looking curious. At the touch of a keypad I blanked the screens.

"That's where we're going," I said.

"Prime?" she squeaked. "But that's the Hegemony's capital!"

The four others on duty in the bridge turned and stared at us.

"I have secret orders," I told her. But I didn't say who the orders had come from. "We're on a mission of diplomacy to Prime."

"They'll blow us out of the galaxy the instant we drop out of superlight," Frede said.

"Let's hope not."

Reluctantly she followed my command to set course for the Hegemony capital. I planned to send out message capsules ahead of us once we neared the Zeta system, so the Hegemony defenders would be warned that we were coming and that our mission was a peaceful one. Frede and the rest of the crew thought the Hegemony ships would shoot first and check on our story after we were safely dead. The almost happy air about the ship dissolved into soldierly griping and dread.

There was something more that I could do, of course. That night, while Frede slept, I tried with all my energies to reach across the span of space-time and contact Anya. Nothing. It was like facing a blank wall too high to climb, too wide to go around.

So I reached out to Aten, instead. Concentrating on my memory of the Creators' city, I translated myself to its timeless stasis in the continuum. I found myself standing atop a Mayan pyramid in the heart of the city, high enough to look out across its broad empty avenues toward the eternal sea. The sun's warmth was tempered slightly by the shimmering golden dome of energy that encased the city.

Aten looked surprised when I appeared. He and several other of the Creators were apparently locked deep in conference, there at the top of the steep stone pyramid. They were all standing together before the sacrificial altar: Aten in a white and gold military uniform; the dark-bearded one I thought of as Zeus in a comfortable tunic and slacks; rust-haired Ares; slim, sharp-eyed Hermes; and the beautiful redheaded woman who had styled herself Hera in an earlier age.

It was Hermes who spied me first; the others had their backs to me as they talked earnestly among themselves.

"Look who's here," Hermes said, touching Aten on the shoulder.

They all turned toward me, wide-eyed with surprise.

Hera smiled maliciously at me. "Who invited you, Orion?"

"The Old Ones," I answered.

That stifled any complaints or gibes they intended to make. "What do you mean?" Aten snapped.

"They have given me a message for you. A warning," I said. "If you try to use the star-destroying weapon the Commonwealth has developed, the Old Ones will destroy you."

Ares glared at me. "How could they know about the star-wrecker? You told them, Orion! You're a traitor!"

"I didn't know about the weapon until they told me of it," I retorted.

"That's true," Aten said. "Orion knew nothing of the weapon."

"Then how could the Old Ones know?"

"They know," I said. "And they will eliminate all of us if you try to use it."

"How credible is this threat by the Old Ones?" Zeus asked.

"What threat?" Aten sneered. "How could they destroy us? We can avoid them by traveling through time whenever we wish. If necessary I can go back to their time of origins and eliminate them."

"I wonder," Zeus muttered.

"Your meddling with space-time has caused us enough trouble," Hera complained.

"My meddling," Aten retorted, "is what created us. Without me, we would never have come into existence."

Zeus said to me, "Orion, you must give this warning to Anya and her cohorts, too."

"The Hegemony—"

"Is developing a similar weapon," Hera told me. "What did you expect?"

"I am trying to reach Anya now," I said to them.

Aten fixed me with an angry look. "I never told you to do so."

"But I told you that I would find her," I said. "That's what I'm doing."

"In the era of the war?" Zeus asked.

"Yes. I am flying my ship to the Hegemony capital to tell her that you have the star-weapon."

"I told you he was a traitor," Ares snapped hotly.

I ignored him. "Now I must carry the Old Ones' warning to her."

"No," Aten snapped. "You mustn't do that."

"I am already doing it."

"I'll put a stop to that! And to you, too, Orion."

"Wait," said Zeus. "Perhaps your creature can accomplish what we cannot."

"Nonsense!"

"Anya has been close to this one in the past," Hera said, sneering. "Maybe she will listen to him where she refuses to speak with us."

"It's worth a try," said Hermes.

Ares glowered at me and rubbed his chin. "Aten, if this creature is yours, you ought to control him better than this."

"I can control him!"

"No, you can't," I said. "Not entirely. I came here on my own power, not because you summoned me. I decided to find Anya even when you told me it was impossible."

He smirked at me. "So you think you have free will? That you are not under my command every instant of your existence?"

"I've gone against your commands in the past," I countered.

"Pah!" spat Zeus. "Stop this posturing, both of you. Aten, I suggest you use your creature to make contact with Anya. This threat from the Old Ones must be taken seriously."

His eyes never leaving mine, Aten replied, "Perhaps you're right. Perhaps this pitifully flawed wretch can be useful to us in spite of himself."

I seemed to fall asleep then, as deep and restful a sleep as I have ever known. When I awoke, I was back in my bunk aboard the *Apollo,* with Frede drowsing peacefully beside me. A wonderful warm feeling of joy filled me. I was going to find Anya, I was going to see her again! And I knew that she loved me as much as I loved her. Nothing else mattered.

Chapter 23

Frede computed our course to the Zeta system with conspicuous reluctance. When on duty in the bridge she was crisp, efficient, and knowledgeable. She checked her navigation constantly by having us drop out of superlight velocity at random times so that she could take an observation of the stars. It took only a few seconds; then we accelerated back into superlight again.

At night, in bed, she tried to talk me out of entering the Zeta system.

"It's suicide, Orion! They'll blast us before we have a chance to blink our eyes. The system must have automated defense bases all around it, belts of them orbiting the star. They'll be programmed to shoot the instant any unauthorized vessel pops out of superlight within range of their weapons."

"We'll send message capsules ahead," I repeated each time she brought up the argument. "We'll tell them exactly when and where we'll appear."

"Great! Then they'll know exactly where and when to shoot!"

"Our mission is a peaceful one," I said. "Surely the Hegemony can understand that one scout won't be a threat to their capital."

Frede huffed at me. "No, they'll see it as an opportunity for target practice."

Every night we came to the same deadlock. And every

night I would end the matter by saying, "Lieutenant, the time for argument is finished. As your commanding officer, I order this discussion closed."

Frede would grumble and give it up. Until the next night. We made love infrequently during that flight to Prime; it was difficult to work up any ardor when each of us was convinced that the other was being pigheaded.

And then, the night before we were scheduled to start sending out the message capsules, Frede told me what was really bothering her.

"You call out to Anya in your sleep, you know."

She was undressing. I did not feel at all sleepy. I did not answer her.

"That's the reason you want to go to Prime, isn't it?" Frede asked me. "She's there."

"Yes," I admitted.

"You're willing to get us all killed, for her?"

"She can stop the war," I said.

"Dogshit she can. Nobody can stop this war. It's going to go on forever."

"Is that what you want?"

"It's the reason I'm alive, Orion. All of us mutts. Stop the war and they freeze us."

"Continue the war and you'll be killed, sooner or later."

She ran a hand through her short-cropped hair. "Some choice, huh?"

"Maybe I can change things," I said, not really believing it myself, but wanting to give her some glimmer of hope.

She smiled weakly at me. "You asked me what I wanted. I want you, Orion. I want to get off this damned dogshit of a life and run away and find some happy little world that the Commonwealth and the Hegemony have never even heard of and live a normal life there. With you."

The look on her face. As if she expected to be hit. Cringing, almost. She had revealed herself to me knowing that there was nothing she could expect except to be hurt.

As gently as I could I took her in my arms and held her for a long, long silent time.

At last she disengaged a little and smiled up at me again. There were tears in her eyes. "Some soldier, huh? I ought to be popped back into a freezer and given a long course in discipline and loyalty, right?"

"You ought to be allowed to live a normal life," I murmured.

"Yeah. Right." She pushed entirely away from me and began to strip off her army brown undershirt. "Well, a normal life for us mutts is to follow orders, fight the enemy when we're awake, train for the next fight when we're in the freezer. Right?"

There was nothing that I could think of to say. As I watched, Frede stripped naked, stamped barefoot to the bunk and pulled down the top sheet.

"Well, I know my rights. I may be just a mutt, but I know my rights as a soldier. Get your gorgeous ass into bed, sir. It's time for you to do your fucking duty."

I made myself smile and say, "Aye, aye, sir."

Next day the tension on the bridge was thick enough to chew on. We slowed out of superlight one last time, and Frede used the few seconds to snap panoramic views of the star fields around us. Once we were safely back in superlight, she checked our position, made a slight course correction and announced in a loud, brittle voice:

"Next stop, Zeta system."

The others on the bridge said nothing, but I could see their bodies stiffen and they avoided looking me in the eye.

I ordered the message capsules sent out, one every four hours for the next twenty-four. Thirty hours from now we would slow to relativistic speed at the edge of the Zeta system. We would either be greeted warily as ambassadors under a flag of truce or blown out of existence in a few nanoseconds.

It was a tense thirty hours. The Hegemony could deduce

the direction from which we were approaching Zeta by back-tracking the message capsules as they appeared in normal space. Thus they could focus their defenses on the area where we would appear. What they could not do was to send us a message in return. I would have given a lot to hear either that they were willing to accept us as ambassadors or that they were waiting to destroy us if we should enter the Zeta system. It would have saved thirty hours' sweat.

"Lightspeed in one minute," the navigation computer announced.

"Still plenty of time to turn around, sir," said Emon, the weapons officer. I glared at him, then saw he was trying to grin at me. It was supposed to be a joke.

"Forty-five seconds."

"I wonder what it's like to be a plasma cloud," Magro, the comm officer, muttered, loud enough for everyone on the bridge to hear.

"Peaceful," Frede said.

"Mind-expanding."

"Just plain expanding."

"Thirty seconds."

I said, "Just in case you didn't know, I've enjoyed serving with you."

"We know, sir!"

"A mutt gets to sense when his commander's having a good time."

"You've got to be born to it. Sir."

"Ten seconds."

I glanced at Frede at the instant she happened to look at me. No words. Not even a smile. But we understood one another.

"Lightspeed," said the computer.

All the screens on the bridge lit up to show a sky full of dazzling stars. And Hegemony dreadnoughts.

"COMMONWEALTH SHIP, YOU WILL ESTABLISH CIRCULAR ORBIT AT FIFTY ASTRONOMICAL

UNITS FROM STAR ZETA AND STAND BY FOR
BOARDING AND INSPECTION."

They were not going to shoot first.

I punched the communications keyboard and answered,
"We will comply with your instructions."

They sent Skorpis warriors aboard to inspect us and disarm our ship's weapon systems. Then they confiscated all our
sidearms and assault rifles. I accompanied the boarding team
as they went through the *Apollo*. They were very thorough in
their search for weapons, but equally careful not to tear up the
ship.

"You will wait aboard your ship until further orders," the
chief of the Skorpis boarding party told me, after his team had
finished.

We were standing at the main air-lock hatch. He towered
over me by a full head, his shoulders so wide he would have
to go through the hatch sideways. I hoped he would remember
to duck his head. As it was, his furry skull was bare millimeters
from the metal ribbing of our overhead.

"We are Commonwealth military personnel on a diplomatic mission," I replied to him. "We will accept instructions
from your superiors, not orders."

His lip curled in what might have been the Skorpis equivalent of a smile. "Instructions, then."

With that, he turned, ducked low, and went sideways
through the air-lock hatch to return to his own ship.

I let out a breath of relief.

"I thought they were going to take our butter knives,"
Jerron piped when I returned to the bridge.

"Makes you feel kind of naked," said Emon, "without
even a pistol."

"We're here to talk, not fight," I reminded them.

"Yessir, I know. But I still feel naked."

For two days we waited inside our ship as it swung in orbit out
at the far end of the Zeta system. Prime, the capital planet, was

far closer to the star Zeta. We were out in the cold and dark, the closest planet a gas giant almost as large as the one at Jilbert.

I wondered if the Old Ones inhabited that huge world, as they did Jilbert's gas giant. But when I tried to probe for them with my mind I received only silence.

With little else to do, I called up the ship's information system for data about the gas-giant worlds of the Zeta system. There were three of them. No native forms of life had been found on any of them, as far as the ship's computer knew. Only the largest, the one closest to the star, bore an ocean of liquid water. The others were too cold for water to remain liquid, even under the pressure of their heavy gravity fields.

I studied the information about Prime, instead, looking for all the details I could find about that gray, grim, rainswept world.

Then we received a message that we would be boarded again. I told the crew to spruce up and look snappy for the Skorpis. They complained loudly, their fears of instant annihilation long since forgotten, and grudgingly put on their best uniforms.

"Trying to impress the Skorpis is like trying to train a cat to fetch a stick," one of the troopers grumbled.

This time, however, it was a human team that came through our air lock. Two male soldiers carrying sidearms and a young woman bearing a red sash across her tunic.

"I am Nella, of the Hegemony diplomatic corps. I am instructed by my superiors to bring your representative to Prime."

I introduced myself and told her that I was the representative. She looked me over and I did the same to her. Nella was small, almost tiny, and seemed very young. I thought she must have been a very junior member of the diplomatic corps, an expendable, sent to fetch me by superiors who were still worried that I might be some sort of Commonwealth trick.

I noticed that Frede was studying her even more intently

than I. Only then did I realize that Nella was rather pretty, youthfully charming.

"It will be my pleasure to escort you to the capital," Nella said, with a sparkling smile.

Turning to Frede, I said, "Lieutenant, you're in command while I'm gone."

"Yessir," she said, snapping a salute.

Startled by her formality, I returned Frede's salute, then told her, "Take care of the ship. And yourself."

Her face a frozen mask, Frede only repeated, "Yessir."

The capital city on Prime was a stunning surprise to me. True, most of its buildings were made of heavy gray stone quarried from the nearby cliffs, but everything else the ship's computer had shown me seemed to be a carefully edited pack of lies—or at least, a terribly slanted view of Prime.

The sky was thick with clouds, but they scudded past on a warm wind from the sea with plenty of blue sky showing between them and sunshine beaming down on the gray old stones of the city. The avenues were thronged with people, vehicles skimming lightly over the guideways, pedestrians strolling past shop fronts displaying brightly colored fashions and all sorts of wares from hundreds of worlds.

There were Skorpis warriors in sight, but not in battle dress. They were easy to spot, their heads bobbing along well above the rest of the crowd. They seemed to be on leave, not on duty. Plenty of other aliens, too, some of them fully encased in space suits to protect themselves from an environment that was hostile to them.

The city seemed happy, busy, engrossed in the everyday matters of shopping, dining, meeting people, finding romance, earning a living, enjoying life. Not at all the grimly forbidding view painted by the Commonwealth's computer. I was shocked by the contrast. And then I realized that the city did not seem concerned at all about the war. If these people knew that their soldiers and allies were fighting and bleeding and dying for them, they certainly did not show it. Just a few hundred kilometers above their heads orbited dreadnoughts and battle stations ready to blast an invader into subatomic particles. But down here on the busy avenues life went along in sunny unconcern.

I saw all this from inside a luxurious limousine. Nella had brought me straight to the capital's spaceport, and then we had ridden in this spacious, well-appointed skimmer into the heart of the city. I got the impression that she was enjoying the ride tremendously; she did not often get to ride in such elegance.

We drove through the crowded shopping district, then past long rows of buildings that looked almost like ancient temples. The traffic here was lighter.

"Government offices," Nella replied when I asked her what they were. She pointed to one as we swept past. "I usually work in there, back in the rear, you can't see it from here. I don't have a window, anyway."

The street climbed up a steep hill.

"That's the capitol, up in the old castle," Nella told me. "That's where we're going."

A full honor guard of Skorpis warriors lined the steps as we disembarked from the skimmer and entered the capitol building. I saw that they were fully armed. They fell in step behind us as Nella led me through a large and beautifully furnished entry hall toward a narrower corridor that ended in a metal door.

It was an elevator. The doors slid open to reveal two human soldiers, wearing sidearms only. Nella ushered me in, then came in behind me. The doors shut, leaving the Skorpis detachment outside.

We rode down, not up. "Medical exams," Nella murmured when the elevator stopped. "We must make certain that you're not carrying any disease organisms."

Or bombs, I added silently. The examination was swift and almost completely automated. I was walked through four different scanning archways; then a white-coated human doctor watched as still another automated archway recorded my full-body scan.

"Completely normal," the physician pronounced, running a finger across the readout display screen. "And extremely healthy."

Satisfied that I was not a walking bomb, Nella and the two human soldiers led me back to the elevator. Again, we rode down, deeper into the bedrock upon which the city was built.

At last I was led to a massive blastproof parasteel door.

"I'll have to leave you here," Nella said, almost apologetic. "When the doors open, step right through. The Director is waiting for you on the other side."

She hurried away, back to the elevator. I stood in front of the heavy doors, feeling a little silly to be standing there all alone.

Then the doors swung open as silently as the lid of a jewel box. I walked into a dimly lit room. I saw a long highly polished table that seemed to be made of granite or perhaps onyx. High-backed padded chairs lined both sides of the table. All of them empty.

The doors swung shut behind me, casting the room into even gloomier shadows.

There was someone sitting at the far end of the table, at its head. Alone, barely discernible in the dim lighting. I realized that I was bathed in light from a lamp in the ceiling high above, bathed in a cone of light while whoever it was at the head of the table hid in the shadows.

I stepped forward and the cone of light moved with me. Very well, I thought, I'll go to the head of the table and see who's there.

But I stopped before I had taken two steps. My eyes adjusted to the dimness and I recognized the figure watching me from the head of the table.

My knees sagged beneath me.

Anya!

Chapter 24

She did not smile at me. She did not give the slightest inkling that she knew who I was. She watched me with those incredibly beautiful gray eyes as I slowly, hesitantly, came toward her. Anya was wearing a simple cream-colored sleeveless dress; her hair was pulled back tightly, highlighting the sculptured plane of her cheekbones, the delicate yet strong curve of her jaw.

As I approached her, slowly, like a penitent making his awestruck way to a shrine, her face began to change. Her skin wrinkled, lost its youthful luster, began to look like faded parchment. Her hair turned gray, then white and lifeless, her hands became knobby claws, spotted with age.

"I am dying, Orion." Her voice was the croak of a feeble old crone.

I rushed to her side. She barely had the strength to hold up her head. I reached out to take her in my arms, but found myself frozen in place, immobile, helpless.

"Aten and the others have sent you," she said, her voice a weak, rasping wheeze. "They want to finish the work they began long ages ago."

I could not even speak. I strained to break free, to reach her.

"Don't struggle, Orion. You are in a stasis field and you will remain there until I determine what to do with you."

But I'm not your enemy! I wanted to tell her.

Her withered face cracked into a sad smile. "My poor
Orion. Of course you're not my enemy. Not consciously. Not
willingly. But you are Aten's creature and you will do his
bidding whether you want to or not. You have no choice. And
I have no choice except to protect myself as best as I can and
fight against the others with the last atom of my fading
strength."

You can't be dying, I said silently.

"I am dying, Orion. It takes a long time, but the strength
ebbs away a little more each day, each hour. It took an enormous effort for me to appear young, the way you once knew
me, when you first entered this chamber. Now you see me as
I am, with very little time left."

No, I thundered silently. *No!*

Anya shook her head painfully. "I don't want it to end
this way, my beloved. I don't want it to end at all. But I am
trapped. Aten has won."

"Never!" I roared. And with all the willpower in me, with
all my anger against the smug self-styled Creators, with all the
rage against my being used as a witless pawn in this battle
across the millennia, with all the blood lust that had been built
into me so that I would be a useful hunter, assassin, mur-
derer—I broke free.

I tapped the energy of the stars, the energy of the
continuum. Just as Aten and the others had sent me across
space-time I reached out for Anya and leaped through the
continuum, through the endless cold of absolute nothingness,
across eons of time and parsecs of space.

And found the two of us standing in a forest. Tall trees
dappling the warm high sun, colorful birds flitting through the
foliage, squirrels scampering, insects buzzing.

"Orion!" Anya gasped. "How could you . . ."

Then she looked down at her hands and saw that she was
young and strong again. I pulled her to me and kissed her
tenderly.

"Do you know where we are?" I asked her.

She took in the entire world in a single glance. "On Earth," she said. "In the forest of Paradise."

The wide woodland that someday would become the Sahara Desert. We had lived here with a Neolithic band, happy and content once we had escaped Set and his reptilian invaders.

"You remember that we thought about staying here forever," I said.

"Yes," Anya replied. But she pulled slightly away from my arms. "Yet we decided that we could not enjoy Paradise when there were so many conflicts in the continuum that had to be resolved."

"Perhaps we were wrong," I said. "Why can't we stay here and let the continuum solve its problems without us?"

She fixed me with those lustrous eyes of hers. "Because then Aten would solve the continuum's problems. And he would take all this away from us. He hates you, Orion. He fears you. And he hates me for loving you."

Aten fears me? That was a new concept for me to consider. "My powers are still growing," I said. "Perhaps I could protect us, protect this whole segment of the continuum. We could be safe here."

"Not from Aten. He's robbed me of my power. He is deliberately killing me, and all the other Creators who sided with me."

"But here you're strong and young."

"Yes," she admitted, smiling sadly, "but that's your doing, Orion, not mine. I can't change form anymore; I've lost the power. Aten has stolen it from me. He wants me dead. Me, and all the other Creators who oppose him."

"Why? What's the reason for all this hatred and killing? Why the war? What's this ultimate crisis?"

She almost laughed. "Orion, you're like a little boy, asking so many questions. They're not easily answered."

I gestured toward a sunny glade where a swift stream burbled over rocks, hardly a few meters from where we stood.

"Very well. Let's go sit in the warmth of the sun and watch the deer come down to the stream and drink. And you can begin to explain it all to me."

"I'm not sure that I can," Anya said, but she walked along with me toward the grassy glade.

"Then tell me as much as my limited mind can understand," I coaxed her.

"Your mind is not as limited as Aten thinks," she told me. "He would be shocked to know that you can translate yourself across the continuum, and carry me along with you. And rejuvenate me, too."

"If we go back to Prime and the era of the war, will you remain as youthful as you are now?"

"No," she said ruefully. "I will be a dying old hag there, unless I exert almost all my failing strength to appear young for a few moments."

"How did Aten do this to you?"

We had stepped out of the shade of the trees, into the welcoming sunlight. Walking to the edge of the stream, we sat on the soft grass, our backs against a big sun-warmed boulder.

"This war between the Commonwealth and the Hegemony," Anya said, "is really a continuation of the conflict we had over Troy."

"But why—"

She hushed me with a finger on my lips. And began to explain as much as she could.

The human race had expanded through the solar system and out to the stars, not as a single unified species, but as a pack of squabbling, contending tribes. Humankind had not overcome its tribal animosities merely because we had achieved interstellar flight. The Creators had built that aggressive nature into us, and no amount of technology could remove it. Indeed, the more sophisticated our technology became, the more dangerous our weaponry. We could blast whole planets clean of all life. Now we were ready to shatter stars.

We had found other intelligent species among the stars. Some were far below us in technological and cultural development: cave dwellers or simple herders and pastoralists. By and large these were left alone by the expanding human species; they had nothing to offer us, neither trade nor knowledge nor competition. Scientists studied them, although now and again unscrupulous humans colonized their worlds and despoiled them.

We also found other species that were far beyond us and, like the Old Ones, wished to have nothing to do with humankind or its ilk. But there were several intelligent species among the stars, such as the Tsihn and the Skorpis, who were close to our own level of knowledge and power. With these we could trade. And fight.

Inevitably, the humans who colonized the stars polarized themselves into two competing groups: the Hegemony and the Commonwealth. Inevitably, they sought allies among the aliens of our own level. Inevitably, they went to war.

"Inevitably?" I asked Anya. "Aten told me that this war is actually a struggle to decide how the Creators will deal with the ultimate crisis."

She bowed her head in acknowledgment. "I hadn't realized he had revealed that much to you."

"Have *all* of humankind's wars been caused by the Creators?" I asked.

"No, not all of them. The human species is ferocious enough to start its own wars, without our instigation."

"But what is this ultimate crisis?" I wanted to know. "Why do we have to kill billions of people and destroy whole planets? Why is the Commonwealth preparing to use a weapon that can blow away a star?"

Her eyes blazed. "They're ready to use it? How do you know . . . ?"

"The Old Ones."

"Aten has made contact with the Old Ones?" Anya looked frightened.

"No, they refuse to speak with either the Commonwealth or the Hegemony."

"Then how—"

"They spoke with me. They told me to warn both the Commonwealth and the Hegemony that they will not allow a star-destroying weapon to be used. They said they would eliminate all of us—all of humankind and all our allies—if we tried to destroy a star."

Anya leaned back against the boulder. "They spoke to you?" She seemed unable to believe it.

I assured her that they did and gave her every detail of my contacts with the Old Ones. She probed into my mind and confirmed that it was all true.

"Then the Hegemony is lost," she said at last. "And me with it. Aten will win. We were hoping to develop the star-destroyer ourselves. It was our last chance, a desperation weapon that we hoped would be so terrible it would force the Commonwealth to accept a truce."

With a shake of my head, I repeated, "The Old Ones won't permit it. They'll wipe out all of us instead."

Anya's eyes looked old again, weary and defeated. "Then you'd better bring me back to Prime. I must tell the other Creators before they decide to go ahead with the weapon."

"Tell me first how Aten is killing you. How is it possible?"

She shook her head again, utterly weary. "It's a disease, Orion, a biological weapon that feeds on my metabolism. Aten developed it and planted it in all the Creators."

"All of them?"

"Every one of us, long eons ago. The microbe lies dormant for ages, then slowly awakes and becomes active. Little by little, it saps your strength, slows your powers. Gradually its effects accelerate, until at last you wither and age and finally succumb."

"But Zeus and Hera and the others—they didn't show any signs of aging."

A wan smile. "That's because Aten is keeping them alive.

As long as they stay with him, support his side of this war, he keeps them healthy."

"And there's nothing you can do? No cure? No way to restore yourself?"

"Don't you think we've tried to find a cure? The organism mutates even as we study it; its basic genetic structure changes randomly. Aten spent millennia developing this disease. He experimented with hundreds of generations of humans to perfect it. Half the plagues in human history were his experiments."

"Yet he can protect the Creators who accept his domination."

"Apparently, although I wonder if he doesn't plan to kill them, too, when he no longer needs them."

"He always wanted to be the only god," I muttered.

Anya seemed to grow weaker with the exertion of admitting her helplessness. Yet I could not believe that she and the other Creators could not overcome Aten's treachery.

"If he can protect some of the Creators," I wondered aloud, "why can't you and the others find the protective agent for yourselves?"

"Because it is keyed to Aten himself," she answered. "He reaches through space-time to alter the microbe whenever we attempt to counteract it. We develop a vaccine and he changes the microbe to be immune to it. We move through space-time to annihilate the microbe, and he moves through space-time to revive it. The game is endless and deadly."

"And each time any of you translates across space-time it unravels the fabric of the continuum a little more," I said, remembering what the Old Ones had told me.

"Yes," Anya agreed grimly. "Already the continuum is so disturbed that we can no longer accurately trace the various space-time tracks. We can't probe the cosmos anymore, Orion! We're losing our ability to foresee the results of our actions. Chaos is crashing down upon us all. Absolute chaos!"

She was trembling with fear. I took her in my arms and

held her while the warm sun of Paradise swung westward and
began to set, turning the sky aflame with red and violet clouds.
I watched the deer and smaller animals come to the stream for
their evening drink while Anya remained huddled in my arms,
as if asleep.

As the world grew dark, though, she lifted up her head
and looked into my eyes.

"We must go back, Orion," she said, tearfully. "I must
tell the others that we cannot develop the star-killer. I must get
them to see that we have lost the war."

"And Aten has won?"

"Yes."

I shook my head. "Not while I live."

Chapter 25

"There is one way to save you," I told Anya.

"I know what you're thinking, Orion, but it can't be done. You can't kill Aten."

"He's killing you."

She touched my cheek with her fingertips, there in the gathering darkness of twilight, then kissed me lightly on the lips. "It can't be done. He's too powerful."

I replied, "He's constantly moving through space-time to adapt his bioweapon microbe against your attempts to destroy it. He's turning the entire continuum into a shambles in his mad lust for dominance. He's got to be stopped."

"But if we other Creators, with all our powers, can't stop him, how could you?"

"I almost killed him once, back in the time of Troy. Remember?"

"He was raving mad then."

"And your fellow Creators pulled me off him. I could have snapped his neck, but the others stopped me."

Despite her fears and her weakness, Anya smiled at me. "We may have made a mistake."

"May have? You tried to cure his madness and now he's killing you."

"Orion," Anya said, "I know how brave you are, and how much you love me. But to attempt to kill Aten is worse madness than he himself displays. He will destroy you with the flick of a finger. Destroy you utterly, and never revive you again."

I shrugged. "So what? I don't want to live if it means serving him forever, lifetime after lifetime. I don't want to live if you die, if he kills you."

"It's hopeless, Orion. Useless."

I got to my feet, extended my arms to her and helped her up. "It's not hopeless, my darling. I have hope. That may be all I've got, but I won't give up hope until the life is crushed out of me."

Anya's gaze shifted away from me. She took in the splashing stream, the trees swaying in the evening breeze, the first stars beginning to appear in the darkening sky.

"We'd better go back," she said, with a sigh.

"Yes," I said. "We have work to do."

I closed my eyes and felt the abyssal cold of the interstices in the space-time continuum. It may have been only my imagination but it seemed to me that it took a longer span than usual to translate us back to that chamber beneath the surface of the planet Prime. Time is meaningless in between space-times, but I sensed that the old pathways were coming apart, unraveling like a frayed ball of twine, the ripples of causality churning into a chaotic froth.

Once again Anya sat at the head of the long, polished conference table. I stood beside her, a spotlight of energy still glowing around me in the otherwise shadowed chamber. She was old, weary, gray and dying.

The light around me dissolved and I was free to go to her, take her in my arms. She felt frail and dust-dry, as if she would crumble at my touch.

But her eyes were still luminous, still alive and alert.

"You'll have to be my strength, Orion," she said. "I can't last much longer."

Spheres of energy appeared along the table, glowing fitfully, feebly. They resolved themselves into a half-dozen of the Creators, all of them aged, withered, dying.

"The Old Ones have sent a message through Orion," Anya told them. "They will not permit either of us to use the star-killer. They say they will eliminate us all if either the Commonwealth or the Hegemony attempts to do so."

Like the Creators surrounding Aten, these Creators also scoffed at the Old Ones' threat.

"How could they eliminate us? They don't even have spacecraft. No technology at all."

"None that you can recognize," I said, still standing beside Anya's chair. "But they can control the forces of the universe in their own way."

"It's a bluff," sputtered one of the gray-bearded men. "They're afraid that we'll attack their stars and they're trying to frighten us."

"I don't believe so," said Anya. "They are far older than we. I suspect their powers are far greater than we can imagine."

"If that's the case, then we might as well surrender to Aten right here and now."

"If the Old Ones have taken away our last trump card, then we've lost the war."

"We'll have to throw ourselves on Aten's mercy."

"He'll stop the ravages of this disease of his if we simply agree to follow his leadership."

They were old. They were tired. They had considered themselves immortal once, and now the prospect of painful death had them frightened and cowed.

"I agree," Anya said to them, her voice utterly weary, infinitely said. "There is no further point to continuing this war. Despite the fact that we hold the military advantage at present, we have lost."

"Ask Aten for a truce."

"Call him now."

Anya said, "We don't even have the strength to reach him. The disease has weakened us too much. We'll have to send an emissary to him, physically."

I was about to tell them that I could reach Aten, but something made me hold my tongue. I glanced down at Anya, sitting hunched over beside me. She did not look at me, but I got the distinct impression that she had warned me not to speak.

"I will go to him," Anya was telling the others. "Orion will convey me in his ship. You can return to your hibernation fields until I return."

They nodded among themselves, then one by one became encased in those glowing spheres of energy that they used to move through space-time. The spheres shone weakly, though, as if they barely had enough power to cover the individual Creators. I knew that each of them had once been able to live in the emptiness of deep space in those spheres, drawing energy directly from the stars themselves. Now they looked as if they could barely make it to their separate chambers, deep beneath the Hegemony's capitol, buried alive in hibernation crypts where they hoped they would be safe from the Commonwealth's weaponry. They slept while their creatures fought and died for them.

"Come, Orion," said Anya, "it's time to put an end to this fighting. Take me to your ship."

So all the fighting, all the strategy and battles came down simply to this: Threaten the Creators who had caused this war, and they were willing to surrender. Or at least ask for a truce. They thought nothing of sending millions of cloned warriors into battle, causing billions of deaths among the humans and other species. But threaten them, themselves, and they were ready to give up.

I could barely conceal my contempt for them all, even Anya.

And she knew it. She made a wan smile for me and said softly, "For what it's worth, I never wanted this war."

I had no intention of surrendering to Aten, but I had to obey Anya's wishes. Or at least, appear to obey.

So I watched as Hegemony technicians slipped her inert form into a cryosleep capsule, an elaborately engraved metal sarcophagus, which we loaded aboard the *Apollo*. The technicians and other humans in the spaceport seemed to understand that their leaders had decided to surrender to the Commonwealth. Rumors of defeat hung heavy in the air. They were sullen, fearful, angry. But they did as they were told.

Anya's last waking thoughts warned me, *Don't let the Skorpis know that we are going to surrender. They would blow your ship out of the galaxy if they knew.*

I wondered if the humans of Prime would try to stop us, but they were obedient and allowed us to break orbit and head out of the Zeta system.

But not for long.

We were accelerating as fast as we could, trying to achieve the safety of superlight velocity before anyone could deter us. We passed the rings of defenses that orbited Prime, then flew through the belt of battle stations that surrounded the Zeta system like a globe of bristling hedgehog spines.

Someone back on the capital planet must have passed on the rumors of our intention to surrender to the Skorpis, for as we were clearing the outermost battle stations in the belt, we were hailed by a dour-faced Skorpis admiral.

I took her message in my command chair on the bridge, wearing my best ship's uniform.

"There is ugly talk," said the admiral, her teeth showing in a barely suppressed snarl, "that you return to the Commonwealth to discuss surrender of the Hegemony."

"This ship carries one of your leaders in cryosleep," I answered. "We are transporting her to Loris, the capital of the Commonwealth, at her command."

"To surrender?"

A diplomat would have found evasive words. A politician would have lied. I was simply a warrior. "To discuss an armistice, a truce, an end to the war," I said.

"On Commonwealth terms," the Skorpis admiral rumbled, like a lioness growling.

"On the best terms that can be obtained."

"Surrender."

"Not surrender," I insisted. "An armistice. Peace."

"Surrender," she repeated. And I realized that she meant I should surrender my ship to her.

"This vessel is on a diplomatic mission. We are carrying one of the Hegemony's highest leaders. You cannot order us—"

"Stop accelerating and prepare to be boarded by my warriors," the Skorpis admiral insisted. "Otherwise we will destroy you, your ship, and the traitoress who wants to surrender."

I knew that every moment I could keep her talking was a moment closer to the relative safety of superlight.

"On what authority do you make such an unreasonable demand?" I asked, as indignantly as I could.

Her image in my display screen disappeared, instantly replaced by a view of a dozen Skorpis battle cruisers powering toward us.

The *Apollo* rocked wildly.

"They've opened fire on us!" Emon yelled. He was practically at my elbow; his shout was more from sudden excitement than fear. At least, I hoped so.

"Evasive maneuvers," I said.

You can't evade laser beams, even at relativistic speed. With a dozen battle cruisers within range of us, they blazed away, catching us in a cone of fire that sizzled our defensive screen and sent all the meters on the bridge deep into the red.

It was a race to see whether they could overload our screen and penetrate it before we achieved superlight and winked out of their sector of space-time.

"Cancel the evasive maneuvers," I said. "All available power to the main engines."

We were still shaking and rattling from the blasts of laser

bolts drenching our screen. And in the static-streaked displays I could see that squadron of battle cruisers coming up on us, far faster than we were. I turned to Frede, strapped into the seat beside me.

She knew what I was going to ask before I asked it. "Computer projects complete screen collapse fourteen seconds before we achieve superlight."

"That's enough time—"

"For them to vaporize us, yes," Frede finished for me.

There had to be something we could do.

"Transfer power from the forward section of the screen to the rear. That's where we're being hit."

"But if those battle cruisers maneuver to come in on our forward section . . ." She did not have to complete the sentence. One shot on an unscreened section of the ship would cut us in two like a hot knife going through butter.

"Do it!" I snapped.

Frede's fingers flicked across her keyboard. "Computer projects we'll be in superlight twenty seconds before the screen overloads," she said. Then added, "If nobody hits us forward."

We all held our breaths. The ship rocked and shivered under the pounding of the orbital stations' guns. The battle cruisers were gaining on us steadily. Two of them spurted ahead, trying to get in front of us and attack us from that quarter.

And then we flashed into superlight. All the display screens went blank and our shaking, shuddering ordeal was over.

"We made it!" whooped Jerron, from his engineer's console.

"So far," I said.

Frede turned to me. "They know we're heading for Loris. They can plant squadrons in all the likely places where we'd come out of superlight for navigational fixes. They'll be waiting for us."

"Only if we follow the geodesic to Loris," I said. *"Now* is the time for evasive maneuvers."

It was a gamble. We had to reach Loris before the Commonwealth started using the star-killers, but we could not approach Loris on the shortest route because Skorpis battle squadrons would be lying in wait along that way. So we had to take a more roundabout route, yet not such a distorted one that our arrival at Loris would be delayed too long.

How long was too long? I had no way of knowing.

Watches changed on the bridge, time flowed by, but I remained in my command chair, unwilling to leave. I did not sleep, I ate only what the crew members brought to me from time to time. I reached out mentally to Anya's frozen body in the cryosleeper deep in our ship's hold. She was alive, her mind slowly flickering in the cryogenic cold.

I thought about attempting to contact Aten, but decided that the dangers there outweighed the advantages. He would read my thoughts the instant I reached him and know that although Anya and the other Creators were ready to bow to his will, I was out to murder him.

Is there some way I can shield my thoughts from him? I asked Anya for her help, but her mind was so slowed by her frozen state that I doubted she could hear me.

We remained in superlight velocity as long as we dared, then slowed to relativistic for a quick navigational fix. The course Frede had plotted for us was designed to take us a considerable distance from the direct geodesic route to Loris. But the closer we got to the Commonwealth planet, the more we would have to adhere to a course that the Skorpis could intercept.

I knew what I would do if I were the Skorpis admiral. I would send a major fleet as close to Loris as I dared, keep it in superlight except for scout ships that hop down to relativistic speed, take a look around, and then power back into superlight once more. As soon as one of the scouts spotted us approaching Loris it could alert the main fleet with a gravitational pulse that could be detected in superlight. Then the entire fleet could go relativistic and catch us as we attempted to reach the planet.

They would have to face the massive defenses of the entire Giotto system, I realized. But, as I played the possible scenarios on the ship's tactical computer, it seemed to me that the Skorpis might not only catch us like a minnow in a net, they might be able to surprise the Commonwealth defenses and overwhelm them. It was a slim chance, but knowing the Skorpis, I thought it highly likely that they would grasp at it.

I almost laughed aloud when I realized what was shaping up. Our "diplomatic" mission was going to lead to a sneak attack on the Commonwealth capital. Our effort to surrender and end the war was going to trigger the bloodiest battle of them all.

And there was nothing I could do to avert it.

Chapter 26

Part of me felt almost exultant. A tremendous battle loomed ahead of us, and I was created for battle. The old excitement simmered within, making my innards tremble with anticipation.

Yet another part of me was filled with revulsion. Not fear, but loathing. How many of my command had already died? And for what? How many had I killed, over the eons? I remembered assassinating Ogotai, the High Khan of the Mongols, my friend, my hunting companion. I remembered the slaughter once we had pierced the walls of Troy. And Jericho. I remembered Philip's accusing stare as the blood filled his mouth and gushed from the slash in his belly.

When will there be an end to blood? The Golden One boasted that he created the human race to fight for him. Could we not overcome the aggression he had built into us? Could we not learn to live in peace?

Your sentiments do you honor, friend Orion. It was the voice of the Old Ones speaking in my mind.

I sat in the command chair on the *Apollo*'s bridge, but my eyes saw the depths of the oceans in which the Old Ones lived. And I was there among them, swimming in their midst, safe and warm in the bubble of energy they had prepared for me.

"My sentiments won't solve the problem we face," I said.

"The problem *you* face, Orion, not we."

"You are not willing to help?"

I felt a slight tremor of disappointment among them. "You must solve your own problems, my friend. Otherwise they are not solved, merely postponed."

"Yet you threaten to wipe out any species that tries to use a star-weapon."

A patient sigh. "Our ethical code demands that we leave younger species alone to work out their own destinies. But that same code cannot allow stars to be wantonly destroyed. A species willing to use such power is a danger not merely to itself, it is a danger to the entire continuum."

"Meaning that it's a danger to you."

They fluttered their many tentacles, colors spiraling across the breadths of their huge, undulating bodies.

"Yes," they admitted at last. "Such a species would be a danger to us and everything else in the continuum."

"Does your ethical code allow you to help me to prevent this catastrophe?"

A long delay, while they swam about me and flashed colors at one another.

Finally, "Orion, you are laboring under a misapprehension. You apparently believe that if you could eliminate one of your species, this one you refer to as Aten, or the Golden One, that his demise would solve your problem."

"Won't it?"

"No. We fear not."

"But—"

"Your species is very violent, Orion. It is part of your makeup. Even you, who are struggling to overcome this heritage of blood, can think of the solution to your problem only in terms of murder."

"Aten must be stopped. He is killing his fellow Creators. He seeks—"

"We know. We have seen it in your mind. But suppose you succeed in murdering Aten. Do you believe that will end your war? Hundreds of billions of humans are struggling against one another. They use weapons of constantly increasing power and horror. Will the death of one of you stop the death desires in your entire species?"

I had to think about that for a while. The Old Ones respected my silence.

Choosing my words carefully, I said, "The first step is to stop the fighting, to put an end to this war. That by itself will not end the violence in the human psyche, but it will stop the killing. Then perhaps we can learn how to live in peace."

"Do you think that is possible?"

"Do you see a better path?" I countered.

"No," they answered. "Quite frankly, we do not."

"Then help me to reach Loris."

"The Skorpis will be waiting for you. There is nothing we can do to protect you from them."

"Can you at least transport the cryosleep capsule my ship is carrying safely to the planet's capitol building?"

They seemed to confer among themselves again, then replied, "Orion, that is a task you must accomplish for yourself."

"You won't help even that much? In the interests of peace?"

"You must accomplish peace by yourselves, Orion," they answered. "It is your task, not ours."

I would receive no help from the Old Ones. None at all.

"Your arrival in the Giotto system will set off a massive battle," they warned.

"The last battle of the war," I said, resignedly.

"Let us hope so."

I said, "Thank you." Bitterly.

"Farewell, friend Orion," they replied. "Farewell forever."

Before I could ask what that meant, I found myself back on the bridge of the *Apollo,* with Frede staring at me oddly.

"Don't you want to eat?"

I saw that she was holding a tray of steaming food before me.

"No, thanks," I mumbled. "I'm not hungry."

How could be I hungry when I suspected the Old Ones had just bid me a final farewell because they knew I was going to be killed?

When I finally left the bridge and went to my quarters for a bit of sleep, I dreamed of ancient Byzantium, the triple-walled New Rome that stood against the barbarian hordes for a thousand years after darkness fell on western Europe.

I was a soldier, an officer, returning to the city after a long, hard campaign against the ravaging Seljuks who had swept out of the heartland of high Asia to conquer the ancient provinces of Cilicia, Cappadocia and even Anatolia. Noble cities such as Antioch, Pergamum and Ephesus were all under the rule of the Moslems now.

My cohort had fought for months, always retreating before the remorseless horsemen from the steppes, fighting and dying as the tide of barbarism pushed us constantly back toward the Bosphorus. It saddened me to see villages, towns, whole cities put to the torch by the invaders; to know that churches and even great cathedrals were being turned into mosques by the heathen savages. Our retreat was marked by columns of black smoke, funeral pyres for our empire, that rose into the hot bright sky like accusing fingers.

At last we stopped them, our backs against the narrow sea that separates Asia from Europe. Not much of the old empire was saved, but mighty Byzantium stood still free—barely. The cost was thousands of good soldiers; of my cohort, hardly a full maniple remained able to stand and fight, and most of us bore many wounds. But we could tell ourselves and anyone who might listen that we had given more than we had taken. The Seljuks were just as exhausted as we, and their piles of dead rose higher than our own.

The fighting was stopped, at least for now, and I had returned to the mighty city. Weary, sick at heart, half crippled from an arrow in my thigh.

I passed through the triple gates on horseback, all my worldly goods tied behind my saddle. The guards hardly paid any attention to a returning soldier; they were busy haggling with a merchant who had a long string of highly laden mules. They wanted a good bribe for allowing the caravan to enter the city.

Through the twisting streets of the old city I rode slowly, deliberately, savoring the sights and sounds and smells of it. Vendors hawked their wares. Shopkeepers talked about the weather or the latest fashions with their customers. Men and women strolled along the thoroughfares or lolled in cafés in the city's many open squares. The aroma of roasting lamb and onions and pungent spiced wine made me almost dizzy after months of dried strips of goat or worse.

Beyond the low roofs of the houses in the market quarter I could see the beautiful curved dome of Santa Sophia. I nosed my tired mount toward the cathedral. If I should offer a prayer of thanks for my survival, why not offer it in the grandest church in Christendom?

Somewhere in the back of my mind I wondered if this was real life or a dream. Am I truly living in this era, or is this merely a dream while I sleep somewhere, somewhen else? What does it matter, I thought. I am lucky to be alive and I owe it to God and His saints to offer a prayer of thanksgiving. At last I reached the broad, cobblestoned plaza in front of the cathedral.

"You can't tie that nag here!"

The nasty, rasping voice startled me. I looked down at the hitching rail where several other horses were tethered and saw a mean, wizened, bent old man in filthy rags casting an angry, beady-eyed look at me.

"This rail is reserved for the wedding party," he croaked. "Don't you try to put that flea-bitten animal in among the quality."

I saw that the horses already at the rail were sleek and

groomed and well fed. My own poor mount showed each of its individual ribs.

"Damned soldiers think you can do whatever you want, don't you? Why aren't you out fighting the Saracens instead of trying to butt your way in where you're not wanted?"

Without a word I turned my horse and went to a farther hitching rail, tied her there and walked back to the grizzled old sourpuss.

"I've left my life's possessions on that flea-bitten nag," I said to him, "except for this." And I pulled my jewel-pommeled sword halfway out of its battered old scabbard. "This blade had taken the lives of more Seljuks than you have hairs in your mangy beard, old man. If anyone so much as touches my horse or my belongings, it will take your life next."

His eyes blazed with fury, but he held his tongue. I turned and went into the cathedral. It was strangely chill inside, and dark except far up in front, by one of the side altars, where a small group had gathered for a wedding. The people whose horses the sourpuss outside was watching, I reasoned.

Kneeling on the stone floor, I could barely make out the huge mosaic of the risen Christ that filled the interior of the main dome. Dim light filtered through the high windows of stained glass, dust motes drifting through the slanting shafts. I half expected to see my own breath frosting in the air, it was so cold inside the cathedral.

Here by the main entrance, next to the massive marble baptismal font, stood a statue of Santa Sophia. I gazed at it, in the shadows, and thought the face that the sculptor had carved looked familiar. I had seen it before, on another statue, in Athens. That other statue had been the work of an ancient pagan, the statue purported to be of Athena, the patron goddess of that old, decrepit city.

And here was the same face on Santa Sophia, decked in soft folds of cloth rather than armor and bronze helmet. Offering prayers for the faithful rather than holding a spear and bearing an owl on her shoulder. But the same face. She seemed to be smiling at me, a beatific smile that warmed me deep in my heart.

I did not stay long. Just one swift prayer of thanks for my life, then I limped back into the sunlight, worried that the sourpuss might take it into his head to steal some of my possessions or all of them and disappear into the crowds of the city before I could stop him. But he was still by the rail with the wedding party's horses, and my horse still stood alone farther off. I had to admit, my mount did indeed look very shabby.

The old man grumbled something at me as I passed him.

"I suppose soldiers don't tip a man who's watched their horse, do they?"

"Soldiers don't have any coins until they're paid," I said to him, over my shoulder. "And none of us have been paid since we first left the city, months ago."

"Pah!" He didn't believe my word.

I was billeted with a family that lived outside the walls. They were hardly overcome with joy to see me. I would be an extra mouth to feed, an extra horse to care for, as long as I stayed with them. They seemed to be having enough difficulty making ends meet, with five youngsters in their brood, the oldest a lad barely into his teens.

The man was a metalsmith; he eked out his living by repairing pots and copperware in the bazaar. The army would pay him a pittance for housing me, but he made it clear that my upkeep would cost him more than the government would pay.

The youngsters clustered around me, bursting with questions about the war and the lands I had seen. They stared at my face curiously, and I realized that it was my scars that fascinated them.

Their mother had been taken by a fever that had swept the city half a year earlier. The old man had a young serving girl to cook and take care of the children. A sturdy, redheaded lass from Muscovy, from the looks of her. She was pretty, with clear white skin that had not been roughened from hard work as yet. I wondered if the old man made her sleep with him.

The two eldest boys helped me unpack my meager belongings and dumped them on one of the beds in the upstairs room; then they took my horse down the street to the stable. During the evening meal the boys wanted to hear tales of battle and victory; all I had to talk about was battles that we lost and retreats in the face of the relentless enemy. Their father ate his barley soup and black bread in dour silence, except to cast dark looks at the serving girl whenever she smiled at me.

"How many of the heathens did you kill?" asked the eldest boy.

"Too many," I said. "And not enough."

The serving girl asked me, "What is it like to take a man's life?"

I replied without thinking, "Better to take his than let him take yours."

She shook her head. "I know they're heathen Moslems and the Church has condoned warring against them, but still, the Christos taught us that it is wrong to kill, didn't He?"

Her disapproving frown nettled me. I wanted to tell her what the Seljuks did to Christian women when they captured them, wanted to describe the villages we had seen where the women had been raped and then put to the sword hideously, where babies had been spitted alive and used as footballs, where fire and knives were used for torturing helpless children.

But I said nothing. Because I was ashamed. My own troops had done much the same to the Moslem villages we had sacked.

"They're heathens," the old man snapped. "Servants of the Antichrist. Killing them isn't the same as killing a Christian. The Patriarchs of the Church have told us so. They're not even human, really."

"Their blood's as red as ours," I heard myself mutter.

"Good! Spill as much of it as you can."

Leave as quickly as you can and return to the wars, he was telling me. And I resolved to do exactly that. This was not my home and never could be. As soon as my leg healed properly, I would go back to the fighting, I told myself.

After dinner, the two boys offered to share their bed with me. I laughed and told them that I had been sleeping on the ground for so long that a bed would probably keep me awake. So I unrolled my sleeping blanket and stretched out on the floor next to their bed in the upstairs room.

Just before I drifted to sleep, the older of the two boys said, "Next year I'll be old enough to join the army."

"Don't," I said. "Stay here and help your family."

"There's no glory in staying here."

"There's no glory in war," I said. "Believe me. Nothing but pain and blood."

"But fighting the Seljuks is doing God's work!"

"Living is doing God's work, son. Killing people is the work of the devil."

"But it's all right to kill the Seljuks. The priests have blessed the war."

Yes, I thought wearily. They always do.

"The emperor himself—"

"Go to sleep," I snapped. "And forget about the army. Only a fool goes to war when he doesn't have to."

That shut him up at last. I turned on my side and went to sleep, dreaming of the distant future when ships flew among the stars.

Chapter 27

I awoke in my quarters aboard the *Apollo* with Frede shaking my shoulder roughly.

"You'd better look at the imagery from our last navigation check," she said, once I had opened my eyes and sat up in the bunk.

Blinking the sleep away, I pointed to the display screen set against the bulkhead. "Put it on the screen."

There had been a pair of Skorpis warships among the stars.

"Did they detect us?" I asked.

Frede shrugged. "They had to. We were only at sublight for thirty seconds, but their sensors are as good as ours or better. They picked us up, all right."

"Did they make any move to stop us?"

"In thirty seconds?"

I studied the alphanumeric data at the bottom of the screen. The Skorpis warships had been drifting along on minimum power.

"Looks like they were waiting for us to show up," I said.

"The Hegemony must be covering as many of our potential reentry points as possible," Frede said. "They want to know where we are and how soon we'll reach the Giotto system."

Swinging my legs off the bunk and reaching for my tunic, I asked, "How close to Loris can you put us? If we can come out of superlight well inside the system's defenses we ought to be safe enough."

"Their automated defenses will shred us within microseconds. Same as Prime and the Zeta system, remember?"

"Message capsules worked then. We could send out message capsules ahead of us, tell them we're coming in."

With a frown, Frede added, "And bringing the whole Skorpis fleet with us."

"What choice do we have?" I asked.

She leaned her back against the hatch to the bridge and did not speak for several moments. I wondered if she did not know what to reply, or if she knew so well that she was rehearsing the words she would use before speaking them.

"We could change course," she said at last. "Why do we have to go to Loris? Why put ourselves into the lion's mouth? There are hundreds of other planetary systems, thousands of them. The Commonwealth—"

"We've got to bring our passenger to the Commonwealth's leaders. They're on Loris. That's where we must go."

"We could go to a thousand other planets and send word to Loris," Frede countered.

"And if the Skorpis found us on one of those other planets?"

"The chances of that happening are so low—"

"But if they do, what are the chances of our surviving? Zero," I told her, before she could answer. "At Loris we have all the defenses of the Giotto system on our side. We have a fighting chance."

She looked utterly unconvinced. I could not tell Frede that my real reason for insisting on Loris was that Anya was dying. Even in cryosleep she grew weaker every day. Aten was killing her and the only way to make him stop was to confront him, to overpower him and the other Creators who had allied themselves with him. To kill him.

He would not come to a rendezvous at some out-of-the-way planet. He had made Loris his headquarters, the capital

of the Commonwealth. So I had to go to Loris, I had to bring
Anya there, I had to face the Golden One.

Frede's expression made me realize that I was, in all
probability, about to get all of us killed.

But I pulled myself up to my full height and gave the
order, "Direct geodesic to Loris. No more evasions. We bore
straight in."

"And damn the torpedoes," she muttered.

"What?"

"An old naval expression. From ancient history."

With no external points of reference there was no way for
our unaided human senses to get any feeling for our ship's
speed. The instruments told us we were hurtling along at many
multiples of the speed of light, but for all we could tell the
Apollo was sitting still in the middle of nothingness.

Yet the morning arrived when Frede said to me, "We're
within two days of the Giotto system. Time to start sending
out message capsules."

I got the feeling that out there in that blank nothingness
surrounding us, the entire Skorpis battle fleet was riding along
with us, waiting for us to slow down to relativistic velocity
once again, their weapons primed and ready to blast us into an
expanding fireball of ionized atoms.

Tension on the bridge grew tighter with each passing
moment. We fired off every message capsule we possessed,
then used the ship's matter transceiver to make still more of
them, converting some of our food stocks to do so.

"We won't need more than two days' worth of food," I
told the transceiver crew. "In three days' time we'll be having
our meals on Loris."

"Or in hell," grumbled one of the technicians when he
thought I was too far down the passageway to hear him.

When I returned to the bridge I asked Frede, "How close
to the planet can you put us?"

She looked up from her navigational screens, bleary-eyed
from concentration and lack of sleep. "Fifty planetary diame-

ters," she answered. "Half a million klicks. Right smack in the middle of their major defense belt."

"Good," I said. "Perfect."

Then she added, "If the ephemeris data in our computer's memory files is up-to-date."

"It should be," I said.

With a sardonic grin she replied, "Right. It should be." She put a slight but noticeable accent on the word *should*. "If it's not we could hang our asses on the wrong side of the planetary system. Or crash into the planet's surface."

Pleasant possibilities.

The ephemeris data was correct and Frede's navigation was practically flawless. The only factor that we did not foresee—could not have foreseen—was that the Skorpis had decided to attack Loris without waiting for us to appear.

We slowed out of superlight and into the middle of a full-scale battle. The sky was filled with warships and orbital battle stations slashing at each other with laser beams and nuclear-tipped missiles.

Apollo jounced and shuddered as a Skorpis dreadnought loomed directly before us, firing its main battery at a Commonwealth orbital station, but turning its secondary laser banks squarely upon us.

I barely had time to yell, "Battle stations!" Control of the ship automatically went to my command chair; the keyboards set into the ends of my armrests now directly controlled all the ship's systems. The rest of the bridge crew were there strictly as backup for me.

My intention was to get to the surface of Loris, but in the midst of this battle that was going to be impossible. The planet's defensive shields were up, powered by every megajoule their ground-based generators could produce.

Swiftly I took in the situation. The Skorpis attackers were not bothering with the planet. They were trying to knock out the belts of defensive stations that orbited Loris. With fanatical bravery they had come as close to the planet as we had before slowing below superlight, risking collisions and even crashes into the planetary surface in their eagerness to surprise the Commonwealth defenders.

Their tactic had worked. They had bypassed the outer rings of defenses, farther out in the Giotto system. Those massive battle stations were in fixed planetary orbits tens of millions of kilometers from Loris. They could be moved, but it would take most of the power they needed for their weapons to activate their propulsion systems and bring them into the battle. And it would take time, too much time for them to make a difference in the battle's outcome.

Most of the Commonwealth fleet was elsewhere, fighting the war on other fronts. The Skorpis had gambled virtually every ship they possessed, as I feared they would, for this one killing stroke at the Commonwealth's capital. Now they were fighting to knock out Loris's belts of defenses and the few ships that the planet could send up. Neutralize the Commonwealth's orbital defenses and the planet itself lay open to bombardment and invasion.

No telling how long the battle had been going on. In the display screens I saw the hulks of blasted ships drifting lifelessly, saw an orbital station riddled with holes, its spherical hull ripped open and bubbling hot metal. Fragments of shattered ships and stations swirled past us; some of them might have been the bodies of humans or Skorpis, they blew past us too fast for me to tell.

I saw a Skorpis dreadnought slugging it out with an orbital station, laser beams lancing back and forth, splashing off their defensive screens in wild coruscations of light. I slipped the *Apollo* under the giant Skorpis warship's belly, probing with our sensors for a weak section in her screen. They were putting most of their power into the forward screen, where they faced the orbital station.

I found a weak spot and fired our one and only bank of lasers at it. The screen went blank and the hull of the dreadnought began to blacken and peel back, curling like leaves in a flame. The dreadnought shuddered; then a huge explosion racked its innards and it stopped firing. The orbital station kept on blasting at it, and the dreadnought broke apart into molten chunks of metal and plastic and flesh.

We had killed it like a foot soldier slips his stiletto between the armor plates of a mounted warrior.

"Six o'clock high!" sang out one of the sensors as the ship shuddered from a direct hit. Our screen held, barely, as a deadly battle cruiser sailed past us, firing another salvo. We fired back, to no effect.

The battle lost all semblance of cohesion. It turned into a thousand separate fights between individual ships and the massive orbital stations. I saw one of the few Commonwealth warships capable of maneuver exchanging shots with two Skorpis dreadnoughts at the same time; it bloomed into a brilliant flare of radiance as it exploded. Then one of the dreadnoughts was caught in a crossfire from two orbital stations. The heavy laser beams carved up the Skorpis vessel and left it drifting helplessly. Another ship burst apart in a titanic explosion.

There were no sounds on the bridge except the beeping of sensors, the tight, quick breathing of my crew and the steady background hum of machinery. No one said a word, their eyes riveted to the display screens as ships fired, turned, exploded in the deathly silence of space.

I drove the *Apollo* through the thick of the battle, desperately trying to maneuver closer to the planet's surface, but it seemed as if every ship in the Skorpis fleet stood in my way. I knew that we were no match for dreadnoughts, neither in firepower nor defensive shielding, yet the battle was raging all around us, whether we liked it or not.

We could try to run in the other direction, get away from the fighting and seek safety by accelerating back to superlight velocity. Then a new fear struck at me. If it appeared that the Skorpis were going to win this battle and then attack Loris itself, Aten might very well leave the planet, escape to some other point in the continuum, leaving the rest of us here. Leaving Anya weak and dying.

I had no choice. I had to stay and fight and try to help the Commonwealth win.

I dove the *Apollo* toward the nearest orbital station, a huge massive globular structure studded with sensors and weapons. Hoping that my ship's automated identification signals would keep the orbital station from frying us, I maneuvered as close to the station as I dared, taking up a minutes-long orbit around it like a bee circling its own hive.

Three Skorpis warships approached, firing as they came. Two of them were battle cruisers, the third a dreadnought. While Frede and the rest of the bridge crew watched silently, I darted our ship down below the two battle cruisers and scanned their defensive shields. Just as I had expected, they were shifting power to ward off the heavy blasts coming from the orbital station's main batteries. I located the weakest part of the first battle cruiser's shield and poured everything we had into it. The cruiser veered away, exposing its weakened belly to the orbital station. One salvo from the station's heavy guns blew the Skorpis warship to pieces.

But the second battle cruiser turned to engage us, jolting the *Apollo* with hits from its main battery. Leaving the orbital station to duel with the lone dreadnought, I raced through the swirling carnage of the battle with that determined battle cruiser on our tail, firing at us steadily. No matter how I jinked our ship back and forth that cruiser stuck to us, as if the only thing in its captain's mind was to avenge its sister ship.

Stubbornness is not an asset to a captain. I checked the display screens and saw that the battle had concentrated on one side of Loris's defensive belt. There were stations on the far side of the orbit that were not being attacked. This made good sense, from the Skorpis point of view. They were concentrating all their forces on a part of the Commonwealth's defenses, intending to overwhelm them and then destroy the remainder afterward. The orbital stations could not maneuver quickly; those on the far side of the battle could never reach the attackers in time to do any good.

But I could bring at least one of the attackers to the idling stations on the far side, if the Skorpis captain did not suddenly acquire a dose of good sense.

She did not. She followed me, closing, firing, making the bridge rattle and our defensive screens buckle. But she followed me for a few seconds too long. I zoomed the *Apollo* into range of the quiescent orbital stations and three of them opened fire on the Skorpis warship at once. It blew up in a giant fireball, the scattered fragments like blazing meteors all across the sky.

"Battle damage," reported Dyer, from her damage-control console. "Hull open to vacuum in starboard stern. Sections fourteen and fifteen of deck two have been automatically sealed off."

"Anyone in there?"

"No, sir. Those are food lockers. We emptied them out to make extra message capsules."

Frede giggled nervously. "We wanted to warn Loris that we were coming, so they wouldn't fire on us, remember?"

It seemed like a million years ago.

"Looks like they didn't need our warning," I said as I turned the ship back into the battle.

I headed for one of the orbital stations, hoping to repeat my earlier tactic of gadflying one of the attacking ships to its destruction. But as we came closer to the fighting, swirling, exploding ships I saw that six Skorpis cruisers detached themselves from the battle to aim directly at us.

"Incoming message," said Magro, the comm officer.

I tapped the comm key on my armrest board. A Skorpis commander appeared on the bridge's main screen.

"*Apollo*, I have orders to take your ship. You will surrender. You cannot escape us."

At the velocity we were going now it would take more

than an hour to build back up to superlight. The Skorpis ships could catch us and board us long before then.

"We will not surrender," I said.

The commander bared her teeth. "My orders are to take you alive—if possible. If you will not surrender, you will die."

Chapter 28

Six against one were impossible odds. Especially when the six were battle cruisers, twice the size and firepower of the *Apollo*.

I looked at the stricken faces of the bridge crew. They had been prisoners of the Skorpis once before.

"They'll freeze us," muttered Emon.

"And serve us for dinner," said Jerron, trying to make a joke of it. No one laughed. They all looked grim, frightened.

"They're not going to take us alive," I told them.

"And that's the good news," Frede wisecracked. Everyone laughed, breaking the tension.

Our one chance was to make it down to the surface of Loris before the Skorpis ships could destroy us. I turned the *Apollo* in that direction, hoping that the orbiting battle stations could pick off some of the warships hounding us.

"Take power from the weapons batteries," I told Jerron. "Put every bit of power we've got into the engines."

Emon looked unhappy that his weapons were being drained. I started to say, "Keep the shields—"

The ship was rocked by several hits. Then a massive jolt slammed into us, knocking me against my seat harness painfully.

"Nuclear missile," Dyer yelled out.

I looked at her screen. The engine section had been hit.

"Screens absorbed most of the energy," Dyer reported,

"but the hull's buckled. Section eighteen, deck two is open to vacuum."

"Seal it," I snapped.

"Automatic," she replied.

The ship shuddered again.

"They're hitting that section," Frede said, almost calmly. "They're trying to knock out our engines."

I jinked the ship back and forth, trying to keep their laser beams from overpowering the screen shielding the engine section. But the weapons of six battle cruisers all firing at us were impossible to evade entirely. *Apollo* bounced and shook like a rat in a terrier's jaws.

One of the Skorpis cruisers blew up, victim of a Commonwealth station's guns. But the others pressed their attack even harder. One of my display screens sputtered and went dark. The overhead lights flickered fitfully.

And the surface of Loris still seemed to be a million light-years away. We were diving toward that blue and white planet, hoping desperately that the Commonwealth defenders would allow us through their planetary screen and shoot the Skorpis warships off our back.

"Power drain exceeding safety limits," Jerron said tensely. "The shield isn't going to hold up more than another fifteen seconds."

"More nuclear missiles on their way!"

I saw them in the main display screen and turned the ship to avoid them. But their guidance sensors had locked on to us.

"Hang on!"

Three explosions hit us almost simultaneously. Display screens burst in showers of sparks all across the bridge. The lights blew out. Acrid smoke filled the darkness.

The red emergency lights came on. In the dimness I saw that the bridge crew was still alive, though we would all have bad bruises from our safety harnesses.

"Power's gone," Jerron muttered.

"We're dead meat."

"Not yet, we aren't," I said, unbuckling my harness. "They said they wanted to take us alive."

Frede smiled grimly. "Break out the rifles and sidearms," she said. "We'll make a fight of it."

A wild thought spun into my mind. A memory of ancient days when sailing ships grappled and sent boarding parties to seize their opponents. The Skorpis were going to board us, I knew. What if we ambushed their boarding party and then seized their battle cruiser?

"Come on," I said, getting to my feet. "We don't have much time."

As we were passing out the hand weapons to the entire crew we heard the thump and clang of a Skorpis ship mating its air lock to our main hatch. With our sensors down, I could not tell if it was a shuttle craft or one of the battle cruisers.

"If that's a shuttle," I said, "there can't be more than twenty or thirty warriors on board."

"More likely it's a battle cruiser," said Frede. "They wouldn't risk a shuttle with all the shooting going on out there."

"And they know they'll need more than thirty warriors to take us down," Emon added, trying to sound cocky.

"Good," I said. "Then after we finish the boarding party we can take over their ship."

Someone laughed in the darkness and muttered, "Yeah, the thirty-five of us against a couple hundred Skorpis."

There was no time to worry about the odds. The Skorpis would quickly burn through our locked hatch. I deployed my crew at the end of the short passageway leading from the main hatch to the power ladder that went down to the main deck.

"Let them into the passageway, then cut them down while they've got no place to hide," I said.

I placed Emon and two other crewmen on the rungs of the ladder, where they could pop up and fire along the passageway. I flattened myself on the deck on the other side of the ladder's hatch, hugging a rifle in both arms, behind a metal table we dragged out of a crewman's quarters. Frede and the others were farther down the passageway, at the next ladderway down, ready to fire at the Skorpis boarders or duck down to the main deck and continue the fight there if the Skorpis got past our first line of defense.

We barely had time to get ourselves set. The Skorpis did not bother trying to melt the hatch's locking mechanism with a laser. They attached an explosive charge to the hatch and set it off. The blast knocked the heavy metal hatch inward, banging halfway down the passageway. Anyone standing there would have been flattened.

The Skorpis were so big that they had to squeeze through the hatch one at a time. In the dim lighting of the smoke-filled passage I saw the first one step through, a heavy rifle pointed straight ahead, helmet brushing the overhead, cat's eyes peering into the darkness warily. We could have potted him easily, but I wanted that passageway filled with as many of their boarding party as possible before we started mowing them down.

They were wearing body armor. They trudged down the passageway carefully, their boots as noiseless as cat's feet on the metal deck plates. Emon and his two crewmates kept their heads down, out of sight, waiting as they clung to the ladder's rungs. I huddled behind the overturned table, scarcely breathing.

The Skorpis warriors stood for several moments, as if waiting for something. Then I heard a muffled explosion from somewhere. And another. They were blowing in our auxiliary hatches! They must have assault teams in space suits breaking into the ship from all three hatches at once!

My brilliant plan was mincemeat. We had to get down onto the main deck and fight at least three boarding parties at once.

"Fire!" I screamed as I raised myself to my knees and cut the first Skorpis in half with a bolt from my rifle.

My senses went into overdrive and the world around me slowed into a dreamlike torpor. I saw Emon and his little team raise their heads leisurely above the ladder hatch's sill and squeeze the triggers of their rifles. More laser beams came sizzling over my head from Frede and her team. The Skorpis warriors, huge and clumsy in the confines of the passageway, died in their tracks, slumping to their knees as laser beams burned holes through their armor, falling sluggishly, weapons dropping from their lifeless fingers. Their death screams sounded like eerie keening wails, echoing off the passageway's metal bulkheads. Their bodies even blocked the hatch, making it difficult for more of them to get in.

But they fired as they fell. They died fighting. More of them pushed through the bodies of their own dead to worm their way on their bellies toward us.

"Everybody down to the main deck," I yelled.

Too late. One of the dying warriors pulled a grenade from his equipment belt and tossed it toward the hatch. I saw it wobbling on a lazy arc toward Emon and his crewmen. I fired at it, hit it, and it exploded in a shower of white-hot shrapnel. Howls of pain came from the ladderway. A body thudded down onto the main deck.

I crawled along the deck plates, firing into the crouching Skorpis who were using their own dead as shields for themselves. I rolled headfirst down into the ladder well, grabbed a rail and let myself slide down the rest of the way to the main deck.

Emon's head and shoulders were covered with blood, his own and his crewmates'. One of the men sprawled dead on the deck, the other clutched a shredded arm with one hand.

"I'm okay," Emon said. "I can still shoot." But when he tried to stand he staggered into my arms.

I pulled him away from the ladderway and into the comparative safety of a compartment hatch. Then I went back and got the other wounded man. I saw laser beams zipping past the open ladder hatch, up above.

Sitting the wounded man against the bulkhead of the compartment, I told Emon, "The Skorpis will be pouring down that ladderway in a few moments."

"I'll hold 'em off," he said, hefting his rifle in bloodied hands.

"Do the best you can," I said. I left him there and sprinted down the passageway toward Frede and the rest of our crew.

"They blew the other hatches," I told her.

"I heard it."

"Get those people down here." I pointed to the crew who were still firing from the top of the ladder. "We'll make our stand in the cargo bay."

"Right."

They must know that we're carrying Anya in this ship. For some reason they want her alive. They don't want her to surrender to the Commonwealth, but they'd rather take her back to Hegemony territory, if they can.

I ran past the dead and smoking bridge, ducked down the ladderway to the lower deck and raced for the cargo hold where Anya's cryosleep capsule lay. Her sarcophagus, I thought.

Four Skorpis warriors were already prying the cargo bay hatch open when I hit the lower deck. They were in space suits and did not hear me running up the passageway toward them. I gave them no chance. I fired my rifle from the hip as I ran toward them. The oxygen tanks on their life-support systems exploded, blowing them to sticky shreds.

Twelve more space-suited warriors came pounding up the passageway from the other end, where the air-lock hatch was. Too many for me to handle by myself, especially when they were firing laser rifles at me. I backpedaled, then turned and ran into the nearest protective hatch. I found myself in the transceiver station, a flat open bay with a small console standing to one side.

Using the passageway hatch to shelter me, I fired at the

Skorpis who stood near the cargo bay hatch. I saw one sag and
slide down the bulkhead, his helmet smoking where my rifle
beam had caught him. The others turned toward me, in
dreamlike slow motion, raising their rifles toward me. I fired
twice, shattering a helmet visor and burning a hole through
the arm of another Skorpis. They backed away, firing. I
ducked back inside the transceiver bay hatch.

A standoff. They could not get into the cargo bay; neither
could I.

I wondered if the ship was still hurtling toward Loris, and
if the planet's defensive systems would blast the Skorpis battle
cruiser and us with it. Or had the cruiser's captain maneuvered
us away from our collision course with the planet?

Footsteps running up the passageway. I glanced out and
saw Frede leading the rest of the crew. I counted only thirty.

"Look out!" I yelled. "They're at the other end of the
passageway, by the cargo bay hatch."

Frede and her people flattened out against the bulkheads,
firing and being fired upon as they, one by one, ducked into
the transceiver bay with me.

"We caught the other boarding party coming through the
after hatch," she said. "Took some casualties."

"So I see." None of them were unwounded. Frede's face
was smeared with blood and sweat.

But she grinned. "We wiped them out. Killed every last
one of those damned cats."

That leaves only a couple of hundred, I thought. It was
obvious that the Skorpis battle cruiser had attached itself to
our air lock. We were not dealing with a shuttle load of warriors, not the way they were pouring reinforcements into our
ship.

"They're regrouping down the passageway," I said.
"Probably getting reinforcements before they charge us."

"The first landing party, up by the main air lock—"

"They'll be coming down here the same way you came.
We'll have our hands full."

"Still thinking of taking their ship?"

I laughed bitterly.

Looking over the ragged remains of my crew, I saw that little Jerron was badly burned in the abdomen and left leg. He lay panting, wide-eyed with shock, with our medical officer bending over him.

"Magro," I called to the comm officer. "Can you power up the transceiver?"

He was grimy and breathing hard, like all the others. But he gave me a nod and said, "I can try, sir."

"What are you thinking?" Frede asked.

Peering down the dimly lit, smoky passageway, I could see no Skorpis. They were beyond the air-lock hatch, preparing their next attack on us.

"They want the cryo capsule in the cargo hold," I told Frede. "Maybe we can beam it down to the planet."

"We'd have to drag it in here," Frede objected.

"We could cut through the bulkhead. Are there any flight packs stashed in that cargo bay? That would make it easier to move the capsule."

Clearly, she did not think much of my idea. But she said, "I'll get a couple of people to cut through the bulkhead."

Nodding, I turned my attention back to the empty passageway. The Skorpis could cut through the ship's outer hull and get into the cargo bay that way, I knew. Would they try that, or would they first try to wipe us out and walk into the cargo bay after we were done with?

Why not blow a hole in the hull right here, in the transceiver bay, and kill us all at one stroke? Blow out the hull, expose us to vacuum; none of us had space suits. Explosive decompression, we'd be dead in an instant. The thought startled me. But then I reasoned that if they had wanted to do that they would have done it by now. A blast big enough to puncture the hull would probably damage Anya's cryosleep capsule, as well, and it seemed that they wanted Anya alive. If possible.

Waiting, wondering what would happen next, was harder
than actually fighting. Behind me I heard the crackling sizzle
of lasers cutting through the metal of the bulkhead separating
us from the cargo bay. The passageway remained empty.
Whatever the Skorpis were planning, they were taking their
time about it.

I heard a crewman sing out, "Watch it, the section's
falling."

Glancing over my shoulder I saw a whole section of the
bulkhead, its edges glowing red, fall inward, scattering the
crewmen who had burned it through. It thumped loudly, making me wonder if the Skorpis could hear it.

"Damn," I heard Frede call, her voice echoing in the
nearly empty cargo bay, "not a flight pack in the place. We'll
have to muscle it."

I called Dyer and told her to watch the passageway. Then
I stepped through the jagged hole in the bulkhead to join the
team of sweating, grunting, cursing men and women who were
tugging at the massive cryosleep capsule.

"Heavier than a sergeant's ass," one of the men muttered.

"Heavier than your ass, anyway."

It was like dragging one of the stones for Khufu's pyramid without the aid of rollers. The capsule screeched along the
metal deck plates, moving grudgingly, a millimeter at a time.
I called almost all the remaining members of the crew to help
us, as I watched through sweat-stung eyes while Magro bent
over the transceiver console, a puzzled frown on his face as he
pecked tentatively at the keyboard.

At last we hauled the capsule onto the transceiver stage.
I felt as if I had dragged the planet Jupiter through a light-year
of mud.

Trudging slowly to Magro at the console, I asked, "You
do have power, don't you?"

"Yessir," he said, still frowning at the readouts. "But I
don't know where we are in relation to the planet. I need a
navigational fix."

I turned to Frede, who was leaning against the side of the capsule, mopping her sweaty face. "How can we—"

"Here they come!" yelped Dyer. And a grenade went off at her feet, blowing her legs off.

Chapter 29

I grabbed for my rifle and raced to the hatch just as a Skorpis warrior stepped through, pistol in one hand, grenade in the other. My senses were so hyper that I could see the slits of his irises moving in his eyeballs as he raised his arm to throw the grenade into our midst.

I fired and the grenade exploded in his hand, hot shrapnel streaking through the transceiver bay. I was knocked off my feet by the blast, my arm and chest stung by searing bits of sharp metal. Most of my crew were already diving to the deck. Magro ducked behind the transceiver console as several shards of shrapnel peppered its plastic stand.

The bulkhead along the passageway began to glow a dull red and I realized that the Skorpis were doing what we had done: burning their way through the bulkhead.

"Get them away from the hatch!" I bellowed, scrambling to my feet. Automatically I closed down the pain receptors and tightened the blood vessels where I had been hit.

Almost a dozen rifle beams converged on the hatch, driving the Skorpis away from it. I raced to it, dived onto my belly and skidded partway out into the passage, firing point-blank at the armored warriors grouped around the hatch.

Someone yanked at my ankles and pulled me back into the relative safety of the bay. I kicked free and yelled, "We've got to clear the passageway of them! Otherwise they'll burn through the bulkhead and pour in here!"

We made the hatchway our bastion. Kneeling, lying prone, standing along its curved metal rim, we fired into the passageway and drove the Skorpis back. They were on both sides of the hatch, coming at us from both ends of the passage. We cut down the warriors who were trying to burn through the bulkhead and drove their cohorts back out of range of our rifles.

But they came at us again, behind a barrage of rocket grenades. There were so many that I could pick off fewer than half of them before they exploded in showers of fragments that forced us away from the hatch. I saw my crew mates fall, chests ripped open, blood spewing, faces screaming in the sudden realization of death.

We backed away and the Skorpis resumed cutting open the bulkhead. I saw it all in slow motion, firing, shouting, men and women sinking to their knees, Skorpis warriors in their armored space suits falling as they shot at us, the bulkhead separating us from the passageway glowing cherry red under their laser torches. We retreated to the cryo capsule and hid behind it, hugging its massive flank for protection as the bulkhead finally crashed down in three separate places and scores of Skorpis warriors poured in upon us.

Their laser bolts splashed off the engraved flank of the cryo capsule, making its surface hot to touch. They were too close to us to use grenades without killing themselves, but they advanced, a centimeter at a time, past the bodies of their own dead, crawling along the deck plates to get at us.

I saw that they were trying to outflank us, get around to the sides of the chamber where we would not have the cryo capsule between ourselves and them. I fired at them until my rifle went dead, then started using my pistol.

"We've got to get out of here!" I shouted into Frede's ear.

"Good thinking," she snapped. "How?"

"Transceiver."

"Not me!" She shook her head as she sprayed a quartet of Skorpis warriors with burning laser fire.

"We're dead if we don't."

"We're dead if we do. I don't care if a copy of me lands on Loris."

But I was thinking of Anya. She knew that coming to Loris would mean throwing herself on Aten's mercy. She knew that surrendering to the Commonwealth could mean final, utter, irretrievable death for her. Yet she had come, she had insisted on this desperate gamble for peace, because she wanted to stop the war. I had thought that she—like the other Creators—cared only for their own safety. But now I realized that she also cared about the billions of humans who were enmeshed in this endless killing. She wanted to face Aten and stop the war, no matter what the cost to herself.

And I would do everything I could, anything I could, to help her.

I glanced at the control console. Magro lay at its foot in a pool of blood.

"You don't even know where the planet is anymore," Frede insisted. "You can't jump blind!"

"It's our only chance."

"Orion, don't!" Frede warned.

"We're already dead," I shouted into her ear, over the blasts of the guns and the screams of the fighting, half-crazed humans and Skorpis. "What difference does it make?"

"I'll take down as many of these damned cats as I can," Frede shouted back. "I won't take the coward's way out."

That was her training, I knew. The programming the army pumped into her brain while she was in cryosleep. Fight as long as you can. Take as many of the enemy as possible. Never surrender.

"I've got to try," I said.

She put the muzzle of her rifle under my chin. It was burning hot. "Stay and fight, Orion."

"You'd shoot me?"

"I'd shoot any coward who tried to run away."

Out of the corner of my eye I saw that three Skorpis

warriors were trying to edge across the bay and flank us again. They were dragging the bodies of fallen warriors to shield them.

"There!" I yelled, and fired at them. Frede's heavier rifle beam burned through one of the corpses and hit the warrior behind it. I hit another on the top of his helmet. The third scampered backward, back toward the protection of his mates.

And I jumped out from behind the cryo capsule, crabbing sideways to Magro's body and the slim protection of the console stand. As I raised my head high enough to look at the console instruments, I saw Frede aim her rifle at me.

Time froze. I did not blame her for wanting to kill me. As far as she was concerned, I was killing her. Matter transmission destroyed the thing being sent and assembled a copy of it elsewhere. Did it matter if the Skorpis killed us or the transceiver did? I punched the key that activated the transceiver as I stared at Frede, who locked her finger on the rifle's trigger.

But did not fire.

Everything went black. I recognized the blast of deathly cold that enveloped me. And I realized for the first time that the translations through the continuum that I had undergone were forms of matter transmission; the transceivers being used in this era were actually primitive forerunners of the capabilities that Aten and the other Creators used at their whim.

I had used them, too. Without knowing how it was done, knowing only how to direct such energies, I had translated myself across the continuum more than once.

Now, in this moment of absolute nothingness, I realized that I had to control not only my own translation through space-time, but those of all the others, as well. And I realized something more: Every time I had died and been revived by the Golden One—it was no revival at all. He merely built new copies of me. When I died, that person died forever, as completely and finally as the lowliest earthworm dies. A new Orion was created by the Golden One to do his bidding, and given

the memories that Aten thought he should have. I laughed in
the soundless infinity of the void. I was not immortal at all;
merely copied.

But that meant that Aten and the other Creators were no
more immortal than I. They could die. They could be killed.
Anya would die, unless I found a way to save her.

That way lay on the planet Loris, capital of the Commonwealth, where Aten directed the war.

I saw Loris in my mind, an Earthlike planet of blue
oceans and white clouds. I reached out mentally and sensed
Frede and the others of my crew. And Anya, frozen in sleep
inside the cryonic capsule.

Distantly, I sensed others observing me. The Creators?
Aten? No, I did not feel the snide derision of the Golden One
or the haughty disdain of his fellow Creators. It was the Old
Ones reaching to me. I felt the warmth of their approval, the
strength of their help. This one time they were actually un-
bending from their aloofness to help me.

"Loris," I said without words, without sound or the body
to speak with. Into the blank emptiness of the void between
space-times, I gathered Anya and my crew and willed us to the
planet Loris.

Chapter 30

Voices struck at me.

"What is it?"

"How can it be?"

"They just—appeared! Pop! Just like that."

I opened my eyes, glad that I had eyes and ears and an existence in the world again.

We were in a wide, sunny city plaza, what was left of us. Frede still leaned against the cryo capsule, pointing her rifle at me. The others of my crew were slumped against the capsule's curved flank. The side that had faced the Skorpis's guns was so hot that it steamed in the afternoon air.

The plaza was filled with people. Well-dressed men and women. The buildings that lined the spacious open square were all graceful towers of glass and gleaming metal. The square was paved with colorful tiles. A fountain sprayed water barely a dozen meters from where we had landed. The people gaped at us as if we were ghosts or some strange alien apparition. More people were gathering around us, talking, pointing, staring.

We were a grimy crew. Bloody, sweaty, aching and parched from our deadly battle. Eighteen of us still alive. Our uniforms were torn, our faces streaked with dirt.

"Who are they?" an elderly woman asked.

"How dare they show themselves here?"

"I think they're *soldiers!*"

"Soldiers? You mean, from the army?"

"What are they doing here?"

"They must be soldiers of some sort. Look at the guns they're carrying."

"You're not permitted to carry weapons in the capital," a cross-faced man shouted at us. "I've summoned the police."

"They smell terrible!"

"Yes, we smell terrible and we look terrible," I shouted at them. "We've been fighting and dying to save you from being invaded."

They gasped.

"He's insane!"

"The whole group—look at them! Obvious lunatics."

"Where are the police? I called for them more than a minute ago."

I couldn't believe what I was seeing and hearing. "Don't you realize there's a battle going on in orbit above you? Don't you know you're at war?"

"It's some sort of trick."

"New theater. The younger generation always tries to shock their elders."

One of the gray-haired women stepped up to me, barely as tall as my collarbone. "See here, young man, there's no use trying to frighten us. The war is being fought a thousand light-years away from here."

I shook my head in a combination of disbelief and disgust, then turned away from her and went over to what was left of my crew.

Frede and the rest of my crew were just as stunned as the civilians. She lowered her rifle, slumped against the sleep capsule and let herself slide down to a sitting position. The others sprawled, exhausted, on the brightly colored tile pavement.

"This is Loris?" Frede asked.

I nodded. "The capital of the Commonwealth."

One of the men came over and glared at me. "You can't

stay here," he told me sternly. "This is a public plaza, not an army barracks."

"Where do you suggest we go?" I asked, controlling my temper.

"That's not for me to decide. But—Ah! Here come the police, at last."

The crowd made a path for a pair of gleaming robots that glided on flight packs a few centimeters above the pavement. Legless, they had six arms, cylindrical torsos, and domed heads that bore sensors and speaker grilles.

"Please identify yourselves," said the one on my left.

"We are the survivors of the crew of the scout ship *Apollo,*" I said. "We escaped the battle—"

"One moment, please." The robot put out one clawed hand in a very human gesture. Then it said, "Records indicate that the *Apollo* is on a mission to the Jilbert system. Please identify yourselves."

"We never got to the Jilbert system," I said, starting to feel odd arguing with a machine. "We got involved in the battle now going on here."

"There is no battle under way here."

"In orbit." I pointed overhead.

The crowd murmured at that. I wondered if any of them would take the trouble to look at the sky after dark, when the exploding spacecraft could be seen as flashes of light among the stars.

If a robot could glare, this one did. "Please come with me."

"Where?"

"To higher authority."

Of course, I thought. Where else? Then I pointed to the cryo unit. "This capsule can't be left here. It should be brought to a hospital or—"

"The object will be taken into custody and brought to a proper facility."

"We go with it," I said.

"You will come with us," the robot replied. "The object will be taken by others to a proper facility."

I rested my hand on the butt of my pistol. Frede and my crew got slowly to their feet, unlimbering their weapons. The crowd faded back from us.

"We were assigned to guard this capsule," I lied. "We have carried it across many light-years and fought overwhelming odds to bring it here safely. We will not leave it in a public square for some garbage truck to pick up."

The robot buzzed to itself for several moments. I noticed that its partner edged off to my right slightly, as if to catch me in a crossfire if any shooting started. Little Jerron, half his tunic torn away and his skin blackened with laser burns, stepped up to it and nudged it with the muzzle of his rifle. It stopped and hovered, buzzing loudly.

"A trained and experienced medical team is on its way to handle the capsule," the first robot said. "It will be dealt with properly."

"Good," I replied. "We'll wait for them to arrive; then we will go with you."

Within minutes three aircars glided across the square and landed gently about fifty meters from us. The crowd muttered and chattered as a team of humans climbed out of the cars. One group wore medical whites. The others were in blue, and armed with pistols and stubby rifles.

"I am Captain Perry of the capital police," said one of the blue uniforms. He was almost my height, stocky, muscular. His curly dark hair flowed to his collar; his face was square, with a pugnacious button of a nose in its middle.

"I am Orion, captain of the *Apollo*. We've brought this cryo capsule from Prime, the Hegemony capital. It bears one of the Hegemony's top leaders, who has come here to discuss peace terms."

"While the whole Skorpis fleet is trying to obliterate our defenses?" Perry almost snarled the words.

I fell back on the time-honored refuge of the soldier. "I'm just following my orders, Captain." It was a lie, but it would work—for the time being.

He tried to stare me down, and when that didn't work he said, "All right, we'll take the capsule to our medical facility. But first you'll have to give up your weapons."

I shook my head. "We're soldiers, Captain. We will surrender our weapons to the proper army authorities, no one else."

"On this planet, the police have the authority to disarm anyone carrying a weapon."

"Find an army officer to order us, and we'll disarm," I said.

Clearly unhappy with us, Perry ordered the medics to attach flight packs to Anya's capsule and slide it into their car. Then he bundled my crew into the two police cars. Eight of them went with Frede; I led the remaining nine into the car with Perry. It was a tight squeeze for us all, especially with the rifles poking ribs.

As I strapped myself in beside Captain Perry I heard the robot police officers telling the crowd, "Please disperse. You are impeding traffic flow."

Like good little citizens, they broke up and went their separate ways, buzzing among themselves about this strange event.

All three aircars lifted off the pavement and started down one of the narrow canyons between the glass and metal towers. We climbed above the towers and I could see the city spread out beneath me, a neat geometrical gridwork of straight streets dotted with plazas and green parks.

The white medical car peeled off and headed in a different direction.

"Wait!" I said to Captain Perry. "We're going with the capsule."

"No, you're not," he said tightly. "The capsule's going to the med labs, where it will be examined and tested."

"But—"

"You and your crew are going to an interrogation center. We checked your story. The *Apollo* was sent to the Jilbert system, more than seven hundred light-years from here. Either you're lying or you're a band of traitors. Either way, we'll get the truth out of you."

I slid the pistol from my holster and nudged it under his chin.

Perry's eyes went wide. "Are you crazy?"

"Call it battle fatigue," I said. "Either we go with the capsule or your brains get splattered on the overhead."

The other police officers in the car gripped their weapons. So did my crew. The driver was the only one without a gun in his hands; he clung to the control wheel, gulped and stared straight ahead.

"You'll kill all of us!" Perry snapped.

"That includes you."

He huffed, then said to the driver, "Follow the medic van."

We turned and went after the white aircar.

"They'll hang you by the balls for this, Orion," Perry said. "And I'll be there to cheer them on."

"After the capsule's properly taken care of," I told him, "then we can see whose balls get stretched."

The medical center was a trap.

We landed in the marked pad in the middle of four towering buildings, all three aircars touching down virtually at the same instant. As we climbed out of the cars, four full squads of Tsihn soldiery stepped out of the doors on all four sides of us, guns leveled.

"Lizards!" I heard Frede growl.

"You will drop your weapons, humans," said the Tsihn leader, a huge ocher-colored reptilian whose chest and arms were covered with insignia and decorations.

For a long silent moment we stood there confronting each other.

"I am Colonel Hrass-shleessa," the big reptilian said. "I am duly authorized to command you. Put your weapons on the ground or we will fire."

I glanced sideways at Captain Perry. He did not relish the idea of being caught in a firefight between us and the Tsihn.

We were hopelessly outnumbered. "They'll kill us all," Jerron grumbled. "Damned lizards."

"Put your guns down," I commanded my crew. "We will obey the colonel's order." I had no choice but to be an obedient soldier.

They marched us into another aircar while a medical team guided Anya's capsule, floating on its flight packs, into one of the buildings. This aircar was army brown, and built more like a truck. We were bundled into the back, seated on the two benches running along its sides. I caught a glimpse of Captain Perry standing next to his own aircar as they slammed the hatch shut in my face. He was grinning at me, a malicious grin of triumph.

We flew out of the city, into the mountains to its west, for more than an hour. With nothing else to do, most of my crew flaked out and drowsed. I sat on the hard bucket seat and thought of the crew members who weren't with us anymore: bloodied Emon, Dyer with her legs blown away, so many others. Don't make friends, I told myself. A combat soldier shouldn't make any personal attachments.

We were flown to an army detention center out in the cold, gray mountains. Human prisoners and Tsihn guards. I bristled at the reptilians; every instinct in me told me they were the enemies of humankind. And here in this detention center that certainly seemed so.

They separated me from Frede and the rest of the crew, showed me to a bare little windowless cell. Nothing but a cot, sink and toilet. And a lightbulb set into the concrete ceiling, too high for me to reach.

I was not in the cell for long, however. A pair of Tsihn guards unlocked my door and escorted me to a room where a junior Tsihn officer—its scales were pale lemon and bore hardly any decorations at all—sat on a high stool that was the only piece of furniture visible.

"You will sit," it said to me.

I lowered myself to the concrete floor. It felt cold, clammy. My two guards remained standing by the door.

Satisfied that he could loom over me, the Tsihn officer leaned toward me and asked, "Who are you and where are you from?"

"My name is Orion. I was captain of the *Apollo*."

It bared its teeth. "The *Apollo* was sent to the Jilbert system."

"We never got there. We went to Prime, instead, and brought one of the Hegemony's topmost leaders here to discuss peace terms with the Commonwealth's leadership."

It snorted. I could see the humid air huffing from its nostrils. "Orion, you say your name is?"

"Yes."

"There is no record of you in the Commonwealth military files."

That surprised me only slightly. "Check with Brigadier Uxley at sector station six," I said. "He knows me. Check with my crew; we've done a lot of fighting together. Lunga, Bititu, the battle going on now in orbit."

"That battle is finished," it said grandly. "The Skorpis fleet has been driven off."

"Good."

Those red slitted eyes stared at me. "You see, to me all you humans look alike. How can we tell if you are truly a Commonwealth soldier or a Hegemony spy? The same applies to your crew, as well."

I realized that my true story would sound ludicrously

fraudulent to it. "You have brainwave scanners, don't you? You can easily see if I'm telling the truth."

"Ah, the truth," breathed my reptilian interrogator, almost like a human professor of philosophy. "What is the truth, Orion? You could tell me a tale that you believe to be true, and yet it might simply be a set of memories implanted in your mind by Hegemony intelligence operatives."

I shrugged. "Then what's the point of this questioning?"

It cocked its lizard's head to one side. "Why, to hear what you have to say. To determine if there is any valuable information in your story. That's the least we can do before we execute you and your crew."

Chapter 31

So I told my Tsihn interrogator my whole story, even the truth about Aten and the other Creators. It listened with great interest, I thought, although it was impossible to read any expression on its reptilian face. But it was polite and even seemed curious, interrupting me with questions time and again.

All through my long narration, though, a part of my mind kept repeating to me that they were going to kill me. Kill Frede and Jerron and the rest of my crew. Why? Why execute loyal soldiers who had fought so hard for them?

It was my fault. I had disobeyed orders and taken them to Prime. As far as the Commonwealth was concerned, I was a traitor, and very likely a spy from the Hegemony. My crew was going to die because of me.

But then I began to think of the other factors. Somewhere in this mess was Aten, the Golden One, trying to manipulate the humans, their allies, their enemies, even the other Creators. He would kill Anya now that he had her in his possession. And I had delivered her to him.

"He'll kill you, too," I told my interrogator.

The young Tsihn blinked its yellow eyes. "What do you mean by that?"

"Aten doesn't want his creatures to know that he is manipulating them. He doesn't want the Commonwealth to know that this war is being fought because of an argument among the Creators."

The Tsihn officer was silent for a long moment. Then it said, "Either you are a very creative liar, Orion, or an absolute psychotic. Your invention of the Creators has some aspect of poetry to it, I must admit, but you carry it too far."

"He'll kill you to keep my story from leaking out," I said.

"I am not one of his creatures—if he exists at all."

"How many Tsihn have died in this war? How many more will be killed?"

"That's enough, Orion," said the reptilian. "This session is finished."

I climbed to my feet, legs tingling from sitting so long. "Your life is now in danger," I told it. Jerking a thumb toward the guards at the door, I added, "Theirs, too."

The Tsihn remained on his stool, barely eye level with me. "Nonsense," it scoffed.

"Is it? I presume this session has been recorded, even though I don't see any equipment."

Its eyes darted to a corner of the ceiling.

"Play back the recording. See if it's intact. I'll bet it's already been erased."

"Nonsense," it said again. But it sounded just a bit weaker to me. It ordered the guards to take me back to my cell. They said not a word to me.

As the cell door slammed behind me, I knew there was only one person who could save my crew from execution. I threw myself on the bare thongs of the cot and squeezed my eyes shut in concentration. Aten was nearby; I could feel his presence, almost smell him.

But he refused to make contact with me. As I tried, I sensed a blank wall, like an energy screen he had built around himself to keep me away from him.

Very well, then. I went elsewhere. I gathered my strength

and my knowledge and tried to contact the Old Ones. I called across the light-years for their aid, their wisdom.

Stop the war, Orion, they told me.

"How? What can I do? I can't even protect my own crew; we're all going to be executed."

Find the strength, they said.

"Help me," I pleaded. "If you want this war to be stopped, then help me."

A vague sigh of disappointment. *It is your problem, Orion, not ours. The problem of the human race. We will not make ourselves your guardians, your conscience, your protectors. You must do it for yourselves.*

"You would exterminate us," I countered.

Only if you become a threat to stars themselves. We have no right to interfere unless you begin to threaten the life of the entire galaxy with your violence.

And they showed me why they were concerned. I saw whole stars exploding, one after another. In a closely packed star cluster, a chain reaction began, dozens of stars erupting into shattering cataclysm, the shock waves from each explosion triggering dozens more, hundreds more. I saw whole galaxies torn apart by titanic explosions at their cores that engulfed millions of stars, tens of millions of planets, countless living creatures. Whole civilizations, intelligent species that had struggled for millennia to reach out among the stars, wiped out in smothering waves of explosions that ripped across megaparsecs, destroying everything in their path, reducing flesh and mind and hope to wildly contorted clouds of ionized gas.

This has been done in other galaxies by intelligences very much like your own, the Old Ones told me. *This we cannot permit here. We have no desire to be your guardian angels, Orion, but we will be your angels of death if you try to destroy the stars.*

I opened my eyes and found myself still in my cell, alone, abandoned by the Old Ones, shunned by the Creators, without even a rat to keep me company. Somewhere the Tsihn were interrogating Frede and the others, I knew. Somewhere an execution squad was waiting for us. I wondered if Captain Perry would be invited to watch.

Anya. I reached out for her, to the cryonic capsule where she slept, still frozen, barely alive, her mind pulsing so slowly as the last dregs of her strength ebbed away that I could not feel even a flicker of her presence. I sensed a team of technicians probing her capsule, trying to decide whether they should attempt to revive her or just shut down the cryonic systems and let her die.

"Somebody's gone to a lot of trouble for nothing," one of the techs said. "This capsule's empty."

Empty!

"How could it be empty?" asked the tech's supervisor. "Those soldiers brought it all the way from Prime, they said."

"Take a look. X rays, magnetic resonance, neutrino scan—there's nobody inside this capsule. It's empty."

With a bellow of rage there in my cell I realized that the Golden One had outwitted me once again. He had removed Anya's dying body from the capsule. He had her in his possession. Perhaps she was already dead.

I leaped to my feet and roared like a jungle animal. I howled and threw myself at the heavy door of my cell. Its reinforced steel barely quivered at my pounding. I slid to the concrete floor and leaned my head against the door. Everything we had done, all the blood and killing, all the dead and wounded we had suffered—all for nothing. Aten had Anya in his grasp and we were going to be executed and there was no one in the whole continuum who would help me.

Use your brain, friend Orion, I heard the Old Ones whisper. *Your strength does not avail you now. You must use your intelligence.*

Wonderful advice. Locked in a prison cell, lost and abandoned. I butted my head softly against the door. How could I get out of here? And what should I do, if I could get out?

I could translate myself to another point in space-time, travel across the continuum to another era, light-years away from here. But what good would that do? I had to save my crew. I had to stop the war. I had to rescue Anya, if she still lived.

I closed my eyes. Somewhere in the galaxy, I realized, there is a matter transceiver that the Creators use for their travels across space-time. It must be enormously powerful, compared to the transceivers we are using in this era. Powered by a star, I guessed, or perhaps even a whole cluster of stars. It extends into the continuum, flickers across space-time so that the Creators can tap into its energies and translate themselves whenever and wherever they are. I myself have used that transceiver without even realizing that it existed. The Creators' mystical tricks are nothing more than very advanced technology, after all.

And what they can do, I told myself, I can do.

Is that so? a sneering voice in my mind challenged. The echo of Aten's arrogant disdain.

I pushed myself to my feet, there in my cell. "Yes, it is so," I said aloud, hoping that Aten could hear me, wanting him to see what I was about to do.

I felt the stupendous energy of that immense transceiver pulsating across the waves of space-time, rippling through the continuum like a steady, strong heartbeat. I tapped into that energy, not blindly as I had before, but purposefully, knowingly.

I reached into the cells in this prison where the rest of my crew were being held. I searched across the capital city, across the entire planet of Loris, and found all the members of the Commonwealth's High Council. I extended my awareness across light-years to Prime and located all the members of the Hegemony's Central Command.

I brought them all together, at the place and time of my choosing: the primeval forest of Paradise on Earth, at the end of the last Ice Age.

As I translated my crew there I decked them in dress uniforms of blue and gold and gave each of them a sidearm in a white leather holster. The politicians of the Commonwealth and Hegemony came as they were, some in street clothes, some in sleepwear, one in swimming trunks, another in nothing but a bath towel. Not all of them were human, of course. Tsihn reptilians joined my meeting, as did Skorpis generals and several other alien species, including a clutch of Arachnoids.

I arranged a clearing in the forest with a long conference table in its middle. The politicians I placed in chairs along the table, Commonwealth on one side, Hegemony on the other. I set up a ten-meter-high web at the foot of the table for the Arachnoids to cling to. I put scratchpads on the table for the Skorpis and water sprayers for the one amphibian species.

There was a considerable uproar, of course. Humans and aliens alike yelled, screeched, thundered a thousand questions at one another. They ignored me as I stood at the head of the table in a uniform of blood red, my arms folded across my chest. My own crew seemed just as startled and confused as the rest.

I let the politicians babble and called Frede to my side.

"What is this?" she asked, breathless, her eyes wide with stunned surprise. "How did you—"

"I'll explain later," I said. "Right now I want you and the rest of the crew to serve as a guard of honor. And to make sure that none of these politicians leave the table."

Frede blinked twice, a thousand questions in her eyes. But she turned without another word and set up the crew at parade rest evenly spaced around the table, their backs to the trees and flowering foliage of Paradise.

The politicians were still jabbering and bickering among themselves, hurling accusations across the table.

I took the pistol from my red leather holster and fired a sizzling laser beam down the length of the table, burning a hole in its end just short of the Arachnoid web. They all jerked back, shocked into silence.

I smiled at them and put the pistol away as I said, "You're probably wondering why I asked you here this morning."

"Who are you?"

"Where are we?"

I held up my hands to silence them before any more questions could be asked.

"We are on Earth, at a time approximately twelve and a half millennia earlier than your own era."

"Nonsense!"

"A patent lie, no one can travel across time. Our scientists have tried it and—"

"Shut up!" I snapped in my best military voice of command.

They shut up.

"You don't have to believe a word I say," I told them. "That doesn't matter at all. What does matter is this: You are going to sit at this table until you have hammered out an agreement to end the war."

They stirred at that.

"I don't care if take days or years. No one leaves this time and place until you have agreed on peace. Once you do, you will be returned precisely to the times and places you were when I brought you here."

"And what do you propose to do if we refuse to discuss peace?" asked the biggest Tsihn there, a real dragon with multihued scales encrusted with decorations.

"I will shoot you, one at a time, until you do begin meaningful discussions."

Half of them leaped to their feet, shouting.

"How dare you?"

"You can't—you wouldn't!"

But they saw my troopers standing behind them, saw the guns at their waists, the grim smiles on their youthful-yet-aged faces.

"You will make peace or you will die," I said sternly.

"Just as you send your soldiers to be killed in battle, now you can face death yourselves."

"You would kill unarmed civilians?"

"Who killed the people of Yellowflower?" I asked. "Who wiped out the Hegemony colonies? Who gave the orders?"

They sank back into their chairs.

"Listen to me," I urged them. "If the war goes on, one side or the other will begin to use star-wrecking weapons. When you come to that point, the older species of the galaxy will annihilate all of you, without mercy and without remorse. You will all be exterminated like vermin."

That started them arguing. I assured them of the Old Ones' resolve. "Weapons powerful enough to destroy whole stars can set up chain reactions that can destroy much of the galaxy, perhaps the entire galaxy. That will not be permitted."

"Who are you to make such threats?"

I smiled coldly. "In a sense, I am the ambassador from the Old Ones and the other ancient species of this galaxy. They have remained aloof from us because we are too young and too ignorant to be of interest to them. But now that we threaten the existence of the galaxy, they have no choice but to take notice of us—and take action."

They did not want to believe me, but after long hours of debate and argument they began to accept what I told them. The sun sank behind the lofty trees and night came on. I kept them at the table, protected and warmed by a bubble of energy. I produced food and allowed them to leave the table briefly, knowing that there was no place in this continent-wide forest that they could escape to.

"No one returns to their own time and place until a peace agreement has been reached," I said.

Days went by. They argued, they railed at each other, they hurled accusations and threats across the table. I reminded them that unless they began working toward peace I would begin shooting them. And I pointed to the loudest of the loudmouths.

"You'll go first," I said.

His eyes widened, but he stopped his insults and imprecations.

It was like a giant group-therapy session. It took time for them to air their true resentments, their real fears. They accused one another of all sorts of aggressions and atrocities, at first. But gradually, knowing that there was no alternative, knowing that they themselves were facing death, they began to get to the underlying causes of the war.

I knew that the real cause was the manipulations of the Creators. No matter what these humans and aliens agreed upon, the Creators could upset it in the blink of an eye. I realized that after I had finished with these politicians, I would have to face the Creators. Led by Aten, the Golden One.

I was surprised that he did not show himself here, even indirectly, disguised as one of the politicians. Probably he was content to let me work out a peace agreement, and then rip it to shreds before it could be implemented. He enjoyed playing with the human race that way, toying with us, tempting us and then degrading us when we reached for greatness. Like flies to wanton boys, I thought. Except that this fly has no intention of allowing any god to pull its wings off. Not now that I've learned how to use them.

Chapter 32

It took weeks. Seven weeks, plus two days. A hundred times or more I thought my imposed peace conference would see a murder across the conference table. A thousand times the politicians blustered at one another, hurled accusations, threats, turned to me and blistered the air with their rage, promising to flay me alive once they got back to their own worlds.

Each time I told them that no one would leave this time and place until they had agreed upon peace, with a treaty that they all endorsed, a treaty that bound them all to stop the war. And I warned them that if they could not end the war, they would become casualties themselves.

A dozen times they came close, only to have the agreement shattered on some objection, some grievance, some seemingly impossible demand.

But slowly, grudgingly, they inched toward the agreement that I demanded. I used no force, except the threat of execution. That was enough to keep them at their work. I fed them and allowed them to refresh themselves from time to time. I allowed them to sleep when they needed to, although that caused some complications because the Skorpis preferred to sleep in the daytime and the Tsihn and humans at night. The Arachnoids did not seem to sleep at all. But always I brought them back to that conference table, like dragging a puppy to the paper it is supposed to use when you are training it.

After fifty-one days they had the agreement on paper. They were exhausted, all of them, by the effort. But where they had started, fifty-one days earlier, as enemies and strangers across the table, now they knew each other, perhaps even respected each other. Even the incommunicative Arachnoids had used the translating machines I gave them to make certain that their needs and desires were addressed in the treaty.

They were about to sign the document when I made the final objection.

"There is one problem that the human members of this conference have not addressed," I said from the head of the long table.

"What is that?" they demanded.

"Your armies. Your soldiers. What do you intend to do with them?"

The humans on both sides of the table glanced at one another. "Why, put them back in cryonic storage, of course. What else can we do with them?"

"Let them live," I said.

"They don't know how to live! They've been bred for soldiering and that's all they know."

"Find worlds that are not occupied and let them settle on them. You owe them that much."

"They won't know how to survive. The skills of farming and building and living peacefully have never been part of their training."

"Then train them," I said firmly. "Train them as you fly them out to these new worlds."

"They would die off in a single generation," a gruff-faced man pointed out. "They're all sterile; bred that way, you know."

"They can make children through cloning, the way you made them. And their children needn't be sterile."

"But if we sent the troops off to other planets, that would disarm us," one of the women objected. "We would have no army to protect us in case of future need."

"Let your own children train for soldiering," I said. "Defend yourselves."

"That's a ghastly idea! My children, soldiers?"

I leaned on the table with both hands. "Only when your own children are soldiers will you understand that war is not something you play at. These men and women have fought for you and you've rewarded them with *nothing*. No rights, no privileges, nothing in all their lives to look forward to except more fighting."

"But they were bred for that! They don't know anything except the army."

"They know that they want to live. They know that they want more than the prospect of pain and blood and killing. They are human beings, just as human as you are. You must accept them as such."

"It's impossible," someone muttered.

"Do you have any idea of what it would cost to settle our soldiers on new worlds?"

"Ask our own children to join the military?"

I said, "That is my demand for this peace treaty. It is not negotiable. You will release your soldiers from their slavery and allow them to lead peaceful lives."

"That is simply not possible. It can't be done."

I replied, "It will be done, or you'll spend the rest of your lives at this table."

"Now, really!"

"You will learn, in some small way, what it's like to have nothing to look forward to. You will stay here until you realize that this form of slavery is no longer to be tolerated."

One of the Skorpis said, "If you humans are worried that you will have no one to protect you, we can be hired to serve as your army.

"The Tsihn have a long tradition of honoring military prowess," said the largest reptilian. "We could certainly make military arrangements with the Commonwealth." It turned its slitted eyes across the table. "Or with the Hegemony, once we have agreed to end the present war."

Several of the humans objected to hiring mercenaries or placing their safety in the hands of aliens on the strength of diplomatic agreements. Others shuddered at the thought of having their own children put on military uniforms.

"May I say a word or two?" Frede asked, from her station to one side of the table.

The politicians all turned to her, surprised to hear a military officer ask for permission to speak. Since the earliest days of this enforced conference, they had taken their guards for granted, as much a part of the background as the trees or energy bubble that protected us from the weather.

"I know that every soldier would be very grateful for the chance to start a new life, in peace. Maybe we don't know anything except soldiering, but that includes a lot of survival skills, and we'd be happy for a chance to learn how to live normal lives. And—well, if you need us, we'd still be available."

"You would leave your new homes and fight for the Commonwealth, if we called you?"

"If it's necessary," Frede said. "You'd have to tell us why it's necessary."

"The human armies of the Hegemony undoubtedly feel the same way," I added.

It took further hours of debate. The humans asked to discuss the matter among themselves, and for the first time Commonwealth and Hegemony men and women walked off together, talking earnestly, trying to find a solution to a common problem.

The Tsihn reptilians seemed puzzled by my demand. "Why not freeze them if you don't need them?" one of the lizards asked me.

"Because they are human beings," I replied, "and entitled to all the rights that any other humans possess."

A Skorpis commander shook her feline head. "Humans

lon't understand the way of the warrior. They regard the warrior as an inferior person, a slave."

"Regrettable," said the Tsihn.

"That attitude is about to change," I said.

"And we are all being held hostage here until it does," the Skorpis commander replied.

"Regrettable," the Tsihn repeated. I wondered if that was its idea of humor.

Neither the Commonwealth humans nor those of the Hegemony liked it, but at last they agreed to my demand: the existing human armies would remain alive and be resettled on unoccupied planets.

We had peace within our grasp. But only if I could make the Creators agree to it, I knew.

I returned the politicians to their homes, precisely to the times when I had kidnapped them. Frede and the other soldiers gaped when the whole group of them disappeared, together with their conference table and everything else.

"Matter transmission," I told them.

They still shook their heads.

"I'm sending you back to Loris," I told them. Before they could object, I added, "But not to your prison cells. You'll be at the army base, in fairly luxurious quarters. If the politicians keep their word, the process of resettlement will begin soon."

"And if it doesn't?" Frede asked, with a veteran's skepticism.

"I'll come and get you," I said.

She gazed into my eyes. "Who in the name of the seven levels of hell are you, Orion?"

"A soldier, just like you."

"Dogshit you are."

I grinned at her. "I've just been around longer. I know more tricks."

"You're not coming back to Loris with us?"

"No, I've got another problem to tackle," I said.

She frowned slightly, then stepped up to me and, throw-

ing her arms around my neck, gave me a very unmilitary kiss.
"Thank you," Frede said. "Thanks for our lives."

I felt slightly flustered. The rest of the crew was grinning
at us. I called them all to attention, then sent them back to
Loris. They disappeared from the forest of Paradise as if they
had never been there.

I took in a deep breath. The real test was facing me now.
I translated myself to the city of the Creators.

This time I went right into the heart of the city, into its magnificent central square, bordered by temples from the highest
human civilizations: a Sumerian ziggurat, a Mayan pyramid,
the Parthenon in all of its original graceful beauty. The sun
shone brightly through the shimmering golden energy dome
that encased the Creators' city; I could feel the breeze from the
nearby sea wafting by.

They were all there, waiting for me, all of them in perfect
glowing health. All of them in splendid robes, a pantheon of
human physical perfection, the men handsome and grave, the
women stunning and equally solemn. All except Anya.

"Where is she?"

The Golden One stepped forward, regarded me somberly.

"Where is she?" I repeated.

"All in due time, Orion. We have other matters to discuss
first."

My left hand snapped out and I seized him by the throat,
pressing my thumb against his windpipe, forcing him to his
knees.

"Where is Anya?" I thundered. "What have you done to
her?"

The one I called Zeus snapped at me, "Release him at
once!" I saw burly Ares and several of the others advancing
upon me.

I tightened my grip on Aten's throat. "Take another step
and I'll snap his neck."

"What good would that do?" Zeus asked. "We will simply revive him."

"You'll copy him," I said. "This one here will never know it. He'll be dead."

Aten's eyes bulged up at me.

"Yes, I know your tricks. I know about matter transmission and the discontinuities you've created in the continuum. I know that you regard mortal humans as less than the dirt beneath your feet."

"That's not true, Orion," said green-eyed Aphrodite. "We care for our creatures."

I flung Aten to the ground. What was the point of killing him? They would simply make another.

But a murderous anger was surging through me. "Gods, you call yourselves? Liars! Imposters! Murderers! You're nothing but a pack of ravening madmen."

"You go too far," Hera said. I remembered when she styled herself Olympias, the mother of Alexander the Great, the woman who engineered the assassination of her husband, Philip, king of Macedon.

Aten glared up at me with a fury in his eyes to match my own. "If you want to find your precious Anya," he croaked, rubbing at his throat, "you will have to settle with us first."

"What is there to settle?" I demanded. "The war is over—unless you godly murderers start it up again."

"The war is over," Hermes agreed, his gray eyes flicking to Zeus before he added, "We have settled our own differences; there's no need for further fighting among the humans."

I looked at Hermes, then at Zeus and Hera and all the others. My gaze finally returned to Aten, climbing back to his feet, glowering pure hatred at me.

"You must speak to the Old Ones for us," he said, his voice already healing from my throttling.

"Must I?"

Zeus said, "It is important that we establish friendly relations with them. Vital."

"Why?"

"The ultimate crisis, Orion!" said Hermes urgently. "It's here! There's no time to waste."

"You can travel across time and yet you say you have no time to waste? I don't understand."

The Golden One almost put on his old smugly superior sneer, but Zeus spoke before he could. "We are facing a crisis that may be beyond our power to solve. No matter how we move across the continuum, all the time tracks, all the geodesics are being warped beyond control."

I recalled the Old Ones telling me that every passage through the continuum creates disturbances, ripples in the fabric of space-time. Now, looking into the Creators' minds as they stood before me, I saw what they feared. They had torn that fabric with their meddling in the continuum, their egomaniacal desire to alter space-time to suit their own desires. Now those ripples were cascading, threatening a turbulence that could rip apart the continuum itself and shatter the universe into mangled shards of chaos. All the timestreams would be torn apart by a tidal wave of discontinuity, causality would be wiped out as the quantum fluctuations of matter/energy dissolved time itself into an endless, meaningless nothingness.

"It is worse than you know, Orion," raven-haired Istar said to me. "We are not the sole cause of the crisis."

Before her words fully registered on my mind, Zeus said, "There are others who manipulate the continuum. Their exploitations of space-time have been even more severe than our own."

"They must be stopped," Hera said.

"Before the whole continuum breaks apart," Hermes added.

I stared at them, trying to digest what they were telling me.

"It's the truth, Orion," said Aten, the Golden One, who had styled himself Apollo to the Greeks. "We are all in enormous danger; the entire universe is threatened."

"That's why you want the Old Ones," I realized. "You need their help."

Aten nodded. "Theirs, and the help of all the elder races in the galaxy."

"And this war that you put humankind through for three generations? Where you destroyed whole planets? And you were ready to destroy the stars themselves—what was the real purpose of it?"

Aten's golden eyes shifted away from mine momentarily, then he pulled himself to his full height and answered, "We disagreed about contacting the elder species, such as the Old Ones. I wanted to enlist their help; Anya and those of us who sided with her wanted to leave them alone."

"And for that you put the human race through a century of war? And dragged in all those alien races, as well?"

Some of the old arrogance came back into his expression. "Anya can be very stubborn."

"Where is she?"

"She refused to join us in this—" He hesitated, as if searching for a word. "—this peace conference."

"She was dying."

"I was trying to make her see things my way. It worked with the others." He gestured carelessly toward Poseidon, Aphrodite, and several of the other Creators. "But, as I said, Anya is very stubborn."

I suspected that there was more to it than he was telling me. "You say that she objected to contacting the Old Ones?"

"She thought we could face the ultimate crisis without their help."

I turned to Aphrodite. "Is that true?"

"Yes," she said. But as she spoke, her eyes were on the Golden One, not on me.

I looked at each of them in turn, finally resting my gaze

on Zeus. "What's the rest of it?" I asked him. "I know there must be more to this than I've been told so far."

He stroked his neatly trimmed beard for a moment, almost smiled at me. "Accept what Aten has told you, Orion. Help us to gain the trust of the Old Ones."

"How can I tell them to trust you when I myself can't?"

Aten's gold-flecked eyes blazed at me. "You'll never be revived again, Orion. You've outlived your usefulness if you don't help us get to the Old Ones."

Staring into those angry eyes, I thought I finally understood what they had refused to tell me.

"You don't want the Old Ones' help. You want their power. You want to learn what they know so you can use it for your own ends. You talk about the ultimate crisis, but you still dream of dominating everyone and everything, you still aspire to mastering the entire continuum."

Aten smiled coldly at me. "You've learned a lot since I first created you. Perhaps too much."

"Stop this masquerade," I demanded. "Show me the truth."

His smile faded. The sky overhead darkened; clouds boiled up out of the sea and swept by. The other Creators aged and withered before my eyes: Aphrodite's hair went dead white, her face wrinkled; Poseidon turned weak and trembling like a palsied old man; even Zeus and Hermes and Hera sank into decrepit gray-skinned wrecks.

Only Aten retained his youthful vigor. He even seemed stronger than before, glowing in the storm-clouded shadows like the sun.

And the Creators' city itself crumbled before my eyes. The temples turned to dust, the columns cracked and toppled to the ground. The earth shook. Lightning split the sky.

"You think you have learned so much, Orion," Aten sneered at me. "How little you know, creature!"

He waved one hand and the sky cleared as quickly as it had clouded. The other Creators had collapsed into heaps of rags and shriveling, decaying flesh in the midst of the ruined city.

And I recognized the ruins.

"Lunga!" I gasped. I could see past the rubble-strewn square, past the demolished stumps of towers and temples, out to the curving beach where the Skorpis base had been.

"Not Lunga," said the Golden One. "That was a bit of a deception I played on you, Orion."

I realized what he meant. "Earth. This is Earth. It never was Lunga, it was Earth all along."

"Far in the future," he said. "So far that the Moon has wandered away in its orbit until you can't even recognize it unless I point it out to you."

"Then the Old Ones are from Earth!"

"I doubt that. Perhaps from Neptune, originally, but not Earth. Some of them colonized Earth's oceans, apparently, long eons ago."

"Who destroyed your city?"

Smirking, "We did it ourselves. Another of our little family squabbles. No difference, we can build it up again when we're ready."

"And the other Creators? You've killed them all?"

"They're not dead, Orion. I'm merely demonstrating to them—and to you—that I am the mightiest of all. They bend to my will or I take their lives from them."

"That's what you did to Anya."

His face clouded. "She escaped me. Somehow, she got away. I suspect that you were responsible for that, Orion. In another era, another place-time, you rescued her."

I felt a surge of joy at that, not merely because I saved her, but because it angered and frustrated him.

"But I'm canceling that occurrence," the Golden One said. "I'm ending your existence, Orion. You've outlived your usefulness."

"And the Old Ones?" I taunted.

He cocked an eyebrow at me. "Ah yes, the Old Ones."

"You need them, don't you?"

"Not as much as I need to be rid of you," he said. "I created you to be my hunter, to do my bidding, but you've become more trouble than you're worth."

"You'd rather have the universe shatter into ultimate chaos than have Anya challenge your supremacy," I said.

His smile returned. "Better to reign in hell, Orion, than serve in heaven."

Once I thought I had wanted to die, to be released from life, freed of the endless wheel of pain and disappointment. But now I wanted to live, to find Anya and revive her, to reach the Old Ones and ask their help in saving the continuum from utter collapse, to stand in the way of Aten and keep him from realizing his megalomaniacal dreams.

"Götterdämmerung," I said.

"The twilight of the gods," he replied. "The downfall of everything. I will be supreme at the end."

"Never," I said, and translated myself out of the ruins of the Creators' city, away from Earth, far into the depths of interstellar space.

It felt like a death. Yet I knew I would live again to seek Anya, to fight against the Golden One, to find my place in the continuum.

Epilogue

It was a brown, arid world, but not without its beauty.

I stood on the crest of a dusty hill clawed by arroyos, looking out on a desert valley. Millions of years ago this had been sea bottom, but now the nearest body of open water was a thousand kilometers away. Yet there was life here: cactus and dry brown brush, poisonous lizards and tiny darting rodents with beady eyes and long hairless tails. Birds chattered from the few scrawny trees. Insects glinted in the harsh hot sunlight.

There was a patch of green down in that valley, with a village at its edge. A tiny knot of buildings made of sun-dried mud bricks, roofed with gnarled thin branches. Men and women were in the fields nearby, bent over their crops.

At first glance I did not notice any machinery, any sign that this human settlement was more advanced than the Stone Age. But then I caught the glint of sunlight on solar collectors atop the roof of a larger building. I saw a geodesic dome, a small one, but large enough to house a communications antenna.

There were no roads in sight, only footpaths out to the fields where the crops were growing.

I had nothing with me but the tatters of an old uniform and an ancient dagger that I kept strapped to my thigh. With a smile of satisfaction, I started down the eroded bare dirt of the hillside, heading for the village.

BEN BOVA

I arrived as the sun touched the western horizon and the workers were coming back from the fields.

They were startled to see a stranger.

"Who're you?" asked the young woman in their lead. She looked to be still in her teens. Sandy hair, sky blue eyes, a scattering of freckles across her pert nose.

"My name is Orion."

"Where're you from? How'd you get here?"

I waved a hand vaguely toward the hills. "I've come a long way. I'm glad I found your village."

She gave me a strange look, part suspicion, part curiosity.

"You said your name is Orion?"

"Does the name mean anything to you?" I asked.

She shook her head uncertainly. The others had gathered around us. I looked over their familiar faces. Clones of Frede, Magro, little Jerron. I saw that the oldest woman among them was pregnant.

"We don't get many visitors out here," Frede's daughter said to me. "Just inspectors from the Commonwealth, once every other year or so."

"What do you call this planet?" I asked them.

"Its official name is Krakon IV," said one of the teenaged boys.

"Yes, I know that. But what is your name for it?"

They glanced at each other. "We just call it Home."

I smiled at them. Home. Their faces were streaked with sweat and they looked tired from their day's work, but they seemed healthy and contented. Their clone parents had found a Home for themselves, far from the wars that they once knew.

"Well, come into the village," Frede's daughter said. "My mother and the elders will want to see you."

Healthy, contented, and not afraid of strangers. The whole village came out to see the new arrival: gray-haired adults, scampering children, young women holding babies in their arms.

Frede's eyes widened when she recognized me. She ran up and flung her arms around my neck.

"Orion!" she cried. "Orion!"

She could still embarrass me. Gently I untangled from her embrace, while the entire village watched, grinning.

"Why are you here?" she asked, suddenly wary. Her eyes were still bright and alert, although her hair had streaks of gray in it.

"I wanted to see how you're doing, nothing more."

She sighed with relief. They feasted me that night. I saw that the primitive look of the village was deliberate. They had decided to live with their environment as much as possible. Electricity from sunlight, engineered microbes to fix nitrogen for their crops and drive away insect pests, a self-contained nuclear pump to bring up water for irrigation.

"Maybe one day we'll build ourselves an aircar or two," Frede said as we sat at table in their main hall. "But for now, we can walk wherever we need to go."

"You seem contented."

She pointed to a young woman with a baby in her lap. "That infant's my granddaughter, Orion. Our second generation can bear children naturally."

Jerron had died, she told me, of a heart attack. "Magro's our medic now. He's got up-to-date equipment, but Jerron's heart just quit. Nothing anyone could do. We buried him out in the fields. He was our first death."

After dinner, Frede and I took a slow walk beneath the bright stars of their night sky.

"You mean you came all this way, to this lonely little frontier world, just to see us?"

"Why else?"

"I thought for a moment," she confessed, "that you'd come to recruit us as soldiers again."

"You're getting a bit old for that," I said.

"Our children aren't."

"There's no need for soldiers. The peace between the Commonwealth and the Hegemony has held for almost twenty years now."

"And you haven't aged a bit."

"I age much more slowly than you."

She was silent for a while as we walked out to the edge of their cultivated fields.

"You're on your way to find her, aren't you? The woman you love."

I nodded in the moonless dark. "Yes. I've got to find her, no matter how long it takes."

"Do you need help? Is that why you've come?"

"No, no. You can't help me. I've got to do this alone."

"Can't you stay here with us? With me?"

I looked down at her starlit face and saw that she was totally serious.

"I wish I could," I said as tenderly as I could manage. "But I've got to find her. Wherever she is in time and space, I've got to go to her."

Frede shook her head sadly. "You've done so much for us, Orion. Can't we do anything for you?"

I smiled. "Live in peace, Frede."

For me, I knew, there would be no peace. Anya was out there somewhere among the stars and I had to find her before all the timestreams of the universe unraveled and collapsed into a chaos that would shatter the continuum forever.

I was no longer Aten's creature, bound to do his bidding through all the ages of the continuum. I am my own man now, I told myself. But I am still Orion, the Hunter. And my hunt is just beginning.